DAWN OF WAR

Legend of the Gods Book III

AARON HODGES

GW00578241

Edited by Genevieve Lerner
Proofread by Sara Houston
Illustration by Zhivko Zhelev
Map by Michael Hodges

Legend of the Gods

Book 1: Oathbreaker
Book 2: Shield of Winter
Book 3: Dawn of War

The Sword of Light Trilogy

Book 1: Stormwielder
Book 2: Firestorm
Book 3: Soul Blade

The Praegressus Project

Book 1: Rebirth
Book 2: Renegades
Book 3: Retaliation
Book 4: Rebellion
Book 5: Retribution

Copyright © October 2018 Aaron Hodges.
First Edition. All rights reserved.
ISBN-13: 978-0995111431

 Aaron Hodges was born in 1989 in the small town of Whakatane, New Zealand. He studied for five years at the University of Auckland, completing a Bachelor of Science in Biology and Geography, and a Masters of Environmental Engineering. After working as an environmental consultant for two years, he grew tired of the 9 to 5 and decided to quit his job to travel the world. During his travels he picked up the old draft of a novel he once wrote in High School—titled 'The Sword of Light'—and began to rewrite the story. Six months later he published his first novel —Stormwielder.

THE THREE NATIONS

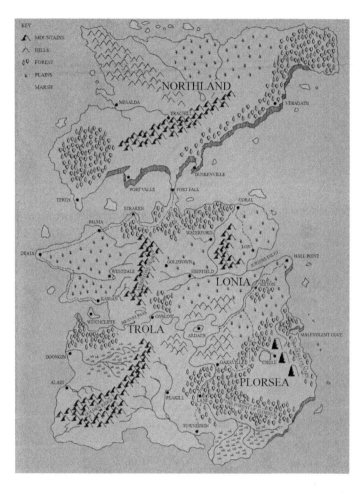

PROLOGUE

Merydith sighed as she entered her bedchamber and swung the door shut behind her. A *thud* followed as the latch caught in the frame, preventing the door from closing. Cursing, she swung back and lifted it more carefully, allowing it to click into place. The faint whisper of laughter from her guards carried through the thick wood. She resolved to have Damyn put them on double shifts for the next few days, but as she turned her back on the door, her exhaustion returned, and the thought drifted away.

The leather sofa beckoned. Staggering across the room, she toppled onto the cushions. She groaned and closed her eyes, giving in to the call of sleep—until the thought of all she had left to do intruded on her peace. Cursing again, she sat back up.

Her quarters had been cleaned while she'd been busy trudging up and down the long corridors of Erachill. Sparsely furnished, the polished walls were mostly of granite, though in places veins of silver streaked the surface. Her room was deep within the mountain city, and there were no windows, but an adjoining chamber led to her washroom. Other than the sofa, her only furniture was a small dining table she used to break her fast, and the double bed in the corner.

The room would no doubt send a southern queen into a fit, but it was all Merydith needed. Indeed, it was far more than her ancestors had enjoyed in the dark days of the past.

Her gaze lingered on the freshly-made bed, but the stench of her unwashed body hung around her like a cloud, and rising, she crossed to the washroom. A smile tugged at her lips as she saw the tub had recently been filled with hot water. Stripping off her long cotton and fur *del*, she lowered herself into the bath.

She sighed as warmth enveloped her, banishing memories of the cold winter draughts that whispered through the tunnels of Erachill. Winter had finally arrived in Northland, and it showed no sign of relenting. Its icy hands would hamper her efforts to muster a defence for their border, but the snows would also slow the enemy, should the Tsar decide to advance.

But then, her enemy's forces were legion, his magic unmatched, and nothing was certain. The man controlled more power than any mortal had a right to.

She and Enala had spoken of the matter many times, about whether her people might find a way to mimic him, but not even Enala's century of wisdom knew how the Tsar had gained such power. So Merydith and her people would face him alone, and pray to the Gods they could match him.

Lying in the hot waters, Merydith's thoughts turned to the old woman. Silently, she wondered where her mentor was now. Enala had been in Merydith's life since before she could remember. After her mother's death, the old priest had become like a third parent to Merydith. But now she needed the woman more than ever, Enala had left, abandoning Northland in the time of its greatest need.

No, Merydith reminded herself, *she has not abandoned us.*

Despite the heat, Merydith shivered, thinking of Enala

and Braidon as she'd last seen them, on the back of the Gold Dragon. They had flown off alone, intent on bringing the fight to the Tsar, on ending his darkness before it could spread beyond the reach of the Three Nations.

No, Enala had not abandoned them. The old woman had placed her trust in Merydith, in the girl she had raised to be Queen, to defend the Northland territories as Enala had since the dark days of Archon.

Merydith was determined not to let her down, and yet... she still longed for the old woman's comforting presence, to know she was there should everything fall apart. Instead, there was only Merydith, only the Queen. If she fell, Northland would fall with her.

She had delivered her message to the Tsar's emissaries the night after Braidon and Enala had left, refusing their request to return the boy. The decision still surprised even her after all, Braidon was the Tsar's own son, though he retained no memory of his past. Yet Enala had been right: Braidon was innocent, and son of the Tsar or not, she could not turn him over to that madman.

The Tsar's people had told her to expect an answer within the day, though they had not mentioned how they planned to communicate her message so quickly across the hundreds of leagues between Erachill and the southern capital of Ardath.

Now, two full days later, she was still waiting for their response. The five southern emissaries had all but vanished, retreating to their quarters. Merydith allowed the faintest of hopes to enter her heart. Could Enala and Braidon's plan have worked? Could they have found a way past the Tsar's defences, and finally put an end to his tyrannical rule?

Merydith quickly quashed the thought. Others could envisage such daydreams, but the fate of Northland rested on her shoulders. She could not afford to indulge in such fantasies. No, until proof of the Tsar's death was placed before her, she needed to prepare as though the man still lived, as though he were planning to march on Northland within the month.

Because in all likelihood, that was the truth.

Rising from the cooling waters, Merydith took a cotton towel from its hook and wrapped it around her body. She wound her long auburn hair in another towel, then wandered out into her bedchamber. A silver mirror hung on the wall above her bed, but she hardly spared it a glimpsed. She didn't need the mirror to remind her of the grey streaks in her hair, nor the faint lines that had appeared around her eyes. At forty-five, she was fitter than most men in their thirties, but even her iron determination could not turn back the slow advance of time.

She started as a knock came from her door. Scowling, Merydith glanced at the wooden panels, wondering who would disturb her at such a late hour. Sleep was beckoning once more, and loath to deny it. She was about to tell them to go away when the knock came again. Grating her teeth, she considered finding something to wear, then decided otherwise.

"Whoever it is, tell them come back in the morning," she called out.

"It's Damyn, your majesty," one of her guards called back. "He says it's urgent."

Merydith closed her eyes and begged the Gods for patience. Damyn was her most trusted advisor and oldest friend, and while he had a habit of overstepping his bounds, even he would not have come to her so late if the matter wasn't truly pressing.

"Send him in," she called back, lifting the latch to unlock the door and then returning to the sofa.

The door creaked as Damyn entered, followed by the click of the latch as he closed it behind him again. He looked as exhausted as she felt as he crossed the room. His black hair was still unwashed, his forty years of age showing in the silver streaks around his temple and the wrinkles across his brow. Shadows ringed his brown eyes, and he grimaced as he looked at her.

"Damyn, what is it?" she asked, sitting up straighter.

Damyn paused when he saw her state of undress, though they had seen each other naked many times while swimming in the mountain rivers as youth. He raised an eyebrow, and she scowled.

"I was just finishing my bath," Merydith replied to his questioning look. She gestured to the space on the sofa beside her. "Now sit down and tell me what's happened."

He nodded and sat, though she noticed there was a distracted look to the way he averted his eyes. "It's Joel, the Tsar's emissary," he said, dispensing with the niceties. "He… he wishes to see you."

Though she kept her expression unchanged, Merydith cursed inwardly. Joel was the Tsar's head ambassador. If he was ready to talk, it meant they had received a reply from the Tsar. Which meant Enala and Braidon had failed…

"He can wait until morning," she replied, her voice hoarse.

"He wants to see you now."

She cast a glare in his direction. "I am the Queen here," she snapped. "Their demands can wait."

Damyn nodded, though the uncertainty remained in his eyes.

Merydith sighed. "Was there something else, Damyn?"

He cleared his throat, obviously uncomfortable. "It's just…he followed me here, Your Majesty."

Merydith closed her eyes in exasperation. "Of course he did." Sucking in a lungful of air, she looked at her companion and shook her head. "It's okay, Damyn. I guess the Tsar's ambassador is not used to being told no." She smiled. "But you will give him my message anyway. With the point of your sword, if needs be."

Damyn grinned at that. His hand drifted to the hilt of the sabre he wore at his side. "It will be as you say, Your Majesty."

Rising, he crossed to the double doors and tugged them open. Before he could step outside, a shadow flickered in the doorway, and a slender man slipped inside. Wearing a sickly smile on his pale face, he sidestepped the startled Damyn. Merydith rose smoothly to her feet as Joel slid towards her, his movements almost snakelike.

"Your Majesty, so nice of you to see me at this late hour," he said smoothly.

"Get out," she snarled, pointing a finger at the door. "Before I have my guards drag you to the dungeons."

The man smiled in the face of her rage. Coming to a stop a few feet away, he spread his hands. "My apologies, Your Majesty," he said as Damyn moved alongside him, eyes narrowed. "But my message could not wait. The Tsar was most displeased with your news regarding his son."

"What message could you possibly have that could not wait until morning?" she snapped.

The smile faded from Joel's face. "Death."

Before Merydith or Damyn could react, a dagger appeared in the man's hand. Caught off guard, Merydith gasped as he lunged forward, the steel blade flashing for her throat. Beside the emissary, Damyn shouted, his hand snaking out to catch the southerner's cloak. But the assassin was already too close.

Reacting with the instincts of a thousand childhood drills, Merydith spun on her heel, twisting into a fighting stance— even as her hand whipped down to strike his wrist. She gasped as fire sliced across her thigh, but she had managed to deflect the dagger from a killing blow.

Her other hand caught her assailant by the arm. Twisting into her attack, she slid her shoulder beneath his arm. He cried out as she thrust back with her hips, heaving him over her shoulder and driving him into the ground. His skull gave a satisfying *crack* as it struck the polished granite, but she still did not release his wrist.

Wrenching his arm, she drove her knee into the back of his elbow, shattering the joint. The dagger clattered to the ground as he screamed. Driving her weight into his chest, she swept up the blade and pressed it to his throat.

"*Traitor!*" she hissed. "Why?"

The man groaned, his eyes whirling in his skull. They had glazed over, but as he looked up and saw her crouched over him, they cleared a little.

"For the Tsar," he breathed.

Before Merydith could say anything else, the man started to shake. His eyes rolled up into his skull, and a long, hissing whisper escaped his throat. Red bubbles burst from his mouth in a sudden cough. Then the life seemed to drain from his body, and he breathed no more.

Dropping the dagger, Merydith stood and staggered back. Her towel had been lost in the scuffle, but she was too horrified to care. She stared at Damyn, seeing the fear in his eyes, a mirror of the terror that had already taken lodge in her heart.

"What does this mean?" he whispered.

Merydith shook her head, her gaze traveling back to the dead emissary. "It means Enala failed. It means war is coming to Northland."

CHAPTER 1

K*eep going, Alana.*
Agony encircled Alana's throat as she followed the voice through the forest, her strength fading with every step. Her shirt was wet with the blood dripping from the wounds around her neck, and the past few hours had turned to a blur. She wasn't sure when the voice had first made itself known— only that in her desperation she had followed it, though she couldn't say whether it was real or a product of her fractured consciousness.

Hardly.

Was it her, or did the voice seem amused by her plight?

Gasping, she continued on, only dimly aware that the light was fading, beckoning in the night. Inside her head, her last moments in the throne room played out again and again, and she saw her father, the Tsar, standing over her, felt the bite of the sword as it wrapped around her neck.

Only Quinn's foolishness had saved her, his weakness showing as he gave in to her pleading. No doubt he would pay for it when her father discovered his part in her escape.

As would the guards she had coerced into aiding her. She had found them while staggering through the endless corridors of the citadel, before the voice had appeared to guide her. The squadron had not heard of her betrayal, and had leapt to obey their princess. They had led the injured Alana deep into the bowels of the citadel, to a private passageway down through the cliffs to the royal docks.

There she had commandeered a skiff and left the guards behind. Unable to summon the strength to wipe their memories with her magic, she had ordered them to remain at their posts until she returned. She wondered how long it had taken her father to find them.

Was he even now searching for her with his power?

No, his powers are exhausted for the moment, the voice came again.

In a moment of clarity, she recalled it had first come to her on the skiff, as she set sail across the lake. In her exhausted state, she had mistaken it as that other part of herself, the gentler, more innocent personality she had created as a mask the first time she'd escaped her father.

Go west, the voice had said, and Alana had obeyed.

On its urging, she had abandoned the skiff on a bend in the Brunei River, pushing it back out into the current after she'd disembarked. Now she was lost in an unknown forest, pursued whatever dark creature her father might send next, still following the voice of some unknown entity, which for all she knew might be leading her into even greater danger.

Not very trusting, are you?

"Oh, do shut up," Alana muttered. She flinched at her own words, her footsteps slowing.

Her voice had echoed loudly in the forest, accentuating the silence blanketing the trees. After a moment she picked up the pace, her thoughts turning to bandits and the dark creatures that might lurk in the night.

Paranoid, too, I see, the voice returned.

"I'm lost in the woods in the middle of the night, I'd

hardly call myself paranoid," Alana replied, then swore beneath her breath. "Great, now I'm talking to myself."

Silent laughter whispered in her mind. Gritting her teeth, Alana resolved to ignore any further instructions from her mysterious guide. She was lost enough as it was.

Branches rustled overhead as a breeze blew down the deer trail she was following. Alana shivered as she tasted ice on the wind, and guessed snow was on its way. This deep in winter, the limbs of the surrounding trees were naked, offering little shelter from the elements. If the snow came, the ground would be covered by morning.

Struggling to ignore the growing cries of her injured body, Alana pressed on, though her every breath seemed to reignite the agony encircling her throat. She needed a healer, someone with the magic to heal her wounds. Unfortunately, the only ones left in the Three Nations were held in her father's sway. Teeth chattering, she continued through the trees, the temperature plummeting around her.

Slowly the last of the light faded, until it was all she could do to keep to the trail. Exhaustion tugged at her mind, calling for her to rest, and she staggered to a stop. Grasping at a tree to steady herself, she sucked in a great, agonising mouthful of air.

You must go on…

"I can't!" she screamed, then groaned as the action tore open her wounds. "I can't," she sobbed again to the empty forest.

The cold seeped through her thin clothing, draining away the last of her strength. She clutched at the tree, knowing that if she sat she would never get up again. In desperation she reached for her magic, for the warming heat of its power, but there was nothing there. Despair gripped Alana as she remembered she'd used the last of it to overwhelm Quinn. Her power was gone, at least until she could stop and rest, recover.

So this is how the Daughter of the Tsar meets her end? the voice sneered. *Lost and defeated, with hardly a whimper of defiance.*

Alana's breath hissed between her teeth as she exhaled. Pushing against the tree, she staggered upright and continued along the trail. She was surprised to see snow on the ground. She hadn't noticed it falling before, but now the air was thick with snowflakes, though Alana hardly felt the cold. A dull thudding began in her temples, spreading outwards across her skull and down the back of her neck.

She staggered as an unseen tree root tripped her, then cursed as the sword she'd taken from one of the guards slammed against her knee. In rage she tore at the scabbard, determined to hurl it into the trees, before sense returned and she only rearranged it on her belt. Without her magic, the blade was her only defence against any unsavoury characters lurking in forest.

"How much longer?" she croaked to the darkness.

Almost there.

Alana shook her head, struggling to hold back her despair. All her life, the Tsar had taught her to be strong, had beaten and tortured her until all that remained was unyielding iron. Yet in the aftermath of the throne room, Alana had been left in pieces. Her father's teachings had done nothing to prepare her for Kellian's death, nothing to ready her for the pain of watching her friend die.

Nor had she been ready for Devon's revulsion. Even now, she could see the loathing in his eyes as he looked at her, his disgust, his hatred. He had seen her suffering and turned his back on her. In that moment, Alana's strength had meant nothing, instead becoming a blade that seemed to drag through her very core.

Now she was lost and alone, at the very edge of her endurance, with nothing but dark forest and silence for company.

The thought brought a frown to her face, and slowing, she

lifted her head to scan the darkness. It was a moment before she realised what had changed—that the trees were no longer silent. A soft whisper carried through the night. Overhead, snowflakes glittered in the faintest sliver of moonlight.

Alana started forward again, the whisper calling her on. The voice had silenced now, and she cursed beneath her breath, her hand drifting to the hilt of her sword. She gripped the pommel, willing strength to her weary limbs.

Squinting, she noticed some of the trees around her had been damaged. Jagged branches stretched across the trail, and it was a moment before she realised that several tree trunks had been snapped in two, as though a giant had come crashing through the canopy.

Her heart beating painfully against her ribcage, Alana stepped from the trail, following some instinct she couldn't quite describe. Moving amongst the broken trees, she scanned the shadows, wondering if a tornado had torn through this section of the forest. Yet they were rare here on the Plorsean plateau, and the area seemed too small…

Alana froze as the trees suddenly gave way to a clearing. Breath held, eyes straining, she watched as a giant shape took form from the gloom. Great, clawed limbs stretched out across the clearing, where deep grooves had torn the earth. Broad wings of scaled skin draped over the broken trees, and a monstrous head lay not too far from where Alana stood, eyes closed. Horns twisted up from its skull, and beyond the body, a massive tail twisted its way into the darkness.

Dragon.

Terror flooded Alana's veins as she recalled her father's Red Dragons, the devastation they had reaped on his enemies. Breath still held, she was about to back away, when she caught the whispering again. It was coming from somewhere in the clearing. She frowned as something moved beside the dragon. With a start, she recognised the sound.

Someone was crying.

A part of her still screamed to run, but another part, one born out of her time with Devon and Kellian, urged her forward. On trembling legs, Alana crept across the clearing. The source of the sobbing came into sight as she moved around one giant foreleg.

An old woman crouched beside the beast, her long robes in tatters, wrinkled skin scorched and blackened from the flames of battle. Her long white hair hung limply against her skull, and there was an air of despair about her as she sat there, head resting against the leather hide of the dragon.

"Tillie..." Alana whispered, then trailed off as she remembered the name wasn't quite right. She swallowed, agony engulfing her throat, and then tried again. "Enala... what happened?"

For a long moment, the old woman said nothing, though the sobbing had ceased at the first word from Alana's mouth. The silence stretched out, heavy with pain, with grief, with anger. Alana opened her mouth, then closed it again when she realised she had nothing else to say.

"Your father happened, girl," Enala whispered, rising to her feet. "My cursed son happened."

CHAPTER 2

Darkness stained the world when Braidon woke, a cry on his lips. Gasping, he looked around, his panicked mind struggling to make sense of his surroundings. Slowly, shapes appeared through the black, shadowy and indistinct. The soft creak of tree branches shifting in the wind seeped into his consciousness, and he shivered as a cold draught touched the back of his neck.

A dull ache began in his lower back as he climbed to his feet. Rubbing his arms, he struggled to recall how he had come to be lying alone in the dark. Images flickered through his mind, disjointed and broken, as though they'd somehow become jumbled as he slept. He remembered a man with sapphire eyes looking down at him, a whisper on his lips.

My son.

The image changed, and he saw the same man in a great gilded room. Flames leapt about him as two aged figures charged, swords extended. Thunder crashed and a great roar filled Braidon's ears as the picture faded to black, leaving one word on his tongue.

Tsar.

Another memory appeared, and he saw himself sitting in

a garden, a young woman beside him. Her steely grey eyes watched him as they spoke, her blonde hair blowing across her face. She smiled down at him, her mouth forming words he could not hear, and another name rose from his scattered thoughts.

Alana.

Sister.

More memories followed then, still jumbled, so that it took time for him to piece them together. He saw a giant of a man with warhammer in hand, facing off against a child with pitch-black eyes, then an older man with kind eyes telling him they would keep him safe.

Devon and Kellian.

As the names came, the flow of memories jolted, flickering forward in time, and he saw his father the Tsar poised over Kellian, golden sword in hand. He watched in horror as the blade descended, and Kellian died. Grief swept through him, turning his legs to water. Sinking to his knees, Braidon wept for the man who had given his life to save him.

The past continued to flow through his mind, faster now, a river that threatened to wash him away. He saw again their journey across the Three Nations, their meeting with Enala, the conflicts with Quinn and his Stalkers, the awful battle in the throne room, his flight with Enala on the back of the Gold Dragon, Dahniul.

Amongst the memories were some he did not recognise, and with a chill he realised they must have come from his other life, from the time before Alana had wiped his mind. Unfamiliar faces rushed across his thoughts, and for the first time he felt a sense of sadness, of loss for the life he could not remember.

Finally, he saw the shining beam of light that had cut across the sky, heard Dahniul scream and Enala cry out, felt himself coming loose from the dragon's back, falling through empty air...

Braidon shuddered, tearing himself from the flow of memories. Turning his mind to his mentor and her dragon, he sent out a silent prayer to the Gods that they had survived his father's attack. There was no doubt in his mind the burning light had come from him—only the Tsar could have commanded magic across such a distance.

There was nothing he could do for his friends now though, and gathering his thoughts, he turned his mind to his own situation. When he'd fallen, it had still been early in the afternoon. He had no idea which direction the dragon had turned as they fled the citadel; all he could recall from before he fell was a sea of green beneath them.

If only he knew which forest he was in, he might be able to find his way out. Many of the forests around Plorsea spanned hundreds of miles. It was said a man could wander lost in the trees for a lifetime, without ever seeing another soul. If he set out without knowing which direction safety lay in, he might end up walking deeper into the abyss, never to be seen again.

Well, not never. It was only a matter of time before his father sought him out. With the magic at the Tsar's command, it didn't matter how many leagues Braidon put between himself and the capital. There was no corner of the Three Nations the man's magic could not reach out and touch his consciousness. Amidst a city of thousands, he might have hidden for a while, camouflaged by the host of other minds, but out here in the wilderness, his mind would shine out like a candle in the darkness.

Unless...

Closing his eyes, Braidon sought his own magic. Breathing slowly, he sank into the void where his power lurked, searching for the flickering white. But he found only darkness, only emptiness where before there had been life. His heart sank as he returned from his trance.

He had used his magic to conceal himself and Enala as

they flew a dragon back from Northland, but the effort had drained his power. Until it regenerated, he could do nothing to hide himself from the Tsar.

Braidon started as a realisation came to him—that Alana had wiped their memories as a way of deceiving their father. Without them, their minds would have been unrecognisable to their father, so that even if he'd touched them with his magic, they would have remained undetected.

A shiver swept through Braidon as he sucked in a breath, tasting the ice on the air. He rubbed his arms and rose to his feet, trying to get his circulation flowing again. The ground crunched beneath his boots, and looking down he noticed a slight sheen to the ground. Brushing his shoulders, his hands came away wet with snow.

His eyes had adjusted to the gloom now, allowing him to cast around for somewhere that would offer shelter. He let out a long breath as he saw the massive buttress roots of a Ficus tree. Twisting away from the trunk, they stood almost a yard off the ground. It was the best shelter he was likely to find in the dark.

He crossed to the tree, and crouching down, crawled into the space between the roots. He moved quickly, collecting as many dry sticks and fallen branches from the grooves between the roots as he could. Protected from the snow, they were still dry, and stacking them in the corner, he started to build a fire between himself and the forest beyond.

Then he paused, realising with a curse he had no way to light it.

As though summoned, a memory came to him, rising from the murky fog that was his past. Born in the citadel atop the cliffs of Ardath, he and his sister had dwelt in luxury—but their lives had never been idle. Their father had wanted them to be strong, ready for any eventuality the world might throw at them.

And Braidon was more than capable of lighting a fire.

Taking out his knife, he cut a slice of bark from the Ficus and placed it on the ground in front of him. Then he took one of the dry branches he'd collected and sliced thin shavings from the wood, collecting them in a pile beside his strip of bark. Selecting a stick from his pile of kindling, he placed its point on the bark, and pressing down, he began to twist it rapidly between his palms.

It took half an hour, several blisters, and Braidon's full assortment of curses before a thin column of smoke rose from the bark. Letting out a yelp of joy, Braidon removed the stick and added the wood shavings to the bark. Carefully he lifted it to his lips and blew gently onto the embers. After a few attempts, the flames leapt to life amongst the kindling. Braidon quickly placed the bark on the ground and added more fuel, until he had a small blaze.

When he was finally satisfied the fire wouldn't go out, Braidon lay back against the tree trunk and closed his eyes, a sigh on his lips as the warmth of the flames bathed his face. Beyond the flickering orange, the forest faded into the darkness, his night vision banished by its light. In that moment he didn't care, so long as he escaped the icy cold creeping through the world beyond his tree.

As his mind relaxed, his thoughts turned back to Enala, and he wondered again at the old woman's fate. She taken him in and taught him to use his magic, had defended him when everyone else had wanted to hand him over to the Tsar. He had wondered why for a long time, but in the throne room Braidon had learned the truth—Enala was his grandmother.

He bit his lip, recalling the moment Enala and the Tsar had faced off. Their words had been bitter, their hatred for one another undisguisable. It saddened him to think of it, and he could only imagine what pain must have come between them to cause such a rift between mother and son.

His mind drifted as the call of sleep beckoned, but he shook himself back awake and added another branch to the fire. The flames leapt at the fresh offering, tongues of orange dancing up to consume the slender wood. He glanced at his small pile, aware it was not enough to last the night. Beyond the flames, the snow was falling faster, piling up in the entrance to his crevice between the Ficus roots. If he didn't want to freeze to death, he'd have to find more before the flames died out. Exhausted as he was, he wouldn't have the strength to relight it.

Even so, Braidon couldn't bring himself to leave the warmth of his shelter. His eyelids drooped again as he leaned against the tree trunk. A loose rock was digging into his backside, but it hardly seemed to matter…

Gasping, Braidon snapped back awake, aware that time had passed but unsure how long. He scrambled up, his heart beating rapidly. The fire was still crackling amongst the wood, and he let out a long sigh of relief. Clutching at his chest, he was about to rise and find more fuel, when a voice spoke from the shadows beyond the flames.

"Evening, sonny."

Braidon gasped as adrenaline burned through his veins. Leaping to his feet, he scrambled for his dagger, until the gentle rasping of laughter reached his ears. Heart still pounding, he paused, squinting into the darkness. The shadows shifted, and a giant of a man appeared. Firelight lit his wiry beard, glinting in his amber eyes. He wore a leather jerkin and steel gauntlets on his wrists, and carried a massive warhammer one-handed. There was a weary smile on his face as he looked down at Braidon.

"You going to stick me with that, sonny, or you gonna invite me to join your camp?" the giant rumbled.

It took an effort of will for Braidon to release the hilt of his dagger. He shook his head, still staring at the warrior in disbelief. "Devon…" He trailed off, swallowing hard. "How… how are you here?"

Devon only grunted. Stepping closer, he brushed the snow

from his woollen cloak. The giant warhammer, *kanker*, made a *thunk* as he dropped it, then Devon lowered himself down beside the fire with a groan. "Oh, but it's been a long day," he said quietly, his eyes on the flames. "Can we leave the questions until the morning?"

Braidon stood for a second longer, before the weight of his own exhaustion drew him back to his seat against the tree trunk. His eyes still did not leave Devon, and after a moment the big man sighed.

"Was there something else?"

Stifling a sob, Braidon darted forward and threw himself at his friend. Until the moment Devon had appeared, he hadn't realised how afraid he'd been, out here in the darkness. He had no idea how the hammerman had found him, but he thanked the Gods for his presence.

Clearly stunned by Braidon's sudden show of affection, Devon tottered backwards beneath his weight. Then giant arms wrapped around Braidon, squeezing him into a bear hug. Unable to hold them back any longer, tears came to his eyes, and he sobbed softly into Devon's chest. The warrior's leather vest was cold from the snowy night, but it was warm in the giant's embrace, comforting. After the gruesome scene Braidon had witnessed in the throne room...

His heart lurched at the memory of Kellian's lifeless body toppling to the marble floor, and he jerked back from Devon. Looking up into the familiar face, he saw the warmth there, but even Devon's grizzled featured couldn't hide the grief that lurked behind his eyes.

"I'm sorry," Braidon blurted out, the words seeming meaningless in the wake of what Devon had lost. "I...we... were too late!"

A sad smile touched Devon's cheeks, and his eyes turned distant, as though he were looking off into some other time, some other place.

"It's not your fault, sonny," Devon whispered. "No one…" His voice cracked, and closing his eyes, he averted his face.

Silence fell, punctuated only by the crackling of the fire beside them. Braidon watched as the giant warrior drew in a long breath. "What brought you back here, sonny? I thought you were safe in Northland."

Braidon swallowed. "Enala and the Queen…" He trailed off, struggling to put together the jumbled memories of the past few weeks. "Enala helped me to master my magic," he started again. "We thought…we thought it might make the difference against the Tsar."

There was a tightness to Devon's face as he forced a smile. "Thank you for trying, sonny. But no one could have saved him. Kellian knew what he was doing when he attacked the Tsar. He knew there would be no going back."

Braidon shivered, remembering the scene. He had witnessed it as he first stepped into the throne room: Kellian surging to his feet as the Tsar towered over Devon, the dagger as it flashed through the air, the Tsar's screams as it struck home. In that one act, Kellian had saved Devon's life. But in doing so, he had paid for it with his own.

"Why did he do it?" Braidon whispered.

"Because…" Devon trailed off. In the light of the fire, his skin seemed pale, his eyes cast in shadow. "Because he was Kellian," he finished with a shrug.

"I don't understand."

Devon nodded. "He was a believer—in the Gods, in humanity, in me. He thought there were things worth more than his own life. Things like freedom, and friendship. He died so that I could live." His shoulders straightened almost imperceptibly, and his brow hardened. "So that I could fight on."

The conversation trailed off with Devon's pronouncement, though the forest no longer seemed so quiet now, no longer so empty. Braidon felt his fear for the morning fading.

The threat of his father still loomed over his future, but with Devon at his side, Braidon felt a sudden faith that things might work out. The call of sleep beckoned, and he wriggled in his hollow, struggling to find a more comfortable position. His eyes slid closed, but as he started to drift off, a thought came to him.

"Devon, where are we?" he asked, cracking open one eye.

The big man chuckled. "Onslow Forest, sonny."

"Onslow...Forest?" Braidon swallowed as lost memories flickered into his mind. He sat back up. "I know it. It's a refuge for outlaws and bandits——"

Devon's booming laughter drowned him out. The sound echoed from the hollow, reverberating out into the trees, as though he were inviting the dark fiends to come for them. A true grin split the hammerman's face as he patted the haft of his warhammer.

"Don't you worry, sonny," he said. "Whatever's out there, it's no match for *kanker*. Now, why don't you get some sleep, you look like you could use it. I'll keep watch."

Seeing the man's immovable confidence, Braidon relaxed back against the tree. Seated beside the fire, with *kanker* in hand, Devon seemed like some hero out of legend, a warrior of renown who could crush any enemy with one hand. Indeed, Braidon himself had watched the man defeat a demon in single-handed combat. Even in his exhausted state, a few bandits were no threat to such a legend.

He nodded wearily, his eyes already flickering closed.

And slept.

CHAPTER 3

"**I**s it dead?"

Alana blurted out the words before she could process what the old woman had said. Standing there before the giant beast, with its dagger-filled jaws large enough to swallow either one of them whole, she could think of nothing else. Alana had seen her father's dragons up close, but none of the Red beasts came close to the size of the creature lying in the clearing.

Her question was met with stony silence. Tearing her gaze from the beast, Alana focused on the wrinkled face of Enala. She frowned as the woman's words finally seeped through her consciousness.

"You're his *mother?*" she gasped.

In all the years Alana's father had trained her, he had never mentioned his parents—not even in her younger years, when there was still some softness in him, and he had still been given to kindness towards his only daughter. Those had been the years when her mother had been with them, before Braidon had arrived and the last traces of humanity faded from their father.

Across from her, the old woman stepped away from the

beast. Despite the darkness, her eyes seemed to glow, and Alana remembered her father's tales of this woman. He may have never mentioned his mother, but he *had* talked endlessly of Enala—the Magicker who had fought against Archon, who with her brother had opposed the Tsar's rise to power.

Now Alana understood why the woman had survived. She had been spared. There could be no other explanation—no one endured her father's wrath.

"You're my grandmother," Alana whispered.

Her words finally drew a reaction from Enala. A tremor swept across the old woman's face, anger replacing grief. "Never!" she snapped. "I know who you are now, *girl*. Your brother may be innocent, but you most certainly aren't. How many young Magickers have you sent to their deaths? How many did you mind wash to do your father's bidding? No, a monster like you will never be a grandchild of mine."

Alana smirked. "On that we can agree."

The old woman glared back. Fists clenched, she advanced a step. "What are you doing here, *girl?*" she spat. "Come to finish the Tsar's dirty work?"

At the mention of her father, Alana's anger flared. Her hand dropped to her sword hilt. "What right do *you* have to judge *me?*" she growled. "The Tsar is *your* making. Everything he is, everything he's done, it's on *you*. If…if…" she stammered, unable to find the words to express her emotions.

She closed her eyes, recalling the pain, the torment of a life spent in thrall of the Tsar, as the enforcer of his will. Even now, memories of her deeds brought Alana a thrill of joy, though they were tainted now with disgust from her other self, from the innocence she had freed when she chained away her own memories. The conflict bubbled within her, until she felt as though she might burst.

"*It's all your fault!*" she screamed, her self-loathing taking voice.

Weariness forgotten, Alana advanced across the clearing.

The old woman watched her come, unmoving. Drawing to a stop, they faced off against one another. Alana flicked a glance at the dragon, wondering whether it might wake, but up close her earlier suspicions were proven true.

The Gold Dragon was dead, its shining scales stained grey. One great eye hung half open, the vacant globe clouded white. Torn scales and blood seeped into the earth around it, and in its stomach a great gash had been scorched deep into its hide. She shuddered, and quickly returned her attention to Enala.

Unnoticed, the old woman had crept forward until their faces were only an inch apart. Confronted by the woman's crystal blue eyes, Alana stumbled back, her heart suddenly racing. A cold smile appeared on Enala's lips.

"If you think to stop me, *girl*, you had best keep your wits about you."

Alana clenched her fists. "I don't answer to my father," she hissed. "Go where you want, old woman."

"You think that's an insult?" She laughed, the sound cold and absent of humour. "Ay, I'm old. I have lived a hundred years and more, seen things you could never comprehend. And I have survived them all. Cross me at your peril, girl."

Her cackling echoed between the trees like the whisper of some long dead spirit, raising the hackles on Alana's neck. Finding herself lost for words, she said nothing, only stood and stared at the woman.

Enala smirked. "A good choice, *girl*," she said, then turned her back. "Now if we're done here, I'm returning to Northland."

Without waiting for a reply, the old woman started around the still body of the fallen dragon. Alana watched her go, a lump lodged in her throat. An image rose from her memories, of her father towering over her with sword in hand. She heard her own pitiful cries for help as she stood alone against him, her sense of powerlessness, and her anger came rushing back.

"That's right!" she shrieked. "Go! Leave the rest of us to clean up your mess. Run, like the coward you are."

Enala froze at the edge of the clearing. Her face was pale as she looked back at Alana, her eyes wide and nostrils flaring. "What did you say?"

"I said you're a coward!" Alana shrieked, advancing. "You ran from your own son, left your nation, your people, your grandchildren alone to suffer under his reign. You could have stopped him, you and your brother, all those years ago, but you did *nothing!*"

"*You* dare to lecture *me*, girl?" Enala hissed. "You, who joyed in enforcing your father's laws, who wielded your power against those who could not defend themselves against it?"

"I'm not the one running away."

"No?" Enala raised an eyebrow. "Then why are you here, in this faraway forest, instead of in Ardath, standing against your father?"

Alana's cheek twitched at the mention of her father, a wave of fear washing through her. She recalled his words back in the citadel, his plans to wipe away everything she was, to expunge her memories and consciousness, and create her anew with his powers. If he had his way, the small shred of good she had discovered within herself would be swept away, leaving only the cold, calculating woman she had become to protect her brother.

Looking at the old woman, Alana saw the satisfied smirk she wore, and bristled. "I can't stop him alone," she snapped, "but I won't let you abandon us, not again."

"Try and stop me," Enala growled.

Steel hissed against leather as Alana's sword leapt into her hand. She lunged forward, the point spearing for the old woman's throat. With a speed belying her age, Enala skipped sideways, and the blade cut only empty air. Carried forward by her momentum, Alana stumbled, her exhaustion returning with the rush of blood to her limbs.

Swaying, she turned to follow the old woman, and barely managed to parry a thrust from Enala's sword. The sharp shriek of steel on steel rang out across the clearing. Alana twisted her blade, slipping the point beneath the old woman's guard and stabbing upward. But again, Enala was too quick, and her blow missed its target.

Alana caught the crunch of twigs beneath boots as the old woman shifted behind her and hurled herself down. A *hiss* came from overhead as Enala's blade cut the space where Alana's head had been. Rolling, Alana came to her feet and spun back toward her grandmother. Face set, Enala strode towards her, blade raised for another blow.

Instinctively, Alana reached for her magic, but there was only the slightest spark of green within. She cried out as she deflected another blow, its impact vibrating down the blade, almost tearing the sword from her grip.

Her breath coming in desperate gasps, Alana switched her attack, seeking to break through the old woman's guard and put an end to the fight. But weakened by blood loss and exhaustion, she was too slow. With each blow, her blade dipped lower, and finally Alana staggered to a stop, allowing the old woman to leap clear.

"Is that all you have, girl?" Enala murmured.

Blood rushed to Alana's head as her face flushed with rage. Roaring, she threw herself forward. She lashed out with the last of her strength, aiming her sword for the old woman's throat. Enala ducked beneath the blow, her shoulder crashing into Alana's chest.

Caught off-guard, Alana was hurled backwards. She staggered on the uneven forest floor, and her feet went out from underneath her. Alana's breath hissed between her teeth as she struck the ground. Gasping, she tried to recover, but her limbs refused to obey her commands. She looked up in time to see a blade flashing towards her face.

CHAPTER 4

The sun was high in the sky by the time the slanted rooftops of Onslow came into view. Standing on the forward rail of the ship, Quinn's heart quickened at the sight. Behind him, the twenty-odd Stalkers he'd selected for this mission were preparing their mounts alongside the fifty soldiers that were to accompany them. Quinn remained where he stood, watching the village's slow approach, already impatient to be underway. Beyond the docks of Onslow, the mountains of western Plorsea slashed the sky, seeming to tower over the land beyond the village.

West, the Tsar had said, and Quinn had obeyed.

That was where the Gold Dragon had fallen, struck down by the awesome power of the Sword of Light. The Tsar's own powers still had not recovered from the battle the day before, when Devon, Enala and Eric had launched their assault on the throne room. They would return though, just as soon as the Magickers in the Tsar's thrall recovered from the drain on their power.

Fortunately for Quinn and the twenty Stalkers he'd chosen for their magic, they had long ago earned the Tsar's trust. They had been spared the bracelets worn by most

Magickers under the Tsar's thrall, which allowed him to siphon off their magic at will. Quinn could still recall their stinging touch from his childhood—and his relief when he'd earned his lieutenant's badge and been freed of them.

Others though were not so lucky. During the assault, the Tsar had drawn on the collective power of his Magickers like never before, driving many to the point of exhaustion and collapse. Several had perished during the hours the battle raged. In the dungeons beneath the citadel, where renegade Magickers were imprisoned, they had died by the score.

With his Magickers in the city drained, the Tsar had mounted his Red Dragon that morning and flown north to join the army as it marched. There, he would have the powers of his Battle Magickers to draw on, to defend their forces against any underhanded attacks the North might mount.

That left Quinn and his Stalkers the task of tracking down his children. Quinn smiled at the thought of having Alana in his thrall once more. He had drained his own magic to save her life, only to have her betray him, leaving him to suffer her father's wrath. In his mercy, the Tsar had spared him, but Quinn was still determined to make the girl pay. While there had been little word of her since she'd fled the citadel, he was confident wherever Braidon was to be found, his sister would not be far away.

His smile faltered as he thought of the old woman who had escaped alongside the boy. The last time they had met, Enala had carved through his Stalkers like a wolf amongst sheep...

He shook his head, dismissing memories of the slaughter. The twenty men and women he had selected were the finest of the Tsar's Stalkers. Each was capable of significant magic and were renown fighters with sword and dagger. If the old woman still lived, even she could not stand against them.

"Sir, your mount is ready."

Quinn found his aid at his side. Nodding his thanks, he

strode across the deck of the barge to where the other Stalkers had gathered. Behind them, his soldiers stood at attention, awaiting their orders.

"The Tsar has commanded us to bring back his children," Quinn boomed. "Their treacherous assault on his person have left his powers fatigued. I do not intend to weary him needlessly with queries on their whereabouts, for are we not Stalkers? Is it not our duty to hunt down renegade Magickers, and bring them before our Tsar?"

He paused, eyeing the men and women gathered before him. They stared back with cold eyes, clearly unimpressed with his speech. His face hardened as he continued more quickly. "I chose each of you based on your reputation. Those reputations were no doubt hard-earned. But do not forget, the Tsar does not accept failure, and his goodwill is easily lost."

There was a stirring amongst the Stalkers now, and he offered them a cold smile. "There has been no word of Alana since she was spotted sailing west across the lake, nor of Braidon since the Gold Dragon he was riding fell from the sky. We know Devon at least took sail on a ship heading for Onslow. Where he goes, I expect the other two will not be far behind. Question the villagers. He will not have gone unnoticed. If they refuse to talk, make them. I expect to be on the road by sunset. Do not fail me, or you will not live to see the Tsar's vengeance."

The Stalkers saluted, their faces carefully blank, their discipline absolute. Many no doubt loathed him for being selected over them to lead this mission. He would have to tread carefully, to ensure they had no cause to offer complaints to the Tsar.

The deck jerked beneath Quinn's feet as their barge banged against the docks. Ignoring the gangplank, he turned and leapt across to the wooden jetty. The *thud* of the gangplank being lowered was followed by the *clip-clop* of hooves as Quinn's aid led his mount across it.

Taking the reins, Quinn vaulted into the saddle and directed the horse down the docks, and out into the town. Several villagers were already gathering. They wore puzzled looks on their faces as they watched the black-garbed Stalkers disembark, before riding into the square to gather around Quinn.

When his entire force was in place, Quinn addressed the villagers from his saddle. "I'm looking for a young woman, a boy, and a renegade soldier by the name of Devon. There's a reward for anyone who comes forward now with information." His hand dropped to the hilt of his sword. "If you refuse…" He trailed off, allowing them to read the threat behind his words.

The dozen or so villagers exchanged glances, their eyes wide with fear, but not a voice spoke. Quinn allowed himself a smile as his horse shifted beneath him.

"Very well then." He pointed to a nearby house and addressed his men. "You can begin there."

CHAPTER 5

The hushed voices fell silent as Merydith entered the room. Her chainmail rattled with each step as she crossed to the granite table, the long sabre slapping against her thigh. Iron gauntlets protected her hands, and on her head, she wore the gold-gilded helm of the Northland Queen. Lantern light lit the room, illuminating the faces of the men and women who rose to their feet as she took her place at the head of the council table.

Merydith reached up and unstrapped her helmet before taking her seat. Her council remained standing, until with a gesture, she indicated they could sit. The rustle of clothing followed as they made themselves comfortable once more, though not a voice was heard.

Studying the men and women around her, Merydith was careful to keep any trace of emotion from her face. Silently, she took note of who was present. The aged faces of the twelve men and women gathered around the table were well-known to her. With their greying hair and wrinkled faces, these were the clan leaders who had presided over Northland after her mother's death, before Merydith herself had come of age. There were other leaders from clans further afield, from the prairies and marshlands and forests that spanned far across Northland, but it would take time for her message to reach them. For the moment, these twelve men and women, chiefs of the mountain clans around Erachill, were all she had.

She had summoned them a week ago to discuss treaties and peace, to deliberate over how best to prevent an invasion from the south. They were long past such talk now though. Winter or no, the Tsar was ready to make his move, and they could no longer afford to delay.

Her messengers had taken wing that morning, summoning their nation to war. Given time, Northland could raise an army twice the size of any the Tsar might field against them. But they did not have time. If the Tsar felt bold enough to strike here, in the heart of their nation, then his forces were already on the march. They could not be allowed to cross the Gap unopposed.

"Thank you for coming here today," Merydith said, finally breaking the silence. "I know things are not as we expected when I first summoned you."

"As expected?" an old woman to Merydith's right snapped. Eyes flashing, she rose to her feet. Merydith did not react as the woman jabbed a wrinkled finger at her chest. "A southerner makes an assassination attempt on you, and your response is to declare war against the Three Nations? Who do you think you are, girl? Archon reborn?"

A strained silence fell over the table as Merydith stared the woman down. "Sit, Dyanna of Clan Clennan," she said, her voice so quiet the others in the room had to lean forward in their chairs, "before you find yourself a guest in my dungeons."

The leader of Clan Clennan bared her teeth, and for a moment Merydith thought she was going to have to make good on her threat. Then with a snort, Dyanna slumped back in her chair. Crossing her arms, she averted her eyes from the Queen.

Merydith nodded, her gaze turning to the others at the table. "Would anyone else here care to question my leadership?" she asked, fixing a glare to her face.

Silence met her question, and smiling, she rose to her feet. "Ladies and gentlemen, you all know me, have seen me grow from a child, to the woman I am today. You know I am no warmonger. This was not a decision I came to lightly, but whether we like it or not, war is coming for Northland. The only decision left is where we choose to make our stand."

"What does it matter?" At the other end of the table, an old man climbed to his feet. His long white hair hung down around his shoulders, and there were more winkles on his face than cracks in his aged leather jerkin. "Your family has always led us with honour, Merydith of Clan Kenzie. So tell us truly, what hope do we have against the Tsar, wherever we face him?"

Merydith swallowed as she looked at the speaker. Murdo was one of the oldest clan leaders, though no less fierce for his advanced years. He came from the Crae Clan, who had been bodyguards to her own family for generations. Murdo himself had served her mother. She could still remember the long winter nights as a child, sitting on his lap while her mother was busy in council, listening to his tales of the olden times, before Northland had been freed from Archon's yoke.

"My family have served yours since long before you were born, Merydith," Murdo continued softly. "Do not seek to mislead me. I say again, tell us truly—what chance do we stand?"

Her mouth suddenly dry, Merydith looked into the old man's eyes, and knew she could not lie to him. "No more chance than the Three Nations when Archon led the greatest army that has ever been known against them."

To her surprise, a smile appeared on the old man's cheeks.

"Very well," he rasped, sinking back into his seat with a groan. "Then my people and I will march with you. I always wished to see the south."

The others at the table stared at her. Unlike the Crae leader, there was open fear in the eyes of many, as the stark reality of what she was asking struck home. Another stood, his hair jet-black, his face as yet untouched by the ravages of age. He stood there for a moment in silence, scratching his beard as his eyes roamed the others at the table.

"There has to be another way," he said at last, the words tumbling from his mouth in a rush. "We should sue for peace, whatever the cost."

Merydith smiled sadly at the young leader of the Cranook Clan. "I'm afraid that is no longer possible, Mokyre," she replied. "Not since I refused to return the Tsar's son."

Mokyre's face turned a mottled red at her words. "And by what right did you make such a decision?" he spat, slamming his fist down on the table.

Beside him, Dyanna was on her feet again, her face twisted with rage. "You would condemn us all to die, for the sake of one life?"

"I offered mercy to a soul in need," Merydith replied calmly, "as we have done for decades."

"Your mercy has doomed us all!"

Merydith's face hardened as she faced the two. Around the table the other clan leaders watched on, waiting to see how she reacted. "I did what was *right*," she hissed, her voice as cold as ice. "Perhaps clans Cranook and Clennan are willing to sacrifice a child to protect their own, but I would rather die."

"Then you are a fool," Mokyre spat.

"Perhaps," Merydith replied with a smile. Stepping away from her chair, she walked around the table until she stood before the man. "But I think always of the future. The moment we handed over the boy, Northland would have accepted the Tsar's authority over our nation. And what would he have asked of us next? If we would sacrifice one boy for our freedom, why not two? Or ten? What fresh atrocities would you be willing to commit, to spare your own life, Mokyre? Where would *you* draw the line?"

As Merydith spoke, Dyanna sank back into her chair, though the Cranook leader remained standing. Eyes burning, he glared at her, but offered nothing in response to her condemnation. Merydith smiled, and with a curt nod, turned her back on him.

"No, this is the only way we remain free," she continued as she circled the table, eyeing each leader in turn. "I will not see Northland become some vassal state for the Tsar. We will not be ground into dust, bowing and scraping to some foreign dictator. I will fight to my dying breath before I see our land succumb to the darkness again."

"Hear, hear!" Murdo replied from the other end of the table.

"What about the Magickers who have come to us?" Dyanna asked softly. "Surely they will fight?"

"They might," Merydith answered as she completed her circuit of the table and resumed her seat, "but I will not ask that of them."

"Surely you jest?" Mokyre shouted. Dyanna only frowned, and slumped further into her chair, but others added their voices to the Cranook leader's objection. Emboldened, he stood and continued. "We have given them food and shelter, safety from the Tsar, surely they have an obligation—"

"*No,*" Merydith snapped, her patience pressed to breaking point. She slammed her palm down on the table. Her gaze swept the room, silencing the old men and women. Sucking in a breath, she prayed to the Goddess for strength. "The Magickers came here with their families to escape the Tsar's persecution—not to be used as a weapon against him."

This time, the room remained silent and Merydith continued. "I'm sorry, my friends. There is no easy path here, but there is no longer any point in debating the past. It is done, set in stone—all we can do now is deal with the reality of the present. And the reality is, the Tsar is coming.

"As I said before, we must decide how best to face him. It is my belief he cannot be allowed to cross The Gap. Northland is too large to defend if he gains a foothold on our lands."

"Then what do you propose, Merydith?" Murdo asked, his eyes aglow with a fresh light.

She smiled. "We march."

CHAPTER 6

S itting by the ashes of the fire, Devon watched as the
morning's light dawned over the forest, illuminating the
snow now lying thick on the forest floor. In their safe haven
amongst the Ficus roots, with the tree's broad canopy overhead, he and Braidon had been spared its icy touch. Even so,
Devon couldn't help but sigh as he felt the sun's warmth on
his face. He'd allowed the fire to die out an hour ago, trusting
that the morning would soon warm his aching bones.

He'd dozed lightly through the night, awakening every so
often to stoke the fire or search for fresh kindling. Now
though, the thought of facing the day filled him with trepida-
tion. Much as he might deny it, the events in the citadel had
left him exhausted, both in body and soul. From the moment
Alana had betrayed them, it felt as though his entire world
had spun out of control. There had been a moment's clarity,
when he had recovered *kanker*, the warhammer passed down
by his ancestors, but even that had quickly been snatched
away by Quinn and his Stalkers.

Then Kellian...

Devon shuddered as his friend's sacrifice played itself out
once more in his mind. He had spent much of the night

trapped in a loop of self-loathing and despair, as he sought again and again for some way he might have changed things.

If only they had left before Alana had betrayed them.

If only Devon had fought Quinn in the corridors, rather than surrendering.

If only, if only, if only…

Clenching his fists, Devon tore his mind from the scene. He found himself staring down at the still sleeping Braidon. Not for the first time that night, he wondered what force could have brought the two of them together once more.

Devon's memories after his flight from the throne room were little more than a blur now. Distracted by the conflagrations rippling out from the throne room, the remaining guards had paid little heed to Devon as he strode down the long corridors of the citadel. Even at the gates to the city, the men on duty had been too focused on the Gold Dragon flying loops around the citadel to notice a single man slipping out the open doors.

From there it had been an easy matter to escape the city. Order within Ardath had already crumbled into chaos long before he made the outer walls, and the guards had already been swept away by the crowd trying to flee the city.

Along with a dozen other panicked citizens, Devon had boarded the first ship he could find departing the island city. A captain heading for Onslow was only too overjoyed to see so many patrons for the voyage. Aided by the afternoon breeze, the passage across the lake had been swift.

The only disturbance had come when a dazzling beam of light sliced across the sky towards the distant shore. Several sailors had thrown themselves flat against the deck, while a few of the jumpier townsfolk had leapt overboard. It had cost precious time fetching them back out of the lake, but they had still reached the river mouth to Onslow before night arrived.

It was only on the Onslow River that the uneasy feeling

had come over Devon. A sense of wrongness had gripped him, a feeling he was traveling in the wrong direction. Farmland stretched away to either side of the river, offering little cover from the hunters that were bound to follow him.

Then around a bend in the river, the first trees of the mountain forests had come into view. The sight had set his heart pounding. Watching the other passengers, he'd tried to ignore the urge to leap overboard.

Devon…

The voice had begun as little more than sigh in his ear, like the whispers of some long-dead spirit. It had grown stronger as the trees approached, until it seemed someone was screaming from the riverbank, begging him to join them.

Before he'd known quite what he was doing, Devon had found himself leaping from the railings of the ship. He had never been a strong swimmer, and the weight of *kanker* on his back had almost dragged him straight to the bottom. Fortunately, the forgiving currents had carried him closer to the shore, and by the time Devon surfaced, he'd had little left to do but reach out and catch an overhanging branch to drag himself from the icy waters.

Standing freezing and drenched on the riverbank, sense had finally returned to Devon, but by then his ship was already disappearing around the next bend in the river. Cursing beneath his breath, Devon had carried on from there on foot. He'd walked quickly, struggling to keep warm as the cold winds cut through his soaking clothes.

By the time darkness fell and the snow began, Devon's teeth were chattering uncontrollably, and he was beginning to lose hope he would ever find shelter. He'd been busy cursing his rotten luck, when the voice returned.

Without any other options, he'd followed its directions without question. He'd been as shocked as Braidon to find the boy sitting beside the flames, though at the time, Devon had been more interested in the heat radiating from the fire.

Now though, he found himself wondering how Braidon had come to be in the forest in the first place. The boy had claimed Enala brought him, that they had meant to make an attempt on the Tsar's life. Yet as far as Devon knew, Braidon's magic was nothing more than illusions. How could the old woman have thought it might prove the difference against the Tsar?

But then, the ways of Magickers were far beyond Devon's understanding, and he had little desire to change that. He wrapped a hand around the haft of *kanker*, drawing reassurance from its presence. It had been passed down from his ancestor Alan, a hero who had once stood upon the walls of Fort Fall and defied the might of Archon. Until recently, Devon had thought it nothing more than what it appeared—a simple hammer—but in the battles of the past few months, he had discovered it had another ability: it could protect its wielder from magic.

It had saved his life on more than one occasion, and while Enala had told him the protection spell would quickly be overwhelmed by the power commanded by the Tsar, he still felt better with it to hand. At least it might give him a fighting chance.

Beside him, Braidon twitched and gave a soft cry. Devon thought again of the voice that had called him through the forest, and wondered whether the boy himself might have summoned him with his magic. Or could it have been the old priest, Enala? Or the Tsar himself, in an effort to gather all his prey in one place?

Devon shuddered at the implications. He glanced out at the snow-covered woods. The light had grown, banishing the shadows beneath the trees. A soft *thump* came from nearby as a clump of snow slid from a branch, but otherwise, there was no sign of movement.

Devon sighed, then sat up and stretched his arms. Braidon jerked awake at the movement, his crystal blue eyes blinking in the dawn's light. Groaning, he started when he saw Devon sitting there, almost making it to his feet before he seemed to realise where he was. His cheeks grew red, and rubbing his eyes he sank back to the damp earth.

"You didn't wake me?" he said with a frown.

Devon smiled. Throughout the night, he'd found himself wondering which version of Braidon he sat beside: the young boy he'd come to know on the road from Ardath, or some other boy, one who had been raised by the cruelty of the Tsar.

"I thought you could use the rest," was all he said.

Braidon's face remained uncertain. "So...how *did* you find me?"

"I don't know, sonny," Devon replied. The first calls of the dawn chorus were just beginning, and Devon watched as a blackbird emerged from a nest in the tree above them. "Something about this forest, it called to me," he added finally. "I should have stopped and made camp long before I found you. Yet something, some presence, called me on. I can't really explain it."

To his surprise, Braidon nodded, as though what he'd said made perfect sense. "Enala said the Gods were still with us, guiding us—"

Devon snorted. "I bet." He chuckled quietly. "Gods, magic, exhaustion-induced hallucinations. Whatever, here we are." He raised an eyebrow in the boy's direction. "So, if you're here...you know the truth about your sister?"

Braidon swallowed visibly. "The news reached us in Erachill, about who she was...who I am," he replied softly.

"So which Braidon am I speaking to then?"

"The only one you've ever known," the boy replied. "If *you* know the truth, then...did you...did you meet my sister?"

Devon's chest tightened. "Best we not talk about that, sonny," he replied bluntly. Before the boy could argue, he rose to his feet, groaning as his joints cracked from the disuse. His stomach rumbled as he looked down at the boy. "How about we walk and talk? I could use a fresh meal, and I don't think we'll find one between the roots of this tree."

Accepting Devon's help, Braidon stood and stamped out the last embers of their fire. Since neither of them knew quite where they were, they set off in a random direction and hoped for the best. Despite Devon's words, they walked in silence, each lost in his own private thoughts.

Thankfully, it wasn't long before Devon caught the distant whisper of running water. The ground sloped down beneath them as they headed towards it, then dropped away sharply into a steep valley. Ivy covered the slope, and moving with care, the two of them picked their way down towards the stream. The dirt beneath their feet turned to loose rocks, and Devon was forced to rely on the thick vines clinging to the slope to keep his balance.

At the bottom, they were rewarded for their efforts by a fast-running stream. Further upstream, the crystal clear waters rushed over a cobble bed, but where they stood, a cluster of boulders had partially damned the flow, creating a small pool around a turn in the valley. Kneeling beside the water, Devon drank gratefully, then sat back and made space for Braidon to do the same.

When he was done, Braidon knelt beside the stream and eyed the water with the intensity of a soldier readying himself for battle. Devon opened his mouth to ask what he was doing, then thought better of it. Moving to a nearby boulder, Devon lay back in a patch of sunlight and watched as the boy lowered his hands into the stream. There he sat, unmoving, as time slowly crept past, until Devon began to wonder whether the boy had lost his mind after all. Coming from far up in the Sandstone Mountains, the waters of the stream must have been freezing.

Still drowsy from the long night, Devon was just beginning to drift off, when a shout snapped him back to wakefulness. Leaping to his feet, he was still scrambling for the haft of his hammer when Braidon's laughter carried to his ears. He frowned. Looking around, he found Braidon standing beside the river, a grin as wide as The Gap on his youthful face. At his feet, a rainbow trout flapped helplessly amongst the gravel, its pink and orange scales shining in the sunlight.

Devon's mouth dropped open. "How?"

Braidon beamed. "It must have been something I knew in my...other life." He gestured up the slope in the direction they'd come from. "It was the same with the fire last night."

Crouching beside the trout, he pulled his dagger from his belt and stabbed it through the eye. Blood gushed onto the stones and the fish ceased flapping. Holding it in the air, he waved it like a trophy at Devon. "Since the citadel, little bits have been coming back to me, snippets of memories. It seems our...father wanted us to be self-sufficient."

Devon could only shake his head. His mind turned back to the night he'd shared with Alana in northern Lonia. The young woman had disappeared for an hour, finally returning with a dead rabbit in tow. She'd claimed to have killed it with a stone. At the time he'd wondered how a girl from the city had learned such a skill.

Now he knew.

His thoughts drifted, turning as they so often did to later that night, when they'd swum together in the moonlit pool. Standing suddenly, Devon forced the painful memory from his mind. "I'll get a fire started," he snapped, then clambered up the slope in search of dry firewood.

He sensed Braidon's gaze on his back, but ignored him. How could he possibly explain his sense of betrayal to the boy, the loss and rage that burned his soul whenever he thought of Alana, and the role she'd played in Kellian's death?

If it hadn't been for her, they would never have been captured.

If it hadn't been for her, they would never have been in

that throne room, and Kellian would never have found himself face-to-face with the Tsar.

Sheltered from the worst of the weather, only a thin frosting of snow had fallen in the valley, and Devon was able to gather a stack of firewood in less than an hour. Returning to the stream, he set about lighting a fire between two boulders that lay on a flat piece of ground just up from the water. He wasn't much of a woodsman, but with his flintstone he managed to get a fire burning.

By then, Braidon had successfully tickled two more trout from the stream. Devon wandered over to help the boy with the fish. They had both lost just about everything but the clothes on their back and the contents of their pockets, but Devon managed to fashion them each a skewer from his stack of kindling. Spearing a fish on the end of each, they braced them over the fire, then sat back and waited, hungry eyes on the roasting flesh.

"Devon..." There was a touch of fear in the boy's voice, and he trailed off without saying anything more.

Devon looked up, knowing what Braidon wished to ask, but not knowing how he should answer him. Their eyes met, and he looked away, a vice closing around his throat.

"What happened to Alana?" Braidon finished in a whisper.

Staring into the flames, Devon saw again those final moments in the throne room, as he'd looked down on the helpless woman. With the twisted sword wrapped around her throat, Alana had begged him to help her, to use his prodigious strength to free her, to carry her clear—anything that might spare her from her father's wrath.

But Devon had walked away.

Guilt wound around his stomach, and clenching his jaw, he struggled to find an answer. "She didn't make it," he said finally, the lie foul on his tongue. "I'm sorry, sonny. The girl we remember is gone."

He looked up as a sob came from across the fire. Tears streaked Braidon's face, and there was desperation in his eyes. In that instant, Devon knew his lie had been the right choice. If he'd told Braidon the truth, nothing in the Three Nations would have stopped the young man from trying to find her, to rescue her.

Just as Devon had done, to his folly.

"I'm sorry," Devon repeated, shuffling around the fire and pulling the young man into a hug. "There was nothing any of us could have done. She was already lost long before we reached that citadel."

"What?" Braidon's question came between sobs, half-muffled by Devon's chest. "But...I saw her in the throne room."

Devon bit his lip, regretting his slip of tongue. He gave Braidon's shoulder a squeeze. "That...that wasn't her, sonny. That was someone else, the woman she used to be, the Daughter of the Tsar. When Kellian and I tried to save her, she betrayed us, had us locked away in the dungeons."

"I'm sorry, I didn't know."

"It wasn't her, sonny," Devon murmured, his eyes burning with remembered pain. "Not the woman we knew, anyway."

The boy fell silent then, his eyes fixed on the running waters of the stream. His face had taken on a faraway look, as though he were recalling some event from long ago. When he spoke, his words were barely more than a whisper.

"But it was," he said. "I have a memory of her, from the old days, sitting with me in some gardens. She...she was kind, loving, vulnerable. She's afraid of our father. It was as though there in that garden, our father's darkness couldn't touch her, and she could let down her guard." He swallowed, his eyes flicking up to look at Devon. "That was why she took our memories. I...I remember now. She was trying to save us, to save *me* from our father."

Silence fell as Braidon trailed off. Devon felt the guilt swell within him as he watched the boy, and saw again the young woman they had travelled with, her sweet smiles and fiercely protective nature. Then he saw her again the night he and Kellian had come for her, how she had tried to tell them to run, to leave her behind.

He looked away as tears came to his own eyes. "I'm sorry," he whispered, struggling to hide his own grief. "I'm sorry I never saw that side of her, sonny."

CHAPTER 7

Alana woke to a sharp throbbing in her temples. Stars danced across her vision as she opened her eyes. A muffled shriek tore from her lips as the light drilled into her skull. Rolling onto her side, her stomach heaved, and she choked as the remains of her last meal came rushing up. A convulsion shook her as she vomited on the forest floor.

It was only when she finally lay back and spat out the acrid taste of bile that Alana realised she was alive. Sitting bolt upright, she looked around for the old priest. Red lights swirled at the edges of her vision, threatening to draw her back down into the darkness. Her stomach swirled again, but she had nothing left to throw up, and a moment later it settled.

Soft laughter came from behind her, and turning, Alana was surprised to find the old woman sitting nearby, the remains of a fire still smouldering between them. Light streamed through the branches above. In the dawn's light, Enala looked younger, less world-weary, and Alana supposed she'd had the night to rest, while she, apparently, had spent it in a coma.

Scowling, Alana pulled herself to her knees. "What are you laughing at, woman?"

Enala grinned and gestured at the mess she'd left on the icy ground. "The Daughter of the Tsar, vomiting in the forest." Still smiling, the old woman reached down and produced a makeshift wooden bowl shaped from tree bark. Within, Alana spied a crude stew of tubers and some kind of meat. She raised an eyebrow.

"It's not poisoned," Enala said when Alana didn't move to take it.

Alana bit her lip, hesitating, until a growl from the void where her stomach was usually located pushed her into action. "Thank you," she muttered as she took the bowl.

The old woman did not reply, and using her hands, Alana set about eating her breakfast. The stew was bland and the meat as tough as old leather, but in her exhausted, injured, half starved and quite possibly half-mad state, she hardly cared. While still warm from the fire, the stew had cooled enough not to burn her fingers, and she wolfed it down in a matter of minutes.

Putting the bowl aside, Alana sat back and contemplated the old woman once more. "Why didn't you kill me?" she asked, her hand drifting to the lump on her forehead. It was the size of a goose egg. Enala must have turned her sword at the last second, striking her with the flat edge of the blade.

The old woman shrugged, her eyes still on the ashes. "Bad luck to kill a grandchild."

Alana snorted. "Glad to know you're so sentimental."

Enala lifted her head. "Care to go again, girl?"

Just the thought of picking up her sword caused the pain in her head to redouble, and Alana quickly lowered her eyes.

"Thought so." Enala cackled.

Branches cracked as Enala lifted herself to her feet and wandered to where Alana sat. She was carrying another bowl, though this one was filled with some kind of green paste speckled with black flakes. Groaning, the old woman crouched beside her.

"Those cuts around your neck don't look good," she said matter-of-factly. "If they get infected, we'll have to amputate."

"Very funny," Alana growled, though she found herself shrinking away from the old woman's presence.

A withered hand shot out and caught her by the wrist. "Where are you going, girl?" Enala asked with a grin as she tried to pull away.

"What do you *want?*" Alana shouted, her panic rising.

"Oh, calm down," Enala snapped. "I'm trying to help." She hefted the bowl of paste. "I'm afraid I can't heal you. Unlike your father, I only command one power, and that tends to have the opposite effect on people." She chuckled at her own joke before continuing: "Luckily for you, I've learnt a few tricks over the years. This should help with the pain, and the healing."

Alana paused, the throbbing around her throat impossible to ignore. Combined with the pounding in her skull, she'd certainly had better days. Her stomach twisted as she eyed the sickly paste, before finally nodding. "Fine."

"So grateful," Enala muttered as she settled herself down and scooped paste from the bowl.

Alana flinched when the poultice touched her skin, a gasp tearing from her throat. It felt as though a burning brand was being pressed into her flesh. She was about to pull away again, when the sensation faded as quickly as it had begun. An icy cool replaced it, radiating out from where Enala had applied the paste, granting instant relief. She sighed at the absence of pain, her eyes flickering closed.

"Thank the Gods," she whispered,

A snort came from the old woman as she applied her poultice to the rest of Alana's wounds. "The Gods have nothing to do with it," she said. "You can address your thanks to me."

"Yes…thank you…Enala." She said the old woman's name reluctantly.

"You're welcome," Enala replied.

Sitting back on her haunches, the old woman inspected her work. Alana watched her, feeling suddenly uncomfortable with the old woman's kindness. She cleared her throat, thankful to find the pain almost completely numbed.

"They're not his powers, you know," she murmured, remembering Enala's comment about her father. "He tried to hide the truth, but it's difficult to keep secrets from me, even for him. He draws his magic from the Magickers in his command. And in the dungeons."

"I gathered as much, after I saw Eric."

"Your brother," Alana whispered, remembering the old man from the throne room. His attack had kept her father from completing his spell, from wiping away her memories and remaking her in his own vision. "He…saved me."

"Yes, he made a habit of doing that," Enala said, and for a moment Alana thought she caught tears in her eyes. The old woman fell silent for a moment, then gestured at Alana. "I can show you how to make more, which plants to use."

Alana nodded her thanks. Without the pain, her mind was growing sharper now. She looked back at Enala, her lips growing tight as a thought occurred to her.

"Devon said you were looking after my brother. In Erachill. What are you doing here?"

"You didn't see him in the throne room?"

For a second, Alana thought she'd misheard. She stared at Enala, a sudden pounding in her ears as her heart began to race. In a rush, she surged to her feet.

"You brought him to the capital?"

For the first time in their encounter, the old woman managed to look ashamed. She quickly looked away, and when she spoke, Enala's words were soft, hesitant. "I thought he might shift the balance in our favour."

"He plays with illusions!" Alana shrieked, lashing out at the remains of the fire. A half-burnt log went flying across the clearing. "*Damnit!* What were you thinking, you stupid hag? What could he possibly have done to stop my father?"

Looking all her hundred-and-twenty years of life, Enala climbed to her feet. "I thought he could hide us. I thought if I could get close enough, my son..."

"You *fool*. His magic protects him."

"No, he must summon his power like any other Magicker. He is not untouchable, not if taken unawares. Did you not see Kellian's blade pierce him?"

Enala hesitated, recalling the bloody dagger jutting from her father's arm. It had caused him pain, but once he had pulled it out, the wound had healed in moments. "But even had you been successful, his magic would have held him to life."

"Perhaps," Enala whispered. There was a haunted look in her eyes, and Alana suddenly realised then what it must have cost her, to try and murder her son. "But I had to try."

A wave of pity swept through Alana, but even so, she shook her head. "So you were willing to put my brother's life at risk, on a hunch? It could never have worked. Even with my brother's power, he would have sensed *you* well before you could strike him."

Enala's eyes returned to the forest floor. "Yes, well, it doesn't matter now, does it?" she muttered to the leaves. "I failed. We'll get no second chances now."

Something in the old woman's tone raised the hackles on Alana's neck. She took a hesitant step towards Enala, ice sliding down her spine. "Enala, where's my brother?"

"He's dead, girl," Enala snapped, swinging to face her. "My son killed him, like he killed everyone else I ever loved. And he'll be coming for us next. If you don't want to end up like your brother, I suggest we get moving."

Alana hardly heard anything after Enala's first two words.

Blood pounded in her ears, drowning out all other sound. She stood staring into space, her lips parted, breath caught in her throat. She shook her head, slowly at first, then harder, as though something as simple as denying the old woman's words could change what was.

"Did you hear what I said, girl?" Enala whispered, stepping in closer. "Your father is coming, we can't stay here."

Blinking, Alana managed to focus on the old woman's face. "He can't be dead," she croaked. "He's...he's the one good thing...I gave up *everything* for him."

Enala's face softened. Unspilt tears shimmered in her eyes as she reached out and gripped Alana's shoulder. "I'm sorry, Alana," she whispered. "So, so sorry. You're right, I never should have brought him here. But nor could I stop him. When Braidon found out what had happened to you...he said he would come alone if he had to."

Alana swallowed. "That was Braidon," she whispered. "Even before my magic..." She swallowed. "He always cared."

A frown creased Enala's forehead. "Why...why did you take both of your memories?"

"He can find you anywhere, once he knows you," Alana replied in a whisper, barely knowing what she was saying. "But I found a way to deceive him."

Enala inhaled sharply. "You did it to hide," she breathed.

Alana nodded. "Without our memories, our minds were unrecognisable to him." Her vision blurred and she swayed on her feet. "How...how did my brother die?" Her voice broke on the last word, and only Enala's grip on her shoulder kept Alana on her feet.

"He...he fell from Dahniul, when your father struck us down."

"I need to see him," Alana whispered, her eyes on the trees.

"Your father—"

"*I need to see him!*"

Alana's eyes flashed, and her magic stirred within, though it was still far too weak to be of use. Enala stared back, and for a long moment Alana thought the old woman would try to stop her. But in the end, Enala closed her eyes, and nodded.

"Very well," she murmured. "Then let us find him."

CHAPTER 8

Sunlight coloured the horizon red as Merydith climbed the crumbling steps up the side of the mountain. Far below, darkness was already creeping over the Northland steeps, and she hoped she could make it to the peak before it reached her. Above, the fractured cliffs loomed, their crevice-riddled stone a maze leading up to her remote perch. She had hoped to arrive earlier, and spend one last quiet evening contemplating the setting sun, but preparations for the coming march had occupied her well into the afternoon.

She shivered, thinking of what was to come on the morrow. At sunrise, she would lead five thousand men and women south through the crags of the Northland mountains, through caves and tunnels and narrow canyons that would bring them out onto the plains above the southern stronghold of Fort Fall.

So few…

"And yet so many," she whispered, trying to reassure herself.

The words only reminded her of the responsibility she now carried on her shoulders. Her legs trembled, and she paused her climb for a moment to steady herself.

Five thousand.

Mothers and fathers, sons and daughters, even a few grandparents, they were the cream of the Northland clans surrounding Erachill.

The Tsar's army would outnumber them ten to one, yet they were all she had. Word had already reached them of a southern army on the march, making their slow way up through northern Plorsea. If they were allowed to reach The Gap and retake the abandoned fortress, the war would be over before it began.

Looking out over the dizzying expanse of the land below, Merydith found herself wishing for the powers of the Dark Magicker, Archon. With his magic, he had swept across the unending span of their fledging nation, summoning his people to war, marshalling them from every corner of the land. But Merydith had no such sorcery, and while messengers had gone out, it would be weeks before there was any response.

She didn't have weeks. So she would make do with her five thousand, and pray it was enough to hold them. At the least, her force was well-trained, with most coming from the warrior clans that guarded the mountain fortress of Erachill.

Merydith was within the cliffs now, making her slow way up towards the mountain peak. Shadows clung to the narrow passageways, making the going slow, and she breathed a sigh of relief when she finally dragged herself back into the sunlight.

Emerging from the crag at the top, she sat herself down on the edge of the cliff. Despite her worries, a smile came to her face as she looked out over the fading plains. This place, more than any other, reminded her of Enala. Scaling these treacherous paths with the wily old woman had become a ritual for Merydith since the time she first learned to walk. Tears welled in her eyes as she remembered the old priest.

"Where are you, Enala?" she whispered to the howling winds. "I need you."

No, you have outgrown me, girl.

Merydith swallowed as she recalled the old woman's words when she'd seen her last. At the time, the old woman's faith had filled her with pride. Yet that had been the day Enala had left. Ever since, things had gone from bad to worse, and Merydith couldn't shake the growing despair in her heart. Without Enala, they were naked in the fight against the Tsar, exposed to his nightmarish powers. The few native Magickers she had under her command could do little against the Tsar.

Demons and dragons and Magickers would come against them, and Northland had only cold hard steel to answer with.

Lowering herself onto a boulder, Merydith pulled her cloak more tightly around her to fend off the cold. The climb up the mountainside had kept her warm, but now that she'd stopped, she was already beginning to shiver. The winds were harsh on the slopes, strong enough to scrape the stones clean of snow and ice.

In the silence, she contemplated the task she faced in the morning. She would be expected to ride at the head of the army, to show no fear in the face of the challenge they faced. There was no one else—certainly no one she could trust. She had already appointed several clan leaders to oversee Northland in her absence, but most of her best were marching south with her. It was there the war would be won or lost.

Even if we win, how many of us will return?

Merydith shivered at the thought. Like most of her people, she had lived her whole life in the north. Now she would lead five thousand men and women south to die on foreign soils, far from the lands of their birth, from those who loved them. If she failed, they might all be lying in the cold hard ground by the summer.

The thought sent a tremor through her soul.

Rising, she was about to start back down to the entrance into Erachill, when a crunch of stones echoed from the crag below. Her hand dropped to her sword hilt as she scanned the shadows. Ever-vigilant since the assassination attempt, her guards had insisted on scouring the mountain paths before her hike, and then taken up position at the exit to ensure she enjoyed the last few hours of daylight undisturbed.

Her heart beat faster as she wondered if her guards had been slain like the ones outside her room, when the Tsar's assassin had come for her. Her fear only lasted a second, as her advisor Damyn appeared on the path between the cliffs. Letting out a long breath, the tension left her body. Another figure appeared alongside him, and together the two dragged themselves clear of the crevice.

It took her a moment to recognise the rugged features of the woman who stood alongside Damyn, and a few moments more to recall her name.

"Helen." She frowned. "What brings you here?" The woman was one of the Magickers who'd fled the Tsar's rein— one of the first, in fact. She and her family had sought passage on a cargo vessel departing Lon. They'd been discovered in the Northland port of Duskendale and brought overland to Erachill to face her judgement. Merydith hadn't spoken with Helen in years, and she wondered what matter was urgent enough for the woman to seek her out now.

Helen shifted on her feet and glanced sidelong at Damyn. Clearing his throat, Damyn stepped forward. While he still looked exhausted, the man seemed to have regained some of his vigour since she'd seen him last. It was a welcome sight, given she had promoted him to captain. He would command a cohort of five hundred cavalry, and she needed him at his best.

"Merydith," he said swiftly, and she was surprised to hear the excitement in his voice. "Helen brings news!"

"Does she?" she asked, her tone a gentle rebuke at his familiarity in the presence of others.

For once, Damyn didn't seem to notice. He gestured the Magicker forward, and Helen hesitantly moved up alongside him.

"Be at ease, Helen," Merydith said gently, trying to dispel the woman's nerves. "Say what you have come to say. It must be important, to brave these mountain paths at so late an hour."

"Thank you for seeing me, Your Majesty," Helen began after another second's hesitation. "I know you must have much on your plate, with the army to march at first light. But…" She trailed off, swallowing visibly. "But I…or that is to say, *we*, have decided, Your Majesty, to accompany you south."

"Accompany me south?" Merydith asked, not understanding.

Eyes downcast, Helen fiddled absently with the cuffs of her robe. "Yes…" she murmured. "We, I, *we* would like to help you, against the Tsar."

Merydith blinked, surprised at the woman's words. Standing there on the mountainside, far from any danger, Helen was as jumpy as a hare in an open field. Folding her arms, Merydith appraised the woman. She must have been fifty years of age by now, though her mousy brown hair had yet to see the streaks of age. At five-foot-five with rounded cheeks and smile lines streaking her face, she was not an imposing figure, and magic or no, Merydith could hardly imagine the woman capable of harming a fly.

Letting out a long sigh, Merydith shook her head. "Helen, that's not necessary," she said, trying to let the woman down gently. She needed Magickers desperately, but she also could not afford weakness in her army. If there was a single fault, a single soul who broke and fled, her entire force might crumble. "I offered you and the others sanctuary, so that you would be safe, so that you might raise your families free of the darkness of the Tsar. I can't ask you to march back into the fire."

"With respect, Your Majesty," Helen replied sharply, "I wasn't asking." Lifting her head, she met the Queen's eyes for the first time. Merydith was surprised to see the ferocity burning there. "I know what you think of me, that I am old and afraid, that I would run at the first clash of swords. Well you're wrong. I have known this day would come since I first came here, that one day the Tsar would set his sights on Northland. And I will not stand idly by when I might do something to stop him. Nor will the others."

"The others?" Merydith asked, shocked at the woman's defiance.

"Yes," the Magicker growled. "When I first heard the news the Tsar was marching, I went to my fellow Magickers, to the other refugees who fled here to escape his wrath. I brought them together, gathered them to see who else wished to fight for their adoptive nation. And I am here to tell you that myself, and a hundred others, are ready to march on the morrow, Your Majesty. And we're not asking."

Helen trailed off into silence, as though suddenly realising she'd gone too far, overstepped her bounds. Silently she dropped her gaze back to the rocky trail.

Merydith was too shocked by her news to care. She stood staring at the woman, struggling to comprehend what her news meant.

A hundred Magickers.

They could prove all the difference, might even be enough to hold off the dark powers of the Tsar. But what Helen was offering went against everything Merydith believed in, everything she'd sacrificed to save the refugee Magickers.

"Are you sure, Helen?" she tried one last time, though her words sounded half-hearted, even to herself.

Helen smiled. "Northland opened its arms for us, took us

in when we had nowhere else to go. This is our home now, and the Tsar threatens it. We will march beside you to defend its freedom, will die if needs be, to ensure our families live on in peace."

Merydith nodded, her eyes shining. "So be it."

CHAPTER 9

A lana swallowed as the aroma of roasting fish drifted to where she sat on a rounded boulder. Her mouth salivated as the old woman turned the makeshift spit they'd erected over the flames. A howling wind swept through the valley, adding to the watery chorus of the running stream and causing the fire to flicker dangerously. Shadows danced across Enala's face, and it seemed to Alana that the abyss was calling to the woman, summoning her to her grave.

An icy draft slid down Enala's spine and shivering, she looked away. They had spent the long day combing the forests around where Enala and her dragon had crashed, searching, seeking, hunting for any sign of her brother…

A lump lodged in her throat at the thought of him lying somewhere in the frozen snow, his face pale with death, staring off into nothing. Closing her eyes, Enala summoned an image of her father. Hatred rose within her, sweeping aside the grief. She shuddered and clung desperately to the emotion, determined not to allow herself the weakness of sorrow.

It was no use though. The other part of her cried out within, her anguish slicing through Alana's hatred like a knife to pierce her heart. She choked back a sob as tears spilt down her cheeks.

She had done her best to hold herself together during the search, to conceal her emotions from the old woman who strode alongside her. Even when they'd broken for the night to set up camp, Alana had thrown herself into the old routine with zest, determined to keep herself distracted. Collecting firewood, tickling a trout from the stream, building the fire—she'd kept her emotions in place through all of it.

Now though, in the silence of the night, they returned to haunt her.

Looking at the old woman, Alana recalled the grief on her aged face as she'd knelt beside the dragon. She had thought it strange at the time, but now she wondered whether her sorrow had been for the beast, or for Braidon. Clutching desperately at the distraction, she rose from her boulder and jumped down beside the fire.

Enala glanced up, one eyebrow raised in question.

"How did you come to know the dragon?" Alana asked tactfully.

"I once knew many Gold Dragons, in my youth," the old woman replied with a smile. "My parents raised me in Dragon Country, when the Gold tribe still ruled that land. They were allied to my family, bound by an ancient pact with the old king of Trola." She paused, her eyes flickering in Alana's direction. "To *our* family."

Alana swallowed. "How did the beast end up in Northland then?"

"Her name was Dahniul," Enala admonished, "and she was there because she came with me. After the war against Archon, Gabriel and I returned to Dragon Country. It was there we raised your father, alongside my brother's family. But the Gold Dragons had suffered terribly against Archon. After losing so many of their numbers, they failed to prosper.

Dahniul was the last of her kind, as I suppose, I am the last of my generation."

"So she joined you when you left for Northland?"

Enala nodded and was about to reply, when a *thump* came from the trees lining the slope of the valley. They were both on their feet in an instant, swords leaping into their hands.

Alana squinted into the darkness beyond their fire, suddenly all too aware of Onslow Forest's reputation. This was a land for rough and wild company. Two women alone in the wilderness would likely be seen as an easy target.

Gripping her sword hilt tighter, Alana smiled at the surprise any wood-be robbers would get if they tried to attack.

The shadows at the edge of their firelight shifted, and a giant figure loomed in the darkness. Alana's eyes widened, her heart skipping a beat. Devon's name was on her lips as the man stepped into the light.

The word died in her throat as she stared at the stranger looming over them. A terrible scar ran from one side of the man's face to the other, and his hazel eyes seemed to glow in the darkness. His jet-black hair had been pulled into a bun that would have been comical on a smaller man, but with this giant it only seemed add to his ferocity. White streaked his matted beard, though with a massive double-blade axe in hand, Alana wasn't thinking about his age.

He stood there in the light of their campfire, appraising them in silence. Alana shifted nervously on her feet, eyes on the axe. Though she didn't doubt the two of them could best him, with such a weapon there would be no room for mistakes. One blow from that monster would end her life.

"What do you want?" Enala asked, her voice edged in steel.

The giant chuckled as he looked over at the old woman. "Such a frosty greeting from a priest," he rumbled.

Enala smirked. "Yes, well, the Goddess didn't see it fit to bless me with much patience."

Their visitor laughed again. "Ay, I bet." He scratched his beard, as though contemplating his next move. "Well, to be honest, I came here to see whether you might have anything of value."

Alana tensed, but the giant continued before she could make a move. "But I see now I've stumbled across the camp-fire of a priest. Seems like it would be bad luck to harm a servant of Antonia, being in her own forest and all. Wouldn't want a vengeful Goddess after me, would I?"

Alana exchanged a glance with the old woman. "Since when does a thief care about the Gods?"

The giant's face darkened at her words. "The name's Joseph," he growled. "And I'm a Baronian, not a thief."

Alana frowned. "Baronian? My father hunt—"

"As far as I recall," Enala interrupted her, "Baronians hunt in packs. Not much of a terror by yourself, are you Joseph?" As she finished, the old woman flicked a glance at Alana, silently reprimanding her for the near-mistake.

"You've got a tongue like acid, priest," Joseph replied good-naturedly. "Glad I don't have to fight you, if you're half as ferocious with that sword." He picked at his sleeve. "And pack or not, I am a Baronian. Why else would I be all in black?"

"You look like a poor knockoff of the Tsar's Stalkers," Alana snapped. She glanced at Enala, irritated the woman hadn't ordered the man to leave yet.

Instead, Enala threw back her head and howled with laughter. Alana jumped, and stared at the old woman, open-mouthed.

"The girl is right, you do look like you've seen better days, Baronian. So sit," she said, ignoring Alana's apocalyptic look. "No need for you to go away with an empty stomach as well as empty-handed."

Shocked into silence, all Alana could do was watch as the giant took a seat on a rock near the fire. Sheathing her sword, Enala joined him, and the two started to talking like long-lost friends who had just been reunited. Alana stood there a moment longer, sword still in hand, but the two seemed to have forgotten her very existence.

Finally she sank back to her seat, though she laid her sword alongside her rather than returning it to her sheath. Enala took the fish from the flames and sliced it into three morsels. Handing Alana her portion, she turned back to Joseph. The two continued to talk as they picked at the soft flesh of the trout that Alana had frozen her hands off to catch.

Alana's anger built as she watched them eat, and she barely touched her own fish. She began to wonder whether the loss of her dragon had caused Enala to snap, if the old woman suddenly had a death wish, inviting the self-proclaimed Baronian to share their fire. The Baronians had been stamped out by her father in the early days of his rein, but she recalled tales of their people well. Great tribes of them had once roamed the wild lands of the Three Nations, harrying travellers and settlements at will. The kings of the time had been powerless to stop them, so great were their numbers.

That is, until the Tsar had come.

"You're awfully quiet, girly."

Alana jumped as she realised the giant had addressed her. She looked up from her food and glared at him. "My name's Alana," she snapped, a scowl curling her lips. "And I'm not used to sharing my food with scum."

"Is that so?" Joseph replied with a hairy grin. "Good to know." His eyes narrowed. "You know, word is there's another Alana in these parts, Daughter of the Tsar or some sort. Lot of folks looking for that one, Stalkers and the like. Causing a lot of trouble in my forest."

Ice ran down Alana's spine. She dropped her hand to her sword, preparing to launch herself at the rogue.

But Joseph only shrugged, another chuckle whispering through the smoke-filled air. "It's a good thing you're not *that* Alana, right?" He looked at her with one eyebrow raised.

Watching him, Alana slowly relaxed, and took her hand from the sword. "I guess so."

Nodding, Joseph turned to where he'd discarded his axe and pack. Rummaging inside, he came back with a bottle of what Alana took to be spirits. He offered it to her, but Alana only shook her head. Grinning, Enala took the bottle instead, and their conversation resumed, though Alana caught the old woman flash her a warning glare.

Alana rose and wandered away. Enala could take care of herself, she decided. Determined not to let her hard-earned fish go to waste, she finished her remaining portion and then tossed the bones into the stream for the crayfish to finish.

As the night grew older, she found a place near the fire and settled herself down. Enala and Joseph were still conversing, but she curled up without offering either another word and closed her eyes. At least the giant's appearance had distracted her momentarily from her brother, though thoughts of him returned now to haunt her. It was a long time before the darkness finally rose to claim her.

IN THE MORNING, Alana woke with a start. Sitting up, she looked around to find Enala already at the fire, a pot of stew bubbling over the flames. She frowned, then suppressed a groan as pain came from her neck.

"I made you a fresh batch," Enala said, as though reading her mind. The old woman nodded to a makeshift bowl of paste sitting beside Alana.

She took it gratefully. The relief as she applied it was

instant, and she closed her eyes, almost willing to sing the old woman's blessings. Almost.

Rising, Alana crossed to the fire. "Where did that come from?" she asked, gesturing to the pot and stew.

"Joseph left it for us," Enala replied, a smile that screamed I-told-you-so on her lips.

"How nice of him," Alana said sarcastically. "You sure it's not poisoned?"

"You need to open your mind, girl," the old woman snapped. She took a breath, her eyes flickering closed, as though she were in pain. "Sorry, I guess I'm not as young as I used to be."

Alana grinned despite herself. "You think?"

"Watch it, girl," Enala shot back, though there was no venom in the words. She sighed, her face turning serious. "Before we start today, I need to know, what are you trying to achieve, looking for Braidon?"

Alana quickly looked away. "I need to see him."

"Is that all of it?"

The words caught in Alana's throat as she looked up to refute the old woman's unspoken accusation. She swallowed them back. "No," she croaked. "I...he could still be alive."

Enala sighed. "I don't think so, Alana. Not with the fall he took."

"Even so...I want to see him, *need* to see him, or I'll never..."

"It won't be long, you know, before the Tsar regains enough magic to sense us. My magic is rebuilding, yours must be too. His own Magickers won't be far behind. Once his power is restored, there will be no place left for us to hide."

"So be it," Alan replied.

"So be it," Enala repeated. She grinned then, gesturing at the bubbling pot. "Well, if I'm to fight alongside someone, I'd appreciate it if she were at least a half-decent swordswoman."

"*What?*" Alana spluttered. "I am—"

"You're competent, I'll give you that, but you're no master, girl," Enala replied.

"I can take you, old woman," Alana growled.

Enala only grinned. Reaching behind her, she lifted two long sticks from behind the boulder she was perched on. She tossed one at Alana's feet.

"Then show me."

CHAPTER 10

Q uinn wore a grim smile as he listened to the crackling of the flames, their roar as they rushed up the sides of the wooden houses, the *boom* as roofs collapsed in on themselves. Great pillars of smoke spiralled upwards, merging with the grey winter sky. His men moved with swift efficiency between each house, dragging out all occupants before tossing flaming torches through the open windows.

The *whoosh* as the new building took light was music to Quinn's ears. He looked at the gathered villagers, on their knees in the centre of the settlement. They wore a mixture of grief and rage on their faces, though none moved to try and stop Quinn and his men. Nor did any come forward with information, and he grated his teeth at their continued obstruction.

Someone had to have seen them. Four renegades could not have gone unnoticed in this forest. With her blonde hair, Alana might have passed for a local, but not the others. Certainly not a young boy barely of age accompanied by an old priest, nor the giant that was Devon. A traveller, a passerby, a villager, someone, *anyone* had to have glimpsed them, even if they had kept to the backtrails.

Yet there had been no word for six days, not since the village of Onslow. There, at least, he had found a witness to Devon's precipitous disembarking from the trading ship. The man was no fool, and had obviously decided making his way through the forest was a better option than taking the Gods Road to Trola.

Of Alana and Braidon and Enala though, there had been not a whisper.

Quinn was starting to grow desperate. This was the fourth village they had burned, and the other Stalkers were becoming restless. They had taken to questioning his orders, challenging his authority at every turn. He was loathe to call on the Tsar's aid, and lose whatever respect he had left, but if there was no word soon he would have no other choice.

Turning to the villagers, Quinn strode across to where they knelt in the mud. "Any sudden recollections yet?" he growled.

The villagers glared back at him, tears streaking their cheeks. Ash fell heavily around them, staining their faces and clothes, all that remained of their livelihoods.

"You would rather see your village burned than betray a couple of renegades?" he asked, shaking his head.

"What can we tell you when we know nothing?" one of the men spat back.

"Liars!" Quinn shrieked, his sabre hissing as it left his sheath. He pointed the tip at the man's throat, but the villager barely moved.

"We do not lie," he replied. "You are mad, Stalker. The Tsar will hear of what you've done."

Quinn smirked. "The Tsar sent me to rat out these traitors. He does not care if I burn a few others along the way."

"But we are loyal—"

The man's protest was cut short as Quinn drove his blade

through the man's throat. Screams went up from the other villagers as the dying man clutched at the wound, trying hopelessly to stem the bleeding. The others tried to scramble up and flee, but Quinn's Stalkers intercepted them and forced them back to their knees. Finally, the man gave a soft groan, and toppled face-first to the ground.

Looking at the next villager in line, Quinn raised his bloody sword. "Well?"

"Please, don't hurt me!" the man screamed. He tried to scramble away, but a Stalker gripped him by the shoulder and shoved him down.

"Where is the renegade known as Devon? The blonde girl, Alana, the black-haired boy, Braidon?"

"I don't know!"

"Then die."

The man cried out, but Quinn's blade took him in the heart before he could put up any fight. He sagged against the impaling sword, then toppled sideways as Quinn dragged back his weapon.

"Who's next?" he growled, swinging his sword in an arc that spanned the remaining villagers.

"The Baronians!" a man at the end of the line shrieked as the blade stopped at an older woman.

Quinn glanced along the line. "What?"

The man paled, and he shook his head as though trying to recall the words. At a gesture from Quinn, one of the Stalkers grabbed him by the scruff of his neck and dragged him across to where the lieutenant stood. Quinn rested the cold point of his blade against the man's chest.

"Well?"

Swallowing visibly, the villager glanced from Quinn to the woman he had threatened. "Please, you have to promise to leave us alone, if I tell you."

Quinn scowled. "First tell me what you know, peasant."

"I…it's not much, only a rumour I heard."

Lowering his sword, Quinn walked around the man to where the older woman knelt. "I take it she is something to you, lad?" he asked, resting his blade against the woman's neck. She flinched away from its touch, though her eyes remained defiant.

"Please don't hurt her!" The man tried to rise, but a shove from the Stalker at his side sent him face-first into the ground.

"Then *speak*," Quinn hissed.

"There's a tribe of Baronians here, they passed by a few days ago, to collect their ransom. I overhead one of them talking about two women he'd met in the forest."

"Yes?" Quinn said, trying to keep the excitement from his voice.

"He said one was a priest, seems she impressed him."

"And the other?"

The villager cleared his throat. "He described her in... some detail," he whispered, "but...he mentioned she had blonde hair."

A fire lit in Quinn's stomach at the villager's words. He had no doubt the so-called Baronian had been speaking of Alana. Who else but she would be cavorting with the thugs inhabiting these woods? He had no idea how she had come to be travelling with the old priest, Enala, but the two of them together presented a serious threat. He would need to find a way to trap them.

If he could find them at all.

"Where?" Quinn grated as he returned to the man's side.

"West of here," the villager replied quickly. "In the forested valleys leading up towards the Sandstone Mountains."

"Very good," Quinn replied. They weren't too far from the western mountains now, though finding the two women in such dense wilderness would be another matter. He was about to move away when another question occurred to him. "You spoke of Baronians? How is that possible, the Tsar hunted them to extinction decades ago. You had best not be lying to me."

"No, I swear!" The man swallowed. "They came here a year ago, took up residence in the forest. Word was sent to the Tsar when they began raiding our villages, but no one ever came. Eventually we agreed to a ransom to keep them away from us."

Quinn stared at the man to the count of ten, but he could see no sign of deceit in his young eyes. Finally he nodded and moved away from the villagers, aware his Stalkers were watching him. This was the first substantial news they'd had since leaving Onslow, and it was still little enough at that. Time was running out and another failure would spell the end for Quinn.

"Mount up!" he shouted, spinning back to his Stalkers.

There was a moment's hesitation amongst the black-garbed men and women of his regiment. Then one stepped forward, a smirk on his face. "Are you sure, Quinn?" the man rasped. "Would it not be better for you to call on your master?"

The anger that had begun with the villager's news of Alana roared. Quinn clenched his fists, struggling to keep control of himself. He would gain nothing by rising to the man's provocation.

"You want me to distract the Tsar from his conquest, Zarent?" he asked quietly. "To call him here when we are still empty-handed? Is that truly what you want, to look him in the eye and tell him *we* have failed?"

Silence answered his question as the man Zarent blanked, and Quinn nodded.

"Very well then. If there are no other questions...? Then *mount up!*"

CHAPTER 11

Topping the rise, Braidon stumbled to a stop, his breathing heavy as he looked up and saw Devon already extending the distance between them. Letting out a groan, Braidon started after him again, trying to ignore the burning in his calves. Six days of marching through the wilderness had taken their toll, and while he thought he'd done a good job of keeping up with Devon's massive strides, he had a feeling the hammerman was holding back now.

Ahead, Devon glanced back at a bend in the narrow game trail, and Braidon picked up the pace, determined not to show the giant warrior any weakness.

A grin spread across his companion's face as Braidon marched up. "You've got stones, sonny," he said, slapping Braidon on the back.

Braidon staggered beneath the blow, his trembling legs barely managing to keep him upright. By the time he recovered, Devon was already several feet ahead. Braidon poked his tongue out at the man's retreating back, then shaking his head, continued after him.

They had no particular destination or goal in mind, and many of their six days on the road had been spent wandering the backtrails of Onslow Forest. All Braidon knew was that they were working their way west towards the Sandstone Mountains. The going was slow in the dense forest, with its low-lying scrub and steep valleys, but Devon was sure that the only alternative, the road through Brunei Pass, would be guarded against them.

Braidon came alongside Devon as the path widened once more. Glancing at the hammerman, he wondered how the man maintained such a pace for so long, seemingly without exertion. Especially with the giant warhammer *kanker* strapped to his back.

"Is it heavy?" he asked, suddenly curious if some spell on the weapon made it lighter than it appeared.

Devon cast him a sidelong look and grinned. "Try it for yourself." Unsheathing *kanker*, he tossed it into the air as though it weighed no more than a sack of feathers, caught it by the head, and offered it to Braidon.

For a full five seconds, all Braidon could do was stare at the ancient weapon, but finally he found his nerve, and reached out to grip the black haft. Still grinning, Devon released the hammer. Braidon cried out as the hammer's weight almost dragged the weapon from his hands. His other arm snapped up to grip the haft in a two-handed grip.

"Gods, how much does this *weigh?*" he groaned.

Chuckling, Devon retrieved the weapon and sheathed it.

"Not so much for a giant like me, sonny," he said. He eyed the dagger on Braidon's belt. "But maybe we can find you something a little more suitable for a growing lad."

Braidon glanced up sharply. "Really?" Alana had never let him have a sword—at least, not that he could remember.

"Why not?" Devon replied, resuming his march down the winding dirt track.

"I don't know how to use one," he mused as he caught up. "Or at least, I can't remember how… It does seem like something my father would have taught me."

"What's it like?" Devon asked, tapping his head. "Having these other memories you can't quite...remember?"

Braidon frowned, his attention distracted by a blackbird as it raced squawking across their path. "It's not easy," he said finally. "What I *can* remember of my other life, they don't seem like my memories at all. It's like they belong to some other Braidon, if that makes sense?"

"I'm not quite sure it does," Devon admitted, scratching his wiry beard.

Closing his eyes, Braidon tried to find some way to explain. "There's only a few, enough for me to know I truly was the Son of the Tsar. I can *see* them as clear as day, I can see myself in them. But I can't remember what I was thinking or feeling when I was doing those things."

"Ah, I think I get it!" the warrior grinned. "So it's kind of like watching bards performing a play, with you as the main character?"

"That seems like a very specific example," Braidon said, eyeing Devon thoughtfully.

"Yes, well," Devon grunted. "There might have been a play or two featuring yours truly after the civil war. All ancient history now, of course. You were probably too young to remember them. There was one, *The Butcher of Kalgan*, think it was. Pretty popular in the local taverns of Ardath. Well, until word got out that I'd rescinded my commission in the army."

"Yes!" Braidon exclaimed. "I *do* remember!" A grin spread across his cheeks as he looked at the hammerman. "They changed the title though: *The Cowardly Hero*, I think they called it."

Devon's own smile vanished as he glared at Braidon. "I prefer—"

Before the warrior could finish his rebuke, a high-pitched scream echoed through the trees. Braidon and Devon shared a glance. The cry sounded again; this time it was clear it came from the path ahead. Reaching up, Devon drew *kanker* and started down the track.

"Stay there," he shouted over his shoulder to Braidon as he leaped a half-buried tree root.

Braidon stood frozen to the spot and watched as the giant charged off. Another scream came from ahead. Putting aside his fear, Braidon raced after his companion. He reached down and drew his dagger as he ran, already wishing he had a larger blade to hand.

Around the bend, Braidon looked ahead, expecting to see Stalkers or soldiers with weapons at the ready. He had been waiting for them for days now, thinking at any moment that his father's warriors would come leaping from the trees. His magic restored, Braidon had hidden them both from the Tsar's powers, but with an army under his command, it was only a matter of time before they were flushed from their hiding place.

Yet as the track straightened and the source of the commotion was revealed, Braidon was surprised to find a very different scene playing out before him.

Devon was still charging ahead, but beyond the giant hammerman, a desperate battle was taking place around a small horse-drawn wagon. A man and woman stood on the seat of the wagon, longswords in hand, each struggling to keep a surging crowd of black-garbed men at bay. They might have been mistaken for his father's Stalkers, if not for their threadbare clothing and half-rusted weapons.

His heart beat faster as Devon shouted a war cry. Chasing after him, Braidon's gaze was drawn to the wagon as one of the assailants leapt, his blade catching the woman's weapon near the handle. The impact tore the sword from her grip, but screaming out in rage, she drew a blade from her belt and plunged it into the man's eye. Blood blossomed as she ripped it loose. Her attacker crumpled in a pile, but another one of his comrades was quick to take his place.

Roaring, Devon surged into the fray, his warhammer clutched one-handed. Braidon watched in awe as he carved through the bandits gathered around the wagon. The first of them went down without a sound, taken unawares by Devon's sudden attack. Next to him, another assailant staggered as the body of his comrade fell across his feet. He spun around in time to catch *kanker* squarely between the eyes. Braidon winced as the man crumpled.

There were still a dozen left, and alerted by their friends' deaths, several turned to face Devon. A man carrying a rust-speckled axe charged, the others reforming behind him. Braidon was still several yards behind Devon. He rushed forward, desperate to offer his aid.

Helped by the narrow path, Devon knocked aside a vicious blow from the axe-man, then reversed his hammer and slammed it into the bandit's chest. Striding over the falling body, he ducked a wild slash of a sword, then caught his attacker with a right hook. The man reeled back clutching his nose, until a blow from *kanker* ended the threat.

Leaping the first of the bodies, Braidon rushed forward, but Devon's bulk filled the narrow animal track, and there was no way for him to enter the fray. The big man was laughing now, his mirth bellowing out with each swing of his hammer.

As Braidon watched, another man came at the giant. A sword thrust beneath Devon's guard, but a swing of his gauntleted wrist smashed the blade aside. Before the bandit could react, Devon's hand flicked out, catching the assailant by the shirt and dragging him into a headbutt. There was an audible *crunch* of breaking bone. Tossing the unconscious man aside, Devon continued forward.

On the wagon, the man had downed one of his assailants, while the woman had recovered a sword and was making short work of a bandit trying to gain a foothold beside her.

Suddenly a cry went up, and as Braidon watched, the

remaining bandits turned tail and fled. Devon dispatched a bandit and then swung around, searching for his next opponent. He blinked, a frown creasing his forehead as he observed the suddenly empty trail.

Seeing the last of the men vanishing into the woods, he bellowed after them, "Cowards!" His cry echoed loudly on the trail, though none of the thieves stopped to challenge his accusation.

"They're thieves, Devon," Braidon muttered, moving alongside him. "It's not like they're the stuff of legend."

The big man glanced down at him. Blood matted his beard, and there were several cuts on his arms, but otherwise he didn't seem injured. His frown faded, and Braidon watched as the tension slowly drained from the warrior's body.

"True," Devon grunted, finally.

A shriek from the wagon drew Braidon's attention back to the couple. One of the bandits they'd downed was climbing to his knees, but before he could stand, the woman leapt from the wagon. Her sword cleaved his spine and he crashed back to the ground. Hurling aside her sword, the woman kicked him in the side.

"Serves. You. Right." She punctuated each word with another kick. "Trying. To. Rob. Us. Good. For. Nothing. *Bastard!*"

"Enough, Elynor!" Sheathing his sword, the man came up behind the woman and grabbed her arm.

She screamed at his touch and swung a fist to fight him off. The man staggered back from the blow, raising a hand to fend off further attack, but seeing it was him, the woman lowered her hand. "Just making sure he got the point."

Braidon glanced at the bandit. Blood slowly spread out around him, forming a scarlet pool in the hard-packed earth.

"I'd say he gets it," Devon rumbled. Braidon nodded his agreement.

On the path, the two spun to face them. The man raised his sword and the woman quickly recovered hers. Braidon raised his hands, but Devon only chuckled.

"Is that any way to treat your saviours?" the giant warrior asked, gesturing to the bandits he'd felled.

The woman scowled. "We had things handled," she snapped, but her sword lowered a fraction. Beside her, the man did the same.

Grinning, Devon wandered towards them, surveying the fallen men as he went. "What were there, a dozen?" He glanced back at Braidon. "How many would you say made it into the woods, sonny?"

"Six?" Braidon replied uncertainly.

"A few more than a dozen then," Devon replied.

Beyond, the couple shared a glance. They were well-dressed in warm woollen coats and thick leather boots. Though the snow from earlier in the week had thawed, Braidon found himself wishing he was similarly attired. However, the clothing worn by the slain bandits was even shabbier than his own fraying jerkin and boots. His eyes settled on a sword pitted with dents and rust. Thinking it might be better than his tiny dagger, he scooped it up.

"Yes, well, whatever our chances were," the man was saying, "I thank you for your help, hammerman." Striding forward, he offered his hand. "My names Carcia, and this is my wife, Elynor. The two of us are in your debt."

Devon shook the man's hand, though Braidon noticed his eyes were on the wagon. The bandits had managed to tear off the blanket covering the back, and Braidon could see a handful of household items lying in a cluttered pile. It looked as though the two had packed in a hurry. They might have been well-dressed, but Braidon guessed they had fallen on hard times to find themselves so far from the Gods Road without so much as a sellsword to help guard their belongings.

"What brings you so far into the forest with a rocking

chain and spindle?" Devon asked, sheathing his hammer on his back. Braidon removed a sword belt from one of the bandits and put away his new sword. With their weapons secured, the couple seemed to relax.

"Elynor and I are running away," the man explained. "We've had enough of the wars, so we're getting out." He paused, his eyes flickering to the hammer on Devon's back. "Just like you, if my suspicions about that hammer are correct."

Devon shrugged. "True enough." He gestured at the wagon. "How about the two of you mount up and we continue this conversation on the road. Who knows if there's more of them scum out there."

Casting nervous glances at the woods, the couple nodded and returned to their wagon. Carcia took a moment to inspect the horse as Elynor climbed into the seat and picked up the reins. A few moments later Carcia joined her, apparently assured the gelding was okay. Braidon guessed the bandits had been intent on taking the beast as their own— after all, it was the most valuable thing he could see in the couple's possession.

With a flick of the reins, the horse started off. Devon strode along beside it, his eyes on the trees, and Braidon hurried to catch up. Now that the adrenaline was fading from his body, his exhaustion returned, and he looked at the back of the wagon with longing.

"Don't suppose you've got room up there for the boy?" Devon asked as Braidon reached them.

Braidon opened his mouth to argue, but the woman was already nodding, and before he could react Devon was scooping him up and tossing him down amongst the wooden chairs and furnishings.

"There's probably room for you as well," Carcia offered, though his face betrayed his doubt.

Devon shook his head. "I'm just as happy walking, sonny,"

he replied. "Good for the heart."

Brushing dust from his clothes, Braidon climbed forward until he could seat himself behind the couple. "Thanks for the ride," he said sheepishly. "The name's Braidon, by the way. I guess you already know Devon's."

"Least we could do after you helped us out," Carcia replied, though beside him his wife snorted. He flicked her a scowl before continuing. "What brings you so far from the capital, young Braidon?" he asked. "That's an Ardath accent, if I'm not mistaken?"

Braidon shared a glance with Devon. "Same as you, I suppose," he said hesitantly, belatedly attempting to add a more rustic tone to his voice. "Devon was a friend of my parents, before...they passed. He's looked after me ever since. I'm fifteen last year, and Devon thought it best we leave before I was conscripted into the war."

Alongside the wagon, Devon's eyebrows rose at the lie, before he quickly nodded in response to the couple's inquisitive stares. "We're heading into the Sandstone Mountains," the warrior said. "See if we can make a life for ourselves out here, least until the war dies down.

"I hear the Queen is marching on us with the Northland army," Carcia said in a hushed tone, as though the woman were close by, and not a thousand leagues to the north."

"That'd be the day," Devon grunted. "More likely, the damned Tsar is looking for an excuse to conquer another kingdom."

Braidon's heart skipped a beat at Devon's treasonous words. A strained silence followed. Braidon looked at the couple out of the corner of his eye, trying to judge their reactions by the expressions on their faces. Beside the wagon, Devon's face blanked and his hands tightened into fists.

"I suppose that could be true," Carcia said, then laughed. "By the Three Gods, it's nice to hear some plain speaking for once!"

The woman was still eyeing Devon closely, but after another moment she seemed to shrug his comment off. "Perhaps, but whatever his faults, I'd still rather have the Tsar ruling us, than those barbarians in the north. Might not be such a bad thing to put them in their place, either. The Gods know they can't be trusted."

Anger flared in Braidon's chest. Remembering the kindness the Northland people had shown when they'd taken him under their protection, the woman's words grated on him. Clenching his teeth, he swallowed back an insult.

"Can't say I've ever had a problem with 'em," Devon said diplomatically. "Their traders have certainly proven more trustworthy than some of the Lonians I've dealt with."

Elynor snorted. "They might pretend they've changed, but a Feline doesn't change its stripes. They've tried to invade —twice. Now that they've got this new Queen, Merydith or whatever her name is, what's to stop them trying it again?"

"Respect, trade, peace?" Braidon asked.

"Those might mean something to a rational leader, little boy, but who's to say we're dealing with someone rational?"

"And what would you prefer?" Devon rumbled. "We invade them unprovoked?"

"If needs be."

"How would that make us any better than those who marched under Archon?" the hammerman asked.

"We're the Three Nations," Elynor replied as though the answer were obvious. "We're the good guys."

"Tell that to Trola," Devon grunted.

An awkward silence stretched out between the four of them as they continued on their way. Braidon shared a look with Devon, but with nothing left to say, they let the conversation drop. Lying back in the wagon, Braidon closed his eyes, pleased for the chance to rest. The soft creaking of the wooden wheels played in his ears like a lullaby, the gentle rocking of the wagon beckoning him to sleep.

CHAPTER 12

"Woah, boy!" Merydith said, pulling back on the reins. Her mount came to a stop on the hilltop, and she allowed herself to glance back over her shoulder. Away to the north, the towering mountains of Erachill rose from the foothills she and her army had just traversed. The tall bows of beech trees rose from the hillslopes, their canopies thick with leaves even in the depths of winter, concealing her forces below.

Turning her gaze to the way ahead, Merydith looked on the empty hillside leading down the last ten miles to the coast. There, the land fell away sharply to the raging waters of two oceans—except where the narrow stretch of land known as The Gap spanned the channel. The ramparts of Fort Fall rose from the earth there, its granite walls standing in defiance of the centuries.

Once, it had been the impenetrable fortress of the Three Nations, the bane of her people. From its gates the south-erners sallied out to raid the clans of the north, crushing any hint of rebellion—until Archon had united them beneath his dark cause. Only once had the fortress fallen, during Archon's first coming.

Now, thankfully, its gates stood open to them. Merydith breathed a sigh of relief to see the Tsar's people had not yet reached the fortress. Her plans relied on crossing into the Three Nations before Fort Fall could be secured against them. Once they had a foothold in northern Lonia, the Tsar would be forced to bring his army against her, or risk having his supply lines cut when he tried to march farther north.

With luck, Merydith and her five thousand would lead him a merry chase, buying enough time for those back in Erachill to gather the rest of their army.

Supplying her own forces would quickly become difficult though, if her allies in Lonia and Trola fell through. She had sent messengers before their departure from Erachill, but so far there had been no word on whether they had reached their destination. Like so many other parts to her plan, all she could do was pray.

"We made it." Damyn brought his horse alongside her.

Merydith smiled at her childhood friend and new captain. "Did you doubt it?"

Damyn rolled his eyes. "Do you have to ask?"

Chuckling, Merydith shook her head. "I hope you didn't let your cohort see it."

She had placed him in command of the vanguard. His soldiers were gathering around them even now, their horses kept in tight formation. Steam rose from their flanks in the morning chill, and the men wore thick woollen coats over their chainmail. Most wore steel helmets and were armed with sabres and iron bucklers for shields. They looked to her in anticipation, awaiting the command to advance.

A smile touched her lips as she raised her hand. With a shout, Damyn kicked his horse forward. The thunder of five hundred horses rumbled across the slopes as the vanguard followed him. Watching them ride, she found herself wondering at the change time had wrought. Whereas a century ago, her people had united with dreams of conquest and destruction, today they rode south in defence of their nation. Her heart swelled at the sight, and with a shout she started down the slope after them.

Ahead, her five hundred cavalry slowed as they neared Fort Fall. Damyn knew his orders well. He was to search the fortress and ensure no ambush waited, before continuing south to scout out the enemy's position. She hoped they had time yet before the Tsar arrived, but she had no desire to be taken unawares.

"The true test begins now." Murdo's dry, rasping voice came from behind her.

Merydith smiled at the sight of the old man in the saddle. In the warmth of the southern sun, he looked younger than she'd seen him in years. Her smile faded as she recognised the figure who rode beside him.

"The beginning of the end," Mokyre said bitterly.

"Did you want Clan Cranook to join the vanguard, Mokyre?" she asked coldly. Distasteful as she found his presence, Merydith had disliked the prospect of leaving the Cranook clan leader behind in Erachill even less. She didn't need enemies stirring things up behind her back while she was risking her life in the south.

The man scowled, but wisely kept his silence. Merydith nodded her approval, as Murdo chuckled, a mischievous grin on his face.

"So, my Queen, the invasion begins. Did you ever dream you'd end up leading an army against the Three Nations?"

Merydith smiled despite herself. "I can't say I did," she replied with a wink, "but after everything they've done for us, I figure it's the least I can do."

Murdo laughed, while Mokyre only scowled and looked away.

Silence fell as they approached the walls. Damyn and his vanguard had already disappeared within the fortress. Merydith took the silence as a good sign. With a glance at her guard, she continued towards the walls.

"I always forget how large this place is," Murdo murmured, his old eyes on the granite walls. "A wonder it was ever taken."

"Hardly difficult with the magic at Archon's command," Merydith replied.

"Do you think he has become more powerful than Archon? The Tsar, I mean?" the old man mused.

"I don't know or care," Merydith answered. "I just hope Helen and her Magickers are powerful enough to hold him back."

"They will be," Murdo said with confidence. Alongside him, Mokyre snorted but said nothing.

"They will or they won't. There's nothing I can do to change it," Merydith sighed. "Much as I might wish it otherwise."

Merydith's thoughts returned to Enala and Braidon. She found herself wondering again what had happened to them, what had gone wrong. Because if the Tsar was marching north with an army, it could only mean they had failed. As for Devon and Kellian, she hadn't heard a single whisper of them since they'd made contact with Enala's connection in Trola.

"She will return to us," Murdo said from beside her. "She always has."

Glancing at the old man, Merydith sighed. She'd forgotten her face was like an open book to him. Her eyes burned at his words and she quickly blinked back the unspilt tears. "This time was different. This time, she said goodbye."

"The woman isn't one to go down without a fight," Murdo murmured. "We'll see her again, you'll see."

Merydith nodded, though she couldn't bring herself to believe the old man's words. The morning Enala had said her goodbyes, Merydith had known in her heart it would be the last time she saw her. But she could not let the others see her despair.

"I know," she replied, forcing a smile to her lips. "I'm just afraid the stubborn old woman has bitten off more than she can chew."

"Better not let her hear you call her that." The old man winked.

As they approached the walls of Fort Fall, Merydith directed her horse towards the open gates. The two clan leaders followed, her guard bringing up the rear. While Merydith had passed this way many times as a child, of the others only Murdo had seen the fortress in person, having been her mother's bodyguard during her journeys south.

Despite his opposition to their quest, the Mokyre's awe for the fortress was clear from the way his mouth hung open as they passed through the first of the gate tunnels. There were three walls in total, each thicker and taller than the last, with wide killing grounds spaced between them. The land rose beneath them as they passed through each gate, so that the defenders did not have so high to climb to reach the ramparts. Beyond the third wall, the gates led into the citadel itself, the tunnel giving way to a series of courtyards overlooked by marble mezzanines and passageways lined with murder holes. Finally, they emerged into the courtyard before the southern gate.

Here Merydith paused to rest her horse, taking the time to look around. For the first time, she saw the damage Enala and Dahniul had wrought when they had come to the rescue of Devon and his friends. A smoky stench still hung around the southern gate tunnel, and a mezzanine had collapsed into the courtyard, as though a giant hand—or a dragon's wing—had smashed it.

Shaking her head, Merydith led her companions into the gate tunnel, eager to be rid of the fortress. Together they rode out onto the plains of northern Lonia.

"Congratulations, Your Majesty," Murdo declared in a solemn voice. "You just invaded the Three Nations."

"Ay," she replied, her eyes on the horizon.

There, ten miles beyond the wasteland, a dust cloud rose from the hooves of racing horses. Silence fell across their company as they watched the horsemen approaching. It was a full minute before Merydith recognised the flashing blue colours of Damyn's scouts. Behind them, the horses of her army slowly formed up beneath the walls of the fortress.

When the first of scout reached them, Merydith rode forward and dismounted, even as the man leapt to the ground before her. Several more were approaching rapidly. There was no sign of the rest of her vanguard, and she prayed Damyn and his force were already safely concealed within the woods south of the wasteland.

"Your Majesty!" the scout gasped.

"Tell me," Merydith said.

The man looked at her, his eyes alive, shining with fear and excitement. "It's the Tsar," he said in a rush. "He has an advance force, already in the forest. They're on foot, but less than a day's march out."

"Did they spot you?"

"No." The man shook his head. "We pulled back as soon as we sighted them."

"Good," Merydith said. "Then I have orders for your captain."

CHAPTER 13

Alana woke, as she had every morning for the last week, to a sharp kick in her ribs. Cursing, she rolled on her side and glared up at the old woman standing over her.

"Enough, I'm awake!" she growled as Enala drew back her foot in preparation for another kick.

Offering a grim smile, Enala tossed a wooden branch down beside Alana and turned away. Alana muttered something choice beneath her breath as she picked it up and climbed to her feet. Around them the forest was still dark with shadow, the first traces of light only just beginning to filter through the canopy.

"Ready?" Enala asked, turning back and raising her makeshift practice sword.

Alana stifled a groan. Wiping the last of the sleep from her eyes, she squared off against the old woman. Over the past few days, the ancient Magicker had shown Alana exactly how little she measured up against a master swordswoman. While the cuts around Alana's neck were now almost healed, her grandmother had ensured she woke to fresh bruises each morning.

Even so, Alana wasn't willing to admit defeat. Spinning

her stick in one hand, she nodded. There were no angry words left to offer now, and she approached the old woman with caution, weapon extended, watching for the slightest hint of movement.

"Show me," Enala murmured.

Alana surged forward, her stick lancing for the old woman's throat. Her grandmother spun away, her own stick leaping up, and Alana was forced to divert her attack to block the would-be deadly thrust. The *clack* of their weapons meeting echoed through the trees as Alana shifted on her feet, seeking to use her height and power to force the old woman back.

Despite her age, Enala was no pushover, and before Alana could bring her weapon to bare, the old woman's shoulder crashed into her chest. The attack sent Alana reeling off-balance. Red flashed across her vision as her grandmother's branch struck her temple. Cursing, Alana thrust upwards, and to her surprise felt the blow connect.

Her grandmother gasped, and Alana took advantage to retreat out of range. They stood staring at one another for a moment, before a smile crossed Enala's face.

"Better," she said, "if you hadn't already been dead."

Alana scowled. Baring her teeth, she brought up her makeshift sword and darted forward in a feint. Her grandmother's branch leapt to meet her, but Alana spun on her heel, aiming low at Enala's thigh. Showing surprising agility, the old woman jumped and Alana's attack sliced empty air. Unbalanced, Alana staggered forward and caught a boot to her jaw.

The blow spun her on her feet, and she had to thrust out a hand at nearby tree to keep from falling. Gasping, she righted herself. The crunch of dry leaves warned her of Enala's approach, and she dived to the side. The old woman's branch careened from the tree trunk with a *thud*.

Recovering finally, Alana surged forward. Trapped by the

tree, Enala spun, her branch coming up to meet Alana's attack. The *clack-clacking* of their makeshift swords sounded sharply in her ears. Fighting desperately, Alana pressed her advantage, trying to force the old woman back against the tree. When her grandmother had nowhere left to retreat, Alana thrust out with her makeshift sword, seeking what would be a killing blow.

Enala's cloak swept up as she sidestepped, entangling Alana's stick in the heavy fabric. Before she could dislodge it, Enala's weapon slammed down on the branch close to where she held it. The force of the strike tore the stick from Alana's fingers, and she cursed as Enala's branch rose to rest gently on her throat.

"Impatience will be your downfall, girl," Enala said, offering Alana her weapon back.

Alana gave a quick nod and snatched the branch from her grandmother's hands. Another thirty minutes of humiliation and defeat followed. Enala was never cruel, nor savage as her father had been, but for Alana, her softly spoken reprimands were almost as bad. All her life, Alana had been taught to conquer, to beat down her enemies with sheer force and unyielding determination, to never give an inch. After all she had suffered at her father's hands, Alana had believed herself skilled with a blade.

Enala had disavowed her of that illusion over the past week. It was galling to find herself squarely outmatched by the old woman, though Alana had to admit she was improving, as her usual battle rage was honed by freshly-taught intuition.

When they finally finished, Alana slumped down beside the dead fire, a fresh set of bruises now covering her arms, torso and fingers. The soft scuffling of boots on broken leaves followed as Enala sat beside her, a weary smile on her lips.

"You were better today," she said. "We may make a swordswoman of you yet."

Alana snorted. "I doubt we have the time," she murmured.

Over the last week, Alana's fear of her father had grown daily, until now it was all she could do to close her eyes at night. She could almost feel him at the periphery of her vision, watching from afar, amused by her feeble attempts to foil him. At least Enala's training proved a distraction, though each day the burnt-out villages they passed through reminded them of his hunters' presence.

So far they had managed to evade the black-clad Stalkers. Signs of them were everywhere in the forest though, and Alana could almost feel the noose closing around her throat. She wasn't sure why they hadn't already found them; the Tsar could have led his Stalkers directly to their campsite with his magic.

Meanwhile, their hunt for her brother had continued through the endless days and nights. At first Alana had despaired at her grandmother's belief that Braidon was dead; now though, Alana found herself clinging to the hope the old woman was wrong. How else could he have just vanished, if he had not survived the fall? The thought of her brother alone out in this forest, defenceless against monsters and Baronian thugs like Joseph, terrified Alana, but it was still better than the alternative.

Alana knew her grandmother still could not bring herself to believe it. Looking at her now, Alana couldn't help but wonder how much life the old woman had left in her. The week in the forest had drained her grandmother of colour, and while she still moved with shocking speed during combat, there was no forgetting the woman was over a century old. During the days, Alana had begun to notice her grandmother struggling to keep up, and their progress had slowed as the week endured.

Sudden warmth bathed Alana's face, and glancing up, she gaped at the gently crackling fire. The surge of magic was already dying away, but Alana looked at her grandmother in horror.

"You used your magic!" she gasped. "My father, he'll—"

"He already knows where we are, child," Enala replied. "If our magic has returned, so has the Tsar's."

"Obviously," Alana snapped. "But…" She trailed off, and her grandmother nodded sadly.

"He's watching us, toying with us. He knows we can't escape him, not with his Stalkers so close. We should have fled long ago. I fear it is too late now. The only way to escape his gaze…"

"No," Alana hissed, shaking her head.

She knew what her grandmother was suggesting, but she couldn't bear the thought of turning her magic on herself again and wiping her memories. The last time had almost destroyed her. She couldn't risk adding a third personality to the two already crowding her mind. It would drive her insane; she was close enough to it already.

Enala nodded. "I thought as much," she sighed. "Then… it's time we left this forest. I'm sorry for what happened to your brother, but we've run out of time."

A lump lodged in Alana's throat. She quickly looked away, struggling to keep the tears from her eyes. Whether Braidon lived or not, there was wisdom in the old woman's words. Braidon could hide himself from their father's magic; Alana and her grandmother could not.

"I…" Thorns of iron wrapped their way around Alana's heart at the thought of abandoning her brother. "No, not yet." She stood suddenly, eyes flashing. "One more day."

Enala looked back at her, a sad twist on her lips, sapphire eyes shining. They were so like her father's, her brother's, that Alana had to look away. Her own granite-grey eyes she'd gotten from her mother—something she had always been glad of. She hated looking into her father's icy eyes, and though she saw only kindness when she looked at her brother, she couldn't help but doubt at times, couldn't help but wonder what else of their father Braidon had inherited.

Alana had done all she could to protect him, to keep him from the Tsar's darkness, but she still feared the monster her father wanted him to become.

Looking into Enala's eyes now, Alana recognised the same hard glint as her father, the unyielding strength that would break before it bent. Enala's son took after her more than the woman cared to admit. Alana dug in, preparing herself to argue, but her grandmother only nodded.

Drawing herself to her feet, the old woman gathered her cloak and gestured to the woods. "Lead the way, granddaughter," she said, not unkindly.

A tingling sensation slid down Alana's spine. It was the first time Enala had called her "granddaughter," and she did not deny the title. Swallowing, she looked at the trees, and picking a direction, set off through the growing light.

They walked for the first hour in silence, as the sun slowly crept higher into the sky. Its heat rarely reached the shadows beneath the canopy, but the light still improved Alana's mood. At least during the day, she could see her father's Stalkers coming. At night, they were forced to take shifts, to sit staring out into the icy dark and pray nothing came near.

As they entered the second hour of their trek, Alana decided to break the silence. Over the last week, she and Enala had settled into a truce, forming a routine between them. Her grandmother would wake Alana each morning to receive her daily bruising, before they broke their fast and set off for the day's search. If they were lucky, one of them would catch a trout or hare for food, but for the most part they walked in silence. Now though, Alana had seen a touch of her grandmother's gentler side, and she found herself wondering at the old woman.

"Did you know?" she asked abruptly as they stopped beside a creek for water. Enala looked perplexed, and Alana elaborated. "Did you know who we were, when you first found us?"

When Alana and her brother had first met the old woman, she'd called herself Tillie. It seemed beyond the realms of coincidence that she should turn out to actually be their grandmother...and yet, no one else had known Alana and Braidon would be in that forest.

Enala straightened beside the creek. "No," she said, "I was only following orders. It seems Antonia still has a sense of humour, even after all these decades."

"Antonia sent you?" Alana asked. Her heart quickened as she remembered the Goddess from her dream, the small girl's awesome rage. She swallowed. "You're...on speaking terms with her?"

Her grandmother smiled. "In a sense," she replied. "She was a part of me once. It is a curse of our bloodline, it seems, that we alone can be hosts for the Gods. Antonia returned my body, but she still drops by from time to time with messages for me."

Alana shuddered. "I see."

So, Antonia had been meddling in her life since long before Alana's dream back in the citadel. A part of her was horrified: their father had raised her to mistrust the Gods. But the other, gentler side of her warmed, reassured at the thought there was something out there, keeping an eye out for her.

The conversation petered out, and leaving the stream, they continued on their way. Feeling more confident now, Alana walked alongside the old woman, asking questions occasionally about her past, of the lands to the north of the Three Nations and the Queen that ruled them. Alana found herself wondering what her life might have been like had Enala been there during her childhood, if she had taken them before their father's cruelty could touch them...

Alana tore her mind from the thoughts of 'what if'. She

pursed her lips. The past was set, and her grandmother had made her choice. It was a long time now since the glory days of the old woman's youth. Once, she might have protected Alana and Braidon from her son's wrath; now though, Enala was a woman out of time, the sole survivor of a generation long since gone.

A lump formed in Alana's throat as she finally realised how lonely it must have been, to watch everyone and everything she'd ever loved wither and die, to see her only child turn from her into darkness, for her grandchildren to grow up without her and suffer because of it.

Swallowing the lump, Alana followed after her grandmother, all questions gone from her mind. The day grew older, as they wandered down goat track after game trail, always searching for sign of the boy who had fallen from the dragon. In the dense forest, they'd encountered no one but the self-proclaimed Baronian over the last week. They had avoided settlements for the most part, except where the buildings had obviously been abandoned or burnt-out.

The last of the light was just beginning to fade when Alana sensed the magic come rushing through the trees towards them. She swung towards the presence, expecting an attack, only realising it was not directed at them when she found empty forest before her. The hairs on the back of her neck stood on end as the metallic taste of magic filled her mouth.

Ahead, Enala had frozen in her tracks and was staring in the same direction as Alana. They shared a glance, though neither could quite put into words the sudden hope that sprang between them.

The magic in the woods was far off, but unmistakable.

It tasted of the Light.

Alana was running through the trees before her mouth could form her brother's name.

"*Braidon!*"

CHAPTER 14

It was nearing nightfall by the time Devon, Braidon and the couple reached a settlement. As the flickering lights of torches came into view between the trees, Devon couldn't help but let out a groan. Their newfound travel companions had been convinced there was a village ahead, but they hadn't known whether it was close enough to reach before dark. Having already fended off one group of bandits that day, Devon hadn't been looking forward to the prospect of spending another night exposed to any would-be thieves.

Thankfully the approaching lights promised a soft bed and hot meal, and he couldn't help but grin. Reaching into the back of the wagon, he gripped Braidon by the shoulder and shook him awake. The boy snorted and looked at him through sleepy eyes.

"What is it?" he asked, fumbling for his sword.

"Easy sonny," Devon said. "We're here. Time for a hot meal and a bath, I think."

Nodding, Braidon climbed from the wagon as Elynor directed the horse into the small square around which the settlement was built around. Taking care not to trip over the short sword strapped to his belt, he frowned at Devon.

"Do we have any money?" he asked.

Devon shook his head and turned towards the couple, but Elynor and Carcia were practically fleeing towards the inn in their haste to avoid them. Devon looked back at Braidon.

"Guess we're on our own on that one," he chuckled. "I'm sure we can manage a bit of work for a bed and meal for the night."

Braidon's eyebrows lifted into his mop of curly black hair, and still laughing, Devon moved off. The settlement they'd found themselves in only consisted of a few dozen wooden buildings laid out in a circular pattern around the square of hard-packed earth in which they stood. The inn stood out as the only building with a sign, though the faded red paint spelling its name could not be read. With Braidon in tow, Devon headed for the wooden steps leading up to the front door through which their former companions had already disappeared.

As they approached, the door swung open and a woman with auburn hair and russet-brown eyes stepped out onto the inn's porch. Her gaze swept the square, settling on Devon and Braidon.

"Suppose you're looking for a room?" she asked, raising her slender eyebrows.

Devon scratched his wiry beard and offered a sheepish grin. "Ay, we are. Got any space?"

"Got any money?" she countered.

"A few coppers…" he trailed off, then spread his hands. "There was trouble in Ardath. We left in a hurry."

"So I heard." Her eyes narrowed, and Devon wondered what the couple had told her. "You'd best not be bringing any of that trouble into my establishment." She jerked her head at the alleyway leading to the rear of the inn. "You'll find some uncut wood rounds out back. When you're done, there'll be a hot meal and straw bed for each of you. Don't go tramping any of that mud inside."

Before either of them could reply, she disappeared back into the building. Devon grinned at Braidon as the door slammed behind her. "What'd I say, sonny?"

Braidon groaned but said nothing, and together the two of them wandered around back. Devon hesitated as he saw the pile of wood waiting for them. Stacked along the rear wall of the building, it came almost up to his shoulders.

"Don't suppose you've got a shilling tucked away somewhere, sonny?" he asked.

The boy grunted, his knitted brow revealing his displeasure. Two blocks of wood had been left out, an axe head buried in each. Unstrapping his sword belt, Braidon wandered over and gripped the haft of the first axe with both hands. He placed his boot on the block of wood and yanked. The haft slipped from his fingers and he went stumbling back, toppling over the second round of wood.

Devon roared with laughter as the boy scrambled to his feet. "This is ridiculous!"

"Oh relax, sonny." He wandered over to the axe Braidon had attempted to free and yanked it clear. Tossing it into the air, he caught it by the head and offered it to the red-faced Braidon. "Here, I'll show you how it's done. Together we'll make short work of that stack."

Braidon studied the axe suspiciously before accepting it. Devon retrieved the second blade, then took a round from the wood pile and placed it on the chopping block.

The axe whistled as he hefted it above his head and slammed it into the round. The power of his swing drove the blade clean through, splitting the wood in a single strike and embedding the axe in the block beneath. Twisting the haft, he jerked it free and knocked the cut pieces aside.

"Grab me another, would ya sonny?" he asked with a grin.

His eyes wide, Braidon leapt to obey. They continued for twenty minutes, Devon chopping, Braidon fetching the uncut rounds and stacking the cut pieces in a fresh pile for firewood. Each worked in silence, content to go about the business of earning their dinner as the last daylight faded beneath the trees at the edge of the settlement.

The woman from the inn appeared at the back door, a lit lantern in hand. She took a moment to inspect the pile Braidon had been stacking before hanging the lantern in a bracket and retreating into the building.

Wiping sweat from his brow, Devon shared a grin with Braidon. "Think it might be time you took a turn, sonny."

Braidon looked at the round he'd just placed on the block, then cast an apprehensive glance at the axe in Devon's hand. "Are you sure?"

Reversing the axe, Devon offered it handle first. "It'll help put some muscle on you. You'll need it if you're gonna use that sword of yours. Promise I won't laugh."

The boy pursed his lips, but he took the axe and moved to stand in front of the block. Casting a final glance at Devon, he hefted the tool above his head and slammed it down on the waiting wood. His aim was poor, and the blade struck with a dull thud, then rebounded from the round and struck the block beneath.

Devon's laughter boomed out across the courtyard, and Braidon's face turned red in the light of the lantern. "Hey!" He pointed the axe at Devon as though it were a sword. "You promised not to laugh!"

Grinning, Devon shook his head. "Sorry, sonny. Won't happen again." Moving to stand beside Braidon, he used his boot to push the boy's feet further apart. "You need to widen your stance," he explained. "Most of the swing comes from your hips. You're far too rigid, so when you swing the axe, you have no power, no accuracy."

Braidon *hmph*ed, but he obeyed, and standing back, Devon nodded for him to try again.

This time the blade struck true, but only made it a third

of the way through the round. Braidon yanked at the handle, trying to free the blade, but the round came with it. Its weight tore the axe from his hands, and Braidon cursed, leaping back as axe and wood toppled to the ground.

Devon retrieved the round and pulled the axe loose as Braidon unleashed a string of words that impressed even Devon.

"Relax, sonny, you'll get it," he said, offering the axe once more.

"I'm not strong enough!" Braidon snapped, eyes flashing. "I'm not a monster like you, I don't have arms the size of a bear."

"Then use what you've got!" Devon replied. "Those legs of yours have kept up with me all this way, *use* them."

Braidon snorted. "Sure. And how exactly can I do that?"

"Like I said, the swing comes from your hips, same as everything else. This time when you go to swing, take a step towards the log. Focus on transferring the momentum from your hips up through your chest, into your arms. Go on, try it," he added, when Braidon still didn't move.

Muttering under his breath, the boy hefted the axe and moved back into position. This time he positioned himself farther back from the log. He paused a moment, the breath whistling in his nostrils, then nodded, as though reassuring himself he could do it. Lifting the axe, he stepped forward and drove it down into the round.

There was a soft *thunk* as the blade sliced clean through the wood and struck the stump beneath. Wandering forward, Devon grinned at the surprised look on Braidon's face.

"Told ya sonny," he rumbled, slapping Braidon on the back. Then he crossed to the stack of uncut rounds, and placed another before the boy. "Now let's see you do it again."

They continued for another half hour with roles reversed. Their pace was slower with Braidon handling the woodcutting, but nonetheless, Devon was proud of the way the boy took to the task. He might have been raised in a palace, but Braidon was no shirker for hard work.

They were toiling by lantern light alone when the woman reappeared at the back door. Surveying their work, she gave a satisfied nod. "I suppose that'll do." She cast an appraising eye over Devon before adding, "There'll be no trouble in my establishment, understood?"

Devon agreed, and she waved for them to join her. They had started up the steps when she suddenly turned back, her nostrils flaring. "On second thought, you'd best take a bath. The smell of the two of you would drive a sow from its pigsty. There's a trough over there. Join me when you smell less like a horse's ass."

She vanished, leaving Devon staring dumbly up at the closed door. Anger rumbled in his chest as he clenched his fists, but beside him, Braidon chuckled.

"She's right you know, you *stink!*"

Devon turned slowly to look at the boy. "Is that so?"

Braidon blanked, but before he could react, Devon scooped him up over his shoulder. The boy's protests range out across the courtyard, but in three quick strides Devon reached the trough. Normally, he guessed it was used to water horses, but Devon had no doubt it doubled for the stable-hand's bath when the crotchety owner demanded it. With a grin, he hefted Braidon and dropped him into the ice-cold water.

The boy vanished beneath the surface and came up screaming. Water sloshed over the sides as he scrambled to his feet. He spluttered wordlessly as torrents ran from his face and clothes. His teeth chattering, he pointed a trembling finger at Devon.

"You *bastard!*" he shrieked.

Devon started to laugh, but Braidon surged forward, using his feet to send a wave splashing up out of the trough. The water caught Devon in the chest, soaking him to the skin, and cursing, he stumbled back. By then it was too late—his pants and shirt were already soaked.

"Thanks," he said wryly.

Braidon glared at him, looking ready to do much worse. Chuckling, Devon stripped off his shirt and pants before any further damage could be done.

By the time the two of them wandered into the warmth of the inn's dining room, they were both frozen to the core. Devon had done his best to wring the water from their clothes, but without anything else to wear, they'd been forced to put them back on still damp. Teeth chattering, they shuffled across to where a fire burned in the giant hearth.

"There, isn't that better?"

Devon turned to find the innkeeper standing behind them, a wry smile on her face. Despite himself, he found himself grinning back. "Not really."

"Oh well, better for the rest of us at least." She carried a bowl of stew in each hand. Handing them over, she wandered off to serve the rest of her customers.

Steaming bowl in hand, Devon followed the woman's path through the dining room. He saw the couple they had rescued at a table in the corner, but the two were now studiously ignoring him. Sighing, he rolled his eyes. It seemed their gratitude hadn't even outlasted the daylight. His gaze continued around the room, but there were only a few locals present, old men mostly, too engaged in their evening meals and the day's gossip to notice Devon or Braidon. It seemed whatever pursuit the Tsar might be mounting, it hadn't yet reached this part of the Onslow Forest.

Not that they had much forest left. They were nearing the mountains now, and he hoped the crevasses and canyons of the Sandstone peaks would be enough to shield them from the roaming eyes of the Tsar's dragons.

The broth the innkeeper had served them was bland, but

its warmth at least helped thaw the ice that had lodged in Devon's chest. When they'd finished, she returned with a tankard of ale and a plate stacked with mashed potatoes, beans and sausages. They accepted both offerings with thanks, their stomachs still aching from the measly rations they'd managed to scavenge on their trip through the forest.

Finally Devon sat back with a groan, his stomach full for the first time in weeks. "Well, sonny, how does it feel to earn your own meal?"

Braidon smiled, but before the boy could reply, a harsh *bang* came from the entrance to the inn. He trailed off, his eyes flickering to the shadow that had appeared in the doorway. Devon followed his gaze, and watched as a man larger than any he'd ever seen stepped into the room. Sharp hazel eyes scanned the occupants from beneath brows as thick as slugs, and a terrible scar ran from one side of his face to another. His hair had been pulled into a bun atop his scalp.

Leather boots thumped loudly on the wooden floors as he strode across the inn. Every inch of fabric he wore had been stained black—even the haft of the giant axe he carried one-handed. Not a man or woman spoke as he came to a stop in the centre of the room.

"You all know who I am," he growled. "I'm here for the bastard that killed my men."

Devon's heart quickened as the hazel eyes found him from across the room. As the newcomer's words trailed off, he rose to his feet.

"That would be me, sonny," he said. "Who's asking?"

CHAPTER 15

Braidon watched in horror as the newcomer came to a stop beside their table. The man was so large, even Devon barely reached his shoulder. A shiver slid down Braidon's spine, and he scrambled from the bench to stand alongside Devon. No one else in the establishment so much as moved a muscle. Then a flicker of movement came from behind the bar, and the innkeeper appeared, her thin lips pursed.

"What are you doing here, Joseph?" she asked, her voice a low hiss. "We have an arrangement."

The giant glanced in her direction. "Ay, we do, Selina," he rumbled. "Last I checked it didn't include you harbouring those who murder my people."

"Murder?" Braidon squawked.

Alongside him Devon chuckled. "Since when is it murder to kill a few good-for-nothings intent on theft and murder?"

"They were *Baronians*, little man," Joseph growled, "and you'd best show some respect."

He swung an arm at Devon, as though to bat him aside, but the hammerman blocked it with his forearm and shoved the giant hard in the chest. Caught off-guard, Joseph staggered back a step. His hideous face twisted and his bushy eyebrows knitted together into a ferocious scowl.

"We doing this here?" Devon snapped before the man could speak. "Or shall we step outside?"

The giant blinked, momentarily taken aback by Devon's forwardness. He stood glowering down at the hammerman for a full second, then glanced at the innkeeper. With a sigh, he shook his head and started to chuckle.

"You've got balls, little man," he rumbled. Turning on his heel, he started for the doorway. "Outside. Selina's paid her due. No need for her to be cleaning your blood off her walls."

Braidon stared in disbelief as Devon followed the giant through the double doors. Hinges squealed as the doors swung shut behind them, loud in the silence that had swallowed the room. Looking around at the other occupants of the inn, Braidon searched for someone that might help, but not a man or woman would meet his gaze.

A steely resolve settled over Braidon as he realised it was up to him to help his friend. He clutched the table for a moment, struggling to control the trembling in his knees. Then he drew his sword and stumbled towards the exit.

The sight that met him outside froze him in his tracks. Standing on the inn's porch, he looked out at the square. A hundred men and women stared back at him, their pitch-black clothing seeming to merge with the night. The swords and axes in their hands shone in the light of a dozen bonfires that now lit the settlement.

A chill spread through Braidon's stomach, and he clenched his sword tight, remembering the man's words inside the inn.

Baronians!

It wasn't possible. The last of the Baronian tribes had vanished decades ago, their brutal traditions expunged from the Three Nations in the early years of the Tsar's rule. A few tribes were said to have fled to Northland, beyond his father's reach, but even those were believed to have died out.

Yet the proof before them was undeniable. With their black-garbed leather armour and rusted weapons, the people gathered below him were like an illustration from the history books, drawn from a time when hordes of Baronian tribes had plagued the wildlands of the Three Nations, waylaying travellers and wreaking havoc at will.

Below, the giant axeman the innkeeper had called Joseph was leading Devon through the horde. The crowd parted before him like he was a king, backing away until a ring formed around the two men. Devon walked a few feet behind the Baronian, his face impassive as he surveyed the surging crowd.

Braidon couldn't understand how his friend could be so calm. With Devon surrounded, there was no way for Braidon to reach him, and he stood frozen on the porch, watching as the two came to a stop in the centre of the square. The doors squealed behind Braidon, and then the innkeeper Selina appeared beside him. Arms crossed, she studied the scene outside her establishment.

"Hope your friend can fight," she said impassively.

Braidon nodded, unable to find the words to speak.

Joseph raised his axe, and a hushed silence fell over the crowd. A grin on his lips, he turned to face Devon. "So, hammerman, how do you wish to die?"

"With *kanker* in hand, as my ancestors did before me." Devon smirked. "But my time hasn't come yet, old man."

To Braidon's shock, Joseph threw back his head and howled with laughter. The sound echoed through the square like thunder as the crowd joined in. The rattle of shields followed as they began to chant.

"*Death, death, death!*"

Braidon wilted as the sound washed over him, the roar of

the crowd's bloodlust draining away his courage, feeding his fear until it was all he could do to remain standing.

Devon watched on, arms crossed, face impassive as the crowd screamed for his death. *Kanker* still hung sheathed on his back, even as Joseph thrust his axe skyward, encouraging his followers to greater excess.

Finally he turned back to Devon. With a gesture of his axe, silence returned to the square. To Braidon, the sudden change was shocking, the absence of sound almost as bad as the screams. He swallowed hard, willing his mind to piece out some escape. His thoughts turned to his magic, and he wondered whether he could make them both invisible and flee. Yet surveying the crowd, he realised that even invisible, there was nowhere for them to run. Looking at Devon, he prayed the man had the strength to prevail.

"My followers disagree, little man," Joseph roared. "But draw your hammer, and I will grant you your final wish."

Devon sighed. His head dropped, and Braidon's heart lurched as Devon spread his empty hands. "What about your final wish, elder?"

Joseph's face darkened. "I don't need one," he snapped.

"Very well."

Before anyone could react, Devon surged forward, his fist flashing up to catch the giant Baronian square in the chin. Taken unawares, the blow lifted Joseph to his toes. He staggered back, and for a second it seemed he would lose his footing and fall. Devon moved after him, but snarling Joseph lashed out with the axe, forcing the hammerman back.

For a moment the two stood facing each other. Then Devon reached up and drew *kanker* from its sheath, and the battle began in earnest.

Air hissed as the axe sliced for Devon's head. Ducking low, the hammerman sidestepped the giant's charge and swung out with *kanker*. Joseph spun, revealing a speed that belied his size, and wrenched his axe down, the massive muscles in his arms rippling with the effort, and an awful shriek rang out as the two weapons collided.

Sparks flew as the warriors leapt back, and Braidon winced at the power behind the blows. He was shocked Joseph's axe had not shattered with the impact, though as the Baronian hefted his weapon, Braidon saw a dent had been left in the steel blade.

Recovering almost as quickly, Devon straightened, hefting his hammer. The magic-blessed weapon didn't show so much as a scratch, and grinning, the hammerman started forward. Braidon held his breath as the two colossal warriors clashed again, the shrieking of their weapons sending shivers down his spine. This was no duel between master swordsmen; there would be no minor wounds inflicted before the end came. One touch with either weapon meant dismemberment or death.

Braidon wanted desperately to tear his eyes away, to turn and flee back into the sanctuary of the inn, to the half an hour earlier when he had sat enjoying a warm meal with his friend. Instead, he stood and watched as Devon battled on. He would not run while the man fought for their very lives, would not leave the hammerman alone to face the Baronians.

In the first clashes of the battle, the two giants had seemed evenly matched, but as the fight drew on, it seemed to Braidon that Devon was gaining ground. Joseph's blows had lost some of their power, and his movements were growing slower, even as Devon ploughed on with seemingly endless vigour. A slight sheen of sweat on his brow was his only sign of exertion, while lines had crept into Joseph's face, as though the fight had aged him a decade. Even the white in his beard appeared more prominent.

The crowd was silent now, the black-cloaked Baronians watching on in awe of the two warriors. Another clash echoed from the settlement as axe and hammer met, the combatants spinning away, each unharmed. They paused, eyes glittering as they faced one another. Then with a dull *thud*, the steel blade of Joseph's axe cracked in half and fell to the ground. The Baronian stared dumbly at the weapon for a moment, then up at Devon.

Adrenaline surged through Braidon's veins and he lifted his fist in triumph. "Finish him, Devon!" he yelled, his voice strained to a shriek by the stress of the fight.

Below, the hammerman looked up at him, his face still impassive. They shared a glance, and then Devon returned his eyes to the Baronian. He lowered his hammer and gestured at his opponent.

"Time for a water break, don't you think, sonny?" he asked, panting softly.

Joseph stood fixed in place, the broken haft of his axe still in hand. After a moment, he nodded. "Good idea."

Tossing aside his broken weapon, he gestured to a Baronian. The man raced forward with a water skin, and wordlessly the axeman pointed at Devon. After a second's hesitation, the Baronian offered the skin to Devon first.

On the porch, Braidon looked on, mouth wide, heart in the pit of his stomach. He shook his head, unable to understand what Devon was doing, why he was sparing the thug's life.

Below, Devon nodded his thanks and placed *kanker* on the ground beside him before accepting the water skin. Lifting it to his lips, he took a long swing and then handed it back to the attendant. The man scampered across to Joseph, who drank deeply as well.

Afterwards, the Baronian gestured at his broken axe. "Mind if I find another weapon?"

Devon grinned. "Won't help you much, sonny," he replied, "but by all means."

Joseph laughed, and shaking his head, he wandered around the circle of Baronians, inspecting their weapons until he found one that suited him. One look at the owner was all it took for the man to hand it over. Hefting the new axe, he returned to the centre of the ring and faced Devon.

"Ready?" he asked.

"Ay," Devon replied, and the battle resumed.

Anger burned in Braidon's chest, and he looked away, cursing Devon for his stupidity. With their lives on the line, the hammerman had thrown away an opportunity to save them both. Worse than that, Devon had given the Baronian time to rest, when it was obvious he was on his last legs. Now Joseph was fighting with renewed vigour and Devon had lost his advantage.

"Noble man, your friend," Selina said from beside him.

Braidon jumped. He'd been so engrossed with the battle he'd forgotten she was there. Shaking his head, he looked up at her in disbelief. "Noble? He had the man! Why did he throw away his chance?"

"Because it wouldn't have been honourable," she replied, her thin lips drawn back into a smile.

"He's fighting a thief!" Braidon countered. "There's no honour amongst such people."

Selina raised an eyebrow. "You shouldn't judge so quickly, young man. Whatever he might appear, Joseph has a code of his own, twisted as it might seem to some. He protects his people, whatever the cost. That is why he is here, why he will continue this fight, even if he may have bitten off more than he can chew."

"Baronian scum," Braidon spat. "I'm glad m…the Tsar drove them from our land."

The innkeeper sighed. "So judgmental for one so young," she said softly. She gestured at the crowd. "Yes, they call themselves Baronians. But look at them, youngster, look at them closely. You think they chose this path, wandering these backroads in the middle of winter, with hardly a cloak between them? Most of those you see here are refugees, runaways from Trola or the capital, where the Tsar's taxes drove them to the edge of poverty. Joseph found them, brought them under his wing. Yes, they might be bandits, but they are only what desperation has made them."

"You defend them?"

Selina shrugged. "Five years ago, before Joseph, the people in this settlement could barely go a month without someone coming under attack. These forests were filled with bandits—vicious, warring factions that were merciless to their victims. Then Joseph came. The worst of the bandits were driven off or brought under his rule. This village, and many like it, came to an arrangement with them. We pay them a small fee, and he and his people do us no harm, nor any harm to those travellers who visit with our permission. It is an unusual arrangement, I admit, but twice as many people live here now, than before the Baronians came."

A cry rang out across the square, and Braidon whipped around, his heart racing once more as he remembered the battle taking place below. Sunlight flickered on steel as the two warriors battled on, but now Devon was being forced back. Joseph's battle cry echoed around the square as his axe rose and fell.

Growling, Devon deflected a wicked blow with his hammer, but using his awesome strength, Joseph wrenched his weapon back and struck again before Devon could counter. The hammerman sidestepped the blow, but lost his footing and stumbled. Joseph rushed forward, his shoulder catching Devon in the chest and hurling him to the ground.

Kanker flew across the dirt. Unarmed, Devon rolled as Joseph's axe bit the earth where he'd fallen. Joseph hefted his axe for another blow, but as Devon scrambled for the hilt of his hammer, he seemed to hesitate for half a second. It was enough, and gripping *kanker* tight, Devon surged back to his feet.

The Baronian snarled and swung his axe, but the blow was wild and clumsily made. Devon deflected it easily and then thrust out with his hammer, catching the black-garbed man in the chest. With its blunted head it did little damage, but in Joseph's tiring state, it was enough to throw him off-balance.

Leaping forward, Devon attacked again. The axe lifted to counter, but Joseph had misjudged his aim, and instead of catching the hammer with the blade, Devon's weapon crunched home into the Baronian's wrist.

A scream of pure agony rang out across the square as Joseph staggered back, the axe toppling from his hand. Then his mouth clamped shut, cutting off his cries as he cradled his right arm against his chest. Head bowed, he sank to his knees in front of Devon.

"Do it quick," he croaked through clenched teeth.

"Ay," Devon replied.

His boot lashed out and caught Joseph in the side of the head. The Baronian toppled silently to the ground, unconscious. Around the square, not a soul moved, as the Baronians stared on in silence.

Devon looked back at them, lips tight, eyes hard. He lifted *kanker* above his head and let out a cry. "Your leader is defeated," his voice boomed. "If any one of you wishes to join him, step forward now, and I will gladly oblige."

Whispers spread around the square as the crowd shifted, the black-garbed watchers sharing glances. Braidon sensed the mood turning dark, the anger of the Baronians building, as hands clenched at sword hilts. Fear gnawed at Braidon's stomach as he watched Devon standing defiantly against the horde. The hammerman could not face them alone, and they knew it. All it would take was one...

Silently Braidon closed his eyes, and allowed his consciousness to plunge inwards. His breath settled into a gentle rhythm, concentrating his mind, carrying his thoughts away to the nothingness within. In an instant, he found himself drifting in the peaceful black at his core, felt the weight of his body falling away. Time seemed to stand still... and then the light of his magic appeared in void.

It formed before him, twisting and morphing into the familiar Feline. Once, the sight of it had filled him with terror, sending him fleeing through the darkness. Now though, need gave him courage, and reaching out, he gripped it with his mind, banishing the beast with the force of his will, making its power his own.

Opening his eyes, Braidon looked out over the square. Only a moment had passed, but he could sense the impasse coming to a close. There were only seconds to spare.

An image flickered into Braidon's mind, of Devon the night he'd appeared beside his campfire. The man had loomed out of the darkness like a giant from of legend. A smile came to Braidon's lips.

Reaching across with his power, he wrapped loops of shining white around Devon, altering his image, changing the appearance of reality.

In the light of the burning fires, it seemed the hammerman grew larger as he stood there. Darkness cloaked him as his iron gaze scanned the watchers, promising death. To every eye in the square, it was no longer a mortal who stood amongst them, but a demigod, his power unrivalled. A crackling filled the air as overhead, thunder boomed, blue fire lighting up the sky.

It was all only illusion, a manipulation of the Light, but it was all Braidon could offer his friend. Looking down at the circle of Baronians, he prayed it was enough.

CHAPTER 16

Exhaustion weighed on Alana as she pushed through the trees, struggling to keep pace with her grandmother. Ahead, Enala threaded through the dense undergrowth as though she were born to it, seemingly untouched by the clinging vines and vicious thorns.

The explosion of Light magic had returned some of the vigour to the old woman, and now it was Alana who was flagging, the endless journey through the dark forest sapping her energies. Several of the cuts on her neck had opened again, and she could feel the steady trickle of blood down her back. Even so, she refused to slow, knowing if her brother had used his magic so blatantly, he had to be in trouble. He needed her, needed them both.

The light of a new day was just beginning around them now, casting light across the forest. A *hiss* came from ahead as Enala tossed aside the burning torch they'd used to light their way, then stamped it out on the damp earth.

Walking up beside her, Alana studied the woods ahead. Shadows still clung beneath the trees, but she could make out the ground clearly now. After spending much of the night being tripped by hidden roots, the sight was a relief. She could still sense the lingering tang of Light magic on the air around them. Its aftertaste was growing weaker by the hour, but they were close to its source now.

"There's still no way of knowing it was him," Enala reminded Alana, though her face said she thought otherwise.

Alana only nodded. Striding past, she took the lead. Whatever lay at the end of their journey, there was no turning back now. All through the night, they had forged their own path through the forest, unable to find a path leading in the direction the magic had come from. It was another hour before they finally came to a wider track of hardened earth.

Enala loosened her sword in its scabbard. "Ready yourself, granddaughter," she said quietly. "It's not far now."

There was a hardness to her grandmother's eyes, and Alana nodded her agreement. Her hand drifted to the hilt of her sword. The old woman's lessons were still fresh in her mind, but she found herself now filled with doubt, with fear she was not the swordswomen she'd once thought herself.

Nonsense, she growled to herself. *You are the Daughter of the Tsar.*

Alana straightened her shoulders. "Let's go."

It wasn't far before the track widened again. Studying the ground, Alana was alarmed to find overlapping bootprints in the hard-packed earth. It looked as though a large force had passed this way not long ago. It was difficult to know their numbers, but she guessed there were at least a hundred. Her stomach clenched as she picked up the pace, her thoughts on her brother.

Around a bend in the track, Alana stumbled to a halt as she found herself facing a small forest settlement. She paused, scanning the nearest buildings, looking for any sign of the owners of the bootprints in the earth beneath her feet. There was no sign of movement or damage, and she shared a glance with her grandmother as the old woman joined her.

"Where is everybody?" she asked.

"There's one," Enala replied, nodding at one of the buildings.

A door had just opened in the only two-storeyed house in the settlement. A middle-aged woman appeared and started down the steps. Her eyes were on her feet, but suddenly they swept up and saw them standing on the other side of the square. She started, then glanced back at the door. It seemed she would retreat back inside, but then reconsidering, she continued her way down.

Enala strode forward, making her way towards the woman. "Excuse me, ma'am," she said, her voice loud enough to carry through the entire settlement. Catching herself, Alana started after her grandmother. "We were wondering if you might help us."

The woman made it to the bottom of the steps, but paused there, looking up at the approaching Enala. "Depends what help you're looking for," she murmured. "Do you need a room for the night?"

Reaching the woman, Enala shook her head. Glancing around at the silent buildings, she raised one eyebrow. "What happened here?"

"We're full-up at the moment," the villager replied, seeming not to hear Enala's question, "if you're looking for a room." Her eyes distant, she turned and started back up the stairs.

"We're looking for a boy!" Alana shouted. "His name is Braidon."

On the steps, the woman froze. Glancing over her shoulder, she pursed her lips. "What did you say?"

Alana's heart quickened. "You've seen him?" she asked desperately. "Please, is he okay?"

The woman bit her lip. "He's alive," she replied.

"Where?" Enala demanded.

The woman looked at them, then at the buildings surrounding the settlement. Alana thought she glimpsed fear in her eyes, but a second later it was gone. With a gesture, she continued up the steps. "Look, we'd best talk inside, okay?" she called down to them.

Enala followed after the woman, but Alana hesitated, her heart palpitating painfully in her chest. Something about the settlement seemed wrong. Where had all the people gone? Why had her brother been here? Why had he used his magic? The woman had already disappeared into the door at the top of the stairs, and Enala was drawing close.

Swallowing her doubt, Alana raced after her grand-mother, catching her just before she reached the doorway. She stepped past her and entered the inn, dropping her hand to the hilt of her sword. Though it was daylight outside, the interior was still dark, the lanterns unlit. In the gloom, Alana could just make out the shadow of a bar and several tables and chairs scattered about the room.

"Light a lantern would you?" Alana asked, searching for the woman who had invited them in, but she was nowhere in sight.

A *bang* came from behind them as the door slammed shut, plunging the room into pitch-black. Alana started back towards the door, when a sudden light erupted through the room. Shocked, she stumbled sideways, struggling to shield her eyes.

"Wha—?" she cried out, as shadows flickered through the room.

Blinking, she strained to see through the brilliant white. Movement came from the tables as black-cloaked men rose from their seats. Her hand was still scrambling for the hilt of her sword when a cold voice spoke from behind her.

"Alana, how good it is to see you again."

SITTING IN THE DARKNESS, Quinn allowed himself a smile as Alana and the old woman came blundering into the inn. The innkeeper had done her job well, as he'd known she would. After all, her life depended on it. Alana and the old priest were nothing to her; she'd had little choice but to accept Quinn's proposition.

Not that it would have mattered in the end. Whether the innkeeper lured them inside or not, he had the numbers to ensure success. Taking them by surprise simply meant a cleaner victory.

His only regret was that they'd missed the boy. Braidon had miscalculated, using his magic on those outside the shield that protected him from magical sight. But at least his mistake had allowed Quinn to flush Alana and the old woman out of hiding.

He'd already sent for the Tsar the night before. Now he had only to capture Alana in preparation for her father's arrival.

Rising, he shielded his eyes and gestured for his Stalkers to make their move. A brilliant white lit the air, illuminating the room and blinding the two women. Silently Quinn moved behind them, cutting off their escape.

"Alana, how good it is to see you again," he whispered when she staggered towards him.

She spun, her hand going for her sword, but Quinn was faster still. His fist flashed out, catching her hard in the base of the skull, and she collapsed without making a sound.

He looked up as warmth bathed his face. Flames crackled in the old woman's hands as she stepped towards him, her face contorted with rage. Quickly Quinn drew his blade and pressed it to the unconscious Alana's throat.

"Enough, woman," he hissed. "One more move, and your granddaughter dies."

"Go ahead!" Enala growled, the fire in her palms leaping higher.

Quinn smiled. "Look around you, woman. You're surrounded. Give up, Enala."

Blinking in the light of his Stalker's magic, Enala hesitated. With fire in both hands, she looked for all the world like an avenging demon, but Quinn knew better. She was weak, the same as her brother. He watched as her gaze swept the room, taking in the dozen Stalkers Quinn had stationed inside the inn. Half stood with crossbows aimed, the other six with magic crackling in their hands. The fight went from the woman's face, but she did not lower her hands.

"I have no wish to kill the Tsar's mother," Quinn said. "I'm sure he has plans of his own for you. But I won't hesitate if you make me. Now, dismiss your magic," Quinn commanded, his voice ringing from the glass windows.

For a moment he thought the old woman would refuse. Crossbows rattled as she stepped towards him, but he raised a hand to halt their release. A low groan came from the girl at his feet, and Enala's gaze dropped to look at her granddaughter. Alana started to move, but froze as Quinn pressed his blade harder against her throat.

"What, oh…" she trailed off as her eyes flickered open and saw Quinn standing over her.

Quinn looked at Enala, and smiled as the fire slowly died from her hands, her eyes returning to crystal blue.

"The sword, too," he ordered.

Unclipping her sword belt, she tossed the weapon to the ground between them. Quinn gestured for one of his Stalkers to retrieve it, then grinned at Enala.

"I knew you would come," he said conversationally, gesturing with his sabre. "I told the Tsar the boy's magic would draw you here."

"You have my brother?" Alana asked from the floor.

Quinn stepped back, allowing Enala to join her granddaughter. Crouching beside Alana, the old woman offered her shoulder, and together the two rose unsteadily to their feet. A scuffling came from across the room as one of his Stalkers dragged the innkeeper forward, one arm twisted up behind her back.

"You said you'd leave us alone!" she snarled as they approached.

"Yes, yes, yes." He and his men had arrived at first light to find the boy already departed, but it had been a small matter of rounding up the villagers to find out where they'd gone. The other occupants of the settlement were currently locked up in the roughshod temple, overseen by a few of his men. "When we're done. Now, would you *please* tell the girl what happened to her brother? She's so eager to hear about his fate."

The innkeeper looked down at Alana. "I'm sorry," she whispered. "The Baronians have him."

"*What?*"

Alana sounded as disbelieving as Quinn had first been. Though he'd heard rumours of a resurgence in the rebel tribes, Quinn hadn't paid them much credence until now.

"So Joseph was telling the truth." Beside Alana, the old woman looked calm. "The Baronians have returned." She smiled at Quinn. "Your Tsar's power fades by the day, Stalker. Or does he no longer care to protect his people?"

Rage bubbled up in Quinn's chest and he pointed his blade at the old woman's chest. "Silence, woman," he growled.

Enala crossed her arms and smirked. "Oh, *now* you're going to kill me are you, Stalker?" she asked. "I thought my son had plans for me?"

Quinn clenched his teeth and sucked in a breath. Struggling to quell his anger, he forced a smile. "Ay, and I hope you live to regret those words." He turned to the innkeeper. Striding forward, he stood face-to-face with the woman. "But you have not told them all of it. Finish the story, innkeeper."

He lifted the tip of his sword and rested it against her chest to emphasise his point.

She flinched away from the steel, but the Stalker holding her only tightened his grip. Terror showed on her face, but with a deep breath, she stilled. She met Quinn's gaze with hatred in her eyes.

"Don't worry, girl," she said, still looking at Quinn, "your brother is fine. His friend defeated the Baronian leader. He leads them now."

"His friend?" Alana asked.

"Devon."

Before the innkeeper could say more, Quinn stepped forward, driving his blade through her chest. She gasped, stiffening as the cold steel sliced through her heart. Collapsing back into the arms of the man holding her, a soft whisper came from her lips. With a jerk, Quinn yanked back his blade and watched the woman's lifeblood pump from the wound. Then he gestured, and his Stalker released her, allowing the innkeeper's body to thud to the floor.

"*Why?*" Alana screamed.

Quinn spun, bloody blade raised. "Because she *lied* to me. It took an hour to get the truth from her, and she thought I would still spare her for finally telling it?" He laughed as he looked at Alana, hatred twisting its cold coils around his soul. "Just like you lied to me, Alana."

Stepping forward, he pointed the tip of his sword at her throat, though he was careful not to touch her with it now that she was conscious. When she was desperate, Alana's magic could transfer along metal, and he had no wish to be used by her again. "You betrayed me."

Alana stared at him a moment, then to his surprise, she bowed her head. "I know," she whispered. "I'm sorry."

Quinn blinked, momentarily confused by her repentance —until he recalled the weakness that had infected her, the soft girl she had become when she'd escaped the citadel. His jaw hardened, his anger returning.

"Sorry? *Sorry?* What do your sorries matter to me? You manipulated me with your power, *used* me, and still I saved you. And how did you repay me?"

"I…"

"You left me to face your father's wrath. By rights he should have killed me a thousand times for allowing you to go free. If not for his mercy…"

Alana snorted. "My father, mercy?"

"Do not speak ill of my Tsar," Quinn hissed.

Summoning his magic, Quinn drew the wind to him. The windows shook, then shattered inwards as the winds gathered around him. With a gesture, he sent them against her, hurling her back against the wall, pinning her there. He walked slowly forward.

"Your father spared me, trusted me to find his children, so that he might lead our army to glory. I will not fail him, not this time. He will have you, and your brother. And I will have my heart's desire."

He lifted a hand to touch her face, but stopped himself at the last second. She stared back at him, her grey eyes set like stone.

"And what is your heart's desire, *my love?*" she asked mockingly.

Quinn scowled and raised a fist, and Alana's eyes flashed. With an effort of will, Quinn controlled himself.

She laughed. "What, are you *afraid,* my love? Go on, *do it,* show me how powerful you are."

Baring his teeth, Quinn swung away from her, and found Enala crouching beside the dead woman. He turned his anger on her. "What do you think you're doing, woman?" he snarled.

"You missed," Enala said, her hands bloody as she pressed a rag to the innkeeper's chest.

Quinn cursed as the woman groaned, her eyelids fluttering. But it was an easy mistake to correct, and hefting his sword, he stepped towards the wounded woman. Before he could reach her, a shout came from outside, followed by a roar that seemed to shake the very foundations of the building.

A smile came to Quinn's lips as he faced the window, and glimpsed the flicker of scarlet scales in the square outside. Lowering his sword, he looked at Alana.

"This should be quite the family reunion."

CHAPTER 17

Merydith sucked in a long breath as she directed her horse into the centre of the Gods Road. The wind swirled around her, kicking up dust and causing the treetops to sway violently overhead. The rustle of leaves against branches was almost enough to muffle the distant tread of marching feet.

Almost.

A shiver ran down her spine and she pulled her cloak tighter about her, though it was not the cold that had her trembling. Her hand dropped to the sword resting across her pommel, and she cast a final glance at the trees, searching the shadows for any hint of movement. But Murdo and Mokyre had done their jobs well, and there was no sign of the Northland force concealed there.

The rhythmic *thump-thump* of boots picked up a notch, and Merydith's attention snapped back to the path ahead. The Gods Road continued straight from where she sat for another hundred yards, before disappearing round a bend in the road. Ahead the road narrowed, allowing only enough room for ten men to march abreast. With fifty thousand soldiers under the Tsar's command, the forest had slowed his advance to a crawl.

Merydith intended to halt them altogether.

Her hunters had already taken care of the few scouts the southerners had bothered to send ahead. The Tsar's advance guard were now marching blind, and she intended to take full advantage. Her people had left their mounts half a mile from the Gods Road, at a confluence of several animal tracks that led further up into the Sandstone Mountains. Now they waited on either side of the path, ready to spring her trap.

At the end of the road, shadows flickered as the first line of soldiers marched into view. Their attention on anything but the way ahead, they continued on a dozen yards before a whinny from her mount finally alerted them to her presence. The *thump-thump* of their marching boots rattled to a discordant stop as the front ranks exchanged bewildered glances. Shouts erupted from the following ranks as men marched unawares into the backs of their companions.

"What's going on here?" a man bellowed, forcing his way to the front. A silver star on his breast marked him as a lieutenant. He pointed a cane at one of the soldiers and opened his mouth to scream again.

"Who dares trespass on my land?" Merydith shouted, her voice carrying on the wind to the soldiers.

The lieutenant spun at the sound of her voice. Lines marked his brow as he frowned. "Who goes there?" he called, taking a step towards her.

Merydith smiled as she edged her horse forward. "The Queen of this forest," she bellowed. "You're trespassing on my land."

Beyond the front ranks of the army, further shouting was breaking out as the sudden halt caused havoc amongst their ranks.

"The Queen of..." the man mumbled, then cursed under his breath. "Get out of our way, woman. This is the Tsar's forest, and he does not take kindly to usurpers." Drawing his sword, he gestured to the men on either side of him. "Take care of the madwoman."

Merydith smiled as the front ranks surged towards her. "Turn back, or you will pay for your insolence," she shouted.

"Kill the b——" The lieutenant's scream was cut short as an arrow blossomed in his throat.

On the road in front of her, the charge faltered as the soldiers glanced back to see what had become of their lieutenant. With their ranks broken and shields still lowered, the first wave of arrows sliced through them like fire in a cornfield. Screams rent the air as men went down, steel-tipped arrows finding their mark in exposed legs and necks and armpits. Only the steel-plated armour of the advance guard stopped the attack from becoming a massacre.

A second volley hissed from the trees, and more soldiers dropped, though fewer this time, as those still standing had turned their shields towards the trees.

Lifting her sabre above her head, Merydith shouted a battle cry. The rumble of hooves came from behind her as a cavalry cohort concealed around the bend came racing into sight. Together, they charged at the enemy.

With their shields turned towards the trees, the Tsar's men were taken unawares, and Merydith's charge carried her people deep into their ranks. Soldiers scattered before her mount or were trampled beneath his iron-shod hooves, and her sabre flashed out, killing any who stood against her. Alongside her, Merydith's people were doing the same, as the Tsar's soldiers tried to flee back down the Gods Road.

As they neared the bend in the road, Merydith's charge slowed, the ranks of soldiers closing in around them. A sword lanced for her chest, and she swung out with her buckler, turning aside the blow. Lashing out with her sabre, she felt a satisfying *crunch* as it struck home, followed by a scream as the assailant staggered back, blood streaming from his severed arm. His shouts were silenced as her guard closed in, and a sabre cleaved his spine.

Merydith nodded her thanks as her guard spread out around her, forcing the southern soldiers back. She swung around in her saddle, taking the opportunity to gauge the battle. Their charge had carried her cohort deep into the enemy ranks, but now that the element of surprise was lost, the Tsar's soldiers were pushing back. Several had managed to join their shields and were advancing up the path towards them.

"Retreat!" she cried, pulling on her reins to swing her stallion back the way they'd come.

Bodies littered the Gods Road behind them, most of them donned in the scarlet robes of Plorsea. Merydith's heart clenched at the sight, though she knew she'd had no choice but to attack, to be the first to strike. They were only five thousand against fifty thousand. To hesitate now was to face certain defeat.

Her mount leapt forward and the northern army followed her, retreating down the Gods Road as quickly as they had appeared. Arrows hissed after them and several of her people fell. Merydith cursed and crouched lower in the saddle until they were safely around the bend in the road. She prayed her archers had already fallen back, but there was no way of knowing until they reached the rendezvous.

Several riders had pulled ahead, forming ranks around her. The leaders dragged their horses towards the trees, where several trails led deeper into the forest. Merydith and the others followed suit, and together they rushed into the darkness of the trees.

The cries of their pursuers died away, muffled by the dense forest. Despite the still pending danger, Merydith allowed herself a deep breath, her heartbeat slowing a notch. A smile tugged at her lips as she estimated the enemy's losses. The Tsar had lost perhaps as many as three hundred soldiers to death or injury, between those killed by her archers and the cavalry charge. She had counted no more than twenty Northerners amongst the dead.

Not bad, for a distraction.

Damyn crouched amongst the scrub and peered down at the wagons rumbling slowly through the narrow valley. The Gods Road was rutted here, the going slow for the steel-shod wheels of the Tsar's baggage train. A ring of soldiers five men thick marched to either side of the wagons, their eyes alert as they scanned the hills. Damyn allowed himself a smile. With the dense bush covering the valley, there was little chance his cohort would be spotted.

Away to their left, the column disappeared around a bend in the road. They had been marching past for an hour now, and the first hundred ranks of the advance guard had only just given way to the baggage train. Damyn followed their progress up the Gods Road in his mind, along the twisting track through the forest, to where his Queen waited.

When his scout had returned with her plan, he'd found himself smiling at her boldness. While he would have preferred to fight alongside her, there had been no time to question the intricacies of her trap. His cohort was in place within the hour, and with scouts riding back and forth, their preparations had been finalised.

Now Damyn had only to wait for the chance to strike. From what he'd seen so far of the Tsar's preparations, it would come soon enough. The man thought Northland weak. He knew they had only five thousand soldiers, and had barely bothered to send scouts out ahead of his army. Those had been easily dispatched. Damyn intended to make the Tsar pay for his arrogance.

The distant cry of a bugle carried through the forest, and

below, the soldiers to either side of the wagons leapt to the alert. The clash of steel on steel and the screams of dying men followed, whispering through the trees like the ghosts of long-dead souls. Those on the road below closed ranks and drew their weapons, their eyes turning to their commanders. The rumble of wagons ceased as the oxen stumbled to a stop. A dust cloud settled around the convoy, hemming them in.

Along the ridgetop, Damyn felt the eyes of his five hundred men on him. He raised a hand, bidding them to wait. Squinting through the dust, he watched the sunlight flickering from the enemy's armour. The screams had set the southerners on edge, drawing their attention to the path ahead and away from the hillside.

Another bugle cried out. Shouts followed from those below as the Tsar's lieutenants started waving their men forward. Half of the force guarding the train surged forward, the others spreading out to fill the gaps they'd left.

Damyn's heart beat faster as he watched the soldiers march out of sight. He did a quick count of those who remained and cursed beneath his breath. They had been more cautious than Merydith had anticipated. She'd warned him not to attack unless the odds of success were overwhelming, but the Tsar had left close to four hundred men below. His own five hundred had them outnumbered, but if things went wrong and they were delayed, Damyn risked the main body of the Tsar's army catching them in the open.

Letting out a long breath, Damyn made a decision. Merydith had ordered him not to take any unnecessary risks, but the destruction of the Tsar's supplies would be a massive blow to the southland army. With the land still in the grips of winter, they would not be able to advance into Northland until they'd been resupplied. It would buy his people much needed time—perhaps even enough to muster an army that could match the southerners in the field.

Retreating behind the lip of the hill, Damyn mounted up.

His five hundred men and women followed suit. Eyes wide, they looked to Damyn for the signal. He swallowed, feeling the weight of their lives on his shoulders. While most had seen combat in the occasional scuffles between clans, none had ever imagined taking on such an army as the one marching up the Gods Road. They knew the odds were against them, but as he looked in their eyes, Damyn knew not a one of them would fail him.

Silently he lifted his sword and pointed it at the valley and army beyond the lip of the hill. A deafening cry went up around him. Damyn kicked his horse into a charge, and five hundred men and woman followed after him.

CHAPTER 18

Reclining in the comfortable embrace of a cowhide hammock, Devon couldn't help but smile as he reflected on his sudden change in fortune. Ever since he'd rescinded his commission in the army, it had seemed as though the Gods themselves were against him. His savings had seemed to evaporate overnight, former comrades had turned against him, and everyone from bards to innkeepers had taken great joy in besmirching his name. Since then, his every action, every decision, only seemed to lead his situation from bad to worse.

Until now. Somehow, saving a couple of selfish townsfolk from bandits had led to his ascension to leader of the Baronians. He could only shake his head in amusement at the turn of events.

"Devon, there you are." Craning his head, Devon watched as Braidon walked up. Wearing a scowl on his face, the boy came to a stop beside the hammock and crossed his arms. "Enjoying yourself, are you?"

Devon grinned. "Immensely." Groaning, he levered himself out of the hammock and stood beside the boy. "Where've you been, sonny?"

Braidon's scowl deepened. "Sleeping in the mud," he snapped.

"Oh…" Devon scratched his beard, a sheepish look coming over his face. "Must have lost track of you somewhere there."

After he'd defeated Joseph, there had been a tense moment when Devon had thought the Baronians were about to tear him to pieces. Strangely, in that moment Devon had felt no fear or anger, only a sense of bemusement that his life would end at the hands of this rabble, rather than the rich and powerful who sought his death.

But instead, the Baronians had one by one fallen to their knees and pronounced him their leader. Devon had felt compelled to accept the title, least their supplication return to rage. Afterwards, they had shepherded Devon and Braidon back to their campsite and shown Devon the hammock. In his exhausted state, Devon had fallen asleep without giving the boy a second thought.

"You think?" Braidon growled.

"Ummm…" Devon was still struggling to produce a satisfactory excuse when a Baronian marched up.

"Hammerman," the Baronian rumbled. "We have prepared your tent, if you'd like to break your fast."

Devon raised an eyebrow at Braidon. "Hungry?" he asked, his tone reconciliatory.

The boy snorted, but eventually offered a nod, and Devon gestured for the Baronian to lead the way. Together they wandered through the roughshod camp the Baronians had created amongst the forest. The undergrowth had been cleared to make space for the cowhide tents, but the trees remained, their upper canopy forming a roof to shield against dragon patrols. Smoke from a dozen cookfires hung heavily in the morning air, and they kept close to their guide as they navigated between the sleeping bodies. It seemed Braidon hadn't been the only one to spend the night without shelter.

Devon wondered how they had survived the harsh winter storm that had passed through a week before.

Wagons lined the perimeter of the campsite, drawn up so they formed a makeshift barrier against the world outside. Looking closer at the tents they passed, Devon saw they were as scruffy as the clothes worn by the bandits he'd encountered on the road. Compared to the tales of old, these Baronians seemed a poor relic, impoverished by the necessity of their concealment from the Tsar.

The camp looked to have been there a while—months, at least. The Baronians of old had moved freely from place to place, never staying in one location for long, spreading their terror across the Three Nations. It seemed Joseph had been content to lead his people down a more peaceful route.

"This is your tent, hammerman."

Devon looked up as their guide spoke. He had stopped outside a large tent set in the centre of the camp. A trail of smoke seeped from the tip of the tent, and Devon grinned as he ducked beneath the flap and found a small fire burning in a rusted camp stove. A rough bed of straw was pushed into the corner and several wooden chairs lay strewn around the tent.

He glanced back as Braidon and their Baronian guide followed him inside. "Why didn't you bring us here last night?"

The man scratched his beard, looking uncertain. "Joseph's...belongings had to be removed."

Devon blinked. "This was Joseph's tent?"

"Of course," the man replied. "It is the best tent in the tribe. It belongs to the one who leads us."

Shaking his head, Devon lowered himself into one of the chairs and gestured for Braidon to join him. He scowled at the Baronian as Braidon claimed his seat. "And where is your former leader now?"

The Baronian cleared his throat. "He is a prisoner. We

have him held in the prison tent, awaiting your judgement, sir."

Devon sighed. "You'd best bring him here then." The man nodded, and was turning away when Devon's stomach rumbled. "Wait!" He shared a sheepish glance with Braidon before gesturing at the camp stove. "On second thought, we'll break our fast first. I'm sure Joseph can wait another hour."

"Of course, hammerman," the Baronian replied with a grin.

After the Baronian had departed, Braidon snorted with laughter. "Glad you've got your priorities straight."

"Damn right," Devon rumbled. Then he sighed and shook his head. "This is already getting complicated, isn't it? What am I meant to do with the big bastard?"

Braidon frowned. "You already spared his life once. Don't make the same mistake twice."

"Mistake?" Devon asked quietly.

In his mind, he saw again the moment the Baronian's axe had shattered, felt again the thrill of victory. Then Braidon's words had carried through the sudden silence that had fallen over the crowd.

Finish him, Devon!

When he'd looked up, Devon had caught the gleam in the boy's sapphire eyes, recognised the familiar bloodlust. His face contorted with hatred, Braidon had looked for all the world like the Son of the Tsar. Kellian's last words had come back to Devon then, about sparing those who could not defend themselves, and lowering *kanker*, he had given the Baronian a second chance.

"What makes you say it was a mistake to spare him?" he said.

"He tried to kill you!" Braidon exclaimed.

"Ay, but he fought with courage, and honour," Devon replied. He searched the boy's eyes as he spoke, seeking... something, but finding only confusion. With a sigh he went on. "He could have ordered his people to slaughter us, but instead he chose to risk single combat. And he lost everything for it. Is that not enough?"

Braidon shook his head, but before more could be said, the tent flap lifted and their guide returned, carrying two steaming plates. Devon studied the contents as they were placed before them, and was slightly disappointed to see they mostly consisted of rice and tubers dug up from the forest. Thin slivers of beef had been sprinkled through the food, with a generous helping of thyme, but there was little else.

His stomach rumbled, and he looked up to ask the Baronian where the rest was, when he saw the anxiety in the man's eyes. Devon's spirits fell as he realised this was the best these people could offer.

"Cheers, sonny," he rumbled, careful to hide his disappointment. "Give us half the hour, then bring the prisoner."

"Of course, hammerman." The man bowed his head and retreated from the tent.

They were just finishing their meal when the Baronian reappeared with Joseph in tow. The former Baronian leader's arms had been tied behind his back, and he glowered down at them as he was ushered into the tent. A bruise darkened his forehead where Devon had knocked him out. With his injured arm tied behind his back, he must have been in considerable pain, but his face remained carefully blank.

With a nod from Devon, their guide retreated from the tent. Standing before them, Joseph smirked. "I trust the new accommodations are to your liking?"

Devon leaned back in his chair and eyed the giant. When he'd first seen the man, he'd thought him in his late thirties. But after a night tied up in the cold winter air, the lines on Joseph's face had deepened, the silver in his beard becoming more prominent, and now Devon wondered if the man was closer to fifty.

If that were true, the fight he'd put up was all the more

impressive. Even now, Joseph refused to bend, facing down his impending judgement with fire in his eyes. Watching Joseph standing there in open defiance, Devon realised he had no desire to see the man killed.

"Seems comfortable enough," Devon mused. "Could use a bit of colour though."

Joseph snorted. "Typical townsfolk."

Beside Devon, Braidon bristled, but the hammerman waved him down. "Strange folks, these Baronians of yours," he mused. "One moment they're cheering for your victory, next they're on their knees proclaiming me their king."

"Baronians don't have kings," Joseph rumbled.

"Leader, whatever," Devon replied, waving a hand.

A strained silence followed, before Joseph sighed and shook his head. "Can't say I understand it myself," he grunted. "Any one of em could have taken my place, if they'd had the guts to put an arrow in ya."

"Glad they couldn't find the courage," Devon replied. Rising to his feet, he gestured at Joseph's bindings. "If I free you, are you going to play nice?"

"I'll make no promises to you, hammerman."

"Then you can rot for all I care," Devon said, starting to sit.

"Fine," Joseph said quickly, betraying his fear for the briefest of moments.

Grinning, Devon fetched a knife from beside the camp stove and cut Joseph's bonds. The man winced as they came free, and lifted his injured arm to the firelight. His wrist had swollen to twice its original size and had turned an awful black colouring. Pulling up a chair, Devon gestured for the giant to sit.

"Where do you keep the ale around here?" he asked as he stepped back.

Joseph chuckled. "Behind the bed, if Jazz didn't pilfer it already."

Devon found the clay jar where Joseph had said, and fetching a couple of mugs from behind the camp stove, he offered ale to Braidon and Joseph. Finally, he filled a mug of his own and settled back in his chair.

"Quite the predicament we've found ourselves in," he said, lifting his ale to Joseph.

The Baronian chuckled. "You seem to have landed on your feet, from where I sit."

"Ay…" Devon trailed off, remembering the information Braidon had shared the night before about the giant warrior and his people. "Who are you, Joseph? Selina says you and your people just showed up here one day, took over the place."

"Selina talks too much," Joseph rumbled. He shook his head and looked away. Then a smile touched his lips. "I might ask the same of you, hammerman. What kind of man leaves his enemies alive? Or sits down and shares a drink with them, for that matter?"

"Who says we're enemies?" Devon replied, taking a swig of his ale. It was strong, the fiery liquid burning its way down his throat, and he grinned in appreciation.

In the other chair, Braidon took his first swig and started to splutter. Joseph threw back his head and howled with laughter, but Braidon was too busy coughing to complain. When the commotion died down, Joseph leaned forward, his eyes dark.

"I'm serious, hammerman," he said quietly. "If you intend to be rid of me, I'd rather not draw this out."

"I don't kill unless I have to, sonny," Devon rumbled. "So the answer to your question is entirely up to you. When we're done here, you'll have your freedom. I'll warn you though, don't cross me. I give no second chances." He eyed the man. "Now, where did you and these Baronians of yours come from?"

Joseph sighed. "They're farmers, mostly. A few of us are

descended from the old folks; have the blood of true Baronians flowing in our veins. But our people have always welcomed exiles, and there's no shortage of those nowadays. I fell on hard times myself a while back, decided the Three Nations could use a bit of the old days."

Devon grinned. "As I heard it, the old days were filled with monsters and Dark Magickers intent on world domination."

"Hasn't changed much, has it?" Joseph replied, sculling his ale. "Just the titles we give em that differ."

Devon gestured for Braidon to fetch the jar of ale. Rolling his eyes, the boy rose and wandered across and retrieved it. Lifting it from the nook where it had been stored, he was just turning back towards them when he stumbled, a sudden cry tearing from his lips.

Throwing back his chair, Devon leapt to his feet. Moaning, Braidon straightened, his breath coming in ragged gasps. His eyes met Devon's, his pupils dilated, as though he were staring away into nothing. Devon took a quick step forward as the boy started to shudder, a low keening coming from the back of his throat.

"Braidon, what's wrong?" he hissed.

Braidon's pale face lifted slowly to meet his gaze. "It's them," he whispered. "It's my sister and Enala. They're in trouble!"

CHAPTER 19

Alana screamed as her magic rose from the depths of her consciousness and wrapped its thorny tendrils about her mind. Daggers of fire tore into her thoughts, dragging her down, trapping her in bonds of agony. Beside her, she could hear someone else screaming, and over it all, their assailant's laughter, mocking her.

The green light of her magic filled her. Its voice whispered in her ear, as her own personal demon took joy in its sudden freedom. Mustering her courage, she tried to face it, as she had so many times before, but now her courage seemed nothing beside the beast. It was as though the gates of its cage had been thrust open, unleashing it on her defenceless soul.

An image flickered into her mind, of her father standing over her, shining white sword in hand. Where once before he had thrust her magic back down, saving her from the demon within, now he was using the power of the Sword to unlock the chains of her own magic, handing the beast its freedom. It was devouring her from the inside out, and there was nothing she could do to protect herself.

Just as Alana was sure her mind would crumble, her magic vanished, its sickly green energies going rushing back down into the void within. Its absence was so sudden Alana gasped out loud. Her body shook, and the metallic taint of blood filled her mouth. Collapsing to the ground, she sobbed into the wooden floor as a voice spoke from overhead.

"That should bring the boy running," her father was saying. "Go prepare for his arrival, lieutenant."

The hard *thump* of boots on wood came from nearby, followed by the *thud* of the door being closed. Alana cracked open her eyes as another set of footsteps approached, and found her father crouching beside her. There was no sign of Quinn or the other Stalkers in the inn. The Tsar's eyes shone as he reached out and stroked her hair.

"Oh, my daughter, why must you torment me so?"

Alana shuddered, but when she tried to move away, she found the bonds of his magic holding her tight. The Tsar was taking no chances on her escaping this time.

"I am sorry it had to come to this," he continued, sadness in his voice. "I searched for so long for another way, but your betrayal has forced my hand. I must complete my task, before my enemies find a way to stop me."

"I won't serve you, Father," Alana croaked. "I would rather die."

The Tsar straightened. "And death is what you shall have," he said, his voice suddenly cold. "You're right, no matter my power, I could never fix what's broken in you. But you can still serve me, one last time."

"Never!" Alana spat.

Ignoring her, the Tsar turned his attention to the figure lying alongside Alana. "And you, Mother..." He trailed off as Enala pushed herself to her knees, pain etched across her aged face. His lips pursed into a thin line. "Why must you fight me? I have only ever done what you raised me to do, to fight for the greater good, to protect our nation from the ravages of war and magic."

Enala's eyes shone like sapphires in the light of the

Tsar's sword. "And how did murdering the God of Light and trapping him in your sword serve our nation?" she murmured, gesturing to the blade. "Did you think I would not recognise his power? No wonder the Goddess came to me."

The Tsar shrugged. "It was only a matter of time before they sought to rule us again."

"You're wrong, son," Enala croaked. "They left because they no longer wanted any part of our world. It is the only reason you exist."

"*Lies!*" the Tsar roared, pointing the Sword of Light at Enala. "You were corrupted by her touch, admit it! You are not the Enala you once were, before Antonia consumed your soul."

Enala smiled sadly. "Perhaps I am not," she murmured. "But that is no fault of Antonia's. It was my choice, to give her my body—and hers to return it."

The Tsar bared his teeth. "And it will be *mine* to finally see an end to her."

The old woman's laughter filled the room. "Antonia is not her brother. You will not fool her so easily, my son. That shoddy copy of a *Soul Blade* will not stop her."

"Copy?" the Tsar cackled. "I spent years studying Archon's work, but I surpassed him long ago. This is no copy, it is an improvement. When I'm done, I won't need others to help me wield the power of the Gods. This blade will contain them all."

"You cannot!" Enala hissed, her eyes widening. "The power will destroy you!"

"I command the magic of five hundred Magickers, Mother. The power of the Gods does not frighten me."

"It should," Enala whispered. She shook her head. "But it does not matter, you will never trap the Goddess. Or do you think she will submit meekly to your blade?"

The smile fell from the Tsar's face as his gaze drifted back to Alana. "No," he whispered. "That is why I need my children. Only they have the bloodline to host their power."

Alana's blood turned to ice at his words. Her mouth fell open, but the words failed to form in her throat. Sword in hand, her father stepped towards her. She tried to scramble back, but at a gesture from him, the bands of power tightened their grip. Slowly they lifted her up, dragging her off her feet until she dangled helplessly before him.

"I am sorry, my daughter," the Tsar whispered. "I wish there were another way."

"Please, don't." Still reeling from the bite of her magic, Alana found herself sobbing. In the past weeks, she had suffered more than she could ever have imagined, and now she could hold herself together no longer. She screamed, fighting to tear herself free of the Tsar's power. Tears spilled down her cheeks as she hurled abuse at the man who dared to call himself her father, and her feet kicked helplessly at empty air.

When she finally stilled, her father stood unmoved before her. Reaching out, he wiped a tear from her cheek, his eyes shining with a grief all of his own. "There is no other way," he whispered. "It is my life's duty to sponge the curse of magic from this land. For years I tried to use the power of the Light to wipe it clean, but the deed requires the Three. I must return the Gods of the Earth and Sky to flesh, so that I might use their power to save our people. You and Braidon are the only hosts left."

"No!" Enala's voice rang from the walls. "I won't let you have them." Flames gathered in her palm as she pointed at the Tsar.

The Tsar only shook his head. "You do not have the power to stop me, Mother. Your brother, your dragon, they're gone now. Look around: you're all alone, there is no one left to help you."

Enala did not back down, but Alana could see the defiance in the old woman's eyes falter, then turn slowly to despair. The soft crackling of her magic died away, and her arm dropped to her side. Her eyes flickered to Alana, her pain reflecting in the light of the Tsar's sword. The lines on her face deepened as she looked back at the Tsar.

"Spare the girl," Enala said. "She and her brother are not the only ones. Take me instead."

CHAPTER 20

"*No!*" Alana screamed at her grandmother. Desperately, she fought to reach her across the wooden floor of the inn, but the Tsar's bonds refused to bend. "Please, don't do this, Enala!"

Enala's face wrinkled into a smile. "Ah, but I must, Granddaughter."

Alana shook her head, her heart burning with newfound pain, an awful ache she had never before experienced. "But... I'm not worth it," she whispered.

The smile fell from her grandmother's face. "Nonsense, girl," she growled. "You are the future."

"No, you can't..."

"I can, and I will," Enala replied. "My time is done; yours is only just beginning, Alana."

Between them, the Tsar chuckled. "If you ladies are quite done?" He flicked a finger in Enala's direction, and the old woman rose ponderously into the air. Another gesture, and she drifted towards him. "And I thank you, Mother. Your sacrifice will allow my daughter to begin her life anew, once I am done shaping it."

"Monster," Enala spat, though she made no attempt to free herself.

Straining her arms, Alana fought to break her father's magic, but the invisible bindings refused to give. She sagged in their grip, a sob tearing from her throat, and watched in despair as the Tsar rested a hand on her grandmother's shoulder.

"Why have you always hated me, Mother?" he asked, his voice reflective.

"I *loved* you," Enala murmured, her voice little more than a croak.

"No." The Tsar shook his head. "I remember your disappointment, the day you discovered the gift wasn't in me, the day you realised I took after my *father*."

"I only ever wanted the best for you."

"*Lies!*" the Tsar snapped, pointing a finger. "I was never enough for you, always lacking, always the magicless son you never wanted. In all your tales and stories, it was always *magic* that brought wonder to your eyes. I could never live up to that. Just like my father."

"I never—"

"You think I couldn't see it?" the Tsar interrupted. "Your scorn for him, your disappointment as he aged, as his mortality began to show?"

The Tsar trailed off, and Enala hung there in silence, her eyes shining. Finally, she swallowed and spoke, her words barely a whisper. "I loved Gabriel until his dying day. Every wrinkle, every new white hair, was a blessing. I love him still. Even now I hope to see him again, to find him waiting for me on the other side. Though I pray he cannot see what his son has become."

"My father would be *proud* of what I have accomplished," the Tsar roared. His fingers bent like claws as he raised a fist. "And you will see him soon, Mother. That I promise you."

Turning away, he reached into his scarlet robes and withdrew a leather pouch. Glass rattled as he slapped it down on the inn's counter and unfurled it, revealing an array of glass vials. A mortar and pestle appeared next. Taking up vial after vial, the Tsar began to add them to the mortar, whispering beneath his breath all the while.

"What are you doing, Father?" Alana asked, her voice laced with venom. "Making us a cocktail?"

The Tsar flicked an irritated glance over his shoulder, and then returned to his work.

"You really think you can face her, son?" Enala cut in.

Slamming the mortar onto the bar, he spun towards them. The Sword of Light leapt into his hand, its blade aglow with power. "I have *this*, don't I?" he snapped. "With power over *all* magic, what chance does the Goddess of the Earth have?"

Enala smiled. "So much knowledge, and yet so little wisdom. Can you truly be so ignorant, my son?"

The Tsar's face turned a mottled red. Baring his teeth, he took a step towards the old woman before catching himself. With an effort of will, he forced himself back to his work. Taking up the pestle, he resumed his muttering as he ground the ingredients into a paste. When he was done, he lifted it to the light, inspecting it closely before nodding to himself.

"It's done," he announced, facing Enala.

"Are you afraid, Father?" Alana asked as he stepped towards her grandmother. A frown crossed his brow as he seemed to hesitate, and emboldened, she went on. "Don't worry, she's only an old woman. Or is it the Goddess who has your knees trembling? I've seen her, you know. She's about ten years old. I'm sure you can take her, though. Go on, get on with it."

The words burned in her mouth, but she felt a moment's satisfaction as her father's face darkened. Baring his teeth, he appraised her with cold eyes.

"Keep it up, my daughter. It will only quicken your fate."

Returning to Enala, he grabbed the old woman's face and

forced open her mouth. As she cried out, he poured half the potion down her throat and then held her jaw closed until she swallowed. Finally he released her and swallowed the rest of the potion himself.

"Bah, but that tastes almost as bad as Jonathan's muck," Enala spat.

The Tsar snorted. "That lunatic knew nothing of magic," he said, leaning casually against the bar. "His experiment would never have worked, not with you dead. Natural magic requires a *soul*. With yours in the void, the power he stole would have withered and died. That is why I am so careful to preserve the lives of my Magickers."

"By condemning them to a life without a past," Alana snapped.

Her father raised an eyebrow. "A task you savoured until quite recently, as I recall."

Alana shuddered as she remembered the part she'd played in her father's reign. Placed in charge of the young Magickers, she had the task of preparing them for their initiation. When the time came, she would take them before her father, and he would unlock their power, forcing them to face the beast within.

Those who survived, she took with her own magic, wiping the memories from them, reshaping them forever as her father's servants. And those who failed...

Her heart twisted as she saw again her charges changing, their eyes darkening to black as they succumbed to the demons within. Even then they could not escape her father's will. Using his power, he had bound their powers to his, to be his creatures, his assassins in the night.

Shame welled in Alana, not just for the horror of her deeds, but for the delight she had taken in them, that she still took in them, in the depths of her soul. She had joyed in her power over the young Magickers—their helplessness in the face of her magic. And when they had dared defy her...

"I was only what you made me," she whispered.

Her father laughed and turned away. She cursed at his back, but with a wave from her father the air changed, and she was hurled backwards against the wall. The breath hissed from her chest as she struck, leaving her gasping desperately for breath.

"Now, now, my daughter," her father's voice carried across the room. "Don't break my concentration. If this goes wrong, you may end up host to the Goddess after all."

"I hope she tears you in two," Alana gasped.

Her father had her back to her now, though, and didn't seem to hear. His voice boomed out in some strange language, and lifting his arms, he advanced on Enala. As he neared the old woman, his eyes became unfocused, and Alana recognised the look of someone reaching for his magic. A second later she sensed it arrive. Its power bubbled through the rundown inn, seeming to set the very air aflame.

Reaching Enala, the Tsar reached out and placed a hand on her shoulder. The old woman flinched at his touch, but wrapped up in his magic, there was nowhere for her to go. Eyes shining, Enala turned to look at Alana. To Alana's surprise, it wasn't fear or anger that shone from her grandmother's eyes, but a look of peace. Her lips moved silently, forming the words she dared not speak.

I love you, granddaughter.

Tears burned in Alana's eyes as the Tsar tightened his grip on her grandmother. A sudden convulsion shook the old woman, her mouth opening wide.

"*No!*" Alana screamed, but the two of them had entered the trance now, and neither heard.

"I summon you, Goddess of the Earth!" Her father's words rang out like thunder. A moan came from the floor near Alana, and she was surprised to see the innkeeper clawing her way towards the door. Another shout from the Tsar returned her attention to the centre of the room. "I summon you, Antonia, return to his mortal realm. I bid you, take host in this vessel, in the body of the woman marked by the name Enala."

His voice dropped to a low hiss then, his words becoming rapid and indistinct, and while Alana strained to hear the rest, she could not make them out. Her eyes were drawn back to her grandmother.

Alana's heart froze in her chest as she saw the old woman's face. Gone was the familiar sapphire of her grandmother's eyes; in its place shone the violet gaze of the Goddess Antonia. An icy fear spread through Alana's veins as she glimpsed the rage in those ancient eyes. When she had met Antonia in her dreams, the Goddess's anger had seemed fleeting, passing in an instant. But here, now, there was a timelessness to her rage, an anger that promised to never die.

The air wavered as the Goddess turned on the Tsar. With a flick of her hand, the forces holding Enala's body in the air shattered, and Antonia dropped lightly to her feet. Folding her arms, she studied the Tsar, her lips twisting into a scowl. Her foot tapped impatiently on the wooden floor as she waited for him to respond.

But Alana's father was still chanting under his breath, his eyes distant, unaware of the change that had come over the old woman. Arms raised, he seemed to be building to a finish. Alana was baffled—why was her father still trying to summon the Goddess, when Antonia was already standing before him? She shuddered as the violet gaze flickered in her direction. To her surprise, the slightest smile touched the Goddess's lips.

"By the *Gods!*" Antonia burst out suddenly. "Are you going to stand there all day mumbling to yourself?" She stamped her foot as though to emphasise her point.

The Tsar jerked as though he'd been stung. His eyes widened when he saw the old woman standing free of his bindings. He cried out as he recognised the violet eyes shining from her face.

"That's…that's not possible!" he gasped. Stumbling back, he lifted the Sword of Light, placing it between himself and the Goddess.

"What would you know, *mortal?*" Antonia growled. She advanced on him, the earth trembling with each step.

Alana gasped as the powers pinning her to the wall snapped as though they'd been severed by an axe. She staggered slightly as she landed, her muscles burning with the disuse. As she recovered, a wave of warmth swept through the room, radiating out from the glowing figure. The magic wrapped around Alana, every pain, every ache vanishing at its touch. Looking at her arms, Alana gaped as her bruises faded away, her cuts and scrapes healing in an instant. The pounding in her head from the blow Quinn had struck vanished.

A groan came from nearby as the innkeeper sat up. Her hands clutched at her chest where Quinn's sword had pierced her, but now the skin was whole. The only trace of the wound that remained was the blood staining her clothes. She looked at Antonia in wonder, tears brimming in her eyes.

"Thank you, Goddess," she whispered.

"*Stop this!*" the Tsar boomed.

He raised the Sword of Light. A brilliant radiance lit the inn, and Alana moaned as the warmth was sucked from the room. It had done its work though, and her strength restored, she crouched down and crept to where the innkeeper sat. Silently she offered her a hand, then turned to watch her father face off against the Goddess of the Earth.

"Your power is *mine*, Goddess," he hissed through clenched teeth. "You cannot harm me."

Antonia only smiled. "I have no wish to harm you, Theo. I never wanted to return to this realm. It was I who first gave up this body, all those years ago, so that you might be born. It pleased me to watch Enala grow, to become the woman I knew she could be. I am only sorry she lived long enough to see her child become a monster." The Goddess's eyes flickered to Alana. "But perhaps it is not too late for her grandchildren."

"Enough!" the Tsar shrieked. "You do not fool me, Goddess. Your tyranny ends today. No longer shall you and your siblings wield your power over this realm."

He lifted the shining sword, but as Antonia stepped towards him, he faltered. Swirling green light appeared in her hands, and the Tsar's eyes widened with fear. A smile touched Antonia's face. With a flick of her finger, power went crackling through the inn. Alana gasped as her ears popped, the pressure building until she thought for sure her skull would crack.

Go, Alana, a voice whispered in her mind. *Save yourself, as your grandmother wished.*

Alana gasped as she recognised the voice as the one who had led her to her grandmother. A sob tore from her as she looked at the Goddess, and saw her head dip in acknowledgement. Eyes burning, Alana swung away, grabbing the innkeeper as she did so. Somewhere behind them was the door to the outside, though how they could avoid Quinn and his Stalkers, Alana didn't know. All she knew was they had to get out, had to escape that room before the end came.

"You cannot defeat the Light!" Alana heard her father bellow. Together with the innkeeper, she staggered toward the door.

"No," came Antonia's reply. The rumbling energies burning through the room went out as though quenched by a bucket of water. Alana glanced back to see the Goddess standing alone, bathed in the eerie white of her father's sword. "But I do not need to."

For a moment her words gave the Tsar pause. He towered over the Goddess, confusion on his ageless face. Then a sneer twisted his lips, and with a bellow of laughter, he lifted the Sword of Light and drove it through the Goddess's chest.

CHAPTER 21

"Y ou sure about this, sonny?" Devon rumbled.

Braidon flicked Devon a nervous grin as they paused on the edge of the settlement. Still in the treeline, he had not yet summoned his magic, and raising a hand, he gestured for the others to halt. The twenty Baronians they had selected to join them came to a stop, their blackened leather armour fading into the shadows beneath the dense canopy.

"As sure as I'll ever be," Braidon muttered.

Movement came from nearby as Joseph crouched beside Devon. Irritation cut through Braidon's fear, but he fought to keep it from his face. The man's injured arm was strapped to his chest, but even wounded, he was a threat. Braidon couldn't believe Devon had let the former leader join them, not when so much was at stake. But his friend had been firm, insisting they needed the man's knowledge of the territory, and of his people.

Shaking his head, Braidon returned his gaze to the settlement. It was too late now to reconsider the Baronian's presence, though looking at what faced them, he wondered if Joseph was already regretting his decision to join them. A dozen Stalkers could be seen wandering the narrow alleyways between the buildings, and in the centre of the square…

"You'd better be, boy," Joseph hissed, his dark eyes transfixed on what faced them.

"Don't worry about the beast," Devon whispered. "It won't lift a claw unless the Tsar wills it."

"How reassuring," Joseph muttered. "But if it's all the same to you, I'd rather not risk my people against a *dragon*."

"Good thing they're not your people anymore, isn't it?" Braidon snapped.

Between them, Devon raised his hands in a consolatory gesture. "Easy," he said. "Don't want to be giving ourselves away just yet." His amber eyes turned on the Baronian. "As for your people, what about the ones in that settlement? Did you not make a deal with the people here to protect them?"

"Against other rogues, not the Tsar himself," Joseph argued, but his head dropped imperceptibly, and after a moment he went on. "The dragon won't attack, you say?"

"Not your people," Devon replied. "Not when Braidon and I have the Tsar's mother and daughter. If everything goes to plan, it'll be coming after *us*. We only need you to free the villagers and distract the Stalkers long enough for them to get away."

"Fine. Just make sure you shake the beast before the rendezvous."

"Don't worry, your safety is our *top* priority," Braidon said spitefully. "Now, if you're done?" Joseph glared at him, but said nothing, and Braidon nodded curtly. "Then we'd better get going, Devon. I can sense something happening in there."

Even as he spoke, the power he sensed in the inn redoubled. Magic rippled through the air, shifting and building, until it seemed his very bones were vibrating with the strength of it. Swallowing his doubt, he reached down and stoked the flames of his own power.

A roar answered his call as it lifted from the depths of

his soul. Ignoring the beast that took shape before him, Braidon gripped it with his mind, forcing it to his will. He reached out with the power in hand and wrapped ghostly threads of white around himself and Devon. As they touched the brilliant blue of Devon's lifeforce, they changed, seeming to merge with the green of the forest. He did the same for himself, and beside them Joseph slowly faded until he was just a silhouette against the world around him.

Blinking, the Baronian looked around as though he could no longer see them. "That's incredible," he murmured. "Are you still there?"

"Remember, ten minutes," Devon hissed.

Then they were up and racing across the open ground between the treeline and the settlement. Braidon held his breath as a Stalker appeared ahead of them, his long strides carrying him around the edge of the square. His eyes swept the forest, fixating for a second on Braidon and Devon, and then passing on. Air whistled between Braidon's teeth as he released his breath.

Moving quickly, they crossed the square and made the inn, taking care to avoid the wings and tail of the Red Dragon. It had taken up residence in the centre of the square, its massive body curled around the couple's wagon. The carcass of their pony lay alongside the beast, its bloody bones all but unrecognisable.

Shuddering, Braidon fixed his eyes on their destination. Checking his spell was still in place, he continued on, Devon keeping fast to his side. Despite the big man's words, Devon had one eye on the beast, and Braidon could sense the fear radiating from his friend.

The magic spreading through the square grew stronger as they approached the stairs to the inn. He no longer sensed Alana or Enala's power, but the confusing mixture of Light, Earth and Sky magic could only have come from his father.

Something else stained the air though, a cold tang of Earth and Light far more potent than even his father's magic.

"You sure they're in there?" Devon whispered.

Braidon nodded and they started up the stairs. The wooden boards creaked beneath Devon's weight, and Braidon glanced back quickly to see if the watchers had noticed. The black silhouettes of the Stalkers continued their slow march around the square. None of the ones hiding in the shadows moved, but the Red Dragon lifted its head, a low rumble coming from its chest. A vile stench carried across to them as it snorted, then took up a piece of bone and began to chew.

"Disgusting creatures," Devon muttered. "I hope Enala still has Dahniul lurking somewhere nearby."

Braidon's throat clenched as he recalled the beam of light that had caught the Gold Dragon, hurling him from its back. Yet both he and Enala had survived; why not the dragon?

He spun back around as an awful shriek came from inside the inn. Braidon's heart leapt into his throat as he felt the magic in the air changing. Gripping Devon by the arm, he raced for the door. As he reached for the handle, a howl came from the forest behind them, announcing the arrival of the Baronians.

Braidon didn't have time to see whether the Stalkers were successfully distracted. If everything went to plan, the Baronians would kill a few and then disappear back into the forest. Hauling open the door, Braidon raced inside.

Green and white light raced out to greet him, and for half a second Braidon felt his power swell, as though fed by some other force. A moment later Devon appeared beside him, *kanker* in hand. Braidon sensed his spell tearing, drained by the spell cast over the hammer—then they were standing in the doorway to the inn for all the world to see.

Before he could restore his illusion, a scream drew Braidon's attention to the centre of the room. His father stood there, glowing white sword in hand, Enala bowed before him.

Before anyone could move, the blade flashed down, tearing through his grandmother's chest.

Braidon's heart lurched and he screamed, reaching out a hand as though by will alone he could undo what his father had done. Another scream came from his right, and Devon rushed past, his face a mask of determination. Braidon was still staring in horror when Devon returned an instant later, Alana now swung over his shoulder.

"Go, Braidon!" he bellowed. Another voice echoed his cry, and Braidon was shocked to see the innkeeper, Selina, racing before the hammerman. "*Go!*" Devon screamed again.

But Braidon was unable to look away from the terrible scene. His grandmother still stood, her eyes burning violet, her body bent around the awful sword. Magic bubbled from the wound up into the Tsar's blade, green and white mixing and merging, seeming to flow into the steel itself.

The Tsar showed no sign he had noticed Alana's rescue, nor his son's presence. Slowly the magic began to fade, then as though she were a fire dashed by water, the light in Enala's eyes died. She slumped against the sword, and wrenching back his blade, the Tsar allowed her body to tumble to the ground. Power swirled as he lifted the sword aloft, awesome, terrifying.

A sudden fear fill Braidon then, and tearing himself free of his shock, he turned away. Tears streamed from his eyes as he chased after Devon. He could feel his grief within, his rage and hatred rising, becoming entangled in the threads of his magic. Unbidden it rose again, igniting a flickering light in his palms. Stumbling outside, Braidon focused on his grandmother's lessons, concentrating on his breathing, seeking the calm within the storm of his emotions.

As his magic came back under his control, he gripped it tightly, seeking to wrap a fresh layer of concealment around the four of them. But as the magic touched Devon, there was a strange sucking sensation, and he realised with a curse that his friend still held *kanker* in one hand.

"Devon!" he called, his voice echoing through the square. "Sheathe your hammer!"

Devon was already at the bottom of the steps. To Braidon's relief, most of the Stalkers had vanished, presumably chasing after the Baronians that had attacked the settlement. Below, Devon looked back, confusion in his eyes, but seeing Braidon's desperation, he did as he was bid. As he reached up to sheathe *kanker*, Alana shrieked, seeming to come alive in his grip. An elbow struck him in the face, and he staggered back as she dropped lightly to her feet. Eyes dark, she started towards the steps.

"You can't help her, girl." Selina blocked the way back to her inn. "And you can't stop him."

Braidon rushed down the steps as Alana raised a hand towards the woman. He sensed her power building and opened his mouth to scream a warning, but at the last moment his sister hesitated. Some of the rage left her face as she closed her eyes, a shudder sweeping through her. She slumped forward, and Selina stepped quickly forwards to catch her.

Reaching them, Braidon wasted only a second to check that Alana was okay, before diving back into his magic. Sensing their peril, it rose in an instant. Acting by a will of its own, the white light wrapped around them, and they faded from view.

"Fine, then I'll make them all pay."

Braidon looked around as his sister straightened once more. Her eyes glowed as she stalked past him. Concealed now by her power, she strode towards the dragon, which had awoke amongst the chaos and was now staring at the space where they had vanished. Just as Devon had predicted, it had made no move against them without being bidden by his father. Casting a quick glance back at the inn, Braidon wondered how long it would be before the command came. Whatever had happened between the Tsar and Enala was obviously still keeping him preoccupied, and he prayed to the Goddess it continued for a while yet.

Alana was approaching the Red Dragon now, and as its tail twitched, she darted forward and gripped it in both hands. Braidon's ears popped as he sensed the power surge from her into the beast. An awful roar rent the air as it threw back its head. Alana leapt away as the tail whipped about, narrowly missing her.

Then the dragon drew suddenly still, the great globes of its eyes fixating on the distant trees. Alana stepped forward again, resting her hands on its foreclaws.

"Go," her voice rang through the square. "Destroy them all, the ones who caged you, the ones who sought to rule you."

The beast roared again, but now the sound was filled with an awful glee. Wings spread, it crouched flat against the dirt, and then bounded into the air. A sharp *crack* sounded in the square as the dragon lifted skywards, its great neck circling to stare down at the settlement. Fire built in the cavern of its jaws as it turned towards them.

"*Run!*" Braidon screamed.

CHAPTER 22

Blood thumped in Alana's ears as she raced through the trees, drowning out the dragon's roar and the screams of dying men. Smoke hung heavy in the air, its stench choking, blinding. Around them the forest was aflame, the world in chaos. Alana cared nothing for any of it.

Enala was dead.

Her grandmother, the woman she had hated until just a few days ago, had been murdered, and there was nothing Alana could do to change it.

"Come on!"

Someone was screaming from ahead of her, but whether it was Devon or Braidon or the strange woman from the inn, she couldn't tell. Head down, she continued through the forest, her footsteps growing shorter as despair ate her resolve. The magic it had taken to break her father's spell over the Red Dragon had cost her greatly, and now the beast was as likely to kill them all as it was her father's Stalkers.

Tears stung her eyes as she finally staggered to a stop, overwhelmed. The fire was somewhere behind her now, but smoke still blanketed the forest. It rose to claim her as she slumped to the ground, stealing away her breath.

How long she crouched there, she couldn't say, but suddenly she sensed her brother alongside her. Her heart beat faster as she looked at him, still hardly believing he was there, that he was alive. After all those days thinking he was gone...

"Braidon," she murmured. "You're alive."

"Of course I am, sis," he said as he knelt in the dirt. "What are you doing here?"

Her vision blurred as the pain of their grandmother's loss cut through her joy. "We have to go back," she croaked. "We have to save her."

The pain in her brother's eyes reflected her own, but he shook his head. Reaching out, he drew her into his arms. Alana sobbed as she breathed in the scent of him, felt his heart beating in concert with her own.

He's alive, he's really alive.

"We can't, sis," Braidon whispered into her ear. "We can't, she's already gone."

"But she's our grandmother," Alana sobbed, trying to pull herself together, to summon the unyielding resolve her father had built within her. Yet the moment Enala had been struck down, all that strength, all that resolve, had been shattered. "She sacrificed herself for me," she burst out, and buried her face in Braidon's shoulder.

Braidon said nothing, only held her tighter. For a while they knelt together in silence, eyes closed, listening as the sounds of the world faded away, until it seemed only the two of them remained. A sweet peace settled around Alana, calming her heart, drying her tears. Finally, she pulled back from her brother and opened her eyes. The forest had vanished, replaced by the softest blanket of white.

"You're doing this?" she whispered.

"It's only an illusion," he murmured. "We have to return, before the fires reach us."

The thought of returning to a world without the crotchety old woman filled Alana with dread. She sucked in a breath, savouring the nothingness around them, the peace of it all, and then nodded at Braidon. With a flick of his fingers, the white vanished, returning them to the chaos of the forest.

Slowly he drew Alana to her feet. "Are you ready?" he asked. "My magic won't hide us forever, not while we're so close."

"I know," Alana whispered.

They started off again. Alana had no idea which direction Braidon was leading her in, but as they continued on, the smoke grew thinner, and the bellows of the dragon faded, until the silence of the forest resumed. It wasn't long before they caught up with Devon and the woman from the inn. Seeing them, Devon turned and started off through the forest without saying a word.

The sight twisted a dagger in Alana's heart, but she said nothing, knowing she deserved every bit of his hatred. Her gaze turned to Braidon, who strode along behind Devon like he knew exactly where they were going. She frowned, thinking back to the last time she had seen him, the young, apprehensive boy she'd left before the gates of Fort Fall.

He had seemed so small then, so frail; she would have done anything to protect him. Now though, it was Braidon who had saved her, who had mustered a rescue from right beneath their father's nose. In the brief time they had been separated, the boy that had been her brother had mastered his magic, had come into his own. He was a man now, though Alana wondered whether she could ever think of him as anything but her little brother.

The roar of the dragon sounded through the quiet of the trees, but it was still some distance away, and after a moment's pause the company started off once more. Between Devon's obvious rage and Alana's shock, little was said amongst the four of them. No doubt there would be time for swapping stories later, though Alana doubted Devon would want to hear a word of what she had to say. For now though, they needed to get away. With Braidon's power concealing them, the Tsar would struggle to detect their minds or magic. But that would not stop his Stalkers from encircling them.

That is, if the Red Dragon didn't burn them first.

They continued on, the trees growing denser around them. After an hour, when they still hadn't heard more from the dragon, Alana sensed her brother release his concealing spell. They shared a glance and she nodded her approval. His magic still protected them from their father's invisible gaze, but the physical concealment required far more energy. Braidon could not have kept up such a magic forever, not without drawing on his own lifeforce.

The trees thinned out again, the light amongst the under-growth brightening as the canopy grew fainter. Brambles appeared, their vines as thick as fingers. Devon took the lead, his leather jacket and pants giving him some protection from their bites. Following behind him, the others struggled through the broken bushes he left behind, cursing as stray thorns cut their flesh.

Dusk approached, and the soft whine of insects arrived. Alana cursed as the creatures slipped through the cracks in her clothing to fasten themselves on her flesh. She slapped her arm, and her hand came away streaked with blood. A few seconds later, another insect took the mosquito's place.

Finally the last of the forest gave way, but as Alana looked around, it wasn't open ground that greeted her, but a towering cliff of blood-red sandstone. Her heart sank as she scanned the mountain range, her eyes alighting on a slightly darker patch of shadow. In the fading light, it wasn't until they grew closer that she realised it was a thin passage leading through the cliffs.

As they neared the crevice, the buzz of voices carried to their ears. Alana slowed, her hand dropping to her empty sword sheath. She cursed, realising she'd left the blade behind on the floor of the inn, but Devon was still striding forward, seemingly uncaring of the voices. Sharing a glance with her brother, she watched as he disappeared into the shadows of the Sandstone Mountains.

Quinn winced as the door clicked shut behind him. In the silence within the inn, the noise seemed unbelievably loud, echoing through the dark interior of the building like a gong. He froze, taking a moment to prepare himself before facing the Tsar.

"They escaped?"

The words were softly spoken, yet they sliced through the silence, filling the room with their power. Quinn's head whipped around, searching the shadows for his master. He found the silhouette of a man near the bar, head bowed, sword still in hand. As Quinn's eyes adjusted, his gaze was drawn to the pile of rags at the Tsar's feet. The slight sheen of blood pooling there was the only hint that the rags were more than they appeared. Swallowing, he looked back at his master.

"Yes, sir—"

The words had barely left his mouth when he sensed an invisible force invade his body. He gasped, the shining blue of his magic rising to defend him. Yet even as it rose, the other force sliced through his resistance as though he were no more potent than a child and wrapped his mind in chains of fire.

A scream tore from Quinn's lips as agony engulfed him. Then, as quickly as it had come, the force departed, and he found himself gasping on the floor of the inn. Shivering, he dragged himself to his knees and looked at the Tsar.

"Speak," came the Tsar's command.

"Yes...sir," he managed. "The Baronians...they attacked. We...chased them into the forest...others were behind us...

they freed the villagers…" He trailed off, his eyes drawn to the dark silhouette of his master.

"And?"

"The Red Dragon, it broke free," Quinn whispered, his voice more steady now. "It burned the forest, half our number, probably the Baronians, too. We…we had to kill it."

Quinn didn't mention the delight he had taken in tearing the beast from the sky. Ever since its mockery of him during his first hunt for Alana, he had despised the creature. He'd been all too happy to combine his magic with the other Stalkers and destroy the Red Dragon, Feshibe.

"And my daughter?"

"One of my men caught a glimpse of her, sir," he replied, "as they left the inn. She was with Devon, and your son."

"So all our enemies, they were here, in this settlement? And you failed to capture them, lieutenant?"

Quinn swallowed. "Yes, sir."

"You disappoint me."

The tone in the Tsar's voice froze the blood in Quinn's veins. He looked up in time to see the soft flicker of lightning as it gathered in the Tsar's hand. Crying out, Quinn stumbled back, but there was no escaping the violence dancing in his master's eyes. With a roar of thunder, it flashed across the room. Catching him around the legs, the blue fire burnt through clothes and flesh alike.

Quinn's back arched, but as he tried to scream he found his jaw clamped tightly shut. The strength went from him as agony engulfed his entire body. Desperately he clawed at his legs, and screamed again as he saw his flesh melting, the shining white of bone peeking through. Another bolt of lightning struck him, and Quinn twisted, his mind falling away…

And then there was nothing.

Blinking, Quinn cried out at the sudden absence of pain. Still clutching his legs, he opened his eyes, and gaped to find the Tsar still standing over him, the Sword of Light pointed at his chest. Except the glow of its power was no longer white, but a brilliant, shining emerald. It streamed from the blade to bathe his legs, cooling wherever it touched. Quinn watched in astonishment as his flesh regrew from nothing, making him whole once more.

"The Goddess is mine," the Tsar whispered. "So I will forgive you this one last time, Quinn." He waved a hand, and light filled the inn, illuminating the broken body of the old woman.

Rising unsteadily to his feet, Quinn bowed. "They won't get far, I promise you."

"I trust not," the Tsar replied. "Take the remaining Stalkers, and the soldiers. There are still more than enough to deal with the hammerman and his newfound allies."

"Yes, sir."

The Tsar regarded him coldly. "Do not betray me, Quinn," he said finally. He gestured to the dead woman. "Or what happened to her will seem a dream compared with your fate."

"Yes, sir," Quinn repeated, dropping to his knees. "I will not fail you."

To his surprise, the man snorted. "You probably will," he cackled. "But for the moment, there is no one else in this forest I can trust." Turning, the Tsar started for the doorway.

"Sir?" Quinn called him back, rising to his feet. "What of the dragon? How will you return to the army?"

"Feshibe's children are already on their way," he replied. His face darkened. "The Northland army has launched an ambush on our forces in Lonia."

"They dare to attack us?"

"Ay, it seems they could not wait for death to come to them. No matter, it will find them soon enough."

CHAPTER 23

Damyn had just moments to glimpse the horror on the faces of his enemies before his force slammed into their flank, driving them back up against the wagons. Hampered by the overburdened vehicles and their own oxen, the soldiers struggled to bring their weapons to bear against the northern cavalry. Scores went down before any sort of resistance could be mounted.

By then, Damyn's forces outnumbered the defenders two to one, yet the enemy refused to break. Soldiers streamed through the gaps between the wagons as those caught on the other side of the baggage train reinforced their comrades. Linking shields, they sought to push back the horses.

Glancing along the road, Damyn cursed as he saw men streaming back through the trees towards them. The forces who'd marched to reinforce the vanguard hadn't gone far, and now Damyn only had minutes before they were surrounded. He looked at the wagons, so close and yet still so tantalisingly far away.

A scream came from one of the oxen in the baggage train, and suddenly it was charging forward. Wagon still attached, it slammed into the men standing between Damyn and his goal, shattering their line. Panicked, another oxen followed suit, the traces holding its load in place shattering as it twisted and leapt away.

The scattered soldiers made easy targets, and screaming an order, Damyn pressed his horse forward. His sabre sliced left and right, cutting a path to the broken wagons. Finally, the southerners broke, first one, then dozens turning and fleeing up the Gods Road towards their reinforcements.

Well-trained, Damyn's men dragged back on their reins when the soldiers were clear of the baggage train, turning their attention to the wagons themselves. Swords flashed, freeing the last of the oxen of their burdens, before torches appeared. Damyn lit his own and hurled it into the back of the nearest wagon. His men did the same, and within the minute thick columns of smoke stained the sky, rising high in the thin winter air.

Turning his horse, Damyn surveyed their work. A grin split his bearded cheeks as he waved to his men.

"Back to the hi—"

An ear-splitting roar drowned out his cry as a shadow passed across the sun. Beneath him, Damyn's horse gave a scream of pure terror and reared. He tugged desperately at the reins as it hit the ground running, seeking to turn it, to bring it back under his control. Around him he sensed others doing the same, even as the *thump, thump, thump* of scarlet wings drove a spike of despair deep into his heart.

Finally, Damyn's horse staggered to a halt, its coat drenched in sweat, its powerful body trembling from head to tail. Hardly daring to breathe, Damyn turned the gelding back towards the hillside. With a shout, he kicked his horse into a run, setting his sights on the distant hilltop.

"Pull back!" he bellowed, though his men were scattered around the Gods Road now, and few could hear him.

The shadow passed across the sun again before Damyn could reach the treeline. The Red Dragon came barrelling down, mouth wide, fire blossoming in the void of its throat. Warmth bathed his face as it gushed forth, engulfing the forest.

A dozen or more of his men had already reached the trees. Their screams were terrible to behold as the inferno swallowed them up. Manes aflame, several horses came racing from the forest, but their riders had already succumbed to the awesome heat.

Damyn's horse stumbled to a stop. Its breath coming in ragged snorts, it stood trembling beneath him, too terrified even to run. Around him, what remained of Damyn's cohort did the same. Each knew there was no longer any point in running; death had come for them, and there would be no escape.

The earth shook as the dragon slammed into the hillside, its wings scattering fire in all directions. Giant jaws stretched wide, revealing endless rows of glistening teeth. Talons tore the earth as it crept towards them, the yellow slits of its eyes speaking of an endless hunger. But it was not the sight of the dragon that filled Damyn with despair; it was the scarlet-cloaked figure perched on its back.

Light flashed from the sword in the man's hand, rippling from white to green. The dragon bent low, offering one awful paw for the man to dismount. Leaping clear, the cloaked figure gestured again with his sword, and the beast leapt back into the sky.

Damyn hardly saw it go. His eyes were trapped in the sapphire gaze of the man before them, in the unyielding gaze of the Tsar. With casual slowness, the man advanced down the hill to where Damyn and his cohort waited. He was one against hundreds, and yet not a single northerner dared raise their sword against him.

The blackened earth crunched beneath the Tsar's boots as he came to a stop before Damyn. Hands clasped before him, he appraised the captain in silence, face impassive. Sitting on his horse, Damyn tried to think of some way of fighting back, but his whole body seemed frozen, as though the man's very presence was enough to rob him of his will.

A crease marked the Tsar's brow as he looked beyond the horsemen at the burning wagons. Raising a hand, he gestured at the flames. A *whoosh* came from behind Damyn as the fires they'd started flickered out.

"I take it the Queen sent you," the Tsar said, his voice deceptively quiet.

Damyn swallowed, his words failing him. The Tsar's rasping laughter whispered through the burning forest as he took a step closer.

"Get down, Captain," he hissed.

"No—" Damyn broke off as he felt something cold pierce his chest.

He gasped and looked down, expecting to see an arrow or blade impaling him, but there was nothing. Yet the sensation was already spreading, seeping out from his chest to fill him with icy fire. Opening his mouth, he tried to scream, even as the cold reached his throat. His shriek came out as a whimper and he slumped in the saddle, his every nerve alive with agony, yet unable to so much as squeak.

"Down," the Tsar repeated.

To Damyn's horror, his body responded without question. His horse whinnied nervously as he dismounted and moved to stand in front of the Tsar. The icy fire still setting his mind aflame, he sank to his knee before the leader of the Three Nations.

Smiling, the Tsar reached down and laid his hand on Damyn's head. Whatever pain he'd felt before redoubled as a terrible force slid through his consciousness. His back arched and he longed to draw his sword and lash out at his assailant, but there was no fighting this man, no resistance against the power gripping his body.

Finally, the Tsar withdrew, his magic going with him.

Crying out, Damyn slumped to the ground. A thousand pinpricks needled his every muscle as he tried to move, to run or even crawl away from the man's awful power. But all he could manage was the pitiful moans of a dying man.

"So the Queen is close," the Tsar mused. "She must have powerful Magickers to have shielded herself from me."

"Bastard," Damyn spat. Finally regaining some of his movement, he managed to drag himself to his knees. "You will never conquer us."

"Conquer?" the Tsar said sadly. He gestured to the burnt-out wagons, a smile appearing on his face. "It was not I who invaded a foreign nation, who ambushed and slaughtered innocent soldiers."

"You left us no choice."

"That is not how history will remember it," the Tsar laughed. "If it remembers you at all."

"You will never win," Damyn choked.

"I have heard that before," the Tsar murmured. Leaning down, he touched Damyn's cheek. His skin was soft, the gesture almost tender, and Damyn jerked away. Chuckling, the Tsar straightened and turned to the other Northerners. "And yet I always do."

"Just kill us," Damyn growled, anger giving his words strength. "You'll get nothing from us."

"Oh, but you have already given me *everything*, young Damyn. Your Queen flees for the Sandstone Mountains, seeking to draw us away from her own people."

"No," Damyn whispered.

An awful rage took him then, fed by hatred and the realisation he had failed his Queen. A scream ripped from his throat as he scrambled to his feet. Sabre in hand, he hurled himself at the Tsar...

He made it two steps before a force like a raging bull struck him in the chest. Something went *crack* as he was hurled from his feet. Agony lanced through his chest as though he'd been stabbed. The breath went from him in a rush as he struck the ground.

Footsteps crunched as the Tsar appeared overhead. "Your loyalty is to be admired," he murmured. "A shame your Queen was unworthy of it."

"She will destroy you."

"She will die, like all the rest." The Tsar lifted his sword. "As will all of your people."

"Get on with it then," Damyn spat.

Lowering his sword, the Tsar smiled. The sight filled Damyn with a sudden dread, even before the man spoke. "Get on with it?" He shook his head, gesturing to the ruined wagons. "But you have brought me such pain, Captain. I cannot simply send you all to the void, without repaying the favour."

Fear spread through Damyn like a poison as he looked into the darkness in the man's eyes and saw his fate. In that instant, he saw what he had to do, and screaming, he surged to his feet. His sword lay just a foot away. He hurled himself at the hilt, sweeping it up and lifting it high.

Then he reversed the blade and drove it into his stomach.

Pain tore through him as the point struck home. The metallic taste of blood filled his mouth as he slumped back to his knees. He looked up at the Tsar, his vision swirling, slowly fading away, and smiled.

"She *will* stop you," he gasped, blood bubbling from his lips.

Darkness closed in as the Tsar leaned down and tore the blade from his stomach. By then Damyn could feel nothing. But as the Tsar knelt beside him, warmth washed over him. He groaned as the darkness receded, the world returning, and with it the pain.

A smile touched the Tsar's face as he stroked Damyn's brow. "Don't go leaving just yet, Captain," he murmured. "I'm not done with you."

CHAPTER 24

Devon waited until darkness before he allowed the Baronians to light their fires, knowing that even in the mountains, the smoke would be seen for miles around. He would have preferred a cold camp, but with the mountains in the grips of winter, half their number would freeze to death before morning without heat. As it was, the threadbare clothing of the Baronians was hopelessly inadequate.

But there was no turning back now. Braidon had been able to cloak their small group of leaders from the Tsar's roaming eyes, but there was no hiding their tracks. Quinn and his Stalkers would not be far behind. It was unlikely the Baronians and their wagons could outrun the hunters, but they could at least make it harder for them.

At least the dragon was dead. Joseph himself had seen it fall from the sky, struck down by magic and a dozen crossbow bolts. They had Alana to thank for that, though Devon would never admit as much to the young woman. He still could not bring himself to speak with her.

Without the beast prowling the skies, Devon only had to concern himself with the Stalkers on their trail. From what he'd seen in the settlement, the Baronians had Quinn and his men badly outnumbered. Even poorly fed and armed, the weight of their numbers might have been enough to overwhelm their pursuers.

If not for the magic of the Stalkers.

Devon had considered setting an ambush further up in the mountains, but quickly dismissed the idea. Even with *kanker* and Braidon and Alana, they were badly outmatched by the powers Quinn and his followers could command. Forcing a pitched battle would be to risk everything on the hope the Stalkers didn't react quickly enough to bring their magic to bear. Sadly, Devon knew Quinn well enough to realise that was unlikely.

No, their only chance for the moment was to retreat into the mountains, and pray to the Gods they could lose the Stalkers in the maze of caves and gullies.

Fat chance of that, Devon thought as he surveyed the camp.

The Baronians had taken the loss of their permanent camp in stride, though they'd been forced to leave many of their tents and wagons behind. A few had refused to come, and had remained behind with their measly possessions, but some five hundred had followed Devon into the mountains.

He had been surprised by their loyalty, though the weight of responsibility hung heavy on his shoulders now. In the brief moments they'd had to plan Alana's rescue, he hadn't thought this far ahead, about what it would mean to lead so many people into the mountain passes. Now though, Devon wondered whether he was escorting them to their doom, if his recklessness had finally caught up with him.

Devon looked up as the flaps of his tent parted and Joseph stepped inside. The former Baronian leader offered a nod, and then wandered over and took a seat on the other side of Devon's camp stove. Holding his hands out to the hot iron, he grinned. "Glad to see this made it into the wagons."

In no mood for company, Devon only grunted and waited for the man's reason for being there. Seeing Alana again had left him feeling confused and dejected. When he'd first stepped into the inn and seen her standing there alive, Devon had experienced a surge of elation, quickly followed by despair as he remembered the Alana standing before him was no longer the woman he loved.

Unlike Braidon, he hadn't been able to move past what had happened, what the woman who looked like Alana had done. When the boy had walked into camp with Alana in tow, there had been smiles all around, though the Baronians did not know what they were celebrating. But Devon had taken no joy from the occasion, and had quickly excused himself. Alone, Devon had found himself longing for the quiet comradery he'd enjoyed with the boy this past week, the tranquil peace as they wandered the forest paths, the silence of the night as they cooked their evening meals.

Instead, Devon now found himself alone but for a man who had tried to kill him just days ago.

"What do you want, Joseph?" he snapped after a minute, when the man still had not spoken.

"Grouchy, aren't you?" The giant chuckled. "And I thought *I* was the old man. Thought you'd be overjoyed to have the woman back."

"I'm happy she's alive," Devon growled.

"Truly?" Joseph asked. "Because you looked ready to scream murder when the boy led her into the camp."

"It's complicated," Devon said. Picking up the iron poker, he stabbed at the coals inside the camp stove.

"Ah, complicated, I see," Joseph replied, as though Devon had just spilled his heart. "Never fun, complicated."

"She killed my friend!" Devon burst out. Jabbing a little too hard with the poker, a coal spilled out and struck the cold earth with a *hiss*. Devon cursed and stamped it out with his boot. "Or close enough to it," he added in a whisper.

Joseph shook his head. "You don't strike me as a man who leaves a friend unavenged." He sat back in his chair, his eyes boring into Devon. "So if she's responsible, why did you rescue her?"

Devon looked away. "Because she reminds me of someone I used to know," he murmured, remembering the fiery woman that had fought her way across the Three Nations to protect her brother. "Because I love her."

"Complicated thing, love."

Unable to find the words to reply, Devon only shook his head, and they fell back into silence. After a few minutes, Joseph groaned and rose to his feet.

"Anyway, she's waiting for you outside," he said. "I'll leave you to it."

"Wait—" Devon started to his feet, but the Baronian had already vanished through the tent flaps.

Alana took his place, a hesitant smile on her face. "Devon," she said formally.

"Alana," he replied, his voice tight.

Her eyes slid to the floor as she let the tent flap fall behind her. Silently she wandered around the tent, her hands trailing over the canvas walls. Circling the room, Alana came to a stop beside the camp stretcher. There she crouched for a moment, then stood again with something in hand. As she turned, Devon saw she now held *kanker*. She pressed it into his hands.

Devon took the weapon with a frown. "What?"

"Use it," she said, the words tumbling from her in a rush. "I can't stand this anymore: the guilt, the pain, the loss. I never loved anything or anyone before, no one except my brother. Now I do, and all it's given me is pain. I saw how much you hate me, back in the throne room. You were right to leave me to die, right to hate me. Kellian died because of me. So do it, please."

Devon's hand tightened on *kanker's* haft. He stared silently into her stone-grey eyes, seeing the tears shining there. Gone was the hardness, the anger of the woman he'd seen in the citadel. Looking at her now, he could almost, *almost* bring himself to believe this was the Alana he knew, the Alana he loved.

"Who *are* you?" he whispered.

She shook her head. "I don't know." Her voice cracked. Sinking to her knees, she wrapped her arms around herself. "Why did she sacrifice herself for me?" she asked, looking up at him. "She *hated* me, and she saved me. *Why?*"

Before Devon could think about what he was doing, he was on his knees beside her. *Kanker* lying discarded beside them, he pulled Alana into his arms, hugging her to his chest. "Because that's who she was," he mumbled. "That was Enala. She dedicated her entire life to others."

"I don't deserve it," Alana sobbed.

"Maybe none of us do," he replied, drawing back from her.

Hiccupping, Alana nodded. She seemed to regain some control over herself then, and wiping the tears from her eyes, she stood. Devon rose with her.

"Devon, I'm so, so sorry." The words came in a rush. "For Kellian, for betraying you, for everything."

Devon nodded, the hope withering in his chest. "So…you are still *that* Alana?"

"No…" She trailed off, her gaze distant. "Yes. I'm her, but also…the other girl as well. Both at once, and neither."

"Not like your brother then," Devon sighed. Wandering past her, he recovered the poker from where he'd discarded it earlier. He added another log to the fire and stirred the coals. "He loves you, you know. Thinks you're a good person, whichever version of yourself you are."

"I—"

Devon slammed the door to the camp stove shut, cutting her off, and then strode across the tent to where she stood. Alana did not shrink away as he towered over her, though her eyes betrayed her doubt.

"He's a good man, your brother," he murmured. "I trust him."

"Then…"

Taking a deep breath, Devon offered his hand. "Why don't we start over?" he said. "The name's Devon. It's nice to meet you…Alana."

There was a moment's pause as Alana stared at his outstretched hand. Then, with a hesitant smile, she reached out and took it.

CHAPTER 25

"**F**orm rank, shields to the front! Archers, nock arrows!"

Merydith's cry carried down the line as her lieutenants passed along her orders. The rattle of metal echoed from the cliffs as her men shifted into position. The horses had already been taken further up the pass with the bulk of the army, but Merydith had remained with the rearguard. After the loss of Damyn and his cohort, she couldn't bring herself to entrust the task to anyone else.

Not for the first time in the past few days, the weight of grief pressed down on Merydith's shoulders. She swallowed it back, unwilling to give in, to admit to her own weakness. The loss of her childhood friend had hit her hard, but worse still was the effect on morale. For a few brief, golden hours, the Northland army had celebrated their triumph on the Gods Road, but their elation had turned to ash when word reached them of the disaster that had befallen Damyn's cohort.

Astride his monstrous Red Dragon, the Tsar had come, and slaughtered them all. Without the northern Magickers to protect them, Damyn's forces had never stood a chance. Her scouts reported his cohort had been slaughtered to a man—though not before the Tsar had had his fun.

A fresh wave of grief swept through Merydith. Clenching her sword hilt, she drew the blade and lifted it above her head.

"For Northland!" Her cry carried down the line, echoing loudly from the cliffs that rose towering above them.

Striding to the front of the line, Merydith looked down on the forces arrayed before them. In their plated armour and cloaks of scarlet and emerald, the army below looked for all the world like their ancestors before them—champions of freedom, defenders of the weak, defiant in the face of evil. She couldn't begin to understand how the once noble lands of the south had become so corrupted.

Yet even as her own nation grew from infancy to adulthood, the Tsar had led the Three Nations into darkness. Now he led them against Northland, and it rested on her to champion the cause of freedom.

"We hold them here!" she shouted.

Even as she spoke, Merydith tasted the bitter tang of despair. The men and women around her knew this wasn't the plan. After their attack on the advanced guard, they were meant to lead the Tsar and his forces on a merry chase through northern Lonia. Damyn was to have rejoined them, and if his attack on the wagons had been successful, they were to retreat to Northland. Without his supplies, the Tsar could not have followed, not while winter still gripped the lands of the north.

But the Tsar had saved his wagons, and sent a cohort of his own north to cut them off from their homeland. With the bulk of his forces to the east and south of them, Merydith had been left with no other options but to forge a path into the Sandstone Mountains.

Now, far from home and with only a week's supplies remaining, their sole hope was to find a pass through to Trola and their allies there. Yet the Sandstone Mountains were a maze, made up of a thousand gullies and hillsides so steep that not even the mountain goats could scale some of them. Without a map, it would take days for her scouts to find a path through.

Until then, all Merydith could do was pray they did not encounter a dead end. Her rear guard could not hold back the Tsar's forces long, only slow his advance. And while Helen and her Magickers had joined their powers to keep the Tsar from attacking them directly, they had nothing left to use against the thousands who marched against them.

Movement came from the men at the bottom of the canyon as their lines shifted, parting to make way for a single man. Merydith watched in astonishment as the distant figure staggered forward, half-tripping on the uneven ground. He wore little more than a loincloth, and his limbs were so emaciated she wondered how he could stand. Bruises marked his chest, where his ribcage stood out starkly against his pale skin.

Only as he neared did Merydith finally recognise him. A cry tore from her throat as Damyn dropped to a knee, his face stretched with exhaustion. His moans carried up the valley to the watching army, and stumbling back to his feet, he continued towards them, eyes wide, mouth gasping.

Merydith stood frozen in place, unable to believe the change that had been wrought on her friend in just a matter of days. There was little left of the man she'd sent to raid the Trolan supplies. Only a shadow remained of him.

As he neared the Northland army, his cry came again. Tearing herself from her shock, Merydith ran to him. He started to fall, but she caught him and lifted him into her arms. Shocked by how little he weighed, she turned and strode back towards her soldiers. Men and women parted wordlessly as she staggered past, then closed together in silence behind her.

Reaching the final ranks of the rear guard, Merydith caught herself. Taking a breath, she looked back. Her people needed her; she could not abandon them to tend to Damyn, not now, with the enemy so close.

Stones crunched as Mokyre appeared alongside her. She closed her eyes, unable to summon the strength to face the man just then. His position amongst the clans had demanded she name him captain, but she'd had little patience for him since the meeting with the other clan leaders.

"Take him," he murmured. Merydith looked at him sharply as Mokyre went on. "He needs you. Don't worry, I'll handle the bastards down there."

Merydith stared at the man, seeing the rage in his eyes as he looked at Damyn. Whatever their differences might be, Mokyre was a Northlander. What the Tsar had done to their people, what he had done to Damyn, was an affront to everything they believed in. Mokyre might not have wanted to go to war against the Tsar, but now that he had joined the battle, he would fight to the end for his nation.

Letting out a long breath, Merydith nodded. "Make them pay."

With that, she turned and started up the valley. From behind her she heard the rhythmic *thump* of marching boots as the Tsar's army advanced. Mokrye's voice rang out in answer, ordering the archers to draw. The *twang* of bowstrings was followed by the whistling of arrows, then the screams of dying men rose from the valley below.

The first clashes of steel sounded as Merydith reached her tent and carried Damyn inside. Her stretcher was unmade but she laid him down over the twisted sheets, ignoring the stains his wounds left on her bedding.

"Your Majesty, is everything okay?" a voice called from the entrance to the tent.

Merydith turned, recognising the speaker. "Helen, what are you doing here? Shouldn't you be with the others, holding off the Tsar?"

The Magicker nodded. "I wanted to check on things

when I heard the battle begin. Then I saw you with... Damyn..." She trailed off as her eyes were drawn to the broken body of her friend. "Gods, what did they do to him?"

"I don't know," Merydith whispered. Away from the eyes of her people, she felt the beginnings of tears. She sucked in a deep breath. "Can you help me?" she asked in a rush.

Helen closed her eyes for the count of ten, and then nodded. "They can cope without my strength, for the moment." She moved to stand beside the bed. "But he may be beyond even my powers to help."

"Just do what you can," Merydith replied. It had been so long since Enala had departed, she had already given the woman up for dead. But she couldn't cope with losing Damyn as well, not now, not like this.

Crouching beside the camp-stretcher, Helen held her hands out towards the captain. Green light spread from her fingers. Where it touched Damyn's emaciated body, he groaned, his face scrunching tight, though he did not wake. Merydith sat alongside the woman and stroked her friend's forehead, whispering quiet reassurances.

Behold the fate of your people, Queen.

Merydith flinched as the words whispered in her ear, the voice as clear as if it had been spoken out loud. She spun, her sword slashing the air behind her, but there was nothing there. Laughter taunted her, seeming to come from all around her. Fear wrapped around Merydith's gut as the voice continued.

Every man, every woman, every child who stands against me will suffer thus. Your Magickers will not keep me from them. Even now they falter. I will crush them and burn your army from my land. I will take you and any who survive and make you my prisoners, to suffer like the good captain has suffered. And I will march into your lands and put an end to your rebellion. Northland will be returned to wasteland, as it was always destined to be.

"What do you want?" Merydith groaned.

Bow, Queen, the voice whispered. *Bow to your Tsar. Hand over your renegade Magickers, and you and your people may live.*

Merydith's eyes were drawn to the hunched form of Helen. Light still seeped from her hands, and she did not seem to have heard the voice whispering through the tent. A knife twisted in Merydith's gut at the thought of betraying the kindly woman, and yet…

Images entered her mind, of her people entombed in the tunnels of Erachill, of the northern steeps burning, and the screams of a million voices ringing out across her land. The clash of steel came again from beyond the walls of her tent, the cries of the dying. Her head bowed beneath the weight of her responsibility.

Then Enala's face flickered into her mind, and she remembered how the old woman had stood against the darkness of Archon, even when all hope seemed lost. No matter how dark things became, she and her brother and the man, Gabriel, had never backed down.

Opening her eyes, Merydith saw a dark fog coalescing before her. Slowly the shape of a man took form, vague and indistinct, and yet unmistakable. The Tsar watched her with ghostly eyes for a long time before he spoke again. This time, his voice rang loudly though the tent, instead of within her own mind.

"What is your decision, Queen?"

Merydith drew herself up and faced the phantom. "I will defy you to my dying breath," she spat.

"So be it." The phantom raised his hands.

Merydith flinched, but beside her Helen staggered to her feet. Terror showed on her face, but her eyes glowed with power. Raising her arms, she cried out.

"Brothers, sisters, on me!"

Light flashed across the tent, and a spiralling vortex of multicoloured magic descended on the woman. It gathered around Helen for half a second, and then rushed from her at the spectre. The air crackled as it sliced through the tent and a cry rang out, followed by a dull *boom*. Darkness swallowed the room as all the lanterns flickered out, followed by absolute silence.

Staggering sideways, Merydith squinted through the gloom. The dark canvas blacked out the daylight, but as her eyes adjusted she saw the Tsar had vanished, and Helen on her knees. Heart in her throat, she stepped toward the Magicker. Groaning, the Magicker rose slowly back to her feet. A frown touched the woman's face as she looked away, but a smile replaced it as her eyes alighted on Merydith.

"You're okay. Thank the Gods."

Merydith nodded. Suddenly weary, she sat on the stretcher beside Damyn. "I thought you said the others could cope without you."

Helen smiled sheepishly. "I guess not."

A voice called to them from beyond the walls of the tent, and then light spilled inside as someone lifted the flap. "Your Majesty!" One of her guards stood there, his face the picture of concern. "Is everything okay? We heard shouting."

Merydith nodded. "Fetch some fresh lanterns, Marcus." The guard nodded and darkness returned to the tent as he departed. Turning her attention to her friend, Merydith reached out and touched his throat. His pulse was erratic but strong. "Is he okay?" she asked the Magicker.

The smile fell from Helen's face. "I've done what I can. Whether he lives is up to him now."

"Thank you, Helen. For everything." She hesitated. "What was that before, when the light appeared?"

"Something very dangerous," the Magicker replied. "While none of us are powerful enough to threaten the Tsar alone, we have been able to combine our magics in a spell, one that keeps the Tsar from entering our camp. Mostly. But just then, when we forced him out, our power needed to be directed. For just a moment, I was its vessel."

"And that's dangerous?"

"If I'd held it a second longer, the force would have torn me to pieces."

Merydith sighed. "So you're saying you couldn't send it against that army down there?"

"I might, though not in the form you just saw. But even if we could manage it, such a feat would cripple us all. It would leave every man and woman here exposed to the Tsar's power." She gestured at Damyn. "And we have seen what he is capable of."

Ice slid down Merydith spine as she nodded. "Very well," she murmured. "Thank you again, Helen, for everything you've done. You should return to the others now, before he tries anything else."

"What about you?" the Magicker whispered, rising to her feet.

Merydith looked down at Damyn. "I will stay with him."

Helen nodded. "May the Gods be with you, my Queen."

Then she was gone, leaving Merydith alone with the man who had stood at her side since she was just a child. Looking at his withered body, she finally allowed her grief to show. Tears burned her eyes as she stroked his cheek.

"Come back to me, Damyn," she said. "I forbid you to die."

Outside, the sounds of battle finally faded away, and silence descended on the tent.

CHAPTER 26

Braidon sat in the darkness staring out over the valley, listening as soft voices carried up from the Baronians gathered below. Their campfires glistened in the moonlight, the flicker of movement betraying the chaos of the camp. Where he was sitting though, the world was at peace. He could almost forget the world was at war, that his father was even now leading an invasion of Northland, or that an elite group of soldiers were hunting him.

In his mind, Braidon pictured the warrior Queen Merydith, and wondered where she was now. The woman wasn't one to sit idly by while her people were attacked, and he hoped she would be ready when his father came for her. She had put her trust in Enala and himself to finish the Tsar, but now that they had failed, Northlands fate was in her hands. Though how she could hope to succeed, he couldn't begin to imagine. The Three Nations were too powerful, the Tsar unstoppable.

And now Enala was gone.

He scrunched his eyes closed and shivered as he saw again Enala fall, cut down by his father's sword.

"Her own son," Braidon whispered, still struggling to come to terms with it all.

While he had learned the truth in Ardath, he'd never had the chance to ask his grandmother about their past, about anything. He wondered now who his grandfather had been, and why Enala had kept herself away from them all this time.

His heart ached for the old woman, but while she had shown him kindness, had protected him and taught him to use his magic, he still could not picture her as his grandmother. There was a gap, a great canyon between the images in his mind, one he could not span. Not now that she was gone.

Sadness touched him as he thought of Merydith. It was the Northland Queen who had truly known the old woman. Enala had helped to raise her, had truly been a grandmother to the woman. Braidon swallowed at the thought of having to tell her the truth, that the old woman was gone. He feared it might break her, after their last conversation in Erachill.

You have outgrown me, girl.

He smiled as he recalled Enala's last words to the Queen. However much the news hurt, Enala had had faith in the woman. Merydith would not break, not when the fate of her nation was at stake.

The crunch of footsteps distracted Braidon from his memories. Alana was approaching, her eyes downcast. He smiled, though it still felt strange, knowing she wasn't entirely the sister he remembered.

"How did it go?" he asked, nodding in the direction of camp.

Alana shrugged and took a seat on the boulder beside him. "As well as could be expected," she said, pulling her knees up to her chest. "I'm alive. It's enough."

Braidon's heart twisted at her words. "Is it, though?"

She looked at him sharply, eyebrows raised. "You've

grown bold, little brother," she said. "Has your magic so changed you?"

Braidon frowned at her words, wondering whether they were true. He'd come a long way in the months since their escape. Though he remembered little of his old life, he sensed the boy he'd been was not much different than the sheltered child he'd become after their escape. But it was not his magic that had changed him; it was his time with Enala. Her training, her quiet faith; they had given him the courage he'd needed, in a way Alana's protection never had.

"Not my magic, no," he replied, biting his lip. "It's... without you, I had to fend for myself. To grow, to master my fears."

"I'm sorry I wasn't there..."

"No." Braidon grinned. "I'm glad you weren't."

He knew his sister's protectiveness came from love, but her lack of faith had drained his own. Looking back now, he wondered whether he ever would have come to terms with his power, had she remained looking over his shoulder.

Alana's face twisted with hurt. "Well, I guess I'll be on my way then."

"No, I didn't mean it that way," Braidon replied quickly. "It's just...Enala showed me I was strong enough by myself." He clenched his fists, allowing a trickle of magic to seep out. Shielded by the power he was already expending to conceal them from their father, it would not be detected by any nearby Magickers. "I even helped Devon, when the Baronians were preparing to attack him. I made him seem a giant, a hero that could not be defeated. And now...here we are."

"I'm proud of you, little brother," Alana said, though there was sadness behind her words.

He looked at her then, seeing her pain, and wondered what she had been through in the time they had been separated. Somewhere along the way, Alana had lost the fire in her eyes. He had glimpsed it for a moment, back in the settlement when she'd set the dragon on their father's Stalkers, but it had not lasted. Bruised and beaten, her neck ringed by scars, Alana no longer seemed the unstoppable warrior he remembered.

"What happened to you, Alana?" he whispered.

She closed her eyes. "I remembered."

"You remember who you were before?"

"No, I *am* who I was before," Alana croaked. "And who I was with you and Devon and Kellian. It's all tangled up, but I know enough now, enough to hate who I was. I deserve everything that's happened to me."

"No, Alana," Braidon whispered. He reached out and gripped her wrist. "I wouldn't be alive if it wasn't for you."

"Braidon…" Alana sighed. "I love you with all my heart. But that doesn't make up for everything else I've done, the people I've killed, the lives I've stolen. You don't remember—"

"Then *help me* remember," Braidon interrupted. His heart pounded in his chest as he took her hand and placed it on his head.

Alana's eyes widened and she shook her head. "No…"

"Please," Braidon murmured. "There's so much missing, I need to see it, to know the truth. Please, Alana."

"What if you don't like what you see?" He could see the doubt lurking behind her stony eyes.

"You'll still be my sister," he insisted. "It'll be okay."

Swallowing, Alana nodded. Her chest swelled as she drew in a breath, and he sensed her power building. He watched it grow in his mind's eye, saw it swell to a bursting point, and then go from her in a rush, pouring down her arm and into him. He gasped at the icy touch of her power, but there was no pain, only a whispered voice, barely audible, as though heard from a great distance.

"Return to me, brother."

All of a sudden, Braidon was a child, standing on the ramparts of the citadel, looking out over the wide expanse of Lake Ardath. Silver threads crisscrossed the plains beyond its waters, weaving through the countryside like some great tapestry of the Gods. To the east, he could just make out the three shadows of Mount Chole and its nameless brothers. Dark clouds swirled around their peaks, sending life-giving rain down onto the plains below. To the west, snow-capped mountains stretched across the horizon as far as the eye could see.

"It will all be yours one day, son," his father was saying. "Your's and your sister's to rule."

A hand rested on his back, powerful, yet reassuring. Braidon looked up at his father with love in his heart, but the Tsar's gaze was fixed on the waters of Lake Ardath.

"It has been my life's goal to make this land safe for you and our people," his father continued, "but I am afraid." His head dipped, his eyes closing for half an instant. "I am afraid I will fail you."

"Father?" Too young to understand his father's pain, Braidon reached out and gripped his meaty hand. "Are you okay?"

The Tsar glanced down at Braidon. Sadness crinkled the skin around his eyes. "No," he muttered, as though talking to himself. "I have not failed, not yet. It will not come to that."

Braidon shook his head. "What are you talking about, Father?"

A smile touched the Tsar's face. He crouched beside Braidon, his grip tightening on the boy's shoulder. "Do you trust me, son?"

"Of course!"

"Good." The Tsar drew him into a hug. "I cannot fail, not with you and your sister beside me. Together, the three of us can do anything. With our magic, we will finally bring peace to this warring land."

"But I don't have magic." At ten years old, Braidon barely knew his place in the world, but he had seen what those around his father were capable of, knew they could do things he could not.

"Not yet, my son," the Tsar replied, "but I can sense it within you. One day, on an anniversary of your birth, it will appear to you. On that day, you must be strong, must be the master, it the servant. Can you do that for me, son?"

Braidon shivered, his father's words filling him with an unknown

terror. Yet he knew the answer his father expected, and nodded. "I can,"
he said, trying to keep the tremor from his voice.

"Good lad," his father replied, coming to his feet. He looked back out
over the lake, a smile on his face. "Every step we take towards a new
dawn, there will be those who fight against us. But we will not fail, the
three of us. We will stand strong against our enemies, and bring a new
era of light into this world."

Braidon shuddered as the vision faded, returning him to
the moonlit mountains. He looked at his sister, opened his
mouth to speak, to ask about this new vision of their father,
but before the words could leave his mouth he was swept
away on a fresh tide, swallowed up by a new wave of
memories.

Now, Braidon found himself standing in a familiar garden. Birds
chirped, and the colours of summer were all around, in the scarlet of the
roses and the blue of the sky, the emerald green of the grass lawns, and
the smiles of the courtiers as they strode past. His thoughts swirled as he
looked up and saw the towers of the citadel spiralling overhead.

Home.

A part of him rebelled at the thought, and yet he knew it to be true.

"Braidon, there you are!" He looked around and saw his sister
walking towards him, a troupe of children following in her wake. "I told
you not to go wandering off!"

Braidon scowled. "But I wasn't doing anything, *sis."*

Alana glared at him. "You're too young to do *anything, little*
brother."

"I'm older than half of them!" he insisted, gesturing at the other
children. "At least let me practice with them."

His sister frowned, and he sensed her resolve wavering. Braidon leapt
on the opportunity with both hands.

"Please, sis, I'll be careful, I swear!"

Alana rolled her eyes. "Fine," she growled in her sternest voice, "but
don't say I didn't warn you." She gestured for him to join the other
children.

They made their way back to the training grounds, where the others collected their practice swords and formed two lines. They eyed his sister nervously as she strode past. Braidon lingered on the periphery, wondering whether Alana had truly meant what she'd said.

Wandering over, she flicked her own practice blade into the air, caught it by the blunted blade, and offered it to him. "You sure you're ready, little brother?" she asked, one eyebrow raised.

Braidon nodded eagerly and took the sword before she could change her mind.

"Be careful with it," she said, a patronising smile on her lips. Before Braidon could say anything, she spun towards the other children. All semblance of kindness left her face. "Anish, get your ass over here!"

A young boy further down the line leapt to obey. "Yes, ma'am!" he said as he joined them.

"Take your new partner through drills one and two. Make sure he's up to speed," Alana snapped.

She walked away before either boy could reply, leaving Braidon staring dumbly at his new sparring partner. The boy nodded, though Braidon didn't miss the fear lurking behind his sea green eyes. As Alana turned, Anish took Braidon through several blocks and counterattacks with the blunted swords, while the other children began to spar.

Braidon was surprised by how quickly he began to pant, the subtle movement required to change stances and heft the heavy blade surprisingly exhausting. Within minutes, sweat was dripping down his forehead, but none of the other students so much as paused for a rest, so he kept on, determined to finish what he'd started.

As he shifted back into the defensive section of the drill, his foot slipped on a patch of mud, and off-balance, he toppled forward. Anish cried out, but his blade was already flashing forward. His head low, Braidon cried out as the blunted edge caught him in the back of his skull. A brilliant red light blinded him and the strength went from his legs, sending him crashing to the ground.

Darkness swirled and for a moment he lost consciousness. When he came to, his sister was crouching over him, her brow creased with concern. She reached out a hand and helped him to sit up. A groan whispered up from his throat as he saw the other students standing in silence, their faces pale as ghosts. They remained behind as Alana helped him to the healer's wing of the citadel, where a kindly man took away his pain with a touch.

Back on the hillside, Braidon smiled at the memory of his sister's concern, even as other memories streamed through his consciousness. Alana had been there through them all: fierce and overprotective, but also caring and compassionate, always ready to defend him.

Then a frown touched his lips. The memories from that day in the gardens continued to flow, streaming through his mind in an endless torrent. He witnessed again the drills, experienced the training, the trips into the forests, where he learned to hunt and fish, to survive. In all those memories, Alana was harsh and unyielding, showing no student other than Braidon an ounce of kindness.

But it wasn't her coldness that scared him, nor her anger or cruelty to those who crossed her. It was the absence he saw now, the missing face he had never noticed in his selfish youth. Because in all the memories he recalled, in all the countless days since his first lesson in the royal gardens, he had never seen Anish again.

At least, not until that fateful day in Lon, when the demon had appeared on their ship, and tried to return them both to their father. Despite the years since their fateful training session, Anish had not aged even a day.

Only his eyes had changed, the sea green giving way to the pitch-black of the demon.

Bile filled Braidon's throat as he staggered to his feet. Alana rose with him, her eyes wide with concern, but as she reached for him he threw her back. Scrambling from the boulder, he slipped on the smooth rock and went crashing to the ground.

"Braidon!" Alana stumbled after him, hands outstretched.

"Stay away from me!" he gasped, holding up his hands to fend her off.

His emotions swirling, he tried to stand. Pain spared his

wrist and he was forced to use his other hand to push himself back to his feet. He stared at her, eyes wide, horror wrapping his stomach in iron bands.

"What did you do to him?" he asked. "To Anish?"

Her eyes widened, then dropped to the ground. She shook her head. "You know what I did."

"Say it!"

"He hurt you!" Alana shrieked. Her head snapped up, her eyes aglow in the moonlight. "So I sent him to our father, to be tested, to be judged."

"And he failed," Braidon murmured.

"He failed," Alana agreed. Her eyes softened and she staggered.

"He failed," she said again, though her voice was touched now by horror. She closed her eyes. "Like so many others."

"How could you?" Braidon whispered.

"Braidon…" Eyes wide, Alana reached for him.

"Don't you touch me!" Braidon screamed.

Tears streaked Alana's cheeks as she watched him back away. Recalling what he'd felt for her just moments before, Braidon wondered how he could have been so blind. He saw now her overprotective nature came not from love, but a twisted sense of possession. Alana had done whatever she could to ensure he did not mature, that he remained inno-cent, and therefore malleable.

Even if it meant robbing him of his own past.

"Stay away," he said one last time.

Turning on his heel, he fled down the mountainside back towards the camp.

CHAPTER 27

For four nights, the Baronians delved deeper into the mountains, their desperation growing with each passing day. With the Stalkers behind them, they could not turn back, yet as the winter closed in, many began to flag. Their supplies dwindled, and they were soon forced to abandon their wagons, the way proving impassable for even the boldest horses. The paths grew narrower as they pushed higher into the snow-capped peaks. In the thin air, men and women struggled, and the weak to die.

Though she kept to herself, Alana could sense the resentment building amongst the Baronians. They had started this journey on a whim. The attack on the Tsar had been an act of defiance against the man who had driven them from their homes. Only now did they realise they might pay for it with their lives.

By the fifth day, a ritual had developed in the mornings, as those who had passed in the night were counted and laid to rest. Finally, on the sixth day, they reached the peak of the winding gullies, and began back down into Trola.

Through it all, Devon kept on, refusing to show the

slightest hint of weakness. He led them through the mountains with his head held high, often with the ancient hammer in hand, as though the weapon could somehow fend off the creeping cold that had stolen so many of his people's lives.

He walked ahead of Alana now, his gaze fixed on the top of the next bend in the gorge. While he showed no outward sign of his pain, Alana was not deceived. She saw glimpses of it in the way he had begun pushing everyone else away, in his sudden bouts of rage when someone questioned him. More than anything, she wanted to go to him, to ease his grief. But while they had developed an uneasy truce, anything more remained beyond them.

As for Braidon, she had hardly seen him since the day on the hillside. Alana had watched him from afar though, seeing how the magic took its toll, and wishing she could help. Their survival rested on his shoulders, on his ability to keep the Tsar and his Stalkers from tracking them with his magic. While their father himself had departed, she didn't doubt he continued to search for them. If Braidon's magic faltered...

She sighed, forcing her mind back to the way ahead. Her brother had made it clear he wanted nothing to do with her. The knowledge ate at her, but she couldn't blame him. She had done terrible, unforgivable things. Each night, memories of the children she had sent to their deaths haunted her. It didn't help that the Tsar had given her no choice, that she had done it to protect Braidon from his darkness.

Because Alana knew in her heart that she had enjoyed it, had savoured the power she held over her charges, the fear she saw in the eyes of the commoners. She had been the Daughter of the Tsar, her power unrivaled, her nobility unquestioned.

Thinking back on the woman she'd been...

"Hello, princess."

Alana's head jerked up as a gruff voice came from alongside her. Her heart quickened, but her excitement gave way to disappointment when she saw it was only Joseph. They hadn't talked since she'd joined the camp, though she hadn't been surprised to learn he was still around. If Devon could set aside his enmity for her, why not a man he'd fought in mortal combat?

"Princess?" Alana asked archly.

Joseph raised an eyebrow as though to ask if she thought him stupid. Her cheeks warmed and she quickly looked away. "Fine, but keep it quiet, Baronian."

"Of course." Joseph chuckled, but his humour didn't last. As the laughter died away, he looked at her again, sadness in his eyes. "I'm sorry about the old woman," he said at last.

Alana swallowed. She tried to speak, but the words lodged in her throat. Shaking her head, she looked to where Devon still strode at the front of the column.

"I wish he'd saved Enala instead," she managed.

"Heard you and the big man were lovers once," Joseph said.

Alana's head whipped around at his words. Her boot caught an unseen rock and she tripped, and would have crashed face-first into the mountainside had Joseph not caught her by the scruff of her tunic and righted her.

"No!" She burst out finally, flashing the giant a glare. "We were *not!*"

Joseph wore a broad grin on his bearded face. "That so?" he chuckled, before setting off again along the trail. "Coulda fooled me."

"There's nothing between us," Alana insisted, chasing after him. "He hates me!"

"Ay, he travelled halfway across the world only to have you reject him. You can hardly blame the man for that."

Alana fell silent, her mind turning back to the night Devon and Kellian had snuck into the citadel to rescue her. She'd been shocked by their appearance, but beyond that, there had been a warmth at seeing the two men again, and an urge to throw herself into Devon's arms.

Unfortunately, her darker side had been stronger then.

"I betrayed him," she whispered. "Even if he still loves me, I don't deserve him."

"Maybe not," Joseph rumbled, "but life rarely gives us what we deserve. And the man is hurting."

At that, the Baronian picked up his pace and strode ahead to walk alongside Devon. Trailing behind them, Alana found herself watching Devon, wondering if Joseph's words were true, if there really still was something between them. Her heart twisted as Devon looked back. They shared a glance, but he quickly looked away, returning his attention to the road.

The day stretched out, the sky darkening as the sun fell below the mountain peaks. Finally a call went up from ahead, signalling a break for the night. Around her, men and women sighed and dropped their packs, sinking to the ground in relief.

People began to gather in groups, doffing packs and pulling out food. A familiar loneliness settled over Alana as she saw Devon sitting in conversation with Braidon and Joseph. She yearned to join them and ask what they were talking about, but as she watched, her brother glanced in her direction. The smile faded from his face as he turned back to the others.

Alana's stomach knotted as a roar of laughter came from the three men. She found a boulder off near the cliff and seated herself so she could look back up the valley. The slope they'd spent the morning traversing stretched above her, empty now of movement. Shadows still slung around the top, and she wondered how long they had before Quinn and his Stalkers caught them.

Quinn.

A shiver swept through her at the thought of him. He'd

been her companion since childhood, first as a friend, then as a teacher. Back then, she had never thought of him as anything more. But as they'd matured, she'd noticed the change in him, the yearning that had appeared in his eyes.

She had finally reciprocated his desires back in Ardath, thinking to satisfy her own cravings. Yet still he had wanted more, seeking to rule her, to make her his own. And that was one thing Alana would never allow.

His words from back in the inn whispered in her mind.

I will have my heart's desire.

Alana's stomach twisted in disgust, a chill raising the hackles on her neck. For a moment, she wished she'd destroyed him back in the throne room.

"Hungry?"

Alana looked up as a woman's voice came from nearby. Her eyes widened as she saw the old innkeeper, Selina wandering towards her, a stale-looking loaf of bread in hand. Alana looked at the bread distastefully, but there was little enough to go around without being fussy, and she nodded.

Drawing a hunting knife from her belt, the old woman cut the bread in two and offered half to Alana. She sat on the next boulder over as Alana tore off a piece of bread and chewed it slowly.

Selina stretched her arms and lay back with a groan. "I tell you, this isn't what I imagined doing in my retirement," she said. "I'm getting a little old for so much adventure."

Alana glanced at the woman, remembering how she'd lain dying on the floor of her own inn. "What are you doing here?" she asked, curious. "You could have gone anywhere. Quinn wouldn't have come searching for you. Why come with us?"

"The Goddess touched me," Selina murmured. Her eyes drifted out to the forested plains far below their mountain perch. "That means something, it has to. I owe her for saving my life." She raised an eyebrow. "And what about you, miss?

Why do you sit alone each day, instead of with your friends and brother?"

Alana shook her head. "It's complicated."

"Step on some toes, did you?"

"You might say that." Despite herself, Alana chuckled at the woman's wording.

"A shame. We need to stand together, us renegades. Tell me, what could you have done to turn even your own brother against you?"

Alana shivered as she ran over the endless list of mistakes that was her existence. "Oh, just destroyed his life," she said finally.

The old woman's cackling echoed from the cliffs. "Is that all?"

"I'm serious!" Alana growled, sitting up on her rock. She jabbed a finger at the innkeeper. "Listen, you little—"

The woman's laughter died away, and her eyes flashed as she looked at Alana. "Yes?" she asked, her voice suddenly dangerous.

Alana gulped back what she'd been about to say. She had faced down demons and Magickers and the leader of the Three Nations, but something about the woman's tone brooked no argument. She tore off another piece of bread and chewed it slowly, seeking something else to say.

"I just mean...I earned this," she said lamely. "I deserve this."

"Pff, probably. But then, if my brother and I had stopped talking every time he ruined my life...well, I guess he'd only have destroyed my business once," she chuckled. "But then, where would the fun have been? Besides, he always made up for it in the end. What about you? Is sitting here moping going to change things between you?"

Alana scowled. "Who says I'm moping?"

The old woman raised a spindly eyebrow, and Alana blushed and looked away. "Fine," she muttered, then shook her head. "But you don't understand, I'm not sure there's anything I *can* do to fix things."

"Whatever you did, you're still family, that means something…"

Alana snorted. "Clearly you haven't met my family."

"Girl, I was dying on that floor, not dead," Selina replied. "I know who your father is, who the old woman was to you."

"Then you know family doesn't mean anything to me."

"It meant something to your grandmother," Selina replied.

The words dried up in Alana's throat. Suddenly she found herself struggling to breathe. Shooting to her feet, she gasped in the icy mountain air. "I didn't ask for her to do that!" she shrieked finally, swinging on the innkeeper.

Selina only smiled. "No, but that is what family does, girl. Loves each other. Protects each other."

Pain locked around Alana's chest and she looked away. "Not my father," she whispered.

"Not your father," Selina agreed. "But it doesn't have to be the same for you, or your brother."

"Then what do you suggest I do?"

"Make peace with young Braidon," the innkeeper murmured. "Protect him from your father."

"I always have," Alana whispered. "It's where this all went wrong."

"Then find a way to work with him," Selina replied. "I think you'll find he's a resourceful young man."

Alana swallowed, fear for her brother's life already swirling within her. She had spent so much of her life protecting him from harm, from their father and his magic, that the thought of *using* him, of working with him to face the man…

"Glad to see you two lasses getting along!" Alana swung around as a voice called down to them from above. Joseph moved towards them, his footsteps crunching on the loose gravel. "Just don't piss her off, Alana. Or you might wake up a few marbles short of a brain."

"What do you want, Joseph?" Selina asked, fixing him with one of her scowls.

Joseph held up his hands in surrender. "Peace, woman, I come in peace." He pointed a thumb over his shoulder. "But Devon wants to see the girl," he said. "You'd best get running, missy."

Alana shared a glance with Selina and then rose to her feet. Her eyes dancing, she fixed a scowl of her own on her lips and stepped towards the giant Baronian. He towered over her, but Alana showed no hint of fear as she rested a hand on his chest.

"This *girl* is the Daughter of the Tsar," she murmured, "and I go where I will."

As she spoke, she allowed a trickle of her power to spread down her arm into his chest. Following the green glow of her magic, she swept through his consciousness. His fear rose before her, a knotted tangle of red and orange. With a few quick twists, she unlocked several threads, sending them spiralling out into the void of Joseph's mind.

A scream echoed from the cliffs as Joseph staggered and dropped to his knees, his eyes wide with terror. Grinning, Alana released him and stepped back, allowing her power to fade.

Blinking, Joseph looked around, as though surprised to find himself back on the mountainside. He frowned, realising he was on his knees looking up at the two women. A scarlet blush touched his cheeks, and scrambling back to his feet, he muttered something incomprehensible and fled.

"That was cruel," Selina commented archly.

Alana chuckled. "I could have left him like that for an hour. *That* would have been cruel."

"You're a hard girl," the innkeeper replied. "Guess it's *me* that should be watching where I step."

Remembering the glare Selina had given her earlier, Alana flashed a grin. "Oh no, you're terrifying enough as it is without any magic. Now I'd best go see what Devon wants. I wouldn't want to keep the leader of the Baronians waiting now, would I?"

CHAPTER 28

Exhaustion pressed on Merydith as she forced herself to take a step, then another. Desperately she fought her way up the winding slope, while around her the harsh winds swirled, the sleeting rain whipping at her exposed face. Despite her thick woollen clothing and boots, she had long since lost all feeling in her extremities. But there was no more time to stop and warm themselves, to set camp and cast back the icy chill of winter. The Tsar was coming, and there was no more time for anything.

Her scouts had spotted his forces scrambling up the gullies nearby, seeking to overtake them. If any of his people reached the upper passes first, Merydith and her people would be trapped. While the outriders' numbers were few, they only needed to hold the northern army a day for the Tsar and the bulk of his force to catch them.

Watching her people make their slow way up towards the next pass, Merydith found herself longing for the gentle valleys of the lower foothills. At least there they had been able to ride their horses. Now, the way was so steep that her people had been forced to dismount and lead their mounts on foot.

And even riderless, the horses were struggling. While the

mountain clans around Erachill were acclimatised to the thin mountain air, their horses came from the lowland steeps. Despite their massive lungs, the beasts were falling by the dozen now. If they did not escape the freezing mountain peaks soon, more would die, and the northern army would lose their only advantage against the foot soldiers of the Tsar.

At least they had bloodied the man's nose over the last few days. With the way unclear, Merydith had sent her scouts ahead to map out the passes, while she continued to fight a delaying tactic against the southerners. They had barricaded every pass, set ambushes wherever they could, ensuring the Tsar's advance slowed to a snail's pace. Every inch of ground the southerners gained was paid for with their blood.

But now their stock of arrows was running short, as was their food and other supplies. If they didn't find the pass through to Trola soon, her people would starve.

If the Tsar did not catch them first.

She shuddered as an image of Damyn flickered into her mind. He still had not woken, though his condition had improved slightly. With the worst of his injuries healed by Helen, the camp doctors had taken over his care; but it was the scars left on his mind that still haunted him.

Merydith had moved him into her tent, and often she would wake to him screaming in the night, though he never regained consciousness. The Tsar's cruelty had torn apart the bold, humorous man she had known half her life, leaving only a husk in his place. In her darkest moments, Merydith found herself wondering whether she should end his suffering, to offer him the final peace of death.

Yet even as he lay sobbing in her lap, his eyes flickering in the grip of some unknown nightmare, she knew she could never do it. Even if seeing him like this reminded her of the fate the Tsar had promised her, of the fate he had promised all of her people, should they continue to defy him.

Shaking her head, Merydith forced the thought from her

mind. Damyn would recover. Her people would reach the pass through the Sandstone Mountains, and descend into Trola. She would raise the people there to rebellion, and together they would wipe the darkness of the Tsar from the history books.

Merydith looked up as footsteps came from above. Through the swirling sleet, she glimpsed a figure take shape. As he neared, she recognised Mokyre's sharp features. He had proven himself on the day Damyn had returned, fighting hard in the frontlines to see off the Tsar's attacks. Under his guidance, her people had inflicted heavy losses to the enemy. She had sent him ahead with several others to scout out the way. Now as he staggered to a stop in front of her, she found herself holding her breath, barely able to bring herself to hear his news.

"Your Majesty!" he burst out, a grin splitting his face. "I've found it!"

"The pass?" she yelled over the wind, her heart clenched with sudden hope.

"The pass!" Mokyre nodded. "It's close. I've sent Tremyl ahead to scout the way."

Forgetting all protocol, Merydith threw herself forward and dragged the man into a hug. The rest of her advance guard let out a cheer that carried on down the canyon, the noise growing as the news passed down through the ranks. Releasing Mokyre, Merydith beamed at her followers.

"The way lies open!" she called out. "One last push! For Northland!"

"For Northland!" The words echoed from the canyon walls as her people shouted their agreement. Merydith turned back and clapped Mokyre on the shoulder. "Are you strong enough to show us the way?"

Despite the ice frosting his beard, Mokyre nodded, and they began the long slog up towards the distant pass. Her limbs filled with a newfound strength, Merydith followed close behind him, the pain in her feet forgotten. She no longer noticed the weight of her sword or buckler; her mind was already far ahead, planning her next move.

Once they took the pass, she would continue into Trola with the bulk of her army, while a rearguard held their rear against the Tsar. If they could pin his forces in the mountains, it would give them time to organise. She already had contacts in Trola, readying themselves for the final battle. Hope warmed Merydith's heart at the thought of fighting alongside the western nation. While few in number, they were ferocious fighters. With them on her side, they might just stand a chance.

Merydith was so lost in thought she didn't notice the second man emerge from the swirling fog on the slopes ahead. A shout from her guards alerted her to his presence, but by then he was almost on top of them. Swords in hand, two guards moved to intercept the newcomer.

A second later they stepped back again as the scout Tremyl stopped before them. Face pale, he stood on the uneven rocks gasping for breath, as though he had run all the way from the pass. Looking into his eyes, Merydith knew what he was going to say before he ever opened his mouth.

"What is it?" she whispered, the wild winds whipping away her words.

"They're ahead of us."

Blood thumped in Merydith's ears, drowning out the words of her guards, the shouts of the other scout, everything but the words he had spoken.

They're ahead of us.

It couldn't be true. The Gods would not allow it. If the Tsar had cut off their escape, all hope was lost. The North-land army would be trapped in this barren canyon, unable to advance, while behind them the unstoppable forces of the Tsar drew ever closer. He would reach them by morning. The weight of his numbers would crush them within a day.

A high-pitched whinny rose above the hiss of rain as a nearby horse toppled to the ground. Merydith stared at the fallen animal, watching as the rapid rise and fall of its chest began to slow, listening to the harsh shuddering of its breath as it tried to stand. But its strength was gone. It slumped back to the earth and lay still.

Merydith's throat contracted as she looked around and saw the eyes of her people on her. She clenched her jaw, struggling to hide her own terror. Death called to them all, but they could not simply lie down and wait for it to take them. If her people were to die here in these barren mountains, they would die as lions, their voices raised in defiance.

"Onwards!" she roared. "Let them try and stop us."

Merydith didn't wait for her people to reply. Pushing past her scouts, she started up the slope. In the swirling winds, she could not hear whether her people followed and she did not risk glancing back. They needed her to be strong now, for their Queen to lead them. After a moment, Mokyre pulled alongside her. She exchanged a glance with the man, remembering his rage back in Erachill, when he had called her a fool. Yet whatever had been said then, he marched with her now, undaunted by the challenge ahead, and she nodded her thanks.

As her guards closed around them, she finally risked a look back. Her people followed below, their faces determined as they marched up through the valley. Tears stung her eyes, and Merydith quickly looked back at the trail.

An hour passed before Mokyre edged alongside her. "Not far now," he whispered, "just over that ridge."

"Front ranks, form lines!" she shouted.

The rattle of steel followed as her guards and the rest of the vanguard formed up around her. She waited a moment, allowing the hundred men and women a chance to catch their breath, and then shouted the order to advance.

As one, the line surged forward. A hundred paces still

separated them from the lip of the slope, but as they advanced the pass slowly came into view. To either side the cliffs of the canyon drew closer, narrowing until only half a dozen men could walk abreast. Merydith scanned the fog and shadows that clung to the pass, seeking the first sign of the Tsar's forces.

Weighed down by their armour and the endless days of marching, their charge slowed as they neared the top. Merydith waited for the answering screams of the enemy, the twang of bowstrings and hiss of swords being drawn.

Instead, there was only the howling of the wind through the jagged rocks.

"Draw swords!" Merydith shouted as they topped the rise.

The whisper of blades leaving leather came from around her. Merydith narrowed her eyes, the hackles on the back of her neck lifting. Still, there was no sign of the Tsar's force, and she turned her gaze to the clifftops around them, wondering now whether she was leading her people into some fresh trap.

The ground flattened out as the pass neared. Merydith slowed her advance, shouting an order for her people to do the same. Together they crept towards the shadows, swords in hand, eyes wide as the walls of the canyon rose up around them.

Then they were through, and the ground was falling away before them, sloping back down towards the distant plains of Trola. Merydith stumbled to a stop, unable to believe it, to understand how they had taken the pass. Her gaze drifted out over the mountains, and then froze as movement came from the slopes below.

Merydith frowned as she saw a man standing alone, his woollen cloak billowing around him. Beyond him the land fell sharply, the stark mountains giving way to rolling green hills. For a moment she thought he was alone, until she glimpsed movement against the cliffs further down the slope. Straining her eyes, she spied a large group of men and women camped in the shadows. She could not tell their number, but only a handful would have been needed to hold the pass.

Yet inexplicably, they had made their camp in the most indefensible spot on the mountainside.

Biting her lip, she turned her attention back to the man standing alone. Merydith started as she saw him advancing, but a quick glance at her guards reassured her. Raising a hand to warn them to stay put, she sheathed her sword and stepped towards the man.

"That's far enough," she called when he was still a few paces away, before adding, "What do you want?"

The man came slowly to a stop. He contemplated her in silence for a long time. Anger grew in Merydith's chest as she waited for him to respond, still keenly aware of the Tsar's forces advancing from behind them. Finally, her patience worn to a thread, she dropped a hand to her sword hilt.

"I said, what are you doing here?" she growled.

The man smiled. "Heard there was a war coming."

"Ay," Merydith snapped, "and if you and your men don't move, you'll soon find yourselves in the middle of it."

The man laughed. "I see." He stepped aside and held out an arm, as though to indicate the way was open. "Please, be my guest. Trola stands open for you, my Queen."

"You know who I am?" Merydith asked, blinking.

"Who else would you be?" the man asked.

Merydith opened her mouth, and then closed it, unable to come up with a reply.

"They say you've come to grant freedom to the Three Nations." He paused, a roguish grin crossing his face. "You've got a strange way of going about it."

Speechless, Merydith could only stand and stare at the man. Finally, pulling herself together, she shook her head. "Who in the Gods' names *are* you?"

The stranger crossed his arms. "You don't know me?"

"Should I?"

"Devon and Kellian might have mentioned me?"

"Devon…and Kellian?" Merydith repeated dumbly. "How…I haven't seen either of them in months."

"Oh." The stranger seemed to deflate at the news. "I was sure they'd escaped…" He sighed. "I guess I shouldn't be surprised. It'll be up to us then, I guess." He held out a hand and smiled. "Betran, at your service, my Queen. I helped Devon and Kellian break into the citadel. Now I'm here."

"Betran…" the Queen mumbled, still struggling to catch up. Her eyes flickered to the men and women camped below. They had begun lighting campfires, and laughter now whispered up the valley to where they stood. "And they are…?"

Betran grinned. "Why, that would be the Trolan rebellion, my Queen. We thought we'd come see if you could use some help."

CHAPTER 29

As Alana approached the entrance to Devon's tent, the leather flaps lifted and her brother stepped out into the night. She froze, her heart lodging in her throat. Opening her mouth, she tried to voice the words Selina had urged her to say, but they would not come out. Braidon staggered to a stop as he noticed her standing there, and an awkward silence stretched out between them.

Finally, Alana could take it no more. "Is Devon in there?" she blurted out, saying the first thought that popped into her head.

Braidon nodded. "Yes…" he responded, and she cursed herself. It was Devon's tent; where else would he be at this hour?

"Umm, I'd better see him then," she replied.

Her brother shrugged. "Suit yourself." He wandered off without so much as a 'good night.'

Alana watched him go, her throat slowly relaxing. A sudden urge came over her to run after him, to pull him into a hug and beg for his forgiveness. But the tent flaps rustled again, and Devon stepped out into the night with a scowl on his face. He looked as though he was about to call out after his departing guest, then he saw her standing there.

"Alana," he said, a little too forcefully. "What are you doing here?"

Her anger flared as she realised the man had forgotten her. She crossed her arms and glared at him, waiting for him to realise his mistake. It took to the count of ten before his eyes widened and he cursed.

"Sorry, I thought you weren't coming," he grunted, as though that explained his memory lapse. "I wanted you to talk some sense into your brother, but there'll be no getting through to him just now. Come inside, enjoy some warmth." Turning, he disappeared inside without waiting for a response.

Left standing in the darkness, Alana had no choice but to follow him. Devon was already lowering himself into a camp chair as she hesitated in the doorway, suddenly uncomfortable. Silently she gave herself an internal shake.

You are Alana! A voice hissed in her mind. *You fear nothing!*

She dragged a camp chair across the room to the iron brazier and parked herself there, with legs stretched out towards the coals. Leaning back into the fabric, she eyed Devon, taking in the rings beneath his eyes, the added wrinkles that seemed to have appeared overnight. His hair was unkempt, his beard even worse, though he'd never kept either particularly neat.

"You're looking well," she commented wryly.

Devon blinked, rubbing his eyes. Seeing her smile, he chuckled. "I've had better days. Better years, for that matter." Reaching behind him, he lifted a bottle of what looked like malt liquor and swigged a mouthful before offering it to her.

Alana accepted it with a grin, enjoying the burning sensation that spread down her throat as she swallowed a mouthful. Despite the fire, her insides were still frozen, but the liquor was quickly changing that.

"Cheers," she said, then coughed as the aftertaste caught her. "Or maybe not," she gasped finally, wrinkling her nose at the bottle.

"Blame Joseph. Apparently he likes the stuff."

"Better than nothing, I suppose," Alana replied, helping herself to another mouthful.

"Hey, leave some for me, would ya!" Devon laughed, snatching it back.

After they'd passed the bottle back and forth a few times, Alana finally began to feel more...herself. She wasn't sure what that meant nowadays, but sitting with Devon in the quiet of his tent, she could almost imagine herself the inno- cent girl who had travelled with him all those weeks ago. The girl who had swum and hunted and fought with him, who could never have imagined sending an innocent child to his death because he angered her.

Almost, but not quite.

Eyeing Devon across the tent, she wondered at his words outside, and her encounter with Braidon. She had been too occupied with her own self-loathing at the time, but thinking back now, he had seemed flustered, not the cool young man he had come to be in her absence.

"Why did you want me to talk to my brother?" she asked.

Sitting back in his chair, Devon sighed. "I'm worried about him," he said at last. "Whatever you did with his memories, it's changed him. Before, he told me he remem- bered a few bits and pieces, but they were more like a play than his own life. He could watch them, hear them, smell them, but it was through the eyes of an observer. Now he remembers *living* them, *feeling* them; it's like there's a whole other Braidon."

Alana looked away. "I know," she whispered. "It's the same for me. But he asked me to do it—to give him his memories back. After everything I've done, I couldn't refuse him."

"Why did you take his memories in the first place?"

"To protect him," she whispered. "To hide us. Without them, our father couldn't find us."

"I see," Devon replied, though his tone suggested otherwise.

She frowned at him. "What?"

"You didn't have any other motives? To hide from your past, perhaps?"

"Maybe," Alana murmured. "But the woman I used to be, she wasn't much for caring about anything."

"Except when it came to your brother," Devon rumbled, his eyes shining.

Alana swallowed. "I did terrible things, Devon…"

"We've all done terrible things, Alana," Devon replied.

She looked at him sharply. From the depths of her memories, she heard his words ringing out, his admission to the horrors he'd committed during the Trolan war.

I killed a child once, he'd said.

At the time, revulsion had curled around her gut at his words, but now when she looked at him, Alana saw only a man in pain. She shook her head.

"I didn't understand before, when you told me what you'd done," she whispered. "I do now. I'm sorry for how I reacted. You're a good man, Devon. Every act you've done since the war has shown it."

Devon said nothing, only offered her the bottle. She accepted it gratefully and finished the dregs, wondering how Devon survived beneath the weight of so much pain. She hated herself for being responsible for so much of it. Whatever his words earlier, he still hadn't forgiven her. It was in his eyes, even now, in the great gulf that separated them.

Alana swallowed as he looked up and caught her watching him.

"Kellian…he would have been proud of you, helping these people."

Devon grunted. "I'm the reason they're in this mess," he mumbled. "I've led them to their doom."

"No more than if they'd stayed in the forest. Quinn knew about them. When he was done with us, my father would have hunted them down, killed every last one of them."

"It still doesn't seem quite possible, the Tsar being your father."

Alana shrugged. "Perhaps not for you. But for me, for Braidon now, that is who he's always been to us. For as long as I can remember, he has cast his shadow over our lives. My whole life, his way was all I ever knew. Until Braidon came, and I realised I didn't want him to be what I had become. I tried to shield him from it, to protect him…" Alana's throat contracted. "I just wish there had been someone to do the same for me."

"It's really the both of you in there now, isn't it?" Devon whispered.

Despite herself, Alana smiled. "It is, big man," she replied. Then she closed her eyes, and felt a tear streak her cheek. "You still haven't forgiven me, have you?"

"I…I have…" Devon started, but she shook her head.

"Please don't lie to me, Devon," Alana whispered. "It's okay, I understand, but please do not lie."

Devon swallowed, but he nodded, his eyes shining. "How…?"

"You're not a hard man to read, Devon," Alana replied, a smile touching her cheeks. "And you haven't called me 'princess' since the night you came to rescue me."

"Alana…" he started, then trailed off.

Alana looked up, and was surprised to find Devon staring at her. Their eyes met and he quickly looked away. Her cheeks flushed and her stomach clenched. Clearing her throat, she looked at anything but him, embarrassed by her own reaction. The tension built, but still neither said anything.

Then Alana's anger rose to burn away her blush. She

wasn't some innocent teenager, no fumbling girl who couldn't say what she wanted. She was Alana, the Daughter of the Tsar, and she would not be denied.

Silently she rose to her feet. Devon's head jerked up as she crossed the room and stood in front of him. Hands clenched at her sides, she looked down at him.

"You want me," she said.

Devon opened his mouth, but all he could manage was an incomprehensible mumble. Smiling, Alana slid onto his lap and draped an arm around his neck. She watched with satisfaction as the shock in his eyes turned to…something else. He tensed beneath her, one arm lifting to grip her waist, and for a moment she thought he would throw her off.

She stroked his brow, her own eyes caught in his amber gaze.

"You want me," she repeated.

Still Devon did not move, and a sudden fear reared within Alana, that the desire she'd seen in his gaze all that time ago had died. She'd thought it was still there, but what if she'd been wrong, what if he didn't want her, and was about to cast her aside, to reject her? Within, she felt the soft green light of her magic stirring. Temptation rose with it, and she reached for it, feeling its warmth bathe her mind. All she needed was to touch him with her power, to bend his mind as she had done to Quinn and so many others.

Don't.

The command whispered through Alana's mind, two voices as one. In that instant she realised if she tried it, she would lose him. It would be a betrayal of their friendship, a final act of evil that would destroy her in his eyes forever.

"Devon…" she whispered, leaning down to press her forehead against his. "Say something."

His eyes flickered closed as he inhaled. The arm on her waist tightened, but he made no effort to throw her aside. Instead, he pulled her closer, so that she could feel the warmth of his broad chest against her breast, his breath on her neck. She trailed her fingers down his giant arms, tracing the outline of his veins, feeling the thump of his powerful heart. Lifting her head, she found herself trapped in his amber eyes, found herself leaning in…

Heat exploded in her chest as their lips met. Her hands went to his head, drawing him deeper into the kiss, as his arm clenched around her. She shivered as their tongues met, tasting the earthly richness of him, feeling his power beneath her. A moan built in her chest and went rumbling from her. Trailing a hand down his neck, she nibbled playfully at his lip. Her fingers tugged at the buttons of his tunic.

Lust rose within her as his hand slide beneath her shirt. She shuddered as his fingers danced across her naked back, tearing another moan from her throat. She wanted more, wanted his hands, his mouth on her flesh. Searching for his other arm, she found it hanging beside the chair. He flinched as she gripped him, her fingers trailing down in search of his own…

Alana froze as she found his hand wrapped around a wooden haft. Her heart lurched in her chest, and pulling back, she looked down to where his arm hung beside the chair. *Kanker* lay there, its steel head shining in the dim light, his meaty hand wrapped around its handle. A sob caught in Alana's throat as she looked at him.

"You don't trust me," she whispered, her eyes burning with unspilt tears.

"Alana…" he started, but she was already pushing away, scrambling to her feet.

"I would *never!*" she all but shouted, even as she recalled the desire that had touched her, the temptation she'd felt to use her magic on him. She shook her head and looked at him. "Never," she repeated in a whisper.

Devon stared back. "I'm sorry," he murmured, but Alana was already shaking her head.

"I'm sorry, too," she said sharply. "Sorry I ever thought this would work."

He opened his mouth, struggling to speak, but Alana was already spinning on her heel. His words fell on deaf ears as she stepped from the tent and fled into the darkness.

CHAPTER 30

The rising sun found Braidon sitting alone on the outskirts of the Baronian camp. He watched as the scarlet light touched the mountaintops, and then came creeping down the valley towards him. The morning was clear, and so high up in the mountains, Braidon could see far out across the Trolan lands, where the light of the new day had yet to reach.

Shivering, Braidon averted his eyes, his mind returning to the past. Memories flashed through his mind, a lifetime of sights and sounds, of joy and pain. Worst of all was the rift they caused within him, the warring emotions between the renegade and the Son of the Tsar.

Alana had been wrong to mess with his mind, to rob him of his memories. He was sure now she had done it to escape her own guilt, rather than protect them from their father. Either way, it hardly mattered now—the damage was done. His mind had been fractured, and now he feared he would never piece it all back together.

Warmth flickered in his chest as an image of his father passed through his mind, of the man holding him tight, his hand casting wide to encompass the great expanse of Plorsea around them. Then the image changed, and he saw again the sword plunging at Enala's chest, heard the old woman's cry as it speared her. He shuddered, feeling the gulf within him widen.

Braidon's old self had feared the Tsar, but amidst that fear there had also been love, born of the knowledge that everything their father did, he did for them. Yet the Braidon he had become under the spell of Alana's magic had loathed and feared the Tsar in equal measure, and he wondered now whether that had also been of his sister's making.

In fact, he found himself questioning everything she'd ever told him, his every memory, every emotion he'd ever felt for her. As a child, he had seen her as his hero, the avenging angel that struck down any who dared threaten him. Looking back over those memories though, he found himself recalling the terror on the faces of her students, the nervousness of even their father's guards in her presence. Alana had never been one to use her power sparingly—who was to say she had not been using it to manipulate him all along?

The thought sent a cold draught down Braidon's spine. Pulling himself to his feet, he stepped down from the boulder and turned in the direction of camp. He staggered as he found Alana standing on the path, her eyes wide, as though he'd just caught her in the middle of some crime. She wore her thick woollen cloak pulled tightly around her shoulders and a sword at her waist.

His heart suddenly beating hard in his chest, Braidon took a step back. "What are you doing here?"

"I…" Alana paused, casting a glance back over her shoulder at the camp. "I…was leaving."

"Leaving?" he asked. "Why?"

She shook her head, and Braidon was surprised to see tears shining in her eyes. "Because there's no place for me here, Braidon."

Braidon's heartbeat slowed. Legs still shaking from the

shock of finding her there, he lowered himself back down onto the boulder. "What do you mean?"

"Devon doesn't trust me. *You* don't trust me——"

"Can you blame me?" he cut in, his voice sharp. "After what you did, I can't even trust my own memories!"

Alana's eyes dropped to the gravel-strewn path. "I know," she whispered. "I'm so sorry, Braidon. That's why I have to go, before I cause either one of you any more pain."

Braidon opened his mouth to speak more angry words, but they died in his throat when he looked into her eyes and saw she was serious. Alana was leaving, and she hadn't even intended on saying goodbye. He reeled at the realisation, clutching hard to the stone beneath him to keep steady.

"Alana, you don't have to go…"

Staggering to a nearby boulder, Alana sank to the ground and placed her face in her hands. "I do, Braidon," she said. "I won't stay where I'm hated."

"I don't hate you," Braidon burst out, surprised to find the words were true. Her head jerked up, and he saw the surprise written across her face. Braidon sank to the ground alongside her. Tentatively, he rested a hand on her back.

"Why not?" Alana croaked. "I deserve it."

Braidon smiled despite himself. "Because whatever happens, you're still my sister, Alana."

She looked down at that. "I'm still not sure that counts for much in our family."

"It counts," Braidon replied. He trailed off, distracted by her words, by the memories of their father. "Alana…" he murmured, knowing he had to ask, but still wondering if he could believe her answer. "Our father…I have all these memories of him now, of him smiling, happy. And more than that, I remember *loving* him, and remember his own love for us…"

Alana swallowed. Braidon struggled for the words, for the

question he needed to ask. "Why...why is he hunting us? What does he want?"

His sister shook her head, her eyes distant. "He wasn't always so hard," she murmured. "After you came and Mum...died, a part of him died with her. And his ambition, it became everything. I guess somewhere along the way I lost myself as well. But you, Braidon, you were the only pure thing in either of our lives. Yes, he loved you in his own way. That won't protect you though, not so long as you stand in the way of his final goal."

"To end all magic," Braidon breathed. "How do I have anything to do with that?"

Alana shook her head. "The same way I did, until Enala took my place." She looked a Braidon, her eyes gleaming. "He wants you to host the spirit of Jurrien, so he can kill the Storm God and take his power."

"*What?*"

"He already took the power of the Light, when he killed Eric's son. After killing Enala, he has Antonia's God magic as well. Jurrien is the last one left. Once he has all three of the Gods under his sway, he believes he'll be able to wipe all magic from the earth."

"But he needs me to do it?" Braidon asked.

Alana nodded. "He tried to find another way," she whispered, "but after we betrayed him..."

"He no longer cares."

"No," Alana said. She stood sharply. "That's why I still have to go. I can't let him take you, and if I stay here, I'm useless. But if I can get close enough to him, if I take him by surprise, I might be able to—"

"He'll kill you," Braidon said, cutting her off. "He has an army around him, dragons and demons and Magickers. You don't stand a chance."

Alana looked away. A cold wind blew down the valley,

catching in her hair and sending it tumbling across her face. "Then he'll kill me."

She reached up to brush the hair from her eyes, but Braidon grabbed her hand and pulled her around. "Damnit, Alana," he snapped. "You don't need to sacrifice yourself for me anymore."

"But—"

"*No*," Braidon all but shouted. He gestured back at the camp, anger mixing with his terror. "Why can't you see it? Why can't you see what Devon and Selina and all the others can see? I don't *need* you to protect me! I need you to respect me."

Alana opened her mouth, then closed it and swallowed hard. She gave a sharp nod and dragged him into a hug. He held her close, feeling the sobs as they shook her, the silent grief. When they finally broke apart her eyes were wet with tears.

"I'm sorry," she whispered. "You're right, you're not a boy anymore. I should have believed in you back then, given you a chance instead of keeping you from the world. I just…" She trailed off.

"Wanted to protect me," Braidon finished for her. He brushed a tear from her face. "It's okay, sis. But I'm a man now. I won't let you throw away your life for me." He smiled. "Besides, do you even know how to find our father? He could be anywhere in the Three Nations by now."

Red spread across Alana's cheeks. "Not exactly."

Braidon laughed despite himself. "Typical, always leaping before you look."

"And I suppose you have an idea?"

"As a matter of fact, I just might," Braidon replied.

Alana shook her head, biting her lip. "Fine, but even if we find him, how do we *stop* him?"

Braidon smiled. "Together."

CHAPTER 31

A cheer went up from the Baronians as they stepped from
the canyon out onto the rolling hills of Trola. Leading
from the front, Devon forced a smile to his lips, though their
joy did little to warm his heart. He stared out over the green
hills, and wondered whether Alana and her brother too had
survived the mountains, if they had come this way before
them, or if they were still lost amongst the crags rising up
behind the Baronian travellers.

Two nights had passed since he and Alana had spoken,
since their passion had exploded into rage. He had woken the
next morning determined to mend the tear he'd opened
between them, but he hadn't even managed to step from his
tent before the news reached him that she and her brother
had vanished.

Panicked, he'd sent out scouts to search for them, to bring
them back so he might apologise and make things right, but it
had been a hopeless effort. With their memories restored, the
Tsar's children were more than capable of disappearing into
the wilderness. And with Braidon's power, the Baronians
might have been looking straight at them and still never
seen them.

The scouts had returned within the hour with no better idea of where the two might have fled. With Quinn still close on their heels, they could not afford to waste time chasing two ghosts through the Sandstone Mountains. With a heavy heart, Devon had ordered the Baronians to break camp, and they had continued their way down through the mountains.

Now that he'd led them safely into Trola, all Devon could think was to turn around and march back into the face of the storm in search of his friends. But all around him, the Baronians were looking to him for guidance. He could not abandon them now, not after taking them from everything they'd ever known to these strange lands.

"Where to now, hammerman?" Joseph asked as he came alongside him.

Devon glanced at the man. His hand no longer hung in a cast and seemed to be healing well, helped in no small part by a paste Selina had created from moss and mountain herbs.

"I hadn't really thought that far ahead, to be honest," Devon grunted. "I'm not exactly popular here."

Joseph glanced behind them, where the snow-capped mountains still towered above. "You think they're still after us, with the two of them gone? They only wanted to boy, didn't they?"

Devon shrugged. "Quinn and I have a bit of a history ourselves," he rumbled. "I doubt he'll give up until I'm six feet under."

"Sounds like we might be better off with another leader," Joseph replied with a grin.

"You thinking about leading a mutiny, sonny?" Devon asked, raising an eyebrow.

Joseph chuckled, rubbing his injured arm. "No thanks. One beating is enough. Besides, we're not on a ship. It's not half as fun when you can't throw the loser overboard."

Shaking his head, Devon returned his eyes to the road ahead. "You're lucky I like having you around," he commented. "Most kings would have hung you for your insolence by now."

"Ay, probably why I've never been fond of kings. Good thing you're a Baronian, not a king."

Devon's laughter rang from the hills. "I'm not a Baronian, sonny."

"Oh? I suppose you're still a Plorsean then?"

The man's words gave Devon pause. "I suppose not," he sighed.

"You're an outcast—that makes you a Baronian!" Joseph slapped him on the back. "Cheer up, there's worse fates in this world of ours."

"Being stuck with you strikes me as one of them."

"Ay, shame you scared off that blonde lassie," Joseph replied with a laugh. "Don't know how you messed that one up, she seemed fond of you."

Devon flashed him a glare, and Joseph raised his hands in surrender. "Alright, alright, still a touchy subject I see," he said. "I can see when I'm not wanted." He fell back into the ranks of Baronians behind them.

"So *do* you have a plan, hammerman?" Selina asked, appearing out of nowhere.

Groaning, Devon raised his eyes to the sky. "You as well?"

"Me as well," she replied, her thin lips drawn tight. "It's only all our lives on the line."

"It's not like we have many options to choose from, woman," Devon grunted. "We either keep running, or turn and fight."

"I know which I would prefer," Selina growled. "I wouldn't mind taking a few pieces off that Quinn, after what he did to my people."

"You'd have to get in line," Devon said. "It's past time the man got his due."

Selina fell silent at that, her eyes growing distant. Devon shivered as he remembered what Alana had told him of the woman, about Quinn stabbing her through the chest and leaving her to die. Only the Goddess's arrival had saved Selina, her Earth magic restoring her to life.

"Quinn, and the Tsar," Selina whispered finally. Her face twitched as though from remembered pain. "He killed the Goddess. What does that mean? Without the Gods...what hope do we have?"

"We've survived well enough without them until now," Devon replied. "I don't know what the Tsar is planning, but I know there are people here in Trola who will stand against him. If we can enlist their help, maybe we can send Quinn and his Stalkers running back to Plorsea with their tails between their legs."

"That's a lot of maybes," Selina said, raising an eyebrow. "Anyone ever tell you you're not much of a planner?"

"Ha!" Devon smiled sadly. "I had a friend who used to say the same. He reckoned the Gods must like me, or I'd have been killed a long time ago."

"Well if that's the case, you'd better hope you're Jurrien's favourite," Selina replied wryly. "I take it your friend is no longer with us?"

Devon looked away at that, pain gripping his chest as he remembered Kellian's death. "No."

"I see." Selina said, and they walked on in silence for a while. Finally she gestured behind them, to the retreating mountains. "Braidon and Alana, why did they leave?"

"I don't know," Devon replied sharply, his heart twisting again.

Thinking of his friends, he felt suddenly alone. First he'd lost Kellian; now Braidon and Alana had left as well. During their time in the forest, he'd grown fond of the young man, watching him come into his own. And Alana...

His cheeks flushed as he remembered their last encounter. Not for the first time in the last few days, Devon cursed himself for his distrust. The pain in Alana's eyes when she'd realised the truth haunted him. He wanted more than anything to take it all back, to return to that night and cast *kanker* aside, to tell her how much she meant to him.

Yet in the moment, what he'd done had seemed right. With the hammer in his hand, her magic could not touch him, could not alter his thoughts, his emotions.

It wasn't until the moment she'd realised his betrayal, that Devon had realised he loved her. Not just the Alana he had travelled with, but the ferocious, confused, and loyal young woman she had become.

But before he could say any of that, she had fled.

Now all Devon could think about was what he'd say when he saw her again.

If he saw her again.

☸

"THEY LEFT the mountains this morning, sir," the Stalker, Zarent, announced as he rode up.

Quinn smiled, relieved to hear they were finally on the right track. For the past week they had trailed the Baronian force deep into the mountains, seeking to head them off before they reached Trolan lands. But with the boy shielding them, finding them had proven more difficult than he'd expected. In the forest, the Baronians and their wagons had left clear tracks for them to follow, but the bare stone of the mountains told little of their passage. The myriad of crevices and valleys that made up the Sandstone Mountains made their task all the more difficult.

Now though, they were finally within striking distance. On their horses, Quinn and his force of Stalkers and soldiers would catch Devon and his followers by evening. Despite the Baronians' greater numbers, Quinn had no doubt they would make quick work of their quarry. Devon, Alana and Braidon might offer a small pocket of resistance, but their power was small compared to the ten Stalkers remaining in Quinn's command. Together, they would break any illusion the boy created, and bring him before the Tsar's justice.

Devon and Alana though, they were Quinn's to deal with. He savoured the thought of the hammerman on his knees, begging for his life. There would be no mercy for him though, nor for any of the Baronians who had followed him. Only the boy would survive untouched, and after what Quinn had witnessed back in the forest, that was no blessing.

As for Alana, Quinn was determined to ensure no harm came to her during the battle. The thought of her still made his blood boil with rage. She had mocked him back in the village, openly derided him in front of his Stalkers. No, after all she had done, death was too good for Alana. He would see her chained and brought before her father, so that he might petition the great man to restore the girl to some semblance of obedience.

First though, he needed to catch them.

"At the canter!" he called out to his Stalkers.

The clatter of horse hooves echoed from the cliffs as they continued down the valley. The stone walls widened around them, slowly giving way to rolling foothills. Further down, grass began to grow once more. The rocky ground turned back to soft earth, the churned up dirt revealing the passage of hundreds of travellers.

Quinn lifted his gaze to the hills ahead of them, watching for the first glimpse of their quarry. It was still only midmorning, and it would be hours yet before he had Devon and the others in his grip, but already his heart raced with anticipation.

Soon.

As the thought touched him, a cold breeze blew across Quinn's neck. Despite the cloudless sky, a shadow seemed to pass overhead. Shivering, Quinn looked up as his gelding gave a cry and staggered to a sudden halt. Around him, the other horses were doing the same. Their screams rolled across the hillside as several reared, throwing off their riders and bolting.

As the downed men chased after their mounts, Quinn dragged back on the reins, bringing his own horse under control. Whispering gently to the panicked beast, he looked around, seeking out whatever had so disturbed the animals.

His heart lurched in his chest as he saw the shadow of a man standing on the path ahead. Cloaked all in darkness, nothing could be seen of his face, yet Quinn recognised him instantly. Hardly daring to breathe, he slid from his horse and dropped to one knee before the Tsar. Seeing him, the other Stalkers abandoned their mounts and did the same.

"Your Majesty," Quinn whispered. "Why are you here?"

Soft laughter whispered across the hillside. "You are too slow, Lieutenant."

"No, sire!" Quinn cried. "We almost have them! No Baronian will be left alive come nightfall, and the boy will be yours."

The figure shook its head. Slowly, the Tsar approached. His feet made no sound on the earth, and Quinn realised with a start that the man was projecting himself from a hundred miles away. He shuddered at the power such a feat must have cost.

"You might catch the Baronians," the Tsar murmured, "but my *son* is no longer with them."

"*What?*" Quinn exclaimed, coming to his feet. "How?"

"Their camp is no longer protected," the Tsar murmured. "Their minds are open to me. My daughter and the boy have abandoned them."

"Why——?"

"*Enough!*" the Tsar's voice boomed, sending their horses bolting again. Quinn staggered back and again dropped to his knees as the shadowed figure loomed. "You have failed me for the last time, Lieutenant," he whispered. "Return to my camp at once."

"What about Devon?" Quinn demanded. "We are so close, I can still destroy him."

"No, Lieutenant," the Tsar growled, blue eyes flashing within the shadows of his hood. "*You* will not. My children are coming here, and I would like my Stalkers at hand to detain them, rather than wandering the countryside carrying out your personal vendettas."

"Devon is dangerous!"

"The man is mortal. He cannot hide from me. I will deal with him when the time is right."

"But—"

"*You!*" Cutting Quinn off, the Tsar turned to a nearby Stalker. Zarent's head jerked up as he realised the Tsar was addressing him, his eyes widening. "You are in charge now. Arrest Quinn. Bring him and the rest of my company to my camp."

The man hesitated, his eyes flickering from Quinn to the other Stalkers, then back to the Tsar. He nodded slowly, his mouth opening and closing as he struggled to adjust to his sudden change of fortunes.

"Can you I trust you to do that, Stalker?" the Tsar asked dangerously. "Or should I find someone else?"

"No, sir!" the Stalker shouted, standing to attention. "It shall be done at once."

"Excellent," the Tsar murmured. His shadowed gaze turned back to Quinn. "Then I shall see you soon, Lieutenant."

With his words, the dark figure faded from sight, leaving Quinn and his Stalkers alone on the hillside.

Except they were no longer *his* Stalkers.

His heart still hammering hard against his ribcage, Quinn faced his former followers. Zarent grinned, reaching for his sword. "You going to come easily, Lieutenant?" he asked as the sword slid free. "Or shall we do this the hard way?"

"Oh, please say hard," another Stalker added as he joined Zarent, blade already in hand.

Panicked, Quinn took a step back. He glanced around, searching for his horse, but in the turmoil inspired by the Tsar's appearance the gelding had galloped clear. Power built in the air as he sensed the black-garbed Stalkers nearest him drawing on their magic, readying themselves for a fight. Slowly they closed in on him.

Silently vowing revenge on his treacherous men, Quinn raised his hands. "I surrender."

"How disappointing," Zarent said, before stepping forward and slamming the hilt of his sword into Quinn's skull.

CHAPTER 32

Merydith paused as a breeze blew across the hilltop, savouring the warmth in its touch, the promise it carried of winter's end. The northern army had set up camp on a lonely hilltop overlooking a narrow valley. Her people were busy fortifying their camp for the coming battle. Men and women were hard at work digging a trench along the northeast slope of the hill, facing the distant mountains from which they'd escaped just a few days before. Still trapped in the grip of winter, snow glimmered on the stark peaks.

It was from there the first attack would come. A rider had reached them that morning—their rearguard had been over-run, the few hundred soldiers tasked with slowing the Tsar's advance massacred. Now he was coming for them, and there was nowhere left for the northern army to run.

Merydith had thought to reach Kalgan and make her stand there, but Betran said the city now stood empty, abandoned by its citizens in anticipation of the coming war. Those who believed in the cause had marched with Betran to join her, while the rest had dissipated into the countryside, spreading the news of the rebel Queen far and wide.

In the two days since escaping the mountains, more

Trolans had joined them, in ones and twos and groups large enough to fill an inn, though none as great as the thousand Betran led. Many were veterans from the civil war, hard men and women with little give in them. She had given Betran the title of captain and set him to work alongside Mokyre to ready their two forces to work in concert. Together with those who had joined them on the road, her force now numbered a little over six thousand.

Still barely a fraction of what the Tsar would field against them.

Merydith continued along the ridgetop, casting an expert eye over the defensive trench and rampart they were erecting. Unfortunately, the rolling farmland of northern Trola offered little in the way of wood for a palisade, and the rocky soils on the hilltop were making the going hard. At least they still had a day before the Tsar could bring the full force of his army down on them.

Terrified farmers and displaced villagers were already streaming down from the north, fleeing the coming army. Many chose to skirt Merydith's force altogether, seeking to disappear into the wildlands of southern Trola. She could hardly blame them; they had already witnessed first-hand the wrath of the Tsar. It would take a brave soul to face him again, after the devastation he had wrought on the nation during their first rebellion.

Satisfied the ramparts and trench would be completed by nightfall, Merydith returned to her tent.

"How's it looking out there, Merydith?"

Blinking, Merydith's eyes took a few moments to adjust to the gloom. A smile touched her lips when she found the aged figure of Murdo seated in the corner beside Damyn's stretcher. His strength normally unquenchable, Damyn's fate had sapped the old man's spirit. Both members of clan Crae, Damyn was as much Murdo's family as he was Merydith's.

Merydith crossed the room and pulled up a stool beside the clan leader.

"We'll be ready," she murmured, her eyes drawn as always to Damyn. His complexion remained pale, but his breathing was easier now that they had left the mountains. Over the last few days, they had managed to feed him a gruel made of roots and tubers, but still he would not wake.

"He's a strong lad, Merydith," Murdo said, as though reading her mind. "He'll be alright. Just make sure you win this war, so he has something to wake up to."

Merydith smiled. "If only it were so easy."

"Ha!" Murdo cackled. "Don't tell me our relentless Queen is having doubts now?"

"I've had doubts all along, my friend," Merydith replied. "I just keep them to myself."

"Ah, well, don't go bringing down this old man's hopes then, would ya?" he rumbled. "You're of the Kenzie Clan, woman. As far as us Craes are concerned, you're unstoppable."

Merydith snorted. "I never said *I* was the problem," she replied. "I'm just hoping the rest of you can keep up with me tomorrow!"

"You won't have to worry about the Trolans!" Merydith swung around as Betran's voice came from the entrance to the tent. The young Trolan wandered inside, followed a second later by Mokyre.

The latter nodded, adding his agreement: "Ay, they're tough bastards out there. We'll give the Tsar's army something to think about."

"They'll have to do more than that," Merydith replied, waving for them to pull up stools and join her. "Our scouts report the Tsar's force still numbers close to forty thousand."

The mood in the tent turned sombre at the reminder of their odds. Mokyre was the first to break the silence. "You'll find a way, my Queen," he said softly. "And even if we fail, at least we bought the rest of our people some time." He eyed her through the gloom. "Come what may, you were right to lead us here."

Merydith nodded her thanks as Betran voiced a fresh worry. "What about the Tsar's magic?" he murmured. "Last time, our cities only held as long as our Magickers' stamina."

"Helen and the others remain strong, for now," Merydith replied, thinking of her meeting with the woman earlier in the day.

A great tent had been set in the centre of the camp for Helen and her hundred Magickers. Within, the shadows were lit by a single torch. Men and women sat in circles spreading out from the centre, legs crossed and eyes closed. Even magic-less, Merydith had felt the power bubbling on the air as she entered.

Helen had set her people to work in shifts through the day and night, with a quarter of their number rotating to sleep every six hours. Even so, the effort it was taking them to keep the Tsar from the camp was obvious. In the time since they'd stepped foot in the Three Nations, the flesh had vanished from Helen's bones, so that she seemed but a shadow of her former self.

Even so, the Magicker had greeted Merydith warmly, and reassured her they would hold the Tsar to their dying breath. But it was not that for which Merydith had visited them. She had gone in search of a way to attack.

In the end, she'd left without an answer, but Merydith prayed to the Gods that Helen and her people could find a way to turn the tables on the Tsar. Because without *something*, she feared no matter how brave, how daring her people, in the end the sheer weight of numbers would overwhelm them.

"How much longer can they hold for?" Mokyre asked, disturbing her train of thought.

"Helen could not say," Merydith said.

"Then it's a good thing we face them on the morrow," Murdo put in.

"Agreed," Merydith replied. "I just wish we'd found a more defensible position."

"We're on a big hill surrounded by valleys and steep sides," Murdo rumbled. "What more could you ask for?"

"Walls, a well or two, some food or supplies might have been nice."

"Ha, well, beggars can't be choosers, can they?" Murdo laughed.

"Another group of farmers just came in," Betran added. "They brought their livestock with them. A few dozen sheep and a couple of cows. We won't go hungry before the fight."

"Your people are a gift that keeps on giving, Betran," Merydith replied with a smile.

"It is our pleasure, my Queen," he said, stroking his beard. He eyed her closely. "All we have desired for this last decade is our freedom."

Merydith took note of his tone. "And you shall have it, my friend," she responded. Her eyes travelled around the room, taking in the ancient eyes of Murdo, the youthful fire of Mokyre, the unyielding stare of Betran. Unlikely friends, in normal times, but common cause had united them under her banner. "First though, we must win it back. For all of us."

The others nodded. With a wave from her, they departed, each returning to the myriad of tasks needing to be completed before the day was out. Before the Tsar and his army arrived.

Finally alone, Merydith turned and looked down on the sleeping face of Damyn. Gently, she stroked his brow, feeling the warmth of his skin, the cloying dampness of his hair. His cheekbones stood out starkly in the candlelight, so that it seemed he were already half-skeleton.

"Where are you, my friend?" she murmured, a shiver touching her.

They had spent so much of their childhood together, she could hardly imagine a world without him. Back then, before she was Queen, they had just been boy and girl. Two troublesome youngsters, they'd often slipped her guards and disappeared into the winding tunnels of Erachill.

Together they had explored the deepest crevices and highest tunnels, venturing even up to the high peak beneath which the city was built. Upon that viewpoint, it had seemed they could see the entire world, from wild steeps to dense forests to rugged coastlines. Even to far the north, the three jagged peaks of Mount Chole and its volcanic siblings had just been visible.

As a child, it had scared her sometimes, standing on that peak and looking out on their realm, knowing one day it would be hers to govern. When she'd told Damyn of her fears, he had stood there beside her with a roguish grin on his youthful face, and laughed. He'd told her she had nothing to fear, that her parents and Enala and he would all be there beside her, that together they would lead Northland to greatness.

Now her time had come, Merydith found herself deserted. Her parents were long dead, Enala she knew not where. Even Damyn had abandoned her, his mind fled, leaving Merydith alone to face the darkness that was the Tsar.

"You said you would be here," she whispered, her voice cracking. "You promised."

Closing her eyes, Merydith let the tears fall. How had everything gone so wrong? For the thousandth time, she wondered if she'd made the right decision, protecting the boy. If she had simply handed Braidon over to the Tsar, Northland might never have needed to fear the Tsar's wrath. All those who had given their lives to her cause these past few weeks would still live, happy and safe in the mountains of Erachill.

And the boy would be dead, she tried to convince herself.

Yet still she had heard nothing of Braidon and Enala,

nothing but rumour and whispers. It was said a Gold Dragon had been spotted in the skies above Ardath, but it had fled across the lake, never to be seen again. Now she wondered if even her one small act of defiance had been in vain, if the Tsar had taken the boy all the same.

"Was I wrong?" she whispered to the shadows in the tent.

"You could never be wrong, Merydith," a rasping voice responded from beside her. Her head flicked around as Damyn groaned and struggled to sit up. "It's just the rest of the world hasn't figured it out yet."

CHAPTER 33

Evening was setting on Devon and his followers as they
topped a rise and found themselves looking down on
the ruins of Westdale. Devon remembered the town well from
the civil war. Close to the mountains, it had once been a place
for revellers of all race and creed. Its popularity had done
nothing to save it though. The inhabitants had surrendered in
the early days of the Tsar's conquest, and been spared, but
the city itself had still been gutted.

Now though, Devon was surprised to see fires glowing
amongst the burnt-out buildings. A quick count in the dying
light estimated there were well over a hundred people camped
out in the ruins. Though the Baronians outnumbered them
five to one, Devon considered skirting them. On closer inspec-
tion though, he realised the people below were kitted out
much the same as his own. They sported worn woollen cloaks
of various colours, and their weapons consisted of rusted
swords and farm hatchets. After a brief discussion with the
others, he decided to risk approaching.

No watch had been set, and he was halfway to the ruins
by the time anyone within noticed the approaching tribe. A
warning cry carried up the slope as chaos descended on the

camp. Devon watched as people rushed in all directions; some gathering up fallen weapons and racing in his direction, while others fled for the wilderness.

"Who goes there!" a voice called up to him.

In the growing darkness, Devon could not make out the man's face, but after a quick check that the Baronians weren't far behind, he lifted *kanker* and shouted a reply. "An enemy of the Tsar!"

Below, the figure staggered to a stop. "Oh!" Before Devon could say anything more, he swung around and shouted to those further down the slope. "It's okay! They're on our side."

Now it was Devon's turn to halt midstride. He frowned, staring at the men and women now gathered on the slope below them. A few carried torches, their soft glow illuminating the hillside. By their light, the first man who had spoken continued forward, a roguish grin on his youthful face. "In that case, well met, stranger!" he said as he strode up.

Devon could only shake his head. The Trolans who'd rushed to defend the camp were already heading back to the ruins, leaving only a few to stand in their path. Beyond, those who had run in the other direction had paused where they stood, and now watched on in silence, as though awaiting the outcoming of the meeting on the hillside. As far as Devon was concerned, they were the smart ones.

"Awfully trusting of you," he said, looking back to the young man. "We might have been lying."

The man looked suddenly unsure of himself, but Devon sheathed *kanker* on his back and waved for his people to do the same with their weapons. Their newfound friend relaxed visibly. Devon was just glad the man hadn't recognised *kanker*. The weapon was infamous amongst the Trolans, and he doubted his reputation had improved at all in the last few months.

"There's not many brave enough to declare themselves enemies of the Tsar," the stranger replied.

"Then what drove a young lad like you to do so?" Devon asked.

"The battle, of course!"

"Battle?" Devon asked.

"You haven't heard?" The man frowned. "Where've you been, mate? The whole of Trola has been talking about it. The Northland Queen has come to liberate us. She's just a little way north of us, camped out on Turkey's Knoll. The Tsar is marching to meet her. We're hoping to reach 'em before the battle begins!" His frown deepened as he glanced over Devon's shoulder, his gaze taking in the Baronians gathered above. "You...aren't from Trola, are you?"

A grin split Devon's matted beard. "No, sonny, but if the Queen's here, that's the best news I've heard all year. What was your name?"

"Corrie." He paused, his eyes narrowing. "And what did you say yours was?"

"I didn't," Devon laughed.

Slapping the man on the shoulder, he strode past, gesturing for the Baronians to join him. Beyond the ruins, the Trolans who had fled were returning to the city. Watching them, Devon wondered what would have happened had it been Quinn who'd come across them first. There were children below, and old men and women bowed with age. Most weren't soldiers at all, though many sported the signs of the last civil war.

They would have been swept away had it been the Tsar's people who came across them first, the earth stained with their blood. And if Trola was in open rebellion again, there would be no mercy this time. His soldiers would slaughter every man, woman, and child they found.

Walking through the broken walls of the city, Devon wondered at the desperation that had brought these people here. Amongst the crumpled buildings and burnt out hovels, there was no escaping the devastation the last war had left.

Their population had been decimated by the Tsar and his army. Devon had played no small part in that massacre. Looking around now, he tasted the familiar tang of guilt in his mouth.

"Where have you all come from?" he asked as he watched a one-armed man walk past him, carrying a stack of firewood.

"Kalgan, Palma, Drata, everywhere in between," Corrie said as he joined Devon.

"And you lead them?"

Corrie shrugged. "No one leads us. I was just the first to notice your people."

"You should have a watch set," Devon grunted. "If the Tsar is in Trola, he will have raiding forces scouring the countryside."

Corrie looked doubtful, and Devon shook his head. "Joseph!" he shouted, turning to the small retinue of Baronians that had followed him into the city.

Joseph stepped forward, his bulk making the young Trolan look tiny. "Yes…sir." He said the title hesitantly, and Devon nodded his thanks at the man for not using his name.

"Take a dozen men and set a watch on the approaches to the city," Devon said, and the man moved away.

Selina stepped up to join them, and the two of them exchanged glances. "Is there room in the city for our people?" she asked the young Trolan.

Corrie shrugged. "There's only a few hundred of us here. The city used to host a thousand. If your people wish to join us for the night, we won't stop them."

Devon chuckled. "It would have been a bit late if you wanted to," he commented, gesturing to where the Baronians were already streaming through the fallen walls. "Anyway, if your people were intending to join the Queen, we'll march with you." He hesitated, casting another glance around them.

"Though I think many of your number would be best left here."

"They'll come, or they won't," Corrie replied. "As I said, I don't lead them." He eyed the black-garbed Baronians. "You still haven't told me where you came from, or who you are, for that matter."

"Ay," Devon replied, his stomach tying in knots.

Clenching his fists, he took a breath. He saw a sudden look of panic on Selina's face, but he could hide the truth no longer. If he was to fight alongside these people, they deserved to know who he was.

"Because I am Devon," he said softly. Reaching up, he drew his hammer. "Because this is *kanker*, and its head is stained with the blood of your people."

Corrie's eyes widened and he took a quick step back. He looked from the fabled weapon to its wielder. Devon watched as hatred blossomed in his eyes.

"You dare to stand here and claim yourself an enemy of the Tsar?" he whispered. "An ally of Trola?"

"I do," Devon rumbled. "Every day since the war ended, I have regretted the part I played in your fall."

"And what is your regret to us, butcher?" Corrie snapped. A crowd was starting to gather around them now. Devon glimpsed men reaching for sword hilts as they realised what Corrie was saying. "Can your regret help to rebuild our cities, or bring back our Magickers? Can it restore our loved ones to life?"

"No," Devon replied. He stepped towards Corrie, so that he stood just an inch from the man, and looked down at him. Beyond the crowd, several Baronians had taken notice of the commotion and were moving towards them. "But you'll find no greater warrior for your cause, sonny."

"We don't need help from the likes of you."

"You do," Devon snapped, his anger flaring. He threw out an arm, gesturing to the men and women that had gathered around them. "Your army is made of old men and cripples. They're brave, I'll give them that, but it is the *Tsar* you face. His army cannot be defeated by bravery alone. You need warriors, fighters with the strength to see an empire fall. You need me."

As he spoke, Devon had watched the doubt enter the young Trolan's eyes. Like many in his nation, Corrie was hotblooded, quick to anger, but now that he found himself facing the Butcher of Trola, Devon could see his hatred turning to fear. He looked around, seeking strength in those around him, but the crowd had taken an unconscious step back at Devon's outburst.

Selina still stood nearby though, and she advanced, her face radiating calm.

"Devon is not the only one here who carries the weight of your people's fate on his shoulders, Trolan," she said quietly. "I too have Trolan blood on my hands."

"You fought against us, lady?" Corrie asked, taking the chance to retreat from Devon.

"I doubt Devon remembers me, but it was not just legends who fought beneath the Tsar's banner," Selina replied.

Devon stared at her in disbelief. With her greying hair and slim frame, he'd never guessed for a moment that she too might have fought in the ranks of soldiers who had marched against Trola. Her eyes flicked in his direction, and a knowing smile touched her lips.

"Very well." Devon looked around as the words burst from Corrie. "You and your people may remain, *Butcher*. But do not expect our friendship." With that he turned and vanished through the crowd.

Despite his claims he was not their leader, the crowd dispersed after that, leaving Devon standing alone with Selina.

"Was that true?" he asked when the last of the Trolans had faded away.

Selina raised an eyebrow. "Is that so hard to believe, hammerman?"

Chuckling, Devon shook his head. "No, I should have guessed it sooner, the way you ordered us around back at the inn." He gestured to where several Baronians had already finished setting up his tent. They started towards it as he continued. "So you decided to retire and set up an inn after the war?"

"It was more for the quiet of the forest, but yes," Selina answered, and Devon chuckled.

"I think my friend would have liked you," he said as he ducked beneath his tent flaps.

Selina followed him inside, and Devon waved for her to join him in the camp seats already laid out by the brazier.

"I'll give 'em this," he said as he sat, "at least the Baronians are more organised than these poor souls."

Selina said nothing, and Devon found her staring at the fire. After a moment she blinked and looked around. Catching Devon watching her, she sighed.

"We never learn, do we?" she said softly.

"What?" Devon asked, nonplussed.

"The folly of war."

Devon frowned. "The Tsar hasn't exactly given us a choice."

"There is always a choice." Selina sighed and leaned forward in her chair. "Tell me, Devon. If you win this fight, what will change? After all this blood and death, after all the orphans you create, what will be left?" There was anger in her voice as she looked at him.

"What do you want from me, Selina?" Devon asked, taken aback. He shook his head, his own anger rising. "I'm no king, no ruler. Those aren't my decisions to make. You think I like this any more than you? I *left* all this, threw everything away to escape it."

"Ay, and what did you do then? What good did you create

in this world, to atone for the death you dealt with that hammer of yours?"

"I..." Devon trailed off as the innkeeper's eyes drilled into his.

"Truth is, you did nothing," Selina hissed. "And you expect the Trolans to be grateful, because after you slaughtered them like so many pigs, you hung up your weapon and said, 'Well that's enough.'"

"I lost my *friend*," Devon snapped, surging to his feet. "I might have been late, but I *have* fought for their cause. I have bled and bled for it, gone up against Stalkers and demons and dragons for it. Don't you *dare* say I have done nothing!"

Selina was on her feet now as well. "You have killed for the cause, Devon, but what have you *built?* What legacy will you leave this world, other than one of death and destruction?" She gestured to the people outside in the ruins. "Those people out there, the Tsar destroyed their lives, took everything from them. But every one of them has built more than you. They have families and farms, a home to return to. They are here to protect their own, to strive for a better world for their children."

"So am I—"

"No, Devon," Selina said sadly, "you are here because after the war, you were empty." She slumped back into her chair, the fight going from her in a rush. "I know, because it was the same for me," she said quietly. She swallowed, her eyes on the walls of the tent, as though she could see straight through the fabric, out to where the Trolans made camp. "If men and women like them ruled this world, there would be no more wars. But instead, it's men and women like us who are worshiped. And so the evil spreads across mountains and rivers, on down the centuries, unending."

Devon sank back into his chair, all anger draining from him. "What can I say, Selina, except that I think you are wrong? I know what I am: a soldier, a warrior, a fighter. It's all my family has ever known. Perhaps someday that will change, but it will not change the way of the world. The powerful will always seek to conquer. Some will fight for the light, others a different shade of grey. But when the dark ones come, it's up to men like me to stand against them, to give our lives to ensure men and women like *them*—" he gestured to the unseen Trolans, "can live their lives in peace."

Selina's eyes were sad as she watched him. "I know that, Devon," she murmured. "But do you not think the soldiers who fight for the Tsar believe the same? To them, you and the Baronians and the Trolans are traitors, the Queen a foreign invader, coming to take their land and enslave their families."

"I know, believe me, I know," Devon said. "By the Gods, I fought alongside many of them. And who knows, maybe they're right." He sighed, staring into the dead brazier. It was growing cold in the tent, but he would have to find fuel before it could be lit. "I can only go by what my eyes tell me, Selina. Those Trolans out there, they have suffered because of the Tsar, because of us. And I have met the Queen and the northerners. She's a hard woman, but Northland is no longer the devil it once was. They are thriving and have no reason to invade. She did not come here unprovoked. So I will fight alongside the Trolans, and Northland, and the Baronians, against my former comrades. It may not be what you or I want, but it is what it is."

"Who says that is not what I want?" Selina chuckled.

Devon frowned. "Understanding your words is like wrestling piglets in the mud; soon as I think I have a handle on them, another one slithers free."

"I'm sorry, Devon, if I took my own frustration out on you. It's just, after all our Three Nations has suffered, I thought we were finally done with war. To sit here now, watching more young men and women marching off to fight for their freedom…" She shook her head. "It's hard to see how it will end in anything but more grief."

"Ay, the Tsar will show them no mercy this time."

"You were right, what you said out there," Selina put in. Devon only shrugged, but she went on. "But they will need more than your courage if they're to stand a chance."

"What do you mean?"

"They need a leader, Devon, one who believes in them, who will fight for them to his dying breath."

"Me?"

"Who else?" Selina whispered.

"Rubbish," Devon rumbled. "They despise me."

"Ay, they hate you, because of what you've done. But that is not who you *are*, Devon. Who you are is the man who led the Baronians through the mountains. Show them *that* Devon, and they will follow you to the gates of hell."

"If the Tsar is marching, hell doesn't begin to describe what we face."

"They need you, Devon," Selina said, cutting across his deflection. "You'll see that, come the morrow."

CHAPTER 34

Merydith sighed as she sank onto the grass behind the hastily erected ramparts. Silence fell over the men and women stationed there as they broke off their conversations to look at her. She offered them what she hoped was her most reassuring smile. The fear in their eyes told Merydith she was only halfway successful.

"They're beautiful from here, aren't they?" she said, gesturing at the mountains.

The rising sun stained their snowy peaks scarlet, a sign amongst many of her people that a bad day was to come. Bad for whom, though, was yet to be decided. Slowly the red gave way to gold as the burning globe topped the mountains, bathing them all in its warmth. She let out a long breath, her eyes fluttering closed for a moment. They might have left the mountains behind, but winter's chill still lingered over Trola.

"Do you really think we can hold them?" a Trolan woman crouched nearby asked her.

Merydith flashed a grin in her direction. "Hold them? They should be so lucky! Today we'll see the Tsar's empire fall, I promise you that."

The woman swallowed visibly. Betran moved alongside

Merydith. "Trust her, Beth," he murmured. "The Queen has a plan."

"It's just…I never knew there would be so *many*."

"Don't worry about the numbers," Merydith answered in her calmest voice, even as she recalled the sight of the Tsar's horde marching towards them in the fading light of the evening. They had just kept coming, hour upon hour, long after the sun had set and torches were needed to light their way. "We have the high ground, and the courage to use it. When the time comes, we'll slice them in two like a knife through butter."

"I hope so," the Trolan murmured.

"Don't hope, *know*," Merydith said, patting the woman's shoulder as she stood.

Nodding to Betran, the man joined her and they bid the woman and her comrades good luck. Together they moved down the line, Betran greeting men and women he recognised and introducing her. They stopped several more times to talk with the troops, letting them see her, to speak with the Queen they would soon be risking their lives for. Most of those stationed along the ramparts were the Trolan rebels that had joined with Betran, or the volunteers they'd picked up along the way.

If her plan failed, it would fall on these men and women to hold the ramparts long enough for the wounded to be evacuated. Merydith prayed it would not come to that, but she knew if the worst were to happen, it was unlikely she would live long enough to witness the aftermath.

Reaching the end of the northern defences, they climbed the earthen mound that was their ramparts. Merydith looked down at the land below, and the dark shadow that spread around their hilltop. Nestled within the valley, the Tsar had not even bothered to take the slopes to either side of his force. He had stalked her across Lonia, far through the mountains, all the way to this lonely hilltop. And like the wolf at the end of a hunt, he knew they were done, that they did not have the strength to flee any longer.

Or at least, she hoped that was what he thought.

If her plan were to succeed, they needed him to be over-bold, to throw caution to the wind and attack up the long, open slope below their hilltop. He would expect her to sit and wait, to defend her makeshift ramparts and trench to the last man and woman. Looking down at the mass of humanity below, Merydith shivered, and wondered if she were mad to think of attacking such a monster.

The emerald and scarlet of the Lonian and Plorsean soldiers wound up the valley and disappeared out of sight, uncountable, though she knew they numbered around forty thousand. Against her tiny force, the odds seemed insurmountable.

Her eyes drifted to the sky, and she wondered whether the Three Gods were looking down on her today, if they had given their blessing to this desperate gamble.

The *thump* of marching feet rumbled up from the valley below as the first wave of soldiers started forward. Row upon row of ironclad men and women stretched across the valley, wide enough to engage the defenders across the entire rampart.

Despite herself, Merydith allowed herself a smile. The Tsar's battle plan was obvious. He would launch a frontal assault upon their hillside, sending wave upon wave of southern soldiers until the defenders were overwhelmed. A less confident commander might have ordered his forces to surround the hilltop, cutting off their escape. But the Tsar knew she had nowhere left to go, that even if the Queen fled, she would only be delaying the inevitable.

No, the fate of their two worlds would be decided here, and neither the Tsar nor the Queen wished to delay its conclusion any longer.

The rumbling grew as the first wave of soldiers

approached the base of the hill. The sound carried up the slope to where the Northland army waited, breaking over them like thunder. Merydith glanced along the line, and smiled when she saw the Trolan defenders standing strong.

She was surprised to find her own fear had evaporated. Looking out at her nemesis, she realised she had been waiting for this day for what felt like a lifetime. Now that it had finally come, she felt a strange indifference to the odds they faced, an acceptance of whatever fate would bring that day.

Even were they to be defeated, Merydith knew the northern battle cry would live on. They had hurt the Tsar these past few weeks, damaged his aura of invisibility. Today, every southern soldier her people slew was one less for their kin back home to face. And if Merydith herself were to die, her death would ring out through the Northland clans, becoming the rallying cry of the free.

The thought brought a sudden melancholy to Merydith, and she pushed it aside.

Death could wait.

Today was for living.

As the sun crept higher into the sky, a single figure broke away from the southern army and started his way up the grass-torn slope. He walked slowly, a white flag flapping above his head. Waving Betran back, Merydith rose and strode down to meet him. Two of her guard followed close behind, the memory of her attempted assassination still fresh in their minds.

"That's far enough," she boomed when the man was still ten paces away.

"I come to discuss terms of surrender!" the man bellowed.

"Excellent!" Merydith shouted back. "Then my terms are this: surrender now, and all but the Tsar may live."

The man stared at her for a long moment, his mouth

frozen open. Finally he seemed to shake himself free of his shock. "Pardon?"

"Do you need me to repeat them, sir?" she asked with a laugh. "I thought they were quite simple. Surrender, and you and your soldiers may live."

His face coloured, and baring his teeth, he took a step towards her. "I have not come to negotiate *our* surrender, witch," he spat, "but the surrender of you and your army of heathens!"

Merydith twisted her lips into a pout. "Oh, that *is* shame. You seem like such a *nice* man. Really, there's no need for you to die here. In fact, I'd rather not see anyone die today, it's such a beautiful morning." She paused. "Other than the Tsar, of course."

"The Tsar is immortal," the man snapped, "and I come under the flag of truce. You cannot kill me."

"Is that so?" Gesturing her guards to remain where they were, she stepped towards the man, her long legs eating up the distance between them. She looked at the white flag he carried. "You think your little flag protects you?" Her sword flashed out to rest against his throat.

The envoy jerked back, his legs stumbling on the uneven ground. With a cry he crashed onto his back. Merydith quickly planted her boot on his chest. Gently she touched her blade to his throat again. He had lost his grip on his flag, and Merydith bent down and picked it up.

"You know, another like you came before me under such a flag." Taking it by the haft, she slammed it into the earth beside his head. "I welcomed him into my city, honoured him as my guest. And how do you think your Tsar repaid me?"

"You...you can't!" the negotiator stuttered.

Lifting her sword, Merydith touched it to his lips, silencing him. "That man tried to kill me," she continued conversationally. "He took his sword and murdered my guards. His assassination almost succeeded. Now another comes before me with a white flag; what am I to do?"

There were tears streaming down the envoy's face now. He managed to blurt out several nonsensical words between sobs.

"Honestly, you're not much of a negotiator. I can't understand a word you're saying. Please, pray, speak more clearly."

The man stilled, his terrified eyes fixing on her. "I have only one message to deliver, witch," he said, his voice hoarse. "Surrender to the Tsar's mercy, and he shall spare half of your people."

Anger rose in Merydith's throat. Teeth bared, she pressed down with her blade, until blood ran from the man's cheek. Silently, she fought the urge to skewer him, aware her people were watching. Whatever crimes the Tsar had committed, she must not let herself sink to his level, lest she become the monster she fought to destroy.

With an effort to will, she withdrew her sword and stepped back. "We reject your terms. Northland will stand to the last against evil."

Turning, Merydith started back towards her people, leaving the man lying in the muck.

His words chased after her, echoing up the hill to the watchers beyond. "Then you will all burn!"

She glanced back, and saw him flinch from the rage in her eyes. "Then you will burn with us."

CHAPTER 35

It took a day and a night for the Stalkers to lead Quinn into the Tsar's camp. Quinn had been surprised to learn the army was already in Trola, but the other Stalkers had been able to ascertain the Tsar's location using their connection to him through their silver bracelets. Their horses were puffing hard by the time the sun broke over their company. Zarent signalled a halt as they topped a rise and looked down at the army camped in the valley below.

Sitting on his horse with his hands tied to the pommel, Quinn realised with a conflicted heart that they had arrived just in time to witness the final battle. Already the Tsar's forces were gathering at the head of the valley, above which the Queen had set her fortifications. An earthen rampart impeded Quinn's view of the rest of the camp, but several hundred soldiers could be seen waiting, their eyes on the army below.

"We're just in time," one of his former Stalkers said with a grin. "Maybe you'll get lucky, *Lieutenant*. The Tsar might send you to the front lines, to die with honour."

Quinn smiled darkly. "Maybe he'll send *you*."

The Stalker's eyes burned into Quinn. "If my Tsar

requires it of me, I will ride into battle with laughter on my lips."

"Of course you would," Quinn spat. "I doubt you've ever had an original thought in that tiny brain of yours."

The Stalker bared his teeth, but the boom of drums drew their attention back to the battlefield. On the hillside beneath the Northland army, a single figure could be seen retreating back to the mass of men and women camped in the valley.

"Guess the negotiations fell through," Quinn commented dryly.

"Let's go," Zarent snapped from the front, urging his horse forward.

Another Stalker held Quinn's reins, leaving him with no choice but to follow the others down the hillside. They rode down towards the camp, where a guard stationed on the outskirts moved to intercept them. The man quickly backed down, though, when he recognised the slick black uniforms of the Stalkers, and they continued on through the campsite, following the familiar layout that was used by the Tsar's army during all campaigns in hostile territory.

Anger coiled around Quinn's gut as they approached the massive tent erected in the centre of the camp. He wanted to hate the Tsar for this betrayal, to rage against Zarent and the other Stalkers, but in the end it was his own failure that had spelt his end. Yet again, the Tsar's children had eluded him. Now the time had come for him to face his judgement.

The other Stalkers dismounted outside the tent, but Quinn was forced to wait until Zarent came and cut his bonds. Clenching his fingers to restore their circulation, he glared down at the Stalker, before climbing from his saddle and joining the others on the ground. Two men took a firm grip on his shoulders and pushed him towards the entrance. Grinding his teeth, he shook them off and strode ahead of them.

Cursing, Zarent pushed past him and took the lead.

Quinn followed a step behind as they approached the Tsar's tent. Two guards stood outside, but they parted without hesitation upon sighting the black-garbed Stalkers. A third stood within, spear held at the ready. He retreated into the gloom to announce their arrival. A moment later he reappeared, and waved them forward.

Standing on the threshold, Quinn hesitated. For a moment he wondered whether he should flee, if he should summon his power and blast the Stalkers from his path, and use the chaos that ensued to disappear into the hills. Yet even as he considered it, he dismissed the idea. His doom might wait within the darkness of the tent, but it was a doom to which he had dedicated his entire life. Whatever his fate, Quinn could not abandon the Tsar now, not when he was so close to his final goal.

Besides, where would he go? The Queen, with her reckless defence of Magickers, was anathema to him, and Devon and his Baronian thugs were even worse.

Straightening his shoulders, Quinn strode into the gloom of the tent. Zarent marched eagerly at his side, while the others waited without. Inside, the tent was huge, and it took a moment for Quinn's eyes to adjust. Marble tiles, packed in an oaken trunk and carried by the army each day, covered the floor, their smooth white surfaces a stark contrast to the churned-up mud that was the rest of the camp. A massive poster bed stood on the far side of the tent, while two iron braziers burned to either side of them.

In the middle of the Tsar's quarters, the man himself sat at an ornate table fashioned from polished steel. He looked up as they entered, a frown on his face. There was a plate before him, heaped with steak and sliced potato. Finishing his mouthful, he sat back in his chair and steepled his fingers.

"Lieutenant," he said, ignoring Zarent. "I take it you have news for me."

Surprised at the Tsar's casual words, Quinn glanced at

Zarent. The other man said nothing though, just stood staring at the Tsar, his face hard. Clearing his throat, Quinn faced the table. "Ahh, no, sir, you ordered us to return?"

The Tsar stilled at his words, his brow knotting into a frown. "Did I?" he asked, his voice dangerously low. "And how, pray, did I do that?"

"You…you appeared to us, sir," Quinn replied, his stomach suddenly a knotted mess. "You ordered Zarent to take command, and bring me here to face your judgement…didn't you?"

"I did not," the Tsar rumbled.

Face dark, he came slowly to his feet. Quinn opened his mouth, searching for a way of explanation. Around him, the temperature in the tent plummeted, as though all substance were being drawn away. He staggered, his breath misting on the air as he struggled to inhale. Strength fled his muscles as the Tsar walked slowly around the table towards him.

"I…I…it was him!" Clutching at the lifeline that was the other Stalker, Quinn stabbed a finger at Zarent.

Zarent stood staring back, his face impassive, his sapphire blue eyes fixed on the Tsar. Quinn frowned, sensing a wrongness to the man…

"I grow weary of your ineptitude, Lieutenant," the Tsar grated as he came to a stop in front of Quinn. "I have been patient, given you chance after chance, but this final disappointment…it cannot be forgiven."

Blue fire appeared in his palm as he raised his hand. Its heat radiated through the tent, the only warmth in the suddenly frigid air. Quinn gasped, his mind racing, struggling to put sense to what the Tsar was saying.

"We…were tricked!" he gasped.

He tried to inhale, to regain his strength, but it was as though all substance had been drained from the air. His legs shook, and then collapsed beneath him, sending him toppling to the ground. Chest heaving, he looked up at the flame dancing in the Tsar's hand.

"Of course you were, Lieutenant," the Tsar murmured. "Now, goodbye."

"Don't!"

The Tsar swung around as a high-pitched voice shouted from across the tent. His eyes straining, Quinn struggled to find the speaker. He frowned, unable to make sense of the light swirling around Zarent. Then suddenly his vision seemed to clear and the lights faded away. Quinn blinked, struggling to comprehend what he was seeing. Zarent had vanished. In his place now stood the boy, Braidon, his arms folded and sapphire eyes burning with spent magic.

"Please, father," he said, taking a step towards the Tsar. "This is not his fault."

"My son," the Tsar said softly. The fire in his hands died as he faced the boy. "So it was *you* who tricked my lieutenant."

"I needed a way to find you."

The Tsar looked around, searching the tent. "And where, pray, is your sister?"

"Safely away from here," he replied.

"Really?" The Tsar's cocked his head. "That seems unlike her." He raised a hand.

"Stop!"

Quinn looked around as another voice spoke from the corner of the tent. For a moment, he saw nothing, and then Alana stepped forward, a swirling mist falling away from her as she moved.

"I'm here, Father," she said, her eyes on the floor.

"A happy reunion," the Tsar murmured, turning back to Braidon. "You impress me, my son. But pray, what sudden change of heart has brought my children before me?"

"We didn't come here to fight," Alana said, stepping towards the Tsar.

Before she could come close, he lifted a hand and pointed

it at her chest. The gesture froze her in place, and Quinn recognised the familiar look of panic on her face as the Tsar's power trapped her. Her mouth opened and closed, but nothing more than a squeak came out. Quietly, Quinn rose to his feet and edged backwards into the shadows.

"I spared your life at Enala's request, daughter, but you no longer play a part in this," the Tsar said. He turned back to Braidon, leaving Alana immobilised. "Now, why have you come, my son?"

Reaching into his belt, Braidon drew a short sword. He stared at the blade for a moment as though deep in thought. Then he tossed it aside.

"My sister thought we might take you by surprise," he said solemnly. "I never thought it would work." He took a step towards the Tsar. "I thought I would call on your mercy, instead."

"My mercy?" the Tsar murmured.

Braidon swallowed. "Yes, Father," he replied. "I know my past now, I've seen the truth. I know you love me, love both of us in your own way."

"And how do you know this, my son?"

"I remember…" Braidon's voice broke, and Quinn glimpsed tears in his eyes. "I remember a day you took me to the top of the citadel, and showed me our world. You told me that everything you did, you did it for us. Was it not true?"

Shadows hid the Tsar's eyes as he shook his head. "Ah, my son, how I have yearned all these years for you to stand at my side." Moving across the room, he knelt beside Braidon and placed a hand on the boy's shoulder. "I remember that day well. It was the day of my greatest despair, when I thought I had failed."

"What do you mean?"

"That was the day I learned the Sword of Light was not enough to accomplish what I desired, that I would need the power of the other Elements to succeed."

"But why did you despair? You had already claimed the power of one God as your own."

"Because I knew I did not have the strength to do what was needed."

Braidon swallowed. "You knew we would have to be sacrificed."

"Ay," the Tsar replied, standing. "On that day I discovered the true weakness of humanity: not magic or hate or war, but love."

"No," the boy murmured. He tried to take a step back, but the Tsar's magic bubbled through the air, freezing him on the spot.

"Yes," the Tsar whispered. "Fickle, relentless, *dangerous*, it was love that stopped me then. But not now, not ever again." Steel hissed on leather as the Tsar reached down and drew the Sword of Light and Earth.

"Father?" Braidon whispered, staring up at the man.

Tears shone in the Tsar's eyes as he towered over the boy. "Oh, my son," he said, his voice taut. "How this pains me, but I will not stop now. The stakes are too great. My enemies surround me, but with your death, their powers will be dust in the wind before us."

Fear showed on Braidon's face as he struggled in his father's bindings. "Please, you don't have to do this, Father!"

"But I do," the Tsar replied. He raised the Sword, studying the flickering green and white light emanating from the blade. "It is the only way. Jurrien will not possess your sister. Only you can host the God of the Sky. I am sorry, my son, but you must die to seal magic's fate."

CHAPTER 36

The Tsar's envoy had barely reached the bottom of the hill before the southern army began to move, its ranks advancing to the rhythmic stomping of boots. Merydith watched from her vantage point atop the earthen ramparts for a few moments, and then retreated beyond the line of Trolan defenders.

"Your mount, Your Majesty," Mokyre said, stepping forward and handing her the reins of her horse.

Merydith nodded her thanks and swung into the saddle. After taking a moment to adjust her buckler, she straightened. Around her, four thousand northern soldiers did the same. The soft whinny of horses whispered across the hilltop, coupled with the ring of steel and creaking of leather.

"Are we ready?" Merydith asked as Mokyre appeared alongside her, freshly mounted.

He nodded, and she turned to look for Betran. She found him standing nearby, his lips twisted in a grim frown. Edging her horse towards him, she shouted to draw his attention.

"Don't look so miserable, Betran," she called when he looked up. "The day is finally here that you get to spit in the face of the Tsar!"

"Oh I know it," said Betran, forcing a smile. "I'm just disappointed I don't get the first stab at him."

"Your time will come, my friend," Merydith replied, though she knew the man did not mean the words.

She glanced back to where the Northland clans were still forming up. Beyond the horses, she could just make out the red steeple of the Magickers' tent. The day's efforts would hinge on not just the courage of those on the battlefield, but on Helen and her people. If they failed, Merydith's gamble would fail with it, and they would all be left exposed to the Tsar's power.

From beyond the ramparts, a distant bugle call drifted up to them. One of the soldiers on watch glanced back at them, his eyes wide with fear. "They're coming!" he called.

Merydith nodded and lifted the gold-enamelled helmet from her saddle. She placed it on her head and then drew her sword. But as she opened her mouth to shout the order to advance, a cry came from behind her, followed by the *thump* of hooves approaching. She swung around, her determination giving way to sudden fear as she saw Damyn riding up.

His face was pale and streaks of red still stained his eyes, but he sat straight in the saddle, a sabre resting across his pommel. He wore no helmet, but his chainmail shone in the morning light. A smile touched his lips when their eyes met, and Merydith's heart gave another twang as she realised there would be no talking him out of joining the fight. Murdo came up behind him, his face more alive than she'd seen it in a decade.

"Save me from the folly of men," Merydith muttered under her breath as the two drew up beside her.

"Were you going to leave without me?" Damyn asked, his voice tight. There was still a greyness to his face, and she wondered where he'd found the strength to leave his stretcher.

Merydith edged her horse closer to the two. "Please don't do this, Damyn," she whispered, trying to keep the panic from her voice. She looked at Murdo, seeking an ally, but the old man only shook his head and gestured at Damyn.

"Please don't try and stop me, Merydith," he replied, his voice shaking slightly. "I can't…I can't just lie here and wait to find out what happens. If we…" His voice broke and he shook his head. "I have to do this."

Understanding touched Merydith as she saw the fear behind his eyes, and she nodded quickly. "Stay close, my guards will protect you." Before he could respond, she turned and lifted her sword once more. "For freedom!"

Trumpets rang out from their camp, and as one, the northern cavalry surged forward. Up the earthen rampart they raced, and down the other side where planks had been tossed across a section of the trench. Then they were on the open hillside for all to see, racing down towards their approaching foe.

Below, the Tsar's forces were already halfway up the hillside, but their charge faltered when they glimpsed the cavalry come pounding into view. The glee on their faces turned to sudden terror as realisation spread through their ranks. In their eagerness to reach the defenders, they had broken ranks and charged in open formation.

A grin touched Merydith's face as she urged her steed onwards, watching as the panic spread through the Tsar's ranks. The southerners had expected Merydith to hide behind her barricades and wait for them to come to her. Now they found themselves facing a charging horde, the frontmost soldiers were hurriedly staggering to a stop. Some even tried to turn back, but the ranks of soldiers coming up behind prevented them from fleeing the field.

As chaos descended on the southern army, Merydith swung towards the right, so that their charge would strike the enemy's flank. Sabre raised in one hand, the reins in the other, she shouted a cry as the last few yards vanished in the blink of an eye.

Then she was amongst them, her sword hacking and cutting, her momentum hardly faltering as her mount smashed aside a man and trampled him beneath iron-shod hooves. A crash like thunder echoed across the hillside as the rest of her cavalry struck, sweeping aside the leading ranks of footmen like leaves before the autumn winds.

Screaming a battle cry, Merydith charged on. Those beyond the first ranks were still struggling to link shields, and they collapsed inwards as she sliced through their midst. A desperate rage built in Merydith's chest as a man leapt at her, grabbing at her leg and trying to drag her from the saddle. Her sabre flashed down, half-severing his arm before dancing clear. Another cried out as she plunged it through his eye.

Suddenly her horse went down, but she leapt free of the saddle and rolled to break her fall. Surging to her feet, she deflected a wild blow from a charging soldier and then drove her blade into his chest.

Tearing it clear, she swung around and saw one of her men topple from his saddle. The horse reared, scattering the enemy, and she leapt for it. From the corner of her eyes she saw a scarlet-caped Plorsean raise his sword and begin to swing, then Damyn charged into view, and the man disappeared in a flash of hooves.

Catching the riderless horse by the reins, Merydith swung herself into the saddle. She nodded her thanks as Damyn pressed closer. Amidst the sudden calm, she looked around, surprised to find them deep in the enemy formation. Behind them was a broken field of corpses, while ahead the endless ranks of the Tsar's army stretched on towards his distant tent.

A shout came from away to their left, and glancing around, Merydith saw the leftmost ranks of the Tsar's force pressing forward to sweep across the hillside. If they succeeded, the northerners would be cut off from their camp, their flanks exposed. With the impetus of their charge broken, the Tsar's forces would be free to surround them, and cut them down at will.

Watching the advancing ranks, Merydith held her breath, and sent up a silent prayer to the Gods—and Helen. For a moment it seemed time stood still, and she sat there in silence, watching the slow advance of the soldiers as they crossed the hillside behind them, like a giant set of jaws stretching out to swallow the northern soldiers.

Then a *boom* echoed across the churned-up hillside. The sound swept through the battle like a ripple on a lake, as every man and woman paused to seek out its source. Confusion appeared on the faces of those around her, and even Damyn looked in the direction of the Tsar's tent with fear.

A terrible scream tore from the earth as the earthquake struck, hurling men and women from their feet. Merydith's horse screamed and bucked beneath her, but she dragged back on its reins, refusing to give it a second's control. Around her, the northerners struggled to do the same.

An ear-rending *boom* echoed across the battlefield like thunder, drawing the eyes of all to the hilltop. Together as one, they watched as the earth itself split in two, and a crack raced down towards the Tsar's army. Screams came from the men gathered there, but it was amongst them before any could regain their feet and flee. Like an axe parting a melon, it tore through the centre of the Tsar's forces, hurling hundreds into the void and continuing down the valley towards the distant camp.

Slowly the thunder of the earth faded away, to be replaced by the screams of the dying. Drawing back on the reins of her unfamiliar mount, Merydith brought the gelding under control. Her guards were already doing the same, and she glimpsed Damyn and Murdo nearby, their eyes on the damage Helen and her Magickers had wrought.

Steeling herself, Merydith turned to examine the aftermath of their magic. A gaping crevice now split the slope leading down from their camp, dividing the Tsar's forces clean in two. The left flank that had sought to encircle them was now trapped on the other side of the gulf.

Merydith looked back at the ranks ahead of them.

And smiled.

THE NEXT DAY found Devon and the Baronians on the road north. Corrie and his Trolans trailed behind them in broken clusters, unorganised and unprepared for the march to come. Within an hour, they were lagging well behind, and Devon was forced to call a stop and wait for the intermittent groups to catch up.

Watching them trail up the hill, he was reminded of Selina's words from the night before. He cursed beneath his breath as Corrie marched up with the last group. Overhead the sun was shining, its warmth already banishing the frost that had set in overnight.

"You're in a bad mood this morning," Joseph said as he joined Devon.

Devon mumbled something unintelligible, but the Baronian only laughed and slapped him on the back.

"Saw Selina leaving your tent last night," Quint replied. "That have anything to do with it?"

"The woman's got a way of getting under a man's skin," Devon grunted.

"That she does," the Baronian agreed. "Usually because she's right, of course."

"Well in that case, you might be interested to hear she wants me to lead all of you, and all of *them*." He waved in the general direction of the Trolans. "Against the Tsar's army."

"Wonderful," Joseph replied. "You think I could reconsider that mutiny?"

"You'd be more than welcome."

Joseph shook his head. "We're already on our way, aren't we?"

"Afraid so," Devon nodded.

"You know he has dragons, right?"

"Yes."

"And demons.

"Yup."

"Magickers too. Don't suppose Alana and her brother have shown up in the night?"

"No," Devon murmured.

Joseph drew his axe from his shoulders and gave it a practice swing. His face twitched, but otherwise his injury didn't seem to bother him. He took a moment to inspect the blade before turning back to Devon.

"You really think the Trolans will follow you?"

"We're about to find out," Devon muttered. Drawing *kanker*, he strode across to where Corrie was sitting with several other Trolans.

The man looked up as he approached, his face darkening. "What do you want, Butcher?"

Devon took a moment to inspect the man before allowing his gaze to travel on, taking in the half dozen men that surrounded him. "Listen up!" he bellowed, his voice carrying across the road to where the other Trolans were gathered. Several faces turned to stare at him. "I'm sure you've all heard about me by now."

"Ay, they've heard," Corrie growled, stepping in front of him. "But they don't need to hear *from* you."

"That's too bad," Devon snapped. Corrie opened his mouth to object, but Devon's hand flicked out, catching him by the shirt. He dragged him close and stared into his terrified eyes. "Listen up, sonny," he murmured. "Whatever you think of me, you can keep on thinking it. Tomorrow. But for today, the past, the future, they don't exist. Because if the Tsar wins, you'll all be dead. Trola will burn. Northland will burn. And there will be no one left to remember any of us. Understand?"

His eyes wide, Corrie's head jerked up and down.

Releasing him, Devon straightened and looked out over the gathered Trolans. "I know you hate me," he started. "I don't blame you. But as I just told your young leader here, today we must set aside our differences. Today, I am not the enemy." He lifted a hand to point the way ahead. "Today, our enemy is the Tsar, and he will destroy us all if we cannot stand together."

"What do you want from us, Butcher?" a voice called from the back of the crowd.

Devon sighed. "I am no king, no general," he replied, "but I understand our enemy, and how he works. These people behind me, they're Baronians." A whisper spread through the crowd at his words. Devon drew *kanker* and lifted it above his head. "*Silence!*" He bellowed. He pointed his hammer at the shocked watchers. "These Baronians, they have already fought against the Tsar, against his Stalkers, against his dragon. Together, we struck a blow against the enemy, and then fled through the mountains. They have followed me through hell and back, and they're still here. Do you know why?"

His gaze swept the gathered Trolans, but not a one of them spoke. He smiled.

"They're here because my name is Devon, and I do not lose."

A cheer erupted from the Baronians behind him as he thrust *kanker* skywards. Looking around, he glimpsed Selina standing amongst them, the slightest hint of a smile on her lips. She nodded as their eyes met, and grinning, he turned back to the Trolans. Silence fell as he lowered his weapon.

"Today, I march against the Tsar. Who will follow me?"

CHAPTER 37

Q uinn shivered as ripples formed around the Tsar, sheer energy pouring from his outstretched hands, seeming to bend the very fabric of reality. His chant whispered through the tent, incomprehensible, and yet it sent a tingling down to Quinn's very core. He could feel the magic building, coalescing around the boy in the centre of it all.

Sadness touched him as he looked at Braidon. Alana had always kept him at an arm's length from the boy, but seeing the terror in his steely eyes, Quinn felt a wave of pity for him. The boy had come here to call on his father's love. How it must pain him to see now it was not enough, that the Tsar would sacrifice everything he loved to bring about the change he sought.

Tearing his gaze from the boy, Quinn found himself looking at Alana. She barely seemed to notice him, so intent was she on her brother. Teeth bared, the veins on her neck bulging, she strained against the forces holding her in place. Quinn grinned despite himself, and crossed to where she stood.

"You cannot save him," he murmured. He circled her,

barely able to contain his glee at her sorrow. "You cannot even save yourself."

"Quinn," she whispered. "Please, he never did anything to you. Help him."

"Never," Quinn hissed. "The boy may be innocent, but you are not. You brought this on for the both of you, Alana. I—"

He broke off as the ground beneath his feet began to shake. Staggering sideways, he thrust out a hand, using Alana to steady himself. Locked in the Tsar's magic, she didn't so much as stumble. Slowly the shaking faded away, and he straightened. Quinn jerked back his hand as he realised he was still touching Alana and could have been influenced by her magic, but she only had eyes for her brother.

"What was that?" In the centre of the tent, the Tsar had broken off his chanting and was looking towards the Queen's army.

"Let me check," Quinn said quickly, springing to the doorway of the tent.

Ducking outside, he glanced at the stunned faces of the Stalkers, then at the battlefield. His jaw dropped as he took in the jagged tear in the hillside. Half the Tsar's force had been stranded on the green fields on one side, while those on the left were battling furiously with the mounted forces of the Northland Queen.

"What do we do?" one of the Stalkers was saying.

Quinn shook himself free of his shock and swung on the man. "Join the battle," he snapped, pointing up at the hill. "The Tsar is already engaged in the final summons. When he's done, the Queen and her people will be wiped from the field. In the meantime, make sure she's occupied."

His group of Stalkers stared at him, before one stepped forward, a sneer on his lips. "You forget yourself, Quinn," he said. "You're not lieu—"

He never got to finish his sentence, as Quinn's blade

plunged through his throat. Dragging back the sword, Quinn glared at the others. "Any other objections?"

As one, the remaining Stalkers turned and fled in the direction of the battle. Quinn followed their progress, wondering whether he should take the chance to escape. It was only a matter of time before the Tsar finished with his work and remembered Quinn's folly. Then there would be a reckoning, one which he was unlikely to survive.

Yet if the Tsar succeeded, there would be nowhere in the Three Nations Quinn could run that he would not be found. Closing his eyes, he returned to the darkness of the tent.

"What's happening out there?" the Tsar demanded. He was at the table now, an assortment of potions and herbs sprawled across its surface.

"The Queen's Magickers have struck. I sent my Stalkers to deal with them," Quinn said quickly.

The Tsar waved a hand, "The Queen will wait, this cannot." Returning to his concoctions, he began mixing ingredients into a mortar.

"Quinn, help me."

Quinn looked around as the boy's voice whispered through the darkness. Swallowing, he clenched his fists. Help him? The boy had tricked him, sentenced him to the same fate as his own. Teeth clenched, he watched as the Tsar worked, as outside the distant roar of voices and clashes of steel carried through the camp.

Finally the Tsar lifted the mortar and held the contents up to the light of a lantern. Nodding to himself, he moved across to where Braidon still stood frozen. He came to a stop before the boy, his face twisted in regret.

"I'm sorry it has to be this way, my son," he murmured.

Braidon's eyes flashed with sudden anger. "Just do it!" he snapped.

Nodding, the Tsar reached out and grabbed his son by the jaw. Forcing his head back, he poured half the contents of the mortar down Braidon's throat, then held his mouth and nose until he was forced to swallow. Then he moved away, and swallowed the remaining potion in one gulp.

The chanting resumed as the Tsar wandered the room, the Sword of Light and Earth now gripped firmly in his hand. Light flickered from the blade, at first brilliant and blinding, then dimming to barely more than a spark.

He returned to stand before the boy and gripped Braidon by the shoulder. His voice grew louder, and finally Quinn understood the words he spoke. Magic bubbled through the tent, and Quinn flinched back at its touch, his own magic boiling up in response. It gathered in the air between the Tsar and his son as the Tsar's voice boomed out:

"I summon you, God of the Sky." At his words, a moan rose up from Braidon's chest. He stiffened, his face taking on a look of terror as he sought to tear himself from his father's grip. "I summon you, Jurrien, return to this mortal realm," the Tsar continued. "I bid you, take host in this vessel, in the body of the man marked by the name Theo. Take his mortal body and return your immortal soul to this world."

Quinn's heart lurched forward at the Tsar's words. Standing there, he struggled to understand whether he'd heard them correctly. He took half a step forward, but the magic pressed against him, forcing him back. Stretching out a hand, he tried to call a warning, but it was already too late. With a triumphant shout, the Tsar slammed his hands together.

A blue light burst into life, blinding, crackling with untold energy. Quinn felt a part of himself respond, drinking it in, his magic exhilarating in the touch of its creator. He gasped as the power of the Storm God swept through him—and then went rushing away. Swirling about the room, the blue light coalesced into a single stream, flowing inwards to a point between the Tsar and his son.

Then with a flash, it vanished.

Letting out a long breath, the Tsar stepped back from Braidon and lifted the Sword of Light and Earth. Braidon stared back at him, his grey eyes shining with a new light, with the triumph of victory. A frown touched the Tsar's forehead as he looked around, saw the horror on Quinn's face, and the joy radiating from the eyes of his two children.

"What is it?" he growled.

"You...you said your own name," Quinn whispered.

The Tsar stared at him blankly, uncomprehending. Before he could respond, a harsh laughter rang through the tent, drawing their attention back to where Braidon stood. Except it was no longer Braidon who stood there.

It was Alana.

A smirk twisting her lips, she folded her arms and raised an eyebrow. "Surprised, boys?"

CHAPTER 38

Merydith cursed as her sword caught in the chest of an enemy soldier and was torn from her grip. Screaming, the woman fell back, but another leapt forward to take her place, his spear driving through the thigh of Merydith's horse. The beast screamed and fell, hurling Merydith from the saddle. She came up, dagger in hand, and braced herself as the spearman charged—only for one of her guards to run in and drive a sword through his heart.

Her guard scooped up a discarded blade and tossed it her way. She caught it by the hilt and spun to block a blow from another soldier. Her guard moved alongside her, but another spear came flashing from the ranks of soldiers, taking him in the throat. He staggered back, blood bubbling from the wound, and collapsed alongside her.

Sword and dagger in hand, Merydith killed the second spearman, then leapt back as three red-cloaked soldiers charged her. Movement came from her sides and Damyn and Mokyre stepped up. They had lost their horses as well, and a quick glance told Merydith most of her force were fighting on foot now.

Steel clashed as they met the Plorseans. Turning aside a stabbing sword with her buckler, Merydith lashed out with her adopted sword, catching her assailant beneath the arm. She dragged back the blade as the man cried out, staggering sideways into one of his comrades. Damyn took advantage of the confusion to finish them both, as Mokyre drove his blade through the heart of the soldier to Merydith's left.

Together they pressed forward into the ranks of southern soldiers, desperately trying to turn back the tide of scarlet and emerald. Despite being cut off from half their number, the Tsar's force still stood strong, and was now beginning to press them back. Inch by inch, the ragged front Merydith's people had formed was bowing beneath the pressure.

Only around their Queen did the northerners still stand their ground. But with both flanks bending back, the Tsar's soldiers were beginning to spread out around her force. If the line was not reinforced, their greater numbers would envelope her people in a ring of iron.

"Forward!" she called, desperately willing her people to hold.

A few of those nearby heard the call and hurled themselves into the battle with renewed fury, but those on the flanks were too far away. The line continued to bend, and she sensed the will of her army flickering, about to give.

Then a cry echoed down the hillside behind them. Merydith glanced back, her heart lifting as she saw Betran and his Trolans streaming down towards them. They split in two, reinforcing the flanks to either side of Merydith. With a roar, they hurled themselves into the battle, and the line straightened.

Merydith shared a grin with Damyn. "We're not done yet!" she shouted over the clash of blades, clapping him on the shoulder.

His face pale, Damyn nodded. Looking for all the world

like a dead man walking, he lifted his sword. "Haven't won yet either."

Nodding, Merydith gave his shoulder a squeeze and released him. Stepping back into line, she hurled herself at the enemy with renewed vigour. Damyn joined her, fighting mechanically now, while to her left Mokyre moved with a deadly efficiency. Each time his sword flashed out, an enemy fell back, more often than not clutching at some mortal wound.

Time stretched out unending, but for every southern soldier they slew, another was ready to step forward, fresh and ready for the fight. Hope withered in Merydith's heart as she realised they weren't going to break. The cavalry charge, the earthquake, the Trolan reinforcements, none of them had succeeded in shattering the enemy spirit. Still outnumbered two to one, the only thing the rebels had left to give was their lives.

Merydith's only consolation was the Tsar had not attacked. In splitting his army in two, Helen and her people had burned through most of their strength. Now every man and women on the hillside lay exposed to the Tsar's power.

And yet he had not sought retribution.

Struggling to catch her breath, she stepped back from the line, nodding as another soldier took her place. She looked out over the heads of the enemy, to where their camp stretched out down the valley. The Tsar's tent was easily seen from her vantage point, but it remained silent, dark. A shiver touched her as she looked at the men and women fighting below. Clearly, the Tsar would rather spend their lives to destroy her, rather than waste his own power on so trivial a matter.

A cry went up from the wall of soldiers ahead, and then Damyn was staggering back, Murdo draped over his shoulder. Her heart lurched as she raced forward and helped lower the old man to the ground.

"Murdo!" she called, looking around for someone to carry him back to the camp.

But his eyelids were already fluttering closed, and with a long, rattling exhalation, he died. A sob tore from Merydith's chest as she scrunched her eyes closed, her hand locked in a death grip around the old man's shirt.

"*Damnit!*" she screamed.

In a rage she lurched to her feet and threw herself at the line of soldiers. Her blade flashed as she tore into the enemy. She felt the satisfying crunch of flesh giving way to steel, and watched as a man crumpled beneath the blow. Dragging back her weapon, Merydith advanced.

Men and women launched themselves at her with renewed fury, but her sword and dagger were like extensions of her own body now, their blades flashing out to steal away the lives of her enemies. Decades of training at the hands of Enala flowed through Merydith, turning her into a living weapon that sent opponents falling back in dismay.

But the battle had been raging for hours now, and even she could not last forever. As she began to slow, a man lurched forward, his sword opening up a cut on her arm. Crying out, she drove her dagger through his neck and staggered back. Mokyre leapt to her defence, his sword slamming into the thigh of the next soldier in line.

Gasping, Merydith straightened, surprised to find herself edged on either side by Trolan soldiers. Her gaze travelled back, taking in the scores of Northlanders lying fallen in their wake, the enemy staked high around them.

As she watched, her people on both flanks were thrust aside, and the Tsar's army rush through the gap.

"No," she whispered.

But it was already too late. With the flanks collapsing around them, her dwindling force was pressed back on itself, and surrounded within moments. Shields raised, the enemy launched themselves at their rear.

"Fighting square!" Merydith cried out, desperate now.

The men and women around her moved quickly, those on the flanks and rear of the force spinning to meet the threat. Many of her people had taken up shields from the enemy, and joining ranks, they presented a united front against the mass of humanity surrounding them. As one, the last of the northern army stood and faced the enemy gathering around them.

Her heart hammering, Merydith spun, seeking a way out. Less than two thousand men and women stood with her now. Trolans and Northlanders together as one, they showed no sign of fear as they faced the Tsar's soldiers, though they knew now there was no way out.

Movement came from the ranks of soldiers ahead of Merydith as their line parted, emitting the Tsar's envoy to the front. The two forces were separated now by several yards, and wearing a slick smile, the envoy took a step towards their line. Coming to a stop beside the body of a Northlander, he stared down at the corpse, then back at her.

"Tell me again, Queen, how we will all burn?" he asked softly.

Hatred for the man burned in Merydith's heart. She took a quick step forward and hurled her dagger. The smile on the envoy's face faltered as her blade embedded itself in his unprotected chest. He staggered sideways, looking down at the dagger in disbelief. Without another word, he slumped to the ground beside the dead Northlander.

"Who's next?" Merydith screamed, gesturing at the ranks of Plorsean and Lonian soldiers with her sword.

Not a soul spoke, but with a rattle of steel shields, the front ranks swept closed. A harsh crash rang out as they started forwards.

It was as though a bucket of cold water had been poured over Merydith's rage. Stepping back into line, she lifted her sword and readied herself. The gap between the two forces narrowed, the southern soldiers silent but for the trod of their boots. There were no battle cries or jeering now. The Northland army and their Trolan allies had paid for their respect in blood.

Smoothly, the lines came together, and the screams of the dying resumed.

CHAPTER 39

S tanding on the edge of the valley, Devon looked down at
the battle raging below. The roar of a thousand voices
whispered up to his vantage point, more like the buzz of
insects than the sound of men and women dying. The
morning on the road had stretched out, their progress slowed
by the older members of the Trolan party. Now that they
were finally here, Devon feared they may already be too late.

Below, a great fissure divided the battlefield in two. On
one side, a great force could be seen on the march, seeking to
find a way across to the battle raging on the other side. From
what Devon could see, the crevice stretched out down the
valley for well over a mile, dividing even the massive camp
that had been set back from the battle.

On the side closest to Devon, the Queen's force stood
surrounded by a sea of red and green cloaks. His heart
pounded in his chest as he watched the Tsar's army surge
forward, slamming into the ranks of the defenders and
pressing them back upon one another. If something didn't
change, the Queen would be overwhelmed within the hour.

"Still planning on helping out?" Joseph asked from
beside him.

Stepping back from the edge, Devon turned and looked back at the thousand men and women gathered behind him. Their numbers had swollen as they came across more stragglers heading for the battle. Now, Baronians and Trolans alike watched him with fear in their eyes. They had not yet seen what waited below, but they could hear the distant screams, the bellowing of trumpets.

They had followed him this far, but he was still unsure whether they would take the final step, if they could set aside their grievances and find common cause with himself and the Baronians. Now though, the time had finally come to find out.

"The battle has been joined," Devon called out. "The Tsar's army has been sundered, but a mighty force still remains. They have the Queen and her people surrounded."

A nervous whispering spread through his followers, but he raised a hand, his eyes fixing them with a glare. Silence fell, and he went on.

"She is not finished yet. *We* are not finished yet."

Devon sucked in a lungful of air and drew *kanker* from its sheath. Looking out at the faces of those who had followed him across the mountains and through these rolling hills, he wondered how it had come to this. These men and women were farmers and potters, bakers and butchers—not soldiers. This was not their life, not their calling. And yet they looked at him with trust in their eyes, believing he would guide them through the coming storm.

Standing amongst the crowd, Selina's lips moved, mouthing the words: *Lead them.*

"I know many of you don't want to be here." The words were out of his mouth before he had time to consider what he was saying. "I know you would rather be safe in your homes, back with your families, anywhere but on this barren hillside. This isn't your place, but you're here anyway, ready to lay down your lives for what you believe in."

"And what do *you* believe in…Devon?" Corrie's voice emerged from the crowd of faces.

Devon smiled. "Love, life, a future for us all," he said simply, lifting *kanker* up in the sunlight. "This is *kanker*. You know it well. With it, I carved my name into your legends. But a legend needs an ending. Today, we will carve that ending in the blood of your enemies, and write a new future for the Trolan nation."

An eerie silence fell over the hillside as he lowered his weapon. All eyes seemed to shift to Corrie. The young man stared back at Devon, his eyes shining. Swallowing visibly, he reached down and drew his sword.

"For Trola!" he cried.

"*For Trola!*" the call echoed off the hillside, lifting Devon up, feeding him strength.

He shared a glance with Corrie. Then he turned and strode over the edge of the hill into the valley beyond.

And a thousand warriors followed after him.

CHAPTER 40

Exhilaration swept through Alana as her brother's illusion melted away, revealing her to the room. Across from her, she watched her own face flicker, then vanish, revealing Braidon standing in her place. Beside her brother, horror was written across Quinn's face. Her father still stood poised in shock, struggling to comprehend what she'd just wrought.

She flashed him a smile. It had been so simple in the end. All she'd needed was physical contact, and just the slightest nudge with her magic. Anything more, and her father might have sensed her power, even through Braidon's illusion. But changing one word, one name, and her magic had slid by undetected.

And instead of inviting the Storm God into his son's body, the Tsar had summoned Jurrien into his own.

Alana watched with growing amusement as realisation came to her father.

"You…how?" he stammered.

Almost immediately, rage replaced his shock, and raising the Sword, he started towards her. Before he could complete a step, however, a brilliant light flashed from his eyes, and he staggered sideways, a cry tearing from his lips.

"*No!*" he screamed, clutching at his skull, as though that could possibly save him from the Storm God.

"Not so fun now, is it Father?" she hissed, stepping towards him. "It's not fun, having someone else in your head. How does it feel, when it's *you* being controlled, when it's *your* mind being burnt away?"

Her father had sunk to his knees now. Another scream whipped the canvas as the Sword of Light and Earth slipped from his fingers. He scrambled for its hilt, but she kicked it away, and then drove her boot into his face, flipping him onto his back. Plucking her dagger from where she had tossed it while disguised as Braidon, she crouched beside him.

Groaning, the Tsar looked up and saw her kneeling there. "Please, daughter, help me!" His eyes flickered, the sapphire blue deepening for half an instant.

"Help you?" she hissed, pressing the dagger to his throat. "You were going to *destroy* me, to sacrifice my brother, *your own son*, all for what? So you could have ultimate power? And now, now you dare ask for my help?"

"Please," he choked, and Alana laughed in his face.

"Nothing was ever enough for you, was it Father? No matter how hard I tried, I was never strong enough, never fast enough, never smart enough. All my life, I tried to satisfy you, but now I see it was your own twisted pain that held us apart. You were always second-best to Eric's son, weren't you? To the *true* Magicker in the family. And even when you killed him, you still couldn't achieve what you had planned. Even with all the powers you had accumulated, even with the Sword of Light, still you wanted more." She laughed, the sound harsh and unforgiving.

She stood and stared down at him. "And where is your power now, father? Even after everything you have achieved, you are *nothing* to the Gods."

Her father stilled at her words. His eyes flickered again as he stared up at her, and with an effort of will he pulled himself to his knees. "You're wrong, Alana," he whispered. "I only ever wanted to save us."

"You wanted to save yourself."

"No..." he groaned, his eyes scrunching closed. "I can... feel him, taking control." He looked up at her again, open panic on his face now. "You can't let him live. He must...not, my daughter. His rage...he will destroy all of it, everything I have created."

"You have created nothing, Father," Alana hissed. "Besides, I have met Antonia. She only ever wanted to help us."

"The Storm God is not Antonia..." The Tsar swayed on his knees. "You think he will show you mercy, after what we have done to his siblings?"

"We?" Alana cried. "It was *you* who killed them!"

"Even so..."

The Tsar dragged himself to his feet. Air hissed between his teeth as he stood there. Alana could sense the power building within him now, the raw energies of the Storm God. Her father was fighting Jurrien with everything he had, no doubt draining the energies from all those in his thrall...but even the Tsar could not fight the power of creation.

"Goodbye, Father," she whispered, stepping back from him.

"Goodbye," Braidon echoed.

"Please, Alana——"

Her father's words were cut off as he stiffened, his eyes darkening to the deep blue of the Storm God. Lightning materialised around him, coalescing in his fingertips, staining the tent white. A howling wind came swirling from nowhere, tearing the tent poles from the earth and flinging the canvas skywards. The Tsar's guards cried out as the black fabric slammed into them, hurling them from their feet.

Standing so close, Alana was forced to her knees by the power of the wind. The temperature plummeted as rain hissed into existence and then froze in an instant. Ice lashed at her face as she strained to see through the swirling vortex that had appeared around her father. Amidst the tempest, she could still see the glow of his eyes, sense the rage that burned behind them. Her ears popped as the pressure built.

"*Where are my siblings?*" The words came from the Tsar's mouth, but it was no longer her father's voice. They boomed across the camp, freezing all who heard it in place.

"Jurrien, we are not your enemies!" Alana had to yell to be heard.

"*Where is my sister? Where is my brother?*" the Storm God screamed.

"Here!" a voice cried from behind the God.

Squinting through the vortex, Alana saw Quinn the second before he acted. The warning was on her lips as he lifted the Tsar's Sword from the ground and leapt. White and green rippled from the blade as it slammed into Jurrien's back.

In an instant, the lightning vanished, the roar of thunder dying away. The wind fell to a whisper, and the soft patter of falling sleet whispered in Alana's ears. Light flashed from her father's eyes one last time as his brow wrinkled in surprise.

A final *boom* sounded, then her father's body slumped to the ground, the blade that had ended his life tearing free.

Mouth wide, Alana stared as Quinn lifted the Sword, his face lit by the flickering white, green, and blue of its power.

CHAPTER 41

F ully engaged with the Queen and her soldiers, the Tsar's forces didn't notice Devon barrelling down on them until he was just a few yards away. At the last second, a shout went up from a scarlet-cloaked soldier, but there was no time for them to re-form, and bellowing a war cry, Devon brought his hammer down on the man's skull. The rest of his people followed him, the momentum of their charge driving them deep into the disorganised ranks of the enemy's rear.

Reversing his swing, Devon smashed *kanker* into the chest of another soldier, hurling the man from his feet. Striding into the gap he'd created, Devon lashed out around him, each swipe of his weapon downing another soldier. His people poured into the gap after him, forming a wedge with Devon at its tip.

Then Joseph was alongside him, Selina on the other, and together the three of them sliced forward through the Tsar's forces. Already he could see men beginning to panic, their courage strained to breaking point by the new turn of events. On his left, Joseph was like death itself, his twin-bladed axe rising and falling with terrifying proficiency, while Selina seemed to dance through the southern soldiers like grace embodied. They fell to her blade all the same.

In the ranks ahead, frightened soldiers tried to pull back, terrified of finding themselves crushed between the Queen and this new threat. Beyond, Devon glimpsed the Queen herself. Wearing her gold-embossed half-helm, she hefted a sword in each hand and led her people against the mass of soldiers separating them, fury written across her face.

Throwing himself back into the fight, Devon was swallowed up by the fury of combat. His thoughts, his heartbeat, everything fell away before the rhythm of the battle. A screaming man came at him and died, then another and another, each falling to a single blow.

Joseph and Selina struggled to stay with him as he surged forward, forcing the Tsar's soldiers back. Selina staggered as a blade sliced her arm, but Joseph downed the man with a swing of his axe. Towering over Selina, he dragged her back to her feet.

Devon was barely aware of his comrades' plight. As they pressed the enemy back, his eyes alighted on the black tent peaking up from the campsite. His heart beat faster as he recognised the tent of the Tsar from his days in the civil war. It was there that the battle would be won or lost. Why had the man not acted yet…?

A flash of blue light suddenly lit the distant tent, then a clap of thunder seemed to shake the very earth. Around Devon, men and women froze, turning to stare at the distant campsite. As they watched, the Tsar's tent seemed to lift from its support, as some invisible force hurled it skyward and then sent it crashing down again some half-mile away.

There was a moment's silence as the opposing forces stood staring at the scene in shock. Unsure of what would come next, they stood waiting for the Tsar to show himself, to hurl his wrath down on the Queen and her allies.

But nothing came, and hefting his hammer, Devon shouted a cry.

"Get em!"

It might not have been the most creative speech, but around him the Trolans and Baronians roared and threw themselves at the enemy. Still stunned by their Tsar's absence, the southern soldiers fell back in disarray. An echoing shout went up from the Queen as the Northland army pressed the attack from the other side.

Leaping forward, Devon pushed ahead once more, carving a path through the gathered bodies. For a moment it seemed as though the enemy would hold. Then a man appeared before Devon, his eyes wide with terror. Glimpsing the giant warrior descending on him, he gave a terrified scream and threw down his sword.

"Run!"

His scream carried through the Tsar's ranks like the plague as others picked up the call. Suddenly, what had been a battle turned into a rout, as half the enemy turned tail and fled. Those who remained found themselves alone, surrounded. Devon's people swarmed over them like ants, and they vanished beneath hacking swords and axes.

Across the battlefield, the Queen's soldiers chased the fleeing men, driving them back towards the camp. Men and women stumbled amidst the tents, tripping over canvas lines and scattering ashes from the morning's campfires. Flames leapt up amongst the broken army, and smoke swirled through the valley on broken winds.

Stumbling to a stop, Devon gasped, taking a moment to catch his breath. His people swept on around him, harrying the fleeing enemy, but he remained where he was. Looking back over the ground they had crossed, a chill spread to his stomach at the death he had left in his wake. Bodies covered the churned-up ground, many still moving, their desperate cries sounding on deaf ears. Hundreds of Trolans and Baronians lay amongst the fallen, but the Tsar's losses numbered in the thousands. Bile rose in his throat, and scrunching his eyes closed, Devon sank to his knees.

Baronians rushed past him, screaming their triumph. They leapt on the backs of fleeing soldiers and bore them to the ground. Overcome by their sudden victory, the Trolans ran with them, hacking and slashing at anyone they could find wearing the colours of Lonia or Plorsea. Scores of unarmed enemy were torn apart as they tried to surrender.

Horrified, Devon staggered back to his feet and bellowed an order. "Stop!"

But his cried went unheeded amidst the chaos, and the slaughter continued unabated.

"So the sheep become wolves," Joseph said, stumbling up beside him.

Devon was about to snap at the man, when the Baronian slumped to his knees. The words stuck in Devon's throat as he caught the man by the shoulder and knelt alongside him.

"What happened?" he asked urgently.

"Didn't see the bastard," Joseph coughed. Blood splattered his beard as he slumped into Devon's arms. "Got 'em though. We'll walk the dark path together, he and I."

"No, sonny," Devon growled. "Not today." Desperately he looked around, searching for help, but his slaughtering forces had moved on, chasing after the fleeing Plorseans.

Then movement came from nearby, and he let out a breath of relief as Selina appeared. She still carried her sword and blood coated her jerkin, but none of it appeared to be hers. She moved quickly through the corpse-strewn battle-ground and crouched alongside Devon. Ignoring him, she lifted Joseph's shirt, revealing the tear in his chainmail, and the gaping wound beneath. Blood pulsed down his side, feeding his life to the grassland.

"You were careless, axeman," she murmured, replacing his shirt.

"Too busy keeping an eye out for the boss," he grunted.

"Can you help him?" Devon snapped, lowering Joseph to his back.

Selina shook her head. Her lips twisted in a frown, she gently brushed the hair from Joseph's face. "No, Devon. He's not long for this world." Her eyes flickered up, looking from Devon to the distant screams. "But you are needed elsewhere."

Devon shivered at her words. Looking out at the slaughter, he shook his head. "You were right."

"No, I was wrong," Selina murmured sadly. Devon looked at her sharply, and she went on. "The farmers were as quick to the slaughter as you or I."

"Rubbish," Joseph coughed, blood dribbling down his cheek. "You...watch. Devon'll...lead 'em...home."

Devon squeezed the man's shoulder. "Thank you, Joseph," he said, "for giving me a place in this world."

Joseph forced a grin. "You're welcome, boy." He groaned, his face scrunching with pain. "Oh..." he murmured, "were I...a gambling man...I'd say your woman...had something to do with that." He extended a finger to indicate the Tsar's ruined tent.

Devon's heart clenched at the man's words. Staring out over the campsite, he held his breath, trying to catch a glimpse of what was going on. For a second, he saw flashing lights amongst the tents, but it quickly died back to nothing.

"He's right, Devon," Selina murmured, touching his shoulder.

"Go save the lass," Joseph breathed.

Devon stood. "If you knew her like I did, you'd know she doesn't need saving." His head whipped around as thunder crashed in the camp. "But perhaps she might need a hand."

CHAPTER 42

"Quinn, what are you doing?" Alana whispered, staring at the Sword.

He seemed to take a long time to hear her words. Lowering the blade, he looked at her, a frown touching his forehead.

"Alana…" He said her name like it was foreign to him, as though he had all but forgotten her. Then his eyes hardened, and the Sword came up again, pointing at her from across the tiles that were all that remained of her father's tent. "You betrayed me!"

Instinctively, Alana hurled herself to the side. A bolt of lightning arced towards her and struck the tiles with an awful *boom*. Shards of marble sliced Alana's face as she rolled across the ground and came to her knees. Reaching for her sword, she swung around, readying herself for another attack.

But Quinn was standing staring at the Sword again, as though surprised by what he'd done. "Incredible," he murmured.

"Quinn, I am not your enemy," Alana shouted.

"No?" He glared at her, his eyes shining with the power of the Sword. "Then why are you the source of all my pain?"

Baring his teeth, he pointed the sword again. Alana tried to hurl herself aside once more, but it was not lightning that came for her this time. Vines tore through the tiles, rushing upwards to envelop her. Winding around her limbs, they lifted her from the ground and bound her tight. Suspended in the air, she watched as Quinn approached.

"Everywhere I look, everywhere I go, I find you, haunting me. Even when I thought you dead in an alleyway somewhere, there you were, fleeing with your brother across Plorsea. Even when I saved you from yourself, from your own father, you betrayed me, rejected me. And for what? That... that bumbling *brute?*"

Alana strained against the vines, but they held her like steel shackles. Slumping into their grasp, she looked at him with disgust. "I am not some prize for you to win, Quinn. All these years, I thought you were my friend."

"I *loved* you," Quin growled, his face just inches from hers. "I would have done *anything* for you."

"You're sick," Alana hissed. "Twisted, if you think this is what love is."

Quinn shook his head. "You still do not see." He lifted the Sword, his eyes drinking in its power. "But I do. I see *all* of it now. This thing, it is knowledge purified, the very essence of creation." He grinned at her. "Your father was a brilliant man, you know? I read of these blades, when I was young: Archon's greatest creation. But your father perfected them. Where your ancestors struggled with their powers, this Sword leaps to do my bidding."

A shout came from behind them, as forgotten, her brother charged at him. Quinn spun, and a burst of flame rushing out towards Braidon. Crying out, he vanished, and the flames caught only empty air. Reappearing beside Quinn, he leapt for the Sword.

"Braidon, *no!*" Alana screamed.

Alerted by her cry, Quinn turned back. His fist caught

Braidon in the forehead and hurled him to the ground. A gesture from the sword, and fresh vines sprang from the earth to bind him in place. Quinn stood over him a second, sword poised.

"Don't," Alana whispered. "Please."

Shaking himself, Quinn looked at her, a look of bewilderment in his eyes. "I wouldn't hurt the boy," he murmured.

"Thank you," she said, watching as he approached.

"I'm not evil, Alana," he replied. "You don't see it yet, but you will."

He lifted the Sword and held it in front of Alana's face. She squeezed her eyes closed, but even then its light burned dots in her vision.

"Please, don—"

Alana's words were cut off as the cold steel touched her forehead. A gasp tore from her as the Earth magic of the Sword entered her, burning into her mind. Like a wolf tracking its prey, it twisted through her thoughts, hunting out her memories, her consciousness, trapping them in bands of fire. She screamed as the flames swelled, as she felt her mind being consumed.

Unlike her own power, the God magic sought not to trap her memories and lock them away, but to erase them, to scorch them from her consciousness forever. It was like a holy fire, burning away all that its master considered blasphemy.

Tears streamed down Alana's face as she watched, helpless, as her memories of Devon burnt. His rescue, his bravery, his love, all of it was incinerated by the unyielding fire of the Sword. She screamed as her brother was enveloped, as Enala's weathered face was torn from her. Every piece of hope, of goodness she had kept locked away, was hunted out without mercy, condemned to the flames.

She sobbed as that other part of her, the one who had loved and grieved and felt joy, was murdered before her eyes, cried out until all that was left was the hard, unyielding woman her father had shaped her to be.

"There…" Quinn murmured, stepping back. "Now, we shall see."

Alana slumped to the ground as the vines unravelled from her arms and legs. She landed lightly, looking around to see her father's body, his blood pooling slowly on the marble tiles. She crouched beside him. With the loss of his magic, his face had aged, his hair turning white. Yet there was no mistaking the man who had raised her, who had fashioned her into the woman she was today.

"You always were a fool, Father," she said.

As she straightened, Alana saw the boy lying nearby, unconscious and still wrapped in vines. She felt a pang of recognition, but as she looked at his face, she could not recall ever seeing him before. A sword lay nearby and she collected it before turning to face Quinn. Blood stained the flickering blade he carried.

"So, you killed him?" she asked, gesturing at the Tsar.

The lieutenant shrugged, a weary grin on his lips. "It needed to be done."

Laughter bubbled up from Alana as she looked at the destruction around them. "You don't say?"

She moved to Quinn and wrapped her arms around his waist. Standing so close to the Sword, she could feel its power bathing them both. The Earth magic at its core called out to her own, and she moaned as her own magic rose in response, filling her with the ecstasy of her power. Standing on her toes, she pulled Quinn down into a kiss.

Electricity leapt between them as their lips met, raising every hair on Alana's body. She gasped as Quinn drew her hard against him. Her hands danced along his back, tempting him to greater passions.

Then she paused, noticing the distant sounds of battle, the cry of voices drawing nearer. She pulled back from Quinn and looked around. The tents closest to them had been flattened by some explosion, giving them a clear view of the battlefield beyond the campsite. There, Plorsean and Lonian soldiers could be seen fleeing the field, as Northland soldiers gave chase.

"What is going on?" she murmured.

Before Quinn could reply, movement came from the nearby tents, and a giant of a man stepped into the open. The breath froze in Alana's throat as his amber eyes caught her gaze. She watched his features twist in surprise, even as her own heart leapt in her chest. In her arms, Quinn tensed, and she glanced at him, surprised to see the sudden hatred in his features.

"You're too late, Devon," he laughed. "She's mine." He pushed Alana aside and lifted the Sword of the Gods.

Across the clearing, the man called Devon hurled himself to the ground as lightning slammed into the earth where he had been standing. Moving faster than she would have believed possible for such a large man, he recovered and charged at Quinn. He carried a warhammer with glowing runes carved into its head. With a bellow of rage, he swung at Quinn.

The Sword leapt to meet him, and sparks flew as the weapons collided. A concussion erupted where they met, leaving the men untouched but hurling Alana from her feet. She rolled across the marble tiles and came to one knee, a snarl on her lips. Gaining her feet, she hefted her sword and started towards the intruder.

A harsh shriek sliced the air as the weapons met again, but this time Alana braced herself and remained standing. Devon leapt back as Quinn attempted to slice his head from his shoulders. As he moved, his eyes turned to her. Alana froze in place at the warmth she saw reflected there. She clutched at her chest as something tore in her heart, and closed her eyes, struggling to draw breath.

The sound of battle resumed, the crackling of flames filling her ears, but Alana did not open her eyes. Standing fixed in place, she swayed on her feet, struggling to comprehend the sudden emptiness swirling at her core. The sight of Devon had set her mind adrift, filling her with an awful pain, a loss she couldn't begin to explain.

Across the marble tiles the two men battled. For a moment it seemed the giant warrior might have the best of Quinn. His hammer slammed into the Sword again and again, its shining head absorbing whatever attacks Quinn hurled his way—magic or otherwise. The power in his blows forced Quinn to retreat, his own blade barely keeping measure of the giant.

Then with a curse, Quinn leapt back out of the giant's range. He lifted the Sword and pointed it at Devon. "Your legend ends today, Devon," he screamed.

A beam of pure energy went screeching from the blade, flashing across the tent to strike at the giant. His hammer lifted in response, catching the assault in a tempest of swirling energy. For a moment the energies seemed to vanish—then the hammer started to glow, and a sharp shriek filled the air. Cracks spread through the hammer like the threads of a web, and with an awful *pop*, the weapon shattered into a thousand pieces.

The forces unleashed from the weapon lifted Devon from his feet and hurled him backwards. He landed with a *thud* on the marble tiles and lay still, his desperate gasping the only sign he still lived.

The breath caught in Alana's throat as Quinn strode across the tiles to stand over Devon.

"Did you really think some old spell would protect you from the power of the Gods?" he asked.

Groaning, Devon struggled to sit up, but the giant's prodigious strength seemed to have given up, and he slumped back to the ground. Wheezing, he ignored Quinn and looked again at Alana.

"*Run, princess,*" he whispered.

The hackles on the back of Alana's neck stood up at his words. She opened her mouth and closed it, her heart racing, though for the life of her she could not say why. Her man had defeated the brute, and now stood poised to take the world. What did she care for the barbarian lying at Quinn's feet?

Yet, each time his amber eyes met hers, she felt something stir within her. And when he had called her 'princess'…

The light in Devon's eyes faded as he saw her stand there, unmoving. He looked back at Quinn. "What have you done to her, Stalker?" he whispered.

"I restored her true self," Quinn replied. "Returned her to the Alana I knew before *you* spoiled her."

"You'll pay—" Devon tried to sit up, but a vine erupted from the ground beneath him, catching him by the throat and dragging him back down.

Blood pounded in Alana's ears as she listened to them, her mind a whir. What was Quinn talking about? What had he done to her? Sensing her panic, magic leapt to her fingertips. It bubbled through her veins, drawing her inwards, seeking out the change Quinn claimed to have wrought, searching for her missing memories.

But there was nothing.

Nothing locked away, nothing hidden, nothing shielded.

Yet as she searched, Alana could sense a loss, a void within, as though something she loved more than life itself had been stolen away. She shuddered and looked back at the two men, at the grizzled face of the giant who had called her 'princess.' For half an instant, she caught a glimpse of him on his knees in a throne room, a dead man in his arms.

"Will I?" Quinn was saying. His laughter rang out across the campsite. "Tell me, Devon, how will you make me pay?"

Devon groaned as the vine tightened around his throat.

He clutched at it with meaty fingers, trying to tear it free, but more erupted from the earth. Thorns appeared along their lengths, ripping at his flesh as they wrapped around his muscular limbs. A scream tore from his throat, but he was helpless before Quinn's magic.

"Quinn, stop!"

The two men turned to look at her, Quinn's eyes wide with surprise. Unable to believe she'd spoken, Alana's own mouth hung open. She watched as the surprise on Quinn's face turned to anger. Looking back at Devon, he lifted the Sword.

"Still you corrupt her," he hissed, "but no longer. Good-bye, Devon."

With a cry of rage, Quinn drove the Sword down.

CHAPTER 43

W rapped in the steely vines, his body in agony, all Devon could do was watch as Quinn lifted the Sword above his head. In that moment, he was surprised to find there was no fear, only a deep regret that in the end, he couldn't save the one thing that mattered to him. He had promised Alana once that he would protect her, that he would keep her safe from the Tsar and his Stalkers. But he had failed.

Quinn had taken her, had used his newfound magic to wipe away the ferocious woman Devon loved, and replaced her with a monster. Lying there, he wondered whether he would find that other Alana in the afterlife, if she had a soul all of her own, and if they would walk the dark road together. Or was she tangled up in the woman standing beside Quinn, bound forever within, doomed to witness the atrocities her twin would commit in her name?

With all his heart, Devon hoped it was the former. But as the Sword came rushing down, he knew he might never know the answer. Closing his eyes, he waited for the end to come.

And waited.

Devon frowned as he realised silence had fallen over the world.

Then he heard Quinn's agonised whisper. "Alana, *why?*"

His eyes snapped open to find Alana standing over him. She stood facing Quinn, hands clutched in front of her. Devon's eyes slid down her back, and the tip of the Sword impaling her. Light still flickered along its blade, stained red by the blood coating its length.

Releasing the Sword, Quinn staggered back, his mouth wide with horror.

"*Why Alana?*" Quinn screamed, stretching out an arm as though he might mend the wound with his hands alone.

Blood pouring down her back, Alana staggered, and then straightened. Her hands reached up to grip the hilt of the Sword, as though to draw it from her. She lifted her head to look at Quinn. Sorrow laced her voice as she spoke.

"You took something from me," she whispered. "Now I'm going to take something from you."

"No…" he said, stepping towards her, still reaching for her. "I can save you!"

"Never," she snapped.

One hand still clenched about the hilt of the Sword Quinn had driven through her stomach, she threw out her other arm. Lightning arced from her fingertips and flashed across the room to catch Quinn square in the chest. For a moment he seemed frozen in its light. His back arched as his body went rigid, his mouth opening wide. A deafening *boom* crashed over the campsite, and the lightning flickered again, blinding all who watched.

When Devon's vision returned, he found himself alone beside Alana. Nothing but a scorched patch of tiles remained of where Quinn had stood.

He sat up as the vines receded, his heart lodged in his throat. Desperately he scrambled to reach Alana as she swayed and began to topple backwards. Catching her in his arms, he lowered her onto her side, taking care not to move the Sword any further. A whisper came from her lips as he rested her head in his lap.

"Alana," he sobbed. He reached out to touch her, then paused, his hand trembling with indecision.

"Please," she murmured, her eyes fluttering. "Who…who are you to me?" A gurgling rattle came from her chest as a convulsion shook her.

Devon swallowed at the pain written across her face, the grief. "I love you."

A sigh whispered from her chest. "I can't remember…" she breathed, trailing off. Then her eyes snapped open, sudden clarity in their stony depths. "You called me 'princess.'"

Devon smiled, despite himself. "You have always been a princess to me, Alana."

"Good," Alana murmured. "Don't you…forget it."

A sob tore from Devon. Swallowing his fear, he reached for the hilt of the Sword, but she caught him by the wrist.

"Don't," Alana said. "Its magic is all…that's keeping me alive."

"No…" Devon croaked.

"Thank you, Devon," she said, her voice so low he had to strain to hear her.

"For what?"

"For saving me," she replied, her lips twitching in a smile. "For bringing me back."

"Now *stay*," Devon hissed, gripping her hand tight.

"I can't…" Alana murmured, her eyes lifting to stare past Devon at some unseen point in the sky.

"No…" Devon trailed off, and for a moment he thought the worst. Sobbing, he bent over her, tears streaming from his cheeks onto her hair.

"Run," her voice whispered in his ear, so softly he almost thought it a trick of the wind.

Pulling back, he shook his head. "I'm not leaving you."

"You must."

"Please," Alana replied. "I don't want...."

"Alana."

"Please, Devon. If you love me, *run*."

Groaning, she pushed weakly at his hand and struggled to a sitting position. Her face pale, alive with agony, she looked at him. Devon stared back, seeing her courage, her anger and pain, but most of all her grief. He knew then it was not the Alana he knew looking at him, but the old one, the Daughter of the Tsar.

And she had helped him.

It made no sense, and yet he could not deny the truth.

Slowly he stood, wiping his tears away. "Are you...sure?"

She nodded, tears of her own streaking her cheeks. Her gaze darted to where a hunched figure lay nearby. "Take the boy."

Striding across the marble tiles, Devon's heart lurched as he saw it was Braidon lying there. He swung the boy over his shoulder and then glanced back at Alana. She had both hands clasped around the Sword now, concentration etched across her face. As he paused, she glanced up, and a smile touched her lips.

"Run, Devon!"

CHAPTER 44

Alana let out a long sigh as Devon disappeared beyond the tents, the boy slung over one shoulder. Slumping against the Sword, she let the pain wash over her. A shriek tore from her lips, and shuddering, she prepared herself for the end.

Don't.

The voice whispered in her mind. It sounded distant, yet it rang with undeniable power.

A frown touched Alana's brow as she looked around, seeking out the source. But she was alone in the campsite now. Not a soul stirred in the tents around her, all her father's soldiers and Stalkers having long since fled. Closing her eyes, she gathered herself.

This is not the way.

Her eyes snapped open, but still there was no sign of movement. "Where are you?" she whispered.

Within, came the reply.

"How?" Alana asked, shaking her head.

Let me show you.

Alana sensed the voice wanted her to let go. Hesitation touched her, her old instincts screaming a warning. But then, she was doomed either way. The second she tore the Sword from her she would die—no amount of God magic would be fast enough to bring her back. So what did she have to lose?

Letting out a long breath, she relaxed, allowing the other presence to take hold…

And woke in a glistening garden, its endless rows of roses lit by a golden light. Alana looked around, surprised by the abrupt change in scenery—and the sudden absence of pain. She touched her stomach and found the flesh whole.

"There is no pain here," a voice spoke from behind her.

Spinning around, Alana watched as a young girl approached through the flowerbeds, her eyes aglow with violet light. Two men walked behind her, one seemingly old beyond time, the other muscular and middle-aged, his beard streaked with white.

The three came to a stop before Alana and appraised her with silent eyes.

"You remember me?" the girl asked.

Alana shook her head. "I remember nothing like this," she whispered. "Nothing good."

"Come then," the girl replied, gesturing Alana forward.

Alana dropped to her knees before the girl. The violet glow of her eyes flickered as she reached out and touched a finger to Alana's forehead. A cool power flooded through her, seeping through her skull, filling her up. Alana sighed, rising into the girl's hold, her whole body coming alive.

And one by one, she felt the pieces of the puzzle appear, her memory restored. She saw again Devon facing off against the demon, her brother Braidon as he outlined his plan to defeat their father, she saw Kellian fall in the throne room, and Enala die beneath her father's blade. A sob tore from her lips as she heard again Devon's words in the wreckage of the Tsar's tent, his whispered 'I love you.'

Alana knew she would never see him again, but more than anything she wished she could have returned those words. She had done so much wrong in her short life, caused so much pain. It had been Devon, with his own dark past, who had led her into the light, drawing her out from

313

beneath her father's sway. Not even Quinn, with all the power of his Sword, had been able to burn that light from her.

Alana looked down at the girl. The Goddess Antonia smiled and gestured at her companions. "You and Jurrien met, briefly," she said, indicating the younger of the two. "My brother, Darius, has watched you from your father's Sword for years."

"I'm sorry," Alana whispered.

Darius smiled, his aged face more wrinkles than skin. "It seems to forever be my fate," he murmured. "Until now."

"I am sorry for my anger, young Alana," Jurrien added, stepping forward and placing a hand on her shoulder. "I could sense Antonia's pain, coming from the Sword." He glanced at the Goddess and smiled. "I have a soft spot for my little sister."

Antonia snorted and rolled her eyes. "Don't blame me for your excesses, brother," she replied. "You were wrecking their ships long before we took flesh."

Jurrien offered a roguish grin. "Yes, well, you two never were much fun."

"If only things could have stayed thus," Darius murmured. His pale white eyes looked to Alana. "But now they must change, permanently this time."

"I am sorry, Alana," Antonia cut in. "With my spirit trapped within the blade, I cannot heal you."

"I know." Alana shrugged, swallowing her grief. "I'm ready."

Antonia nodded. "As are we."

Alana shook her head. "Ready for what?"

"For death."

Alana blinked, looking from Antonia to the other two. "What do you mean, 'death'?"

"You shall not walk the dark path alone, Alana," Darius replied. "We shall walk with you, if you would free us."

"Why?" she whispered. "You're Gods, why would you want to die?"

"Because it is our power that corrupts you, all of you," Antonia replied sadly. "Our spirit, our magic, it touches all things. But only humanity seeks to claim it. It calls to them, driving your strongest, your *cleverest, to seek us out. Twice now our powers have been trapped by your people. The last time, we departed the physical realm, in the belief it would be enough. But your father drew us back, took our power for his own."*

"*You want me to destroy you?" Alana asked.*

"*We want you to destroy it all," Jurrien replied.*

"*All magic comes from us," Darius added, "and it will die with us."*

Alana stared into the faces of the three Gods, and realised for the first time there was fear in their eyes. These three beings had lived an eternity beyond anything she could imagine, had watched over humanity for eons before the scrambling priests had first summoned them to flesh.

Now they were asking to join Alana on the final journey, to go with her into the darkness of death, and look upon what waited on the other side.

She swallowed. "Are you sure?"

The Three Gods nodded.

"*Then tell me how."*

CHAPTER 45

By the time Merydith gathered her people near the bottom of the valley, the last of the enemy had either fled or been slain. She had found a fresh horse from the few that had survived the battle, and now sat in the saddle, looking out over the weary faces of her people.

Less than a thousand were left, and of those there were few who had emerged unscathed. Even so, they looked back at her with triumph in their eyes. She knew that every one of them was celebrating their life, that of all those who had perished today, they still breathed the fresh evening air.

Helen and what remained of her Magickers had joined them once the enemy had fallen back. The effort required to split the valley in two had cost them dearly. Helen had informed her with sadness that two dozen of their number had collapsed and died soon after. Their sacrifice had won the day, Merydith knew, and she embraced the woman like an old sister.

Looking over the gathered allies, Merydith searched for their other saviour. The hammerman Devon had appeared at the decisive minute, leading a horde of black-cloaked warriors as he charged the enemy's rear. She could see many of his people scattered amongst her ranks, but of the hammerman himself, there was still no sign.

Damyn and Mokyre stood to either side of her, their watchful eyes on the campsite. Her guards had died defending her amidst the chaos of battle, and the two clansmen seemed to have taken the role upon themselves. Weary as she was, Merydith didn't have the strength to argue with them over it.

Turning her horse to face the survivors, she was about to speak when a voice shouted out from the crowd.

"Devon!"

Merydith let out a long breath as she saw the hammerman stumbling from the last of the tents. Her heart lifted at the sight of Braidon in his arms, and almost without thinking, she looked at the campsite, waiting for Enala to emerge. But as Devon neared, it became obvious the hammerman was alone. Her heart twisted, but she forced herself to dismount and stride out to meet Devon.

"Well met, hammerman," she said, an uncharacteristic grin on her face. "Your timing was impeccable."

He paused, offering a nod, and then continued past her. Merydith's smile faded, replaced with irritation, and she followed the hammerman into a cluster of black-garbed warriors. An older woman stepped out to meet him, and together they lowered Braidon to the ground.

"I think he's okay," Devon murmured as the woman crouched beside the boy.

The woman touched a finger to his neck, waited a moment, and then nodded her agreement. "He's sleeping."

"What happened, Devon?" Merydith cut in, her irritation mounting.

Devon glanced in her direction, and sighed. "Sorry, Queen," he croaked. "I...it's been a long day."

Merydith opened her mouth to snap a retort, and then caught herself. Letting out a long breath, she forced a smile.

"It has," she agreed. "And as I said, I am grateful for your aid."

"Thank them," he said gesturing to the black-garbed warriors scattered amongst her people.

"In time," Merydith replied. "First, what has happened to the Tsar, do you know?"

"He's dead," Devon grunted. "And all his powers with him."

Merydith's heart swelled at his words. "Truly?"

"Ay," Devon replied. "Though it cost everything."

His voice was tight with barely controlled emotion, and Merydith read the pain on his face. Not knowing what to say, she reached out and squeezed his arm.

"Thank you, my friend," she said. "You have given us everything."

"Not me," he murmured, looking past her to the gathered allies. "The Tsar's Daughter. Alana."

Merydith nodded, though in truth she did not understand what he was saying. A cry came from the ground, and the boy lurched up, his sapphire eyes wild.

"Alana!" he cried.

"Easy, sonny," Devon said gently, moving to his side.

"No, what, where am I?" Braidon gasped, pushing aside the helping hands of his friends.

"You're safe, Braidon," the woman said gently.

"Selina?" he frowned, finally taking in his surroundings. "Where is Alana?"

Selina lifted her eyes to Devon, who quickly looked away. "I'm sorry, sonny," he said quietly. "I couldn't save her, not this time. She's—"

Before he could finish speaking, a rumbling noise came from the campsite. All eyes turned back to where the dark tents of the Tsar's army lay empty. A light had blossomed there, stretching up into the sky. Green, blue, red, gold, and a thousand other colours crisscrossed the column, growing more intense, until it seemed the world itself would flicker out before its power.

A sharp *pop* sounded, followed by a terrifying *boom* that shook the very earth. The column of light swept outwards. Her people cried out as the magic rushed towards them. Merydith threw herself on the ground and closed her eyes, but even then the light seared at her eyes. Her ears filled with an awful buzzing, and she smelt burning in her nostrils.

Then as suddenly as it had appeared, the light flickered out, leaving Merydith crouched on the grass, untouched. Sitting up, she saw the bewilderment on the faces of her people as they looked around, in disbelief that they were alive. Merydith could hardly believe it either—for a second, she'd thought Devon had been wrong, that the Tsar still lived and had launched a final attack against them.

A harsh sobbing drew her attention back to the present, and standing, she searched for the source. She found Helen and the other Magickers nearby, each crouched with their faces to the ground. Listening to their cries, Merydith could not understand what had happened to them, but she heard the pain of loss in their voices.

"What is it?" she asked, moving to Helen's side.

The Magicker looked up, her eyes red. "It's gone," she whispered.

"What's gone?"

"The Gods, magic, all of it," Helen cried.

Merydith stared at her, uncomprehending. Before she could respond, another cry drew her attention to the other end of the valley. Men and women there were shouting and running towards her, their eyes filled with panic. Her heart beat faster, though she barely had the strength to stand now. The day had just about consumed her last reserve of strength.

She looked beyond her people, out to where the valley twisted out of sight. The crevice that Helen and her

Magickers had opened ended there. Marching towards them up the valley was the other half the Tsar's army.

Merydith could have laughed. As Mokyre and Damyn formed up on either side of her, she walked towards the approaching force. Her people parted for her, their eyes wide. She felt no fear though, only a strange nothingness, a knowledge that she had done all she possibly could to save her people.

The thud of twenty thousand marching boots rumbled up the valley as the army neared. When they were still a hundred yards away, a trumpet sounded, and the silence resumed. Merydith came to a stop at the front of her people. Folding her arms, she waited for the enemy to make their move.

A gap appeared in the front line of soldiers, and three men stepped into the open. Merydith exchanged glances with Mokyre and Damyn, and then the three of them walked out to meet them. They came to a stop midway between the two forces. Merydith folded her arms once more as the three men stopped before her.

"My name is General Saryn," the frontmost of the three spoke, his voice clear and crisp, carrying with it the air of command. "What happened here?"

"The Tsar is dead. His army is defeated. The empire is done," Merydith said.

A smile touched the general's face. "Is it?"

"It is," Merydith replied. She sighed, her gaze looking out over the men and women aligned against her. "Have enough not died already, General?"

The smile faded from his face. "It has been a grim day indeed."

"Then shall we put an end to this?"

He sighed. "The Tsar is truly dead?"

"He is," Merydith murmured. "And magic with him."

"Then you shall have your peace," Saryn replied, sinking to his knees. "My Queen."

EPILOGUE

Devon walked slowly up the sloping streets of Ardath, taking his time in the stifling heat. His leg still ached where a shard of his hammer had embedded itself in his thigh, and he couldn't go at much more than a slow amble anyway. With magic gone from the continent, it would take months for the wound to fully heal.

Not for the first time in the past few weeks, he wondered what had gone through Alana's head in those final moments. Had she known what she was doing, when she'd turned the Sword on its makers, destroying the spirits of the Gods, and magic with them? It had been her father's purpose in making the Sword in the first place, but…

He shook his head. There was no point in fretting over it. What Alana had done could not be reversed. The moment she'd broken the Sword, it was too late. Now all the Three Nations could do was move on, and forge a fresh future for themselves in a world without magic.

Merydith had decided to remain in the Three Nations for a time, to oversee the transition of power as the empire broke up. Her aide, Mokyre, had been sent back to Northland to oversee the nation in her absence, while the Queen herself was rarely seen without Damyn at her side. They had ridden hand in hand for much of the trip to the capital, and at night had made little secret of their passion.

Along with Braidon and Selina, Devon had joined them for the journey back to Ardath. First though, he had returned to the site where he had last seen Alana. He had needed to see the truth for himself, to know she was not hiding out there somewhere, alone and afraid. But in the end, there had been nothing left to see. The marble tiles that had marked the spot where the Tsar's tent had stood were gone; even the earth beneath had been torn apart, leaving a crater the size of a house where Alana had lain.

He'd known then she could not have survived, that at the end she had made the ultimate sacrifice. Why, they would never know, but he liked to think she had her reasons.

The surviving Baronians had remained behind with their Trolan comrades. With the Tsar gone, the threat of persecution had lifted, and most had been excited at the thought of returning to a stationary lifestyle.

With plenty of land and few hands to work it, the Trolans had welcomed them with open arms. In the days following the battle, Devon had been overjoyed to learn it had been Betran who had raised the rebellion in Trola. If not for his efforts, the Queen's army would have lost long before Devon and his followers arrived.

Much to his protest, the Queen had named Betran as the next Trolan King. Devon smiled at the thought of the timid-looking man he'd first met in a bar beneath the streets of Kalgan ruling a nation. The idea appealed to him, and he began to whistle a familiar tune as he continued through the maze of alleyways.

Braidon had been cool towards him on the journey home. Devon could not fault him for it. The boy blamed him for Alana's death, for not saving her as Devon had saved him. Devon had tried to explain, but the hurt was too fresh. The loss of Braidon's magic had been a double blow, and for days there had been no reasoning with him. Devon hoped that might change, given time.

The Queen intended to give Braidon the Plorsean crown once he came of age. After watching him grow and prosper over the last few months, Devon thought the boy would make a fine king, though he had no doubt there would be those who watched him closely for hints of his father's madness.

Merydith herself planned to stay out the year and then return to Northland next summer. With Lonia already holding elections to bring a new council to rule, only Plorsea needed her help putting itself back together. They had suffered the most during the battle, with most of their leaders dead or missing. It would take time to find someone trustworthy enough to rule in Braidon's stead until he came of age. Personally, Devon was more than glad to know Merydith's hands were at the helm for the moment.

Devon came to a stop outside the blackened remains of a building. Placing his hands on his hips, he cast an appraising eye over the ruin of the Firestone Inn. The stone walls still stood strong, but the fire had consumed the clay tiles of the roof, and there was nothing left of the wooden steps out front.

Climbing up into the building, Devon stood looking on the ruin, remembering the long days and nights he had spent there with Kellian. Sometimes he'd been a customer, others a bouncer, paying off some damage or debt he'd managed to cost his friend. Regardless, they had been good times, simpler and filled with joy, long before they had rescued the Tsar's children and embarked on a quest that would see an empire topple.

Devon chuckled to himself as he studied the gutted interior, and wondered what his friend would think of him standing there now.

"It's going to take a lot of work, you know." A voice came from the doorway behind him.

Turning, Devon smiled as Selina wandered into the ruin.

"Ay, it will." Devon replied. Reaching into his belt, he hefted an old clawhammer. Dented and rusting in places, it told no stories, held no ancient spells. But it would do. He smiled at Selina. "But I'm game to try. Care to join me?"

Selina laughed. "I just might, hammerman."

Here ends book three of
The Legend of the Gods Trilogy
For more adventures in the Three Nations, read on…

For five hundred years the Gods have united the Three Lands in harmony. Now that balance has been shattered, and chaos threatens.

A town burns and flames light the night sky. Hunted and alone, seventeen year old Eric flees through the wreckage. The mob grows closer, baying for the blood of their tormentor. Guilt weighs on his soul, but he cannot stop, cannot turn back. ***If he stops, they die.***

For two years he has carried this curse, bringing death and destruction wherever he goes. But now there is another searching for him – one who offers salvation. His name is Alastair, and he knows the true nature of the curse. ***Magic.***

The Sword of Light

Enjoyed this novel? **Then be sure to share the joy with your friends on Facebook!**

You can also join my VIP group to receive a free short story every month, as well as news about my upcoming novels!

http://www.aaronhodges.co.nz/newsletter-signup/

NOTE FROM THE AUTHOR

Phew, what a ride! I've gotta say, my stories in the Three Nations are still my favourite to write, even after six novels and a novella or two! And as you might have guessed from their ending, there's still more tales left to explore in this brave new world. They'll have to wait a while though - first I plan on writing something a little different. I'll let you know when I figure out what that is!

In the meantime, if you haven't already you should definitely check out my prequel series - **Sword of Light Trilogy. The three books are set a hundred years before events in this series, so they might explain a few gaps you might have noticed in the Dawn of War! Be sure to read on below for a free excerpt...**

FOLLOW AARON HODGES:

Each month I send my followers a **free short story** - so be sure to signup below!

http://www.aaronhodges.co.nz/newsletter-signup/

THE SWORD OF LIGHT TRILOGY

If you've enjoyed this book, you might also like
my prequel trilogy:
The Sword of Light

When Eric was young a terrible power woke within him. Horrified by the devastation he had unleashed, Eric fled his village, and has spent the last two years wandering the wilderness alone. Now, desperate to end his isolation, he seeks a new life in the town of Oaksville. But the power of the Gods is fading, and in their absence, dark things have come creeping back to the Three Nations. Civilisation is no longer the safe haven he once knew, and Eric will soon learn he is not the only one with power…

ALSO BY AARON HODGES

Legend of the Gods

Book 1: Oathbreaker

Book 2: Shield of Winter

Book 3: Dawn of War

The Sword of Light Trilogy

Book 1: Stormwielder

Book 2: Firestorm

Book 3: Soul Blade

The Praegressus Project

Book 1: Rebirth

Book 2: Renegades

Book 3: Retaliation

Book 4: Rebellion

Book 5: Retribution

Printed in Great Britain
by Amazon